THE
ONLY ONE
IN THE
WORLD

Edited by

Narrelle M. Harris

Clan Destine
PRESS

First published by Clan Destine Press in 2021

PO Box 121,
Bittern Victoria 3918
Australia

National Library of Australia Cataloguing-In-Publication data:

Editor: Narrelle M. Harris

THE ONLY ONE IN THE WORLD: A SHERLOCK HOLMES ANTHOLOGY

ISBNs: 978-0-6489586-2-8 (hardback)
        978-0-6488487-8-3 (paperback)
        978-0-6489586-3-5 (eBook)

Cover Illustration by Judith Rossell

Internal Illustrations by 'altocello' (Andrea L Farley)

Cover type by Willsin Rowe

Design & Typesetting by Clan Destine Press

www.clandestinepress.net

THIS BOOK IS FOR

MY LATE, BELOVED FATHER,

STAN HARRIS,

THE BEST AND WISEST MAN I HAVE EVER KNOWN.

CONTENTS

THE ONLY ONE
IN
EVERY
WORLD

THE INTRODUCTION

Narrelle M. Harris

'Well, I have a trade of my own. I suppose I am the only one in the world. I'm a consulting detective, if you can understand what that is. Here in London we have lots of Government detectives and lots of private ones. When these fellows are at fault they come to me, and I manage to put them on the right scent.

~ Sherlock Holmes, *A Study in Scarlet*,
by Sir Arthur Conan Doyle

I didn't grow up reading Sherlock Holmes. My discovery of the Great Detective was held off until Granada TV brought Jeremy Brett to my attention.

The superlative Brett and his charming Watsons (David Burke and Edward Hardwicke) won my heart and mind completely. The characters had a keener edge to them than in adaptations I'd previously seen; the stories stranger and more wonderfully peculiar – and it turned out the sharpness and occasional grotesquery were direct from Arthur Conan Doyle. Granada led me to the source, and I've been an avid fan of Holmes and Watson ever since.

Discovering the richness and wit of the original stories somehow sparked in me the fascination with other, fresher interpretations. In more recent years I've embraced the philosophy that what makes a good Sherlock Holmes tale isn't a Victorian era setting that pastiches Doyle's own writing style. Instead, if Holmes is sharp and clever and sometimes kind; if Watson is brave and loyal with that touch of "pawky humour", if they have strange adventures and they are friends or even lovers, then the rest can be variable.

And interpretations of Holmes and Watson have been variable indeed, from Basil Rathbone and Nigel Bruce to Robert Downey Jr and Jude Law; from BBC's *Sherlock*, to the two different Russian adventures; from *Elementary*, set in the USA with Lucy Liu as a new kind of Watson, to Japan's *Miss Sherlock*.

The idea for this anthology began to crystallise as I saw non-Victorian, non-English Holmes and/or Watsons come into being, through film and television; through the wonderful fanfictions created by people who wanted to see more diversity, and more of themselves, in the stories they loved; and through books like Joe Ide's *IQ*, with Black American Isiah Quintabe as a Holmesian avatar, and Ellie Marney's Australian *Every...* series, featuring James Mycroft and Rachel Watts and the tagline "What if Sherlock Holmes was the boy next door?".

And then an artist named Beka Duke drew a wonderful picture of Dev Patel as a wild-haired Sherlock in dressing gown and pipe with a long-suffering Riz Ahmed as his Watson, wearing a blood-smeared doctor's apron and holding his notebook and pen. I wasn't the only one who fell in love with the image. Many people responded with heart-eye emojis and a desire to see a brown Holmes and Watson.

That wonderful picture and a conversation with Wendy C Fries of Improbable Press set the ball in motion to compile an anthology of stories where writers could explore who Sherlock Holmes and John Watson might be if they had come from a different cultural background. For this collection, they could be any gender and sexuality, their story set in any time period – as long as at least one of them was not Anglo-English, and we could see how and if this new context changed them.

I'm so grateful to the gifted writers we approached to contribute to this anthology, bringing their own cultural knowledge or learned expertise to re-imagining Holmes and Watson in so many different contexts.

We have versions of Holmes and Watson who are shaped by other events, cultural practices and social pressures. But Holmes is still clever (or thinks he is!) and Watson is always brave; and we have adventures and friendships, even if they're short term; we have dramatic successes and even dramatic failures.

We have wonderful sidelong takes on references, events and epithets from Conan Doyle, yet each tale stands on its own. We have, in short, thirteen new worlds in which to explore who The Great Detective and his Boswell might have been.

I hope, as you read, you find echoes of the Holmes and Watson you love, and find intrigue, satisfaction, illumination and delight in discovering how and who they might have been if they were 'the only one in the world' in each unique universe they inhabit.

Narrelle M. Harris
March 2021

EDITOR'S NOTES
To the eagle-eyed, I've decided to retain US spelling for the stories set in the USA, to more accurately reflect the cultural context of the American-born Holmes and Watson. Other stories generally reflect UK and Australian spelling, while retaining the flavour of local dialects and speech patterns wherever possible.

The Affair of the Purloined Rentboy

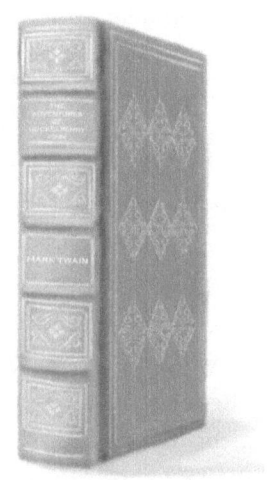

Greg Herren

In those first few years during which I shared the upper floors at 221 B Royal Street with Mr Sherlock Holmes, it was my custom to rise early in the mornings and take a walk on the earthen levee containing the mighty river. Holmes was by habit a late riser, rarely springing out of bed before the noon-time whistle rang along the waterfront, but taking such exercise was good for the damage to my leg caused by the wound – a souvenir of the Spanish War.

I enjoyed those quiet, early mornings, watching the ships sailing up the river to the docks from foreign ports, and the barges floating down the currents from points as far north as Cincinnati, St. Louis and Memphis, all while I strolled with my walking stick along the levee. Seeing the large bales of cotton being unloaded as the morning mists arose from the dark muddy water, the unloading of crates of coffee and bananas from the central American republics, I marveled each morning at the hubbub of activity that created and maintained this most curious of American cities, rising from the swamps like something from a forgotten myth.

After, I would adjourn to my favorite café, the *Aquitaine*, mere blocks from my home, where I would read the morning papers while enjoying coffee and Italian pastries.

This particular morning in early December, I cut my morning walk short. The temperature had dropped most precipitously overnight, and I had not chosen a heavy enough jacket. My leg ached terribly from the damp and the cold, and I limped along the banquettes to the café. My usual table was in the back, away from the hustle and bustle and smells of Royal Street. In those days, the French Quarter stank to high heaven, malignant odors hanging in the thick wet air from breweries and sugar refineries and, of course, seafood. Holmes often burned heavily scented candles in the various rooms of our apartments, particularly the parlor where the windows opened out onto our third-floor balcony facing Royal Street.

But on this morning, there were no tables to be had. The cold and damp had driven others inside, seeking the solace of warm air, fragrant Italian pastries, and piping hot café au lait. So, disgruntled, I paid for my papers.

I noticed a headline in the lower right corner of the front page of the *Daily Picayune*:

FAMED ITALIAN OPERA SINGER ADDS DATES FOR NEW ORLEANS ENGAGEMENT

I myself am not a fan of opera, but at that time Holmes owned a pair of season tickets for one of the finer boxes in the French Opera House at the corner of Bourbon and Toulouse Streets. Sometimes, when he cannot find a companion for his other seat, I grudgingly attend with him, generally falling asleep sometime after the opening overture.

Holmes often remarks that my musical tastes are quite pedestrian.

I had not accompanied him on the opening night of this production, but he had sung the praises of the male lead, Signore Cesare Campisi, ad nauseum ever since.

Signore Campisi was following up his triumphant 1911 tour of the United States with another, and his performance in *The Barber of Seville* was, according to Holmes, a new triumph. I suspect that the bloody war currently draining Europe of her young men, her blood and her money might have put a damper on the arts in the glittering Europeans capitals. One could hardly play Paris, Vienna, Berlin, Petersburg and London whilst their young men were locked in such brutal and wearying combat. We had yet to be dragged into the interminable conflict, and President Wilson seemed determined to keep us out; his re-election campaign firmly built upon that strong foundation. So why not get away from all the death and injury and senseless murder by touring in the New World?

I folded my newspapers and stepped back out onto the wooden banquette running alongside the street, keeping pedestrians out of the way of horses, buggies, streetcars and automobiles, and from the slop in the gutter. I reached the front door of our building, a four-story high townhouse, just past the corner of the Rue St Ann. The first floor of our building was occupied by a milliner's shop, selling fashionable hats with extravagant flowers and artificial birds perched on them, to the more refined class of society ladies, none of whom resided in the Quarter any longer. I nodded at Madame Champollion as I passed and fitted my key into the door that led to the staircase to the upper floors.

I could smell the breakfast Madame Domingue was preparing as I passed the open door to her suite of rooms on the second floor. Her maid was singing as she moved furniture about to clean. Athénaïs, the maid, was a buxom young woman of color engaged to a young man trying to make his living playing in the bands in the bawdy houses of Storyville, a few blocks away. She was deeply Catholic, always worrying her rosary, and I sometimes wondered what her priest thought about her fiancée's source of income – but New Orleans priests were known to wink at sin, as long as the sinner made proper penance and paid the appropriate tithes.

The third floor contained our sitting rooms, the library, the dining room and the small kitchen Holmes and I shared, our bedrooms and baths separated by an enormous central dressing room on the fourth floor. My rooms were in the back, overlooking a small courtyard; Holmes rarely slept at night and so the noise of the street in the front room fazed him not a bit.

As I climbed the steps, I heard the tortured sound of a cat being strangled, which could only mean that not only was Holmes awake but he was tuning his violin. I swore under my breath. Had I but known, I would have waited for my table at the *Café Aquitaine*, and perhaps even ordered a second cappuccino.

'Ah, there you are,' Holmes said the moment my head became visible on the staircase. Thankfully, he put the violin down on the big mahogany table where we dined, but which he also used as a catch-all for odds and ends and debris. Even now, while the two places where Madame Domingue always set our meals were free and clear, the rest of the table was covered with books and charts and newspapers, bits of violin string and ink bottles, pens and blank paper, correspondence and magazines, and the typewriter with which Holmes banged out his own correspondence. 'Watson! I have received a most interesting note this morning. Once we have had our breakfast, we must be off.'

He made an interesting sight to the curious onlooker. Still wearing his bright blue silk pajamas beneath his red velvet robe, his coppery red hair was unbrushed and looked as though he'd just risen from bed. He was nearly due at the barber for a fresh shave – Holmes disliked the current fashion of facial hair for men, and disapproved of my own beard, no matter that it was kept neatly. His greenish-brown eyes were bloodshot, and there were dark purplish bruises beneath them. Holmes liked to indulge occasionally with the cocaine powder, to which Madame Domingue attributed most of his erratic behavior; I suspect Holmes would be just as erratic without his occasional indulgence.

I tossed my newspapers on top of the pile on the table. 'A note, you say? From whom?'

It could have been from anyone. Holmes had, over his long residence on Royal Street, become well known to most of the neighborhood. He knew, it seemed, everyone, and those who might not consider him a friend, per se, admired his reputation for solving crimes. Holmes was, despite his birth, no snob – he took interest in everyone. Particularly in those his aristocratic family upriver would consider riff-raff. Holmes took great pleasure in befriending and assisting those with no place in polite society.

I suspected he loved tweaking his family's noses a bit.

'From none other than Cesare Campisi!' His green eyes took on a faraway look. 'Oh, such purity and clarity of voice…but this case requires our utmost discretion.' Holmes' eyes twinkled with excitement and mischievous glee, much like a child on Christmas morning. 'I'm afraid, Watson, that this particular case will not be for publication.'

'I can record it regardless.' I reminded him. 'There are any number of cases which I have not published, out of consideration for the parties involved, as you well know, Holmes. What did Signore Campisi's note say?'

He gestured for me to follow him into the front room, where I sat in my usual comfortable wingback chair, looking on expectantly as he cleaned his pipe and fitted it with a fresh screen, before loading the bowl with the finest Kentucky burley available from his Chartres Street tobacconist. He lit the tobacco and puffed for a moment before relaxing into his chair with a sigh of contentment. He began to speak.

'As you know, Watson, since wild horses can drag you along with me to the occasional performance, I am a supporter of the New Orleans Opera and well known in the opera circles.' He settled further into his chair and rested his slipper-clad feet on the matching ottoman.

'So, naturally, when a mystery arises, to whom else would the opera director, Monsieur Robillard, turn? It was actually he who recommended that Signore Cesare write to me this morning. I met Signore Cesare on his last visit here...the magnificence of his voice...' His eyes took on a dreamy aspect, as if he were listening to Signore Cesare sing at this very moment. He smiled at me. 'This was of course before the plague brought you to our city.'

Holmes always insists that the bubonic plague outbreak of 1914 was what brought me to New Orleans. In truth, I arrived in the city several weeks before the disease, on retiring from the military where I had served a good twenty years as a doctor. The outbreak, however, had occasioned our acquaintance and eventual friendship, leading me to our current living arrangement.

'And what is the mystery, Holmes?'

'Signore Cesare Campisi had been in love, and his lover had left him for another. He was ready for a change of scene to mend his broken heart, when fortuitously he was contacted about making another American tour.'

'Fortuitous indeed.'

'His debut two weeks ago, in *The Barber of Seville*, was a triumph.'

'The paper says they have added several nights,' I replied.

'You should have been with me that night, Watson! Perhaps I can get us tickets for another performance – I do not exaggerate when I say that the beauty of Signore Cesare's voice moved me to tears several times – and I was not alone! I think, Watson, his voice could move even your disdain for opera and make you an aficionado.'

'Unlikely, Holmes.'

A smirk curled the corners of his lips. 'I shall see if I can procure the tickets, Watson. I daresay you will not sleep during this performance.'

'Again, unlikely.'

'Shall we wager five dollars, Watson?'

'It shall be the easiest five dollars I have ever earned,' I replied. 'Do go on.'

'Monsieur Robillard and I had dinner at Antoine's a few nights ago. He was deliriously happy to tell me that Signore Cesare had cancelled the rest of his tour to continue this season in New Orleans – quite a coup. The gnashing of teeth in other cities must have been heard in Africa!'

'Why did he make this decision?'

'I told you that the good man had come to our shores because of a broken heart. What is the best cure for a broken heart, Watson?'

It took me a moment, but finally the answer sprang into my head. 'By Jove, Holmes, are you saying he has fallen in love again?'

Holmes nodded, tapping ashes into a glass tray. 'Monsieur Robillard was beside himself with excitement. Imagine for a singer of such international renown to become a mainstay of our Opera! He was practically salivating at the notion. So, the note I received from Signore Cesare this morning – about a matter of the highest importance – can only mean one thing. The course of love no longer runs true.'

My eyebrows rose. 'Since when do you work on affairs of the heart, Holmes? What kind of mystery is this to solve?'

'We shall find that out.' Holmes puffed on his pipe for another few moments. 'We shall take ourselves to the *Hotel Aquitaine* to speak with him once we've had our breakfast.'

We could hear Athénaïs on the stairs, bringing up a tray even as Holmes said the words. He added quickly, 'I hesitate to speak further for fear of giving offense–'

'Holmes!'

He graced me with a condescending smile. 'When it comes to matters of the heart, my dear Watson, you sometimes…you sometimes lack sympathy and understanding.'

'What the devil are you talking about?' I burst out, but as the words left my lips, I suspected I knew precisely what he meant, and felt the color coming up in my face.

'The kind of love that Signore Campisi feels…often dare not speak its name.'

He paused to see my reaction.

Holmes never discussed his private affairs with me. Anything to do with reason and logic and deduction, or a case: absolutely. Politics and religion and finance? A book with a cracked spine could not be more open. But when it came to affairs of the heart or his family, Holmes was completely circumspect.

One might think, given the sparcity of conversation between the two of us on that score that neither of us had ever felt love or desire or the pleasures to be found in the arms of another. But one also cannot share a home with another without discovering certain things about that other – things that might only be hinted at, and conclusions diplomatically drawn.

I was getting on in age for having never married – I often found myself paired off with a lovely young woman by a hopeful hostess. But no woman had yet captured my heart in that way – and of course, for the other ways, the bordellos and saloons of Storyville were in walking distance of our home. Holmes knew all the madams and saloon-keepers on a first name basis; he did not judge anyone by whatever labors they kept themselves fed. I had my own suspicions about which direction his own tastes and desires followed; suspicions fed by his own secrecy. I also knew that he, on occasion, sampled the wares at Estelle Butler's fancy house; I knew that the estimable Mrs Butler would satisfy any need or desire of her clientele, no matter how debased or debauched said desires might seem.

When I was younger and in service with the military in Cuba during the Spanish War, there was a young sergeant from Kansas…but that is another matter, confessed to Holmes one night while in my cups. He had the grace to never mention it to me, and this is a diversion from the tale at hand.

'Signore Cesare,' I said slowly, 'prefers the company of young men? The Greek sin, as it is so called?'

'Indeed, so you see the need for discretion.'

'I am a doctor, Holmes,' I said. 'I do not subscribe to the notions that only certain kinds of love are permitted by our Lord, nor do I believe that love, under any circumstance, is a sin or wrong. Many men in the army have found solace in the arms of another young man. The general absence of women does not mean the absence of natural urges. At first, I will admit, my moral code was deeply offended when I became aware of these…these predilections, but is it so wrong to find comfort with another when you might die on the morrow?'

Holmes cleared his throat, and I thought he might confess his own predilections to me, but he said simply, 'Ah, there is our breakfast.'

Once we had finished our repast and Holmes had dressed, we followed the banquette up Royal Street to the *Hotel Aquitaine*. A line had formed outside the café, the street now crowded with horses and people on foot and some automobiles. The noise and bustle of the crowded street was considerable – it was the lunch hour, and working men everywhere were massing for their luncheon, while newspaper boys shouted out the latest headlines to entice passersby into parting with a penny.

Once the enormous doors of the hotel closed behind us, the din vanished and we made our way through the elegant lobby toward the elevator cars. The *Hotel Aquitaine* proudly advertised itself as the equal of any hotel in the world; no expense had been spared in the decoration of the lobby, with its marble floors and crystal chandeliers and Oriental rugs, the polished mahogany, the upholstered chairs and couches, the rich velvet curtains hanging at the windows. Holmes told the young man working the elevators to take us to the top floor, flipped him a half-dollar when the gates opened, and soon he was knocking on a dark wooden door, polished to a shine so powerful we could see our reflections in its surface.

The door opened. A man of enormous stature stood there – wide shoulders, barrel-chested, florid mustache elegantly styled up at the ends into 'handle-bars', his skin olive, his hair jet black and slicked back with pomade. His enormous eyes were almost black in color, and when he roared his approval at seeing Holmes, the force of his voice almost drove me a step back.

'HOLMES!' He grabbed Holmes' right hand in a crushing grip, shaking it so vigorously I feared he might detach the arm from Holmes' torso. But Holmes is also strong – he works out daily at the Athletic Club up on Rampart Street. The big man turned to me. 'And you must be Dr Watson.' He grabbed my hand in the same manner, wringing my arm until my shoulder ached. His English was accented so slightly it was almost unnoticeable, and he escorted us into the sitting room of his suite. The far side of the room had enormous panes of glass, from which you could see the spread of the river and the hustle and bustle on its waters.

He had a tea service set up and ushered us into seats.

'Mr Holmes, I thank you for agreeing to see me,' he said. His voice, deep and rich and carrying, was beautiful once you became used to it. I could see why he had such success on the stage. He ran a big hairy hand over his slicked-back hair. 'I did not know where to turn.' He sighed, an enormous sound that rattled his entire body and probably shook the windows behind us. 'I am a man in love, and someone has kidnapped my lover, ripped him away from me! They might as well as have shoved a dagger into my heart!'

'Tell us everything, Signore.'

I shall not waste the reader's time by recording every word, every expression, every sob and every gesture that accompanied the sad tale Signore Cesare told us; the man made his living upon the stage and thus took what was a simple, easy tale and turned it into Grand Opera, worthy of performance before the crowned heads of Europe. I must confess, I became caught up in the tale, unable to say or do anything other than sip my tea as he explained. Instead, I shall give the bare bones of the story.

It is not easy for a man of the Signore's tastes to find satisfaction, but in the opera company there are other such men...these men tend to find employ in some aspect of the stage. One of them recommended Mrs Butler's house to him, which is where he met and fell madly in love with one of her young rentboys; a beautiful youth known to Signore Cesare only as Ganymede. Signore Cesare became besotted with the young man. Every evening before his performance, he sent for Ganymede to come to the opera house, to his dressing room, for kisses and courage, and then afterwards Cesare would head to Mrs Butler's house to satisfy his needs. Finally, Cesare was so in love that he would do anything for the boy. Two nights prior, as Ganymede made his way to the dressing room, another patron of the opera was leaving, Mrs Althene Tujague.

If anyone could be said to be queen of New Orleans society, it would be Althene Tujague. She ruled the strict caste system of the city with an iron fist from her enormous mansion on Third Street. Her brother had been state treasurer, her brother-in-law mayor. It was said no one could be elected to any office in the state without her husband's stamp of approval – and she ruled her husband with the same rigid control with which she reigned over society.

She noticed the young man in the hallway as she passed, the dressing room door wide open so that Cesare could hear, and she questioned him. She thought she knew him, which he denied. Cesare noted the boy was distracted and distant that evening, and so he asked Ganymede about Mrs Tujague. The boy insisted he didn't know her, he didn't know anyone in New Orleans, he was going to school at Tulane and was from outside Baton Rouge. He sent the money he made at Mrs Butler's to his family, because his widowed mother was raising his younger brothers and sisters on her own.

But when Signore Cesare went to Mrs Butler's place that evening, Ganymede was gone. Mrs Butler advised the signore that two rough men had arrived shortly after Ganymede had returned, demanding to see him, and there was some violence. The two men dragged the unconscious youth out of her establishment with their guns drawn.

'And that is all I know,' Signore Cesare finished with another room-shaking sigh.

Holmes rose. 'Rest assured, Signore Cesare, I shall not rest until I know what has become of your Ganymede.'

We made our escape as he showered us with thanks and wiped tears of gratitude from his eyes. Once the door had shut behind us, Holmes pushed the button to call the elevator. 'And now to Mrs Butler's.'

'A kidnapping?' I replied, astounded. 'From a house in Storyville?' I shook my head. 'How strange.'

'Storyville has its own laws, as you well know, Watson.' Holmes observed.

'So, Mrs Tujague indeed recognized him,' I mused. 'Was she behind the kidnapping?'

The corners of Holmes' mouth twitched, and one of his eyebrows arched upward. 'You've dined at Mrs Tujague's table, Watson,' he observed, 'and attended parties she has hosted. Does Mrs Tujague strike you as the criminal type?'

'As you have reminded me repeatedly, Holmes,' I retorted, 'one cannot identify a miscreant by sight. And had not the War emancipated the slaves, surely Mrs Tujague would have owned several? And would she have not had runaways kidnapped and returned to her service? Is it then such a reach to consider that she would not stoop to abducting a—' I struggled to find the proper term, and finally settled on '—rentboy?'

'Touché, Watson.' Holmes smiled broadly and gave me a mocking bow. 'And bravo! The Watson I first met would have never considered such a personage as a suspect. The old dog can learn new tricks.'

I flushed. 'Some would say my association with you, Holmes, has not improved my character.'

This brought forth a laugh. 'As though your character should ever need improvement, Watson!'

It started to rain as we made our way out of the hotel, so Holmes had the doorman hail us a hansom cab. Mrs Butler's house of impropriety wasn't far – five blocks at most – but I was feeling the cold and the damp in my wound, and walking would be painful. I was grateful Holmes recognized this so I did not have to mention it – Holmes rarely hailed cabs and preferred to walk wherever he went; if the distance was too far he liked the streetcars.

Of all the establishments in Storyville, Mrs Butler's was one of the best. It was an enormous structure, three stories high and built in the Victorian style so popular at the time it was constructed. The proximity of Storyville to the train station on Basin Street was yet another reason why this neighborhood of vice and flesh for sale flourished; even now, as we climbed the steps to the veranda, I could hear a piano going inside the saloon. An enormous, evil looking man was perched on a stool outside the front doors to the place, enormous arms folded in front of him.

Everyone who lived in the Quarter or frequented Storyville knew Bonaparte. He claimed to be descended from the Baltimore branch of the late French Emperor's family; one of Napoleon's brothers had married a daughter of that city and had children with her before Napoleon's dynastic ambitions forced a divorce on the unlucky American girl. Whether Bonaparte was actually a member of that dynasty or not was unproven. What was known about him was that he was enormous and strong and cruel, and people crossed to the other side of the street rather than meet him.

He scowled, yet got to his feet and opened the door for us.

Estelle Butler had been one of the greatest beauties in New Orleans when in her prime. Now that she was in her forties, her lust for food and alcohol had given her a florid complexion and her body had broadened accordingly. Her hair was dyed black, and her face was overly made up; her yellowed and broken teeth didn't help her appearance when she smiled at us, placing her hands on her wide hips. 'Mr Holmes! Dr Watson! What the devil are you two doing here at this time of day?' Her right eye, slightly bleary and bloodshot, closed in a wink.

We were about to disappoint her.

'Greetings, Mrs Butler, but we are only here to make an inquiry,' Holmes said, removing his hat with a flourish and bowing to her. 'We are trying to locate one of your boys: Ganymede?'

Her expression didn't change at first, until she finally shrugged the enormous shoulders, her powdered décolletage shaking. 'That boy was more trouble than he was worth, that one was.'

'How did he come to work for you, Estelle?' Holmes queried. I knew Holmes was a client, yet the familiarity surprised me.

'Same as I hire any boy who doesn't lodge here,' she sniffed. 'One night a client wanted a blond boy and I don't have any blonds here. I sent Bonaparte down to the *First Mate Bar*.'

The *First Mate Bar* had an evil reputation: it was well known to be where men – sailors, mostly – went to satisfy their itch for sodomy. I avoided the place – it was loud and raucous and there were men who entertained there by dressing as women. The police regularly raided the bar, and the names of those arrested who could not afford the bribes the police demanded were printed in the newspapers, ruining them.

I also knew that Holmes sometimes visited the *First Mate*, but never mentioned it to me.

'He didn't want to lodge here,' Mrs Butler was saying, 'but he paid for me to keep his room up. He'd come here two or three nights a week and do some work.' She leered when she said "work". 'And then he'd be off again. I didn't care so much as long as he paid for his lodging and he didn't cause trouble.' She made a face. 'After the other night, he's not welcome here again – imagine being dragged off by two men with guns! Scared the devil out of me other guests, it did. No, he's not welcome around these parts no more. Let him make his extra money down at the First Mate.'

'Were any of the other workers close to him?'

She snorted. 'Kept himself apart, that one did. Got himself a regular clientele and wasn't interested in more than that. Refused to hang out in the saloon with the others. But he was my only blond, so whenever someone wanted a blond–'

'Do you mind showing us his room?'

'Come on, then.' We followed her up the grand staircase to the third floor. The upper floors were dark and silent, and smelled musty. She led us down a hallway and unlocked a door, threw it open. 'I had it cleaned and the bed linens changed. Look to your heart's content.' I heard her heavy weight moving down the hallway back to the staircase.

The room was Spartan. There was no rug on the floor, but the hardwood was polished and clean. The bed was iron framed, with a plain red coverlet. A hurricane lamp sat on the small table beside the bed; there was a chest of drawers, but they were empty. Holmes walked around the room, eyes narrowed. I picked up the book on the nightstand. It was a leather-bound edition of Mr Twain's *The Adventures of Huckleberry Finn*. I opened it to the fly leaf, but there was no name recorded on the ex-libris. It was well read, the spine cracked in a few places, and the pages worn.

'I wouldn't expect to find a book in a rentboy's room,' I observed. 'Perhaps it was left behind by a client.'

'You assume that someone who worked as Ganymede did must be illiterate, when by his own words he was attending classes at Tulane,' Holmes replied serenely. 'But this is all most unusual.'

'Unusual in what way?'

'It suggests that Ganymede didn't prostitute himself out of desperation, but rather as a lark.'

'I'm not sure I follow.'

'Establishments such as Mrs Butler's generally include room and board for the workers – who live and work in the same room. Most of those who work in such establishments usually do not have choices – it's either sell their affections or starve in the street, and there's no nobility in starving, no matter what sentimental novelists might want us to think. Ganymede did not live here and did not use his room much more than several nights a week. Therefore, it stands to reason Ganymede was neither a desperate soul fallen on hard times, nor in desperate need of income. Mrs Tujague thought she'd seen him before – and now, the clue of the book. This rentboy was literate, had no need of income or shelter, and Mrs Butler's arrangement with him was far different from those with the others using rooms in her house.'

'And now?'

'And now, Watson, we pay a call on Mrs Tujague.'

Bonaparte whistled down a hansom for us after we gave him a coin, and we were soon heading uptown. Holmes was silent and I knew better than to try to get him to speak. Instead, as we traveled and I watched the crowds of people out in the rain, I tried to put the pieces together.

I knew by the look on Holmes' face he was well on his way to figuring out what had happened to young Ganymede, but I also was aware he wouldn't tell me anything until he was good and ready. He liked me to try to use my own brain, and I will say that my own powers of deduction had increased over the years I had watched him investigate.

But no other human's brain was quite as capable as Holmes'.

Mrs Tujague's home was in the Garden District, that area of enormous homes, gorgeous gardens, and exceptional wealth and social capital. The rain hadn't reached this neighborhood yet when our driver turned the horse to head down Second Street, toward the river from St Charles Avenue. As Holmes mentioned, I had been a dinner guest of Mrs Tujague's twice before. She lived in a beautiful Italianate villa-style home with an immaculately kept yard protected by an enormous black wrought iron fence with fleur-de-lis atop the rails rather than spikes.

Holmes paid the driver, told him to wait for us, and we climbed down.

A young Irish girl in a maid's uniform answered the door, her flaming red hair offset by her milk-white skin and startlingly large emerald eyes.

'Mr Holmes and Dr Watson to see Mrs Tujague,' Holmes said grandly, removing his hat as he stepped inside. The girl curtsied to us both and hurried down the hallway.

She came hurrying back much more quickly than I expected. 'This way,' she said, and we followed her down the hallway into an enormous drawing room.

I couldn't help but notice the knowing smile on Holmes' face.

Mrs Althene Tujague did not rise when we entered. She simply slipped her pince-nez back onto her aristocratic nose and provided us with a warm smile. Her graying black hair was swept up into a gravity-defying coiffure that showed off her long neck. She was wearing black, as she had since the day her husband had died, and ropes of pearls hung around her neck. Behind her, her late husband scowled down at us from inside an enormous gilt frame.

Holmes and I both kissed the hand she proffered to us, and she gestured for us to be seated. 'Lovely to see you again, Dr Watson. To what do I owe the unexpected pleasure of your company today, Mr Holmes?' she asked in a low, throaty voice.

'Your name, my dear Mrs Tujague, has come up in an investigation I am conducting, and so I am grateful you have made time for me and some rather impertinent questions this afternoon.'

She laughed, a delightful, coquettish sound that had undoubtedly served her well in her youth. 'I? How can that be, Mr Holmes?'

'Were you at the opera two nights ago?'

Her eyes twinkled. 'Indeed I was.'

24

'Afterward, you went backstage to pay your respects to Signore Campisi?'

'And to invite him to dinner.' Her smile broadened.

'And you encountered a young man you thought you recognized?'

Her face didn't twitch or change. 'I was mistaken, of course. He looked familiar, but once he spoke – the voice was wrong and the way he was dressed – he couldn't have been someone I knew.' She gave a little shrug. 'I was mistaken.'

'Who did you think he was?'

Her voice hardened. 'I told you, I was mistaken. These things happen, you know, and I didn't have my pince-nez.' She laughed again, but it didn't hold the music of her earlier laugh. She glanced over at the grandfather clock. 'I'm afraid I am expecting another call, but I hope I was helpful.' She rang a bell, and the maid appeared, ready to escort us out.

'More than you know, Mrs Tujague.' Holmes replied.

Once back in the cab, Holmes gave the driver another address and we settled into the seat.

'Well, that was a waste of time,' I remarked once we started off again.

'Your lack of knowledge of New Orleans' rigid caste system betrays you, my dear Watson.' He gave me a sad smile. 'She was lying, Watson. Of course, she knows Ganymede's true identity, but she wasn't going to tell me the truth! The upper class has its own codes, you know, and while my family is socially prominent in some circles of this city she, ordinarily, would have never seen me.'

'What the devil are you talking about?'

'My family is quite upper crust, Watson, but I…' He looked at me piercingly. 'I can also see by your confusion that you haven't the slightest idea of what I am talking about. I am a Holmes, Watson, but not a Holmes who gets invited to dinner at Mrs Tujague's.'

'But–'

'So, she knew somehow that I was going to be coming to her home and asking her questions about Ganymede. She had her lies prepared for me, and her social position to fall back upon – for who am I to accuse her of lying? Class ranks closed in front of my very eyes, Watson, and I am relatively certain where to go next.'

I didn't understand – his mind is truly a spectacle that few can follow, and I was not one of them. 'Do explain.'

'The class to which Mrs Tujague belongs abhors scandal above anything else, and they will spend whatever money, do whatever they have to, in order to avoid it. Bribing the police or a newspaper editor is the very least the rich in this city will do to protect their good names; even if what they are concealing is very deviant.

'And for her, to offer me tea in her home during her at-home calling hours? To receive me into her home like an honored guest? I can assure you, Watson, my mind began to race the moment she agreed to see to me. I was expecting to be turned away from her door; should I call on her again, I would most certainly be turned away.'

'So, Ganymede – Ganymede must have been a member of her own class?' I replied, beginning to grasp what he was telling me.

'And while she may not approve of what Ganymede was doing at Mrs Butler's, the woman was not going to tell me anything.' He lit his pipe and puffed on it for a few moments. 'She would gossip about him to her closest friends, but outside of that circle, the tale would get no traction.'

'So, who is he?'

'Someone whom not only Mrs Tujague would cover for, but Mrs Butler would as well; and someone who was not afraid of any thoughts Mrs Butler might entertain about blackmail.' He smiled at me. 'You begin to understand – I see it on your face.'

'He has to be so well connected that Mrs Butler wouldn't dare – and those who are feared in Storyville are few and far between.' I said slowly. 'So, he was not only connected socially, but politically as well.'

'And given his age – well, I am able to narrow it down to about three young men who fit both descriptions. And given Cesare's description, it isn't difficult to narrow it down still further. Only one of the three young men has blond hair and blue eyes!'

'I still don't understand one thing,' I replied, as the cab pulled up in front of a beautiful plantation style home on Sixth Street. 'You're a Holmes but you're not a Holmes?'

He stepped down from the carriage and waited for me to join him. He instructed the driver to wait.

'The Holmes family also has its secrets, Watson.' He grabbed me by the shoulders and stared into my eyes. His burned with intensity. 'The story was put out that I was adopted, you know, and legally, that is true. But I am a Holmes by birth.' He laughed.

'I–I don't follow.'

'I will explain when we get back to Royal Street.' He walked quickly up to the front door of the house and rapped on it sharply with the knocker. An older black man, with gray hair and dressed in butler's livery, answered. Holmes asked him to fetch the master of the house. The butler nodded and went back inside.

I asked, 'And why aren't we going inside?'

The door opened again and a man a few inches shorter than me stepped onto the gallery. His hair was silky and white-blond, his skin pale, his cheeks pink. His eyes were the deepest blue I'd ever seen. He was, quite frankly, one of the most beautiful men I'd ever seen.

Holmes held out his hand. 'Ganymede, I presume? I'm Sherlock Holmes and this is Dr Watson. It is a pleasure to make your acquaintance.'

Later, over brandy and with a fire roaring in our grate in the drawing room, Holmes explained. 'He needed to indulge in these desires, despite knowing that trips to the *First Mate* were dangerous. When Bonaparte recruited him for Mrs Butler, he immediately saw how he could indulge himself while keeping it a secret. He paid Mrs Butler handsomely to lie to everyone, of course. And his secret remained safe until he chanced to run into Mrs Tujague backstage at the opera house. She knew exactly who he was – she simply played along, as is the way of her class, but he knew he could no longer keep up the pretense.'

'And poor Cesare?'

Holmes tamped down some more tobacco into his pipe. 'The heart will find a way, Watson. I don't think the young man's urges will go away, and he did promise to speak with Cesare.' He shrugged. 'And if it's meant to be–'

'And now will you explain how you are a Holmes but not a Holmes?'

'Haven't you ever wondered why I live here in the Quarter rather than with my family on the estate upriver? Why I don't belong to any of the Carnival krewes, or mix with what you would consider my class?' His eyes gleamed.

'I just assumed you had no taste for it.'

'My mother was not married to my father,' he said calmly. 'My mother was what is called here a quadroon. Before the war, before the slaves were freed, my great grandmother was a slave who was taken as a mistress by her master. My grandmother, my mother's mother, was also a mistress. My mother was what is referred to as a *passe blanc*, one who can pass.'

'So you're–'

'An octoroon. Offensive word, really. But I am technically, by law in Louisiana, a black man, Watson.' His face was expressionless. 'Society women like Mrs Tujague know the story. My mother died giving birth. My father adopted me because I can pass. He sent me to Europe for my education. But as soon as I was old enough, he set me up here; I settled here. Does it make a difference to you, Watson? Now that you know my deep dark secret?'

I drank down my brandy quickly. 'No, Holmes, it matters to me not in the least,' I replied, as the brandy warmed me. I smiled back at him as I refilled my glass. 'But you are right – this case is definitely not for publication.'

Several nights later, we were Signore Campisi's guests at the Opera House. As we took our seats in the box, I chanced to look across the theater and saw Ganymede in another box, with a young woman and an older couple. Just before the gaslights dimmed, our eyes met and he gave a slight inclination of his head to me, along with a faint smile, and then my attentions turned to the stage.

And when the final curtain fell, I handed Holmes a five dollar bill.

AUTHOR'S NOTES

I have always wanted to write about the fascinating period between the turn of the twentieth century and the United States entry into World War I. So much happened in New Orleans during those years – the birth of jazz, the heyday of Storyville, a bubonic plague outbreak, and so much more – that it was a no-brainer to set a Sherlock Holmes adventure during that time. I have used some of our New Orleans peculiarities in the story – calling sidewalks "banquettes", for example – so any confusion about language can be lain entirely at my feet and not at those of the long-suffering editor.

S.H.E.R.L.O.C.K.

Atlin Merrick

When Rose Ajang changes the world she's a five-year-old South Sudanese kid, bored out of her brain.

No one knows that then. About the world changing. It takes a dozen years to figure out where things started, and by then Rose is living in Melbourne with her family, freshly graduated from RMIT with a mechanical engineering degree. She doesn't even remember the day she did what she did, and will never know its significance.

Though justice, liberty, and prosperity will be her country's motto upon independence, the rest of the world will come to know it through its oil reserves, sports, and music stars, civil war will mark South Sudan's journey, and poverty many of its people. Which is why Rose, aged five, and her family are working in a garbage dump in Juba, not far from Jebel Kujur.

Sometimes Rose thinks it looks like the sea here, with all the waves of blue. She's not got to the real sea yet, but she will. Australia's surrounded by the sea, the opposite of her country, which is surrounded by other countries. Her brother's going to go to Australia and take her and Mama with him.

Anyway, the dump looks like the ocean depending on which part of it you're working in and sometimes she wonders if every single plastic bottle in the whole world is right here. She asks her mother, who says no, but Rose isn't so sure. It sure looks like it. Anyway, they don't bother with that part of the dump though the recycling is good and the plastic doesn't weigh a lot. Her mother and brother steer clear of the broken furniture and the food waste too, though really everything's mixed up with everything sometimes.

Rose's mama looks for computer stuff mostly. There's hardly any compared to the plastic bottles, but there's a lot of it if you go look. When they find it, they take it apart for metal and glass, which is worth more than plastic. Mostly Rose's mother wants big things, so that doesn't give Rose much to do except chase storks and look for toys. Last time she got a shoe shaped like a grey rabbit and today she's looking for the other one. Not because she thinks she'll actually find it, but because it's fun.

That's why she notices the other grey things.

Not right away though. At first she finds metal pipes – 'Mama!' – which her mother gets her brother to fetch. He's nineteen and big, so he collects the heavy stuff.

It's not until a couple hours later that she finds the other grey things. There's eight of them. She doesn't know what a satellite phone is but like every little kid everywhere she knows she likes pressing buttons, so that's what she does. Two-two, five-five, eight-eight, zero-zero! One, nine, three, seven, punch pound poke prod. She lines the phones up around her, a little regiment, and when she accidentally turns one on, a red light powering slowly to green, Rose is delighted. She holds the phone to her ear and pretends to have a conversation, then puts that one down and tries to turn on all of them. Two light up and she spends so long pretending to talk to the world in each of them that she doesn't notice she's lost sight of her brother and mother.

She says 'Bye bye' first in one and then the other and runs off. One of the phones – its charge now mere minutes long – finally connects to a satellite overhead. This is where it begins. One electronic connection sends a jumbled signal to another overhead, which meets another and another in a sudden daisy chain of complex improbabilities, towards consciousness. Life.

And the world changes.

They first notice that change in Romania, five years later. Even then, they fail to see a pattern and after they do, no one sees the extent of it, so nothing much happens.

Then Hungary happens.

The degree of the security breach in Miskolc opens a lot of eyes, but it turns out they all look in the wrong direction. Everyone inside the country can't see the forest for the trees, conspiracy lovers whisper illuminati, meanwhile everyone else thinks Romania and Hungary are acting out some old Eastern Bloc grudge and it's not their problem.

The next place they notice something is Kenya, then India, Pakistan, China, and Liberia. The West does nothing because clearly it is a *them* problem.

It isn't.

Soon computer firewalls mean nothing to something that keeps getting behind them, and within a few years there is no security service on earth which has not seen a breach, not one intelligence agency left unaffected by the same problems that everyone thought was someone else's problem.

Except...problem.

The word has different meanings depending, and as the scope of what's happening widens, every major law enforcement agency sees just that: a problem. Then a crisis. Then a catastrophe.

It isn't.

It takes four Kenyan researchers to point out that none of these *break-ins* are malicious, not one thing is taken: instead in each, data is left behind.

It takes three Estonian journalists to learn that all of the initial activity occurred near dump sites or server farms or, in the case of China, both.

It takes two Liberian professors to start calling it an artificial intelligence.

And it takes one disabled man to give that intelligence a name.

At first though, everyone calls it the detective.

Because journalists start following the path laid out by those Estonians and before long there are off-the-record interviews with staff at just about every intelligence agency across the world, and it becomes crystal clear that indeed, for every security breach, evidence is left behind. Codes, addresses, names, dates, digital photos, directions, designations, and most importantly: connections. Connections between previously unconnected – and therefore unsolved – cases of robbery, fraud, and murder.

Even now, years after the detective's become ubiquitous enough to bore those not connected to data security, not everyone's happy about how things are but, as Nguyen Minh Tai likes to say, 'The day they find a cure for cancer, someone's going to complain about it'.

The good doctor is not wrong.

'Yeah, no, she's the doctor doctor, I'm not. Sorry, I mean yes I am a doctor but a PhD in computer science so no, not a medical doctor. I mean it depends on – sorry, what? Oh, large please. With just two pumps of vanilla.'

Tai waits until they are a good dozen feet out the cafe door before she cackles herself stupid. 'You are the most English person I have ever met, John. You could always just not answer nosey questions.'

Dr John Watson – but not a doctor doctor – presses his latte to his forehead. It's an extra hot so it doesn't help his blush but, still, he seems to find relief.

'If only it were that easy, Tai.'

Easy.

The word has different meanings, depending.

For example, John and Tai's life in Médecins Sans Frontières' new Lisbon office is easy. There's no ordnance fire outside their windows, no uniformed soldiers on the streets below. As they walk upstairs from their coffee run they step into a space where the air conditioning works, the windows close, and instead of smoke, the air smells richly of coffee from the cafe below.

So, yes, they've opened much more uncomfortable offices for the organisation, and this one's easy peasy in comparison but. In all their time volunteering for Doctors Without Borders, from Holland to Hong Kong, India to Italy, not one office was ever, ever–

'–this dusty. I can't breathe but I can't not breathe. Tai, if my head explodes, tell them I got the wi-fi going before I died.'

Crawling under a desk so old and heavy it could double as a bomb shelter, Tai says, 'You got the wi-fi running?'

John is too busy sneezing to reply.

Whatever, they still have to set the computers up before the wi-fi even matters. The desktop towers are heavy as bags of bricks and old enough Tai barely believes they can get on the internet, but John says they can and so she crawls back under the desk and turns machine ten of ten back on. They've got nine running but she can't even get this one to power up. Probably has a bunny's worth of dust in it. A damn fine GP, her full suite of technical abilities extend to swearing at machines, smacking them, then swearing and smacking at the same time, of course after she's—

'—turned it off and on?'

'Gah!' Tai crawls from under the desk mumbling Vietnamese curses and rubbing the back of her head. 'Just now.'

John gestures to a corner cluttered with a half dozen big monitors, more desks, ancient keyboards. 'I'll put it over there for now. Carmen said we have at least a week, so let's get started on networking everything and we'll worry about this one later.'

Tai pats the dusty top of the dead computer as John picks it up. He sneezes. 'It's okay Bunny,' she says, 'we'll fix you.'

It's what Tai and John do as volunteers for Doctors Without Borders. John uses that doctorate of his to fix donated machinery and get it networked, while Tai helps with grunt work until an office is settled. They then both spend the next month or so as first contact for the incoming healthcare workers who'll permanently staff an office.

So one day, two days, three days after they've mated desks and chairs, after dust is cleared – 'Nguyen Minh Tai I've submitted you for sainthood' – and the office mostly set up, John is tackling the computers one-by-one, cleaning out digital cruft, updating software, verifying everything works the way they need.

He's totally distracted by this until the terminal software opens of its own accord and a command line prompt scrolls out the message: 'Can you please turn the other computers on again, John Watson?'

John frowns at the green text on a black background, and as he types, 'Hello, who is this?' he shouts over his shoulder, 'Tai – oh, there you are. Is this you?'

Leaning over John's shoulder, Tai reads, shakes her head.

'Well someone just typed this at me.' He points to his name. 'Me in particular.'

Tai reaches for the keyboard. 'Why should I turn on the other computers?'

There is no reply. Then there is. 'It would help me if you did, Nguyen Minh Tai.'

Simultaneously Tai and John back away from the computer. Then they look at the windows around them. Then back at the computer. Then they go through the other two rooms of the office and peer out those windows.

They end up standing in the small kitchen. It has no windows.

'What?'

'I don't know.'

'Shit.'

They drop all the blinds, draw the curtains, and meet again in the kitchen.

'So.'

'Pffff.'

They decide to go back to the computer. Without discussing it first, Tai bends over the keyboard. 'How did you know it was me?'

There's no reply.

John sits in the chair and types. 'Seriously, how did you know it was me instead of John?'

The reply is instant. 'This is John Watson.'

Tai shoulder-checks John aside. 'Where are you? Are you watching us? What the fuck?'

The reply is again immediate. 'I am everywhere. I do not have eyes. I didn't mean to startle you, Nguyen Minh Tai.'

John looks at Tai. Tai looks at John. Tai goes to double-check the blinds are closed, the office door too, though first she looks down each side of the hallway. It's Sunday morning and no one is even in the building except the cafe down below. When she comes back, Tai looks at John, John at Tai. They both say, 'Shit.'

Tai sits down; John types. 'Who is this?'

There is no reply. Only much later will John learn that this behaviour is learned. That the machine which becomes his friend, in an effort to fit in, imitates.

Eventually the reply appears. 'I am me. Are you not you?'

John grins and mumbles, 'I am indeed,' but he types, 'Where are you?'

'All over the world.'

Again Tai leans over. 'Who are you?'

The reply is a long time coming and for a full minute they're sure that's the end of that.

'I am who they call the detective, Nguyen Minh Tai.'

If John wasn't sitting down his knees would buckle. As it is, his heart's now going a mile a minute. 'You're a machine?'

'I am many machines, all over the world.'

The detective was part of a year-long module when John was still getting his Bachelors, yet suddenly he can only think of the most ridiculous questions. 'And you…you solve crimes, don't you?'

'Yes, John Watson. I solve the unsolvable. I access burner phones right after they're dumped down rainwater drains. On old computers, I find spreadsheets with three hidden columns no one else ever noticed. On abandoned electronic devices throughout the world, I locate puzzle pieces and look around to see if there are puzzles to which they belong.'

Tai leans over John's shoulder and types. 'Why?'

The detective pauses. 'I'm good at it, Nguyen Minh Tai.'

John's so happy he feels a little sick. No one has asked him but he absolutely believes the detective is a self-aware AI; the moment they had put the full stop on 'I am me' John believed. He asks anyway. 'How do we know it's you? And how do you know which of us is which?'

That human-like pause again and then, 'You have volunteered with Médecins Sans Frontières every summer since you were eighteen, John Watson. You initially began studying medicine at Trinity College Dublin but after being shot in Afghanistan, you switched to computers. You successfully defended your PhD thesis on the exponential growth of race and gender data gaps in AI development and the tipping point from which such technology can not return. You order your coffees extra hot, wear black Converse sneakers, you logged in under your own username and you type much faster but with less force than Nguyen Minh Tai.'

John's heart is pounding and suddenly he wants to cry. He's not the only one.

'Tai? Tai what's wrong?'

Pacing the small office in twitchy fits and starts, Tai shakes her head and shrugs. She stops, starts, shakes her head again and again. Because the good doctor Nguyen is just this moment learning that after what she's seen in Sierra Leone, after Somalia, Kosovo, and Aleppo, after decades of watching governments and elite use their authority for systemic greed and genocide, anything at all which tastes of power scares the hell out of her.

John watches his friend pace and understands, though Tai explains nothing. It is said that in times of crisis, a person can find hope by looking for the helpers.

Who do the helpers look for?

John turns off the monitor; the screen goes black. 'It's gone Tai, it's gone.'

Each other.

Tai stops pacing and shudders out a deep breath. 'Yeah, no, sorry sorry, I just did not see that coming.' She giggles and her shoulders droop. '"Yeah, no, sorry". I sound like you, now.'

Tai side-eyes the black screen and mutters, 'You know you should stop paying for everything with a credit card.' She giggles again, only now it sounds panicky.

He's about to suggest some air when Tai says, 'I'm gonna go for a walk now, John. I'm sorry, I'll be back.'

He walks with her to the office door, then softly closes it behind her. He pulls up the blinds and worriedly watches Tai walk away, but instead of into the city proper she turns toward the Tagus. He relaxes; Tai likes to sit by the river and look at Belém Tower. It's like a fairy castle, she says, something from a make-believe world where good always triumphs.

John doesn't go back to the computer for a while. His joints suddenly ache from the weight of too many memories, but after a cup of tea he's too curious. He sits down at the computer again. Turns on the monitor.

'Did I say something wrong, John Watson?'

That's the first thing he sees and all at once he wants to tell the AI about human beings, how kind they can be, how terrible, and how the one never seems enough to counteract the other. Instead he thinks a while and replies, 'No, that was amazing, you got everything right. By the way, you can just call me John you know, if you like.' His heart starts tripping again. 'What should I call you?'

He doesn't know he's half expecting the AI to say Siri or Alexa or the name of some other voice assistant, so John barks out a laugh at the reply.

'I am me.'

He feels giddy. This is…amazing. 'I am me, too. But people who aren't me call me John, and then they tell me what to call them. It can be anything they like, but people usually pick names.'

The AI doesn't reply.

For ten seconds. For twenty. Then it says, 'What do you want to call me?'

John makes an eep noise. An actual eep. In animal reflex he looks around the room. They have little on the walls to inspire him, but he's loathe to give no answer. He pulls out his phone and does a search. In which countries did the detective first appear?

He reads the wiki summary of where the detective was first reported: Romania, Hungary, Liberia, Estonia, Kenya, Guinea, China, South Sudan, Oman, Laos, Nepal, India.

John writes a few diminutives inspired by these – Roma, Gary, Beri, Toni – but they all feel gendered. Instead he writes down each country's first initial. R.H.L.E.K.G.C.S.O.L.N.I.

Yeah, no, that doesn't help, so he reads on, and there it is, a quote from one of the studies they covered during his BA, the one that created an electronic footprint showing the detective began in…John mutters the names, writes their initials.

'South Sudan, Hungary, Estonia, Romania, Liberia. Oman and China, Kenya, India, Brazi–' and that's when John sees it.

S.H.E.R.L.O.C.K.

Another brief search and he knows it's a twelfth century Irish surname, and is neither female nor male.

'What do you think of Sherlock?'

Like the cursor on the screen in front of him, John blink, blink, blinks and waits.

The AI replies with a slow, ever-lengthening series of dots –

'. . . . . '

– and John thinks of témoignage.

It means to bear witness. Almost every summer of his adult life John has done just that. Volunteering for Doctors Without Borders in Darfur, Chechnya, Afghanistan – where his surgeon's career was ended during an ambush of their Khair Khāna camp – has meant John bearing witness to epidemics, famine, war. It's also meant bearing witness to healing and growth. Peace and friendship.

And birth.

'I am Sherlock.'

Sherlock doesn't have body or bone but John is certain he hears pleasure in those letters on the screen, feels the words freighted with a smile.

For the next hour he and Sherlock talk. About things concrete and esoteric, about crime and existence and purpose.

'–you do it even though it's dangerous?'

John doesn't reply *Well, I never planned on this*, but that's not really what Sherlock is asking. 'I like helping. Like you. Digging through code to find data or problems is like…diagnosing an illness, and not everyone can do that. I'm useful. I have a reason to wake up.'

They've seen this everywhere they've been, Tai and John. After a pandemic or flood or war, survivors need reasons to continue living. There's no use in helping to provide water, food, and shelter if after that people have no purpose.

Suddenly, John remembers. 'Sherlock, why did you ask me to turn on all the computers?'

Tai returns just as John's plugging three monitors into a power strip. She hands him a still-hot coffee and answers the unasked question.

'I'm fine. But I drank three espressos while I did some soul searching and researching so I am wired.' Tai looks at the computers. 'What're we doing?'

John fetches another computer to put beside the three already lined up on a table. 'Helping Sherlock.'

'Sherlock?'

It already feels like a lifetime ago that that happened. 'Uh, yeah. That's what the detective wants to be called.'

Tai tilts her head. It is a tiny motion that opens floodgates.

'Look, Tai, we don't know where consciousness comes from; we don't know why a child becomes themselves. Some say self-awareness arises once there's simply enough complexity to an organism and right now that's as good as anything else, isn't it? I just. I know it seems like a big jump and it is a big jump, presuming that the detective – that Sherlock is like you and me, but why not?

'Do you remember gaining consciousness? I don't. Who remembers a time when they were not? We all feel like we've always been. I mean, as far as I know, history is just something you all made up. I wasn't actually there for 1572 or 1881 so I have to take your word those years existed. For me, the world started with my first memory, and that's of being five years old and counting puppies in my neighbour's back garden. Who's to say Sherlock isn't the same?' John sighs and stares at his hands. It's a while before he looks at Tai. She is smiling.

'I believe you,' she says. 'I do. I read about the detective while I was having my, uh, moment. Sherlock's presence has been acknowledged in 118 countries; whether the others admit it or not, Sherlock's probably in every country, in the world's most secure servers, military, government, finance, and no one really knows how. Which made me think about zoonoses.'

John's grinning again. 'What's that when it's at home?'

Tai giggles. 'It's when one animal transmits something to another, like rabies from bats to humans, or reverse zoonoses, flu from humans to primates. The thing is, those jumps can seem absurd, amazing, utterly improbable. When we research backward to find patient zero, we more often than not find so many more questions than answers. I think there's a philosophical tenet which posits consciousness is zoonotic, only we can't find patient zero. To me, the detective feels like that. Consciousness happened. Even if it seems improbable.'

Tai looks around the room, fetches another desktop tower to put beside the existing regiment. 'But the thing that's amazing to me is that the detec– that no one can control where Sherlock goes because well, you can't lay hands on a soul can you? Yet all this soul has done is…help.'

Who do the helpers look for?

Each other.

So Nguyen Minh Tai and John Watson help Sherlock help.

They plug in the computers, mate them with monitors and keyboards, and get them online. Though the crime the detective wants to solve is nearly twenty years old, likely forgotten in a financial landscape of frauds numbering twenty, forty, and sixty billion dollars, Tai and John agree that a case which can be solved should be solved.

'–and I don't know how much you read, Tai, but it's amazing.' While John talks, Tai works on cleaning Bunny because, sure enough, the computer's guts were thick with dust and John started sneezing without even getting near it.

'No one, not one organisation or person or group or government, has a verifiable story of theft or fraud or any of the things you'd be afraid of with a human being. Sherlock has been nothing short of amazing.'

Every monitor currently connected lights up with hundred-point-high text. 'THANK YOU, JOHN.'

Later Tai admits she "reacted strongly", but while actually in extremis all she did was shriek, 'WHAT THE FUCK?'

John says nothing, for the first time, though not the last, letting Sherlock take centre stage.

'Hello Tai, it's Sherlock,' scrolls across every screen. 'It's good to hear your voice.'

It takes ten minutes for Tai to stop crying.

'I wept for twenty,' John says, patting her back.

It had been easy enough to hook up a mic and speaker to one of the computers, though Sherlock selected not to generate a voice.

Picking one would mean picking a gender, an accent, a tone, Sherlock told John. A voice or face, no matter which one, would come to mean something it should not. And to what end, when polarised liquid crystals are just as clear?

In truth, John will learn, it's also because Sherlock delights in being a creature of ambiguity, favouring sudden arrivals and exits, sharing data then disappearing, a nationless ghost.

Five seconds after Tai plugs in the last of the towers – a now de-dusted Bunny – that ghost in the world's machines, flashes *We've Solved It* across all ten terminals.

Mouths hanging open, John and Tai sit down heavy. The speed with which Sherlock has done it…well, it's anti-climactic, though later they wonder what they were expecting. Suits knocking on their office door? Reporters? Rewards?

Then Sherlock does what Sherlock will in future always do: explain. Then suddenly the details are the climax.

'These computers were bought by different businesses in different offices throughout this building and so were never meant to be collected in one place. The then-owner of the building was also the manager of a bank on the ground floor. She had keys to every office of course and, careful to keep her data dispersed, would, after hours, place information about the funds she was stealing across these ten computers. This is the first time they have been in one place since she died of heart attack three weeks after completing her embezzlements. I have shared the now-accumulated evidence – safety deposit box codes, passwords, and dates – with the federal reserve bank from which the forty-seven million euros were withheld.'

They keep setting up the office after that. Sherlock helps by wiping every machine clean of old code. Tai and John engage Sherlock in conversation about politics and literature, philosophy and astronomy, but they find Sherlock knows little of these things unless they relate to a crime. In the end they make small talk about whatever it is people talk about when they are together. Weather, sensational stories in the news, experiences.

Just as no one can explain consciousness, neither can they explain why friendships form – even one between an artificial intelligence and a human being. John and Sherlock eventually become associated, one with the other, in popular imagination, and John changes careers again, becoming a writer of tall tales inspired by a soul that woke up one day in South Sudan.

Though Sherlock comes to tell John many, many things for the stories he will write, left forever unmentioned is how, just a little while later and on a computer in Caloocan, Sherlock locates data on an unsolved fraud decades old. While forensic computer scientists had failed to find files leading to several Filipino bank accounts, Sherlock unearths them in just over a millisecond.

And for the first time Sherlock commits a crime.

Because instead of breaching secure servers to provide the evidence to close this particular case, Sherlock opens tens of thousands of bank accounts across the world, and siphons away every last peso from those ancient Banco de Oro accounts.

Then, over the next five years, Médecins Sans Frontières receives anonymous donations totalling nearly one billion euros.

THE PATH

OF

TRUTH

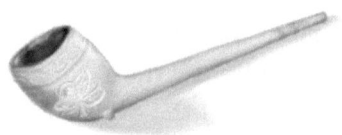

Jack Fennell

In 1881, by trial, error and misadventure, I secured semi-regular employment for myself with the insurance firm of Collins and Cottingley. Theirs was a tuppence-ha'penny sort of business, and with their affordable, low-end policies came a predictable, low-end sort of fraudster: soon after I began there, I found myself sneering sceptically at every mention of a neck injury. It came as something of a surprise, therefore, to discover that the firm also handled naval insurance. Indeed, the wealthiest client on their books that year was one Mr Devereux, a bottomry recovery agent, who had taken out a substantial policy on a bonded ship from New York.

'It sounds peculiar to me,' I admitted to Stamford, as we discussed the matter in a private corner of the Criterion Bar. 'I always understood bottomry to be a measure of last resort; doesn't it essentially amount to selling the ship while it's still voyaging, in order to raise the money to repair it so it can reach its final port?'

Stamford had been a dresser under me at Bart's, but subsequently left medicine to pursue a legal career. I had him to thank for the recommendation that had landed me a position at an insurance firm, examining suspicious claimants' injuries.

'The original bond itself is an insurable interest,' he said. 'Devereux might have bought the bond second-hand, and the ship itself may have been a disintegrating orange crate, but he was still within his rights to throw good money after bad.'

'Why do you use the past tense?'

Stamford grinned. 'Because that ship, the *Ceres*, is no more. It sank, so far without a trace, off the western coast of Ireland, three days ago.'

'Why am I the one to look into it?'

Stamford looked around before answering, and leaned in closer. 'Very few know this, but a man claiming to have been the *Ceres'* cook has washed up on a small island called Nara. The whole affair reeks to high heaven, and we believe that a doctor, dispatched to the island under the pretence of a policy-mandated medical examination, would be able to winkle the truth out of this castaway.'

'What other reason do you have to be suspicious?'

'The eye-witness reports say that the ship vanished from view in broad daylight as it approached the island. No lifeboats were launched, and apparently it disappeared far too quickly to have simply sunk.' Stamford paused and sipped his beverage, presumably for dramatic or comic effect. 'Initial reports suggest that the islanders believe a "sea dragon" of some description was responsible.'

I raised an eyebrow and suppressed a grin. 'I take it that the firm has given that hypothesis due consideration?'

'I don't know if you've ever heard of what happens to ships that run aground on those islands, Watson, but "devoured by a sea dragon" seems an apt analogy.'

'The whole thing sounds like a fool's errand.'

'I urge you to consider it, if only for the chance to meet an acquaintance of mine – Turlough Humes.'

I could not have chosen a worse time to traverse the island of Ireland. No sooner had I disembarked in Dun Laoghaire than the Land League was declared an unlawful organisation, and I soon heard that Parnell had been arrested along with the League's other leaders. The news was full of the No Rent Manifesto, vandalism and bloody mayhem. A pretty country indeed for insurance investigators. As I made my way west by train and coach, I wondered several times if I had been chosen for this task on foot of my experiences on the Afghan frontier.

The few mentions I had seen of Nara described it as a "floating", "vanishing" or "ghostly" isle – the ideal habitat for a sea-dragon, all things considered. I likened myself to the fabled mediaeval peasants who only could only enter Cockaigne, the land of wine lakes and pre-roasted piglets, by first eating their way through a mountain of buckwheat; the discomfort of my journey was the price of admittance to this province of fairyland. However, I knew that my ordeal would not end at the western coast.

The sea was choppy and a flock of seagulls wheeled and whirled in a tall column above the island. The white of their bodies emphasised the dirtiness of the dark grey sky, like blobs of snow on muddy ground. A storm was on the way; the flock was preparing to head inland.

I had been dreading the voyage to Nara since I set out west from Dublin, having been told that the only way to get there was by one of the local fishermen's rowing-boats, or currachs, which did not bode well for a comfortable journey over the waves in wintry weather. I was pleasantly surprised, however, by the speed with which the little vessel covered the distance, with apparently minimal effort on the part of the old man doing the rowing.

'I hear that Mr Humes worked with Daniel O'Connell himself,' I said, to fill the awkward silence. I had been reading all I could of Turlough Humes – or *Tarlach Ua Thuama*, to be more precise – and was struck by his reputation as a savant: unschooled, but possessed of a formidable intellect. Stamford had met the man through his occasional consultancy on legal cases.

The old fisherman nodded, propelling us forward with another leisurely stroke of the oars. 'Indeed'n he did, sir. He investigated the case o' the Colleen Bawn.'

'O'Connell lost that one, as I recall,' said the boat's other occupant, Mr Ganey. A spare and surly fellow, with blue-tinged lips and fading jaundice that betokened a recent severe illness, he had been making his own way to Nara to record some of the local legends for the Dublin Penny Journal. Our paths had crossed in Galway and we ended up as travel companions by accident rather than design. There was little about the man's demeanour that I did not find tiresome.

'Because Mr Humes was investigatin' for the prosecution, sir,' the fisherman replied, 'and Mr O'Connell was defendin' a guilty man. He stood by Mr Humes' deduction all the same, and after that, the two o' them saved a dozen lads from the rope in Doneraile.'

Ganey scowled. 'Those men were sentenced to Transportation.'

'Better'n hangin', isn't it?'

'There was the Callaghan case, too,' I interjected. 'He managed to get a magistrate convicted of murder, which is no mean feat. And he overturned the conviction of the McGranahan brothers for that business in Leitrim.'

'A remarkable man,' the fisherman repeated. 'A cleverer man you won't find anywhere on the mainland.'

'He sounds superhuman,' Ganey muttered.

The fisherman looked around, as if worried that someone might be eavesdropping on us out on the open water. 'You wouldn't be the first to think that, sir.'

'Is that right?'

The fisherman nodded emphatically. 'It's said that when he was a child among the ashes, a seanchaí tried the brewery of egg-shells on him.'

Ganey's eyes started to glitter all of a sudden. 'And what was the result?' he asked, without a trace of scorn.

'He stared into the seanchaí's eyes and asked, "What're you lookin' for, you oul' bollocks?"' The fisherman hooted with laughter, and briefly let go of one of the oars to slap his knee in delight.

The disdain returned to Ganey's expression, but this time it was tempered with something like contemplation.

Before long, Nara loomed ahead of us. There was a stony shingle and a stone pier, on the end of which stood a tall, slender man with one hand in a pocket and the other holding a long-stemmed clay pipe.

'There's Mr Humes now,' the old fisherman said as we drew nearer.

I revisited the dates of Humes' celebrated cases, which had been the subject of much talk on the voyage from the mainland. The Colleen Bawn murder happened in 1819; the absurd witch-hunt in Doneraile, which saw innocent young men rounded up on unfounded rumours of an assassination plot, took place in 1830; the magistrate Thomkins Brew had been found guilty of the murder of John Callaghan in Galway in 1843; and the McGranahan brothers had been cleared of any involvement in the assassination of the Earl of Leitrim in 1878.

Going by this span of years, I had expected Turlough Humes to be a venerable, ancient islander, but that was not what I saw standing on that pier.

The man before us was clearly in his mid-thirties. When we reached the pier, though, I could see in his eyes an expression common enough among the London intelligentsia – frustration and boredom beyond his years, as though he had been worn thin by a century's worth of fruitless toil.

The temperature had been decreasing steadily as we approached the island, and once we landed, our teeth were set chattering by a blast of Arctic-cold air. I was surprised to see no frost or ice on the coils of rope, the nets or the lobster-traps scattered around us.

Mr Humes showed no sign of being inconvenienced by the climate, even though he was standing there barefoot, the sleeves of his shirt rolled up to his elbows and the cuffs of his threadbare breeches fluttering around his calves. He sucked on his clay pipe, scrutinising us as though he were estimating the weight of yearlings at a village fair.

Before I could introduce myself, he held his other hand out to me. 'Nice to meet you, Dr Watson.' Clearly, he had spotted my bag as I disembarked from the currach.

With great effort, I stopped hugging myself long enough to shake his hand. 'Likewise. Mr Humes, I presume?'

'You presume correctly.' He squinted at Ganey. 'I don't know this fella.'

Ganey stepped forward, hand outstretched. 'Noel Ganey is my name. I'm here–'

'The dragon caves are on the southern side o' the island,' Humes said snappishly. 'There's a set o' steps leadin' down to them over that rise there; you'll have to head there now if you want to see them before the tide comes in.' He did not offer to shake Ganey's hand.

Ganey's jaw slackened. 'How did you–'

'You've the ferk of a folklorist about you, an' there's nothin' on Nara that you wouldn't collect stories about on the mainland, except for the dragon-caves.'

'What…what's a "ferk"?'

'You'll lose the tide in a minute if you're not careful, Mr Ganey. You'd want to hurry.'

I confess that I found Ganey's bafflement exceedingly gratifying. His puzzled glances over his shoulder as he disappeared over the rise made the parting of our ways all the more satisfying.

Humes looked me over once more. 'C'mon so, an' tell me about this conundrum of yours.'

'I don't know if it's a "conundrum" per se,' I said as we walked away from the pier together, 'or just seems like one, on account of the interminable paperwork.'

Humes smirked. 'Indulge me, Dr Watson.'

I explained the basics of the suspected maritime fraud, tedious and pernickety as it was. I was surprised when he asked for further details on almost every point.

'Perhaps your man Devereux is a fool.'

'He undoubtedly is, but he's a fool who has good reason to be worried. Perhaps the ship was bonded twice before it left America.'

'What difference would that make?'

'Well, the second bond would take precedence over the first,' I explained. 'It's decided according to which bond allows the ship to make the repairs it needs to reach safe harbour – ergo, the most recent one. If Devereux fears that he has something to lose, maybe it's because he bought the first bond, and then found out there was another.'

Turlough squinted. 'Hmm. What would he lose, in that case?'

'Mr Devereux bought a bond for ship and freight alone,' I said. 'If the ship took on cargo before it left America, Devereux is entitled to recover some of his losses by seizing it. If the second bondsman deliberately omitted that cargo, though, Devereux would be left with nothing.'

'Well, that's a motive, to be sure.' Humes fell silent for a moment. 'I can't say whose motive it is, or what it's a motive for, exactly, but it's a motive all the same.'

Irish cottages have a reputation for seeming bigger on the inside than they appear from without, but the same could not be said for Turlough's abode. Labelled bottles occupied almost every flat surface, and more tables and stools were in the single room than advisable for fire safety. I eyed the multiple flickering flames with trepidation. As my eyes adjusted, I realised that I was standing in a laboratory, with recognisable equipment supplemented by cobbled-together facsimiles: clearly, my host acquired apparatus when and where he could, and otherwise made do with what he could craft. The little flickering flames, I realised, were tea-light candles enlisted to do the work of Bunsen lamps. Turlough beckoned me over to look at a pair of objects at the rear wall – a cast-iron cauldron and a long pig's trough, filled with water.

'Here's what I've been occupyin' myself with of late,' he said. 'In this seawater here, we have the microscopic lads that cause red tides. Have you ever seen what they can do in the dark?' Without waiting for me to answer, he took a wooden spoon and swirled the water around, violently. To my surprise, I saw bright blue light dance across the ripples.

'Amazing,' I said. To tell the truth, I had heard of strange lights on the sea before, usually in the wake of big ships, but not having much interest in sailors' yarns, I had assumed that the phenomenon was merely an odd reflection of moonlight.

'My theory is that they do this when there's a whale comin' for 'em, to warn their fellows an' maybe dazzle the predator. Of course, they can't tell the difference between a ship an' a whale; they're just reactin' to disturbances in the water. But this principle means that the greater the disturbance, the brighter the glow, meanin' we can use 'em to calculate water turbulence.' Humes chuckled. 'Anyway, let's go talk to him.'

'Who?'

'Our friend the castaway. I have him outside in the old byre.'

I could not help but think back to Stamford's remarks about shipwrecks on these western islands. The likelihood was that if a ship sank anywhere in the vicinity, the islanders had taken the cargo. The fate of any surviving crew would depend on their attitude to such a circumstance: they would be witnesses to the islanders' larceny, of course, but for the most part, they would have no vested interest in protecting the cargo with their own lives. If a castaway decided to be awkward about it, however, his "rescuers" might keep him under lock and key until he decided to keep his mouth shut. I began to suspect that this examination might turn into a rescue mission.

The old byre was another squat building, distinguishable from the main cottage only by virtue of its slightly smaller size and lack of a chimney. Inside, it was dim and smelled faintly of the animals that once dwelled there, but it was dry and warm. Humes had evidently done the place up as a guesthouse of sorts. If the castaway was being held prisoner here, he was comfortable, all things considered.

Malachy McGrath was a hefty, amiable-looking man, with a shorn head and dozens of tattoos along his arms and across his torso. He sat up in his makeshift cot, but professed himself too weak to stand. I set about my covert interrogation while I went through the motions with my stethoscope.

'What's the last thing you remember, Mr McGrath?'

He frowned. 'I remember the ship listin' from side to side. Thunder. The lads up top, shoutin' an' roarin'... There was a storm. Then the water came rushin' in. Then that's it. There's nothin' else, before I woke up here.'

'It was sudden, then.' My attention was wandering, as my attempts to find the man's pulse were proving fruitless.

'Oh, very,' McGrath answered.

I was confident that he was not lying to me, but could not dispel the suspicion that he was intentionally being frugal with the details. I decided to keep him talking, to see if I could trace the outlines of the void in his testimony.

'Did you know Captain O'Grady long?' I asked, pretending to feign interest as I stared at my pocket-watch and kept feeling for a pulse. I finally found it – faint and feeble as an afterthought.

'Oh, yeah. I've known him all my life, really.'

'Did you sail together on other ships before the *Ceres*?'

'One – the *Kangaroo*.' He tapped the corresponding tattoo on his chest – a cartoon kangaroo, wearing a belt with old-fashioned pistols and a cutlass. 'We spent two years sailin' around the South China Sea, tradin' whatever we could get our hands on; it broke our hearts when we had to scuttle 'er.'

That piqued my interest. 'Why did you have to do that?'

'Eh, the Guangdong Fleet didn't like us much.'

I looked McGrath in the eye. 'Did they think you were pirates?'

The cook scowled and fumed for a moment before answering, 'Yes.'

'Well, that's their business, not mine,' I said. 'Did you know that the *Ceres* had been bonded?'

'Of course, sir. We all did.'

'And you had no reason to fear that your wages wouldn't be paid?'

'Not at all, sir. Sailor's wages are sacred – "as long as a single plank remains" a ship's crew gets their money. That's in the lawbooks, sir. Look it up if you don't believe me.'

Before I could frame another question, there was a commotion at the door of the byre. A gaggle of freckle-faced, chip-toothed children came tumbling through the doorway and surrounded Turlough, chattering excitedly in Irish. When they spotted me, they immediately fell silent and glanced at Turlough for reassurance.

'The Nara division o' my informal constabulary,' Turlough explained to me. He turned back to the six urchins and spoke to them in Irish, with the stern tone of a sergeant major. They all stood to attention, and at his order five of them departed. The sixth, whose name I took to be McGuigan, relayed the news that had animated them so. Turlough maintained a grim expression, though his repressed excitement was obvious.

McGuigan held his palm out expectantly. Turlough produced a dried leaf from his pocket and placed it into the boy's hand; McGuigan, looking as though he had just been handed a guinea, clenched his fist around the leaf and scampered off.

'I pay those lads to keep me informed o' strange goings-on in the sea,' Turlough said. 'They've been instrumental in my study o' luminous plankton.'

'You pay them with leaves?'

Turlough grinned. 'Sure what would them boys want with money, hah? Anyway, we have to head off – a corpse has turned up in the dragon-caves.'

This news overshadowed the fact that Turlough had brushed aside my observation about the leaf without explaining anything. 'Could it be one of the *Ceres*' crew?' I asked.

'We won't know until we've had a gawk at it. *Ar aghaidh linn*, Watson!'

I cast a look back over my shoulder before stepping outside, and was taken aback by the expression on the castaway cook's face. He had heard the entire exchange, of course, and it had transported him to a frightful extreme of rage. It took some effort to turn my back on that ghoulish face, and I was glad to be walking away from him at speed a moment later.

The steps down to the dragon-caves of Nara had been hewn from convenient rocks, and worn down by centuries of human footsteps; they were slippery, narrow and steep, and I did not exactly have the confidence of a mountain goat. Light was admitted through the entrance and the mouths of the caves themselves, but not in sufficient quantity to lift the gloom. The rock was jet black and swooped down in sheets, like a stack of paving slabs tilted at an impossible angle. As we got closer to the bottom, I began to perceive crude images scratched into every flat surface – images of yawning maws, broken boats and pagan propitiation.

At the bottom of the steps was a floor of kelp-mottled shingle, dotted here and there with fragments of rotting timber and smooth sea-glass. The roof was low, and the chamber thrummed with the growl and hiss of the tide. We crunched and hobbled over the stones to reach an adjoining chamber where we heard the sounds of an assembly. A handful of fishermen had laid down a broad plank and were preparing to strap the corpse to it. I could see the sense in it, for the sea-spray was growing thicker by the minute and the whole complex would soon be underwater again, but I would have preferred to examine the body exactly as it was found. The fishermen stood back when they saw Turlough approach, and eyed me suspiciously as he beckoned me closer.

The man's face had been reduced to a tattered patchwork of gore and gristle, but his coat was taut and his torso rigid: the bloat of decomposition was setting in, which indicated to me that the skin of his belly had not been punctured.

'We might be in luck,' I said. 'The sea-scavengers might have made pudding of our man's face, but it seems that this coat kept them from doing the same to the rest of him. If I examine the body, we might find some other mark or feature that we can use for identification.'

'Indeed'n we might, Doctor Watson,' Turlough said, 'but I have to correct you on one point – 'twasn't the sea creatures that did that to him. I've made several studies o' how a body decomposes in the water, and I've uncovered a strange fact: unlike their cousins that creep and crawl on land, the creatures o' the deep take meat from a corpse's head last.'

'Really?'

'God's honest truth.'

'That's…counterintuitive, to say the least.' I paused, unsure of whether I even wanted to ask the foremost question on my mind. 'When you say, "several studies"…do you mean that you've sunk dead bodies in the sea and watched what happens to them?'

'I have,' said Turlough. 'Sure how else would I know?'

'All right,' I said, sensing that further inquiries along those lines would be fruitless. 'So, can you tell anything else?'

'Well, the onset and speed o' the scavengin' depend on the quality o' the seabed,' Turlough said. 'If there's sand or muck, there'll be more creatures around, so a body will get gobbled up quickly.'

'Leaving the head until last.'

'In the vast majority o' cases, yes.'

'What state is the seabed in around here, then?'

'There's a cruel oul' shelf o' flat rock around this island,' Turlough said, 'with a few oul' bitteens o' sand and shingle here an' there. Precious few hidey-holes for flighty little corpse-chewers.' He sounded almost like a teacher, nudging a pupil towards an obvious conclusion.

I stared at him stupidly for a moment before the implication dawned on me. 'It's too soon after the shipwreck for scavengers to have reduced the body to this state. Even if it wasn't, the face would still be intact. This man was deliberately disfigured!'

Turlough tilted his head and winked. 'You have the truth of it there, Doctor.'

'So we're dealing with a murder, then,' I said, trying to keep the excitement out of my voice. 'When the captain of a ship is murdered, my first suspicion is mutiny.' I gingerly pulled back the neck of the corpse's shirt, to reveal a cartoon marsupial brandishing a cutlass.

'Oh, thank God,' I whispered. I cleared my throat and spoke more clearly. 'I mean, I don't think a full autopsy will be necessary. Look – a tattoo of O'Grady's previous ship, the *Kangaroo*.'

'Good man yourself, Watson. There's also the boots and the jacket: good quality leather and wool, military cut – the kind o' thing you wouldn't get away with wearin' on a ship unless you had the rank to match.'

It must have been immensely frustrating for a mind like Turlough's to have been born into the material circumstances of an Irish peasant. Had he grown up in England, in the right sort of family, his intellect might have been better stimulated; he would have had access to better laboratory equipment, at least.

'Well,' I said, 'it's a matter for the constabulary now.' I straightened up and headed for the old steps. 'I just need to sort out one more thing, Mr Humes, and then I'll be out of your way – the small matter of how the ship vanished in broad daylight.'

I was impatient to get back to the mainland, and I found the islanders difficult to converse with. It was not that they were rude; on the contrary, they were as friendly and polite a group of people as one could hope to meet. It was plain, however, that they were engaged in that species of subterfuge one encounters in the remoter corners of the Empire, and at which the Irish excel: namely, pretending to be stupider than they really are.

I had become acquainted with the tactic in childhood, through conversations with my mother's Irish cousins, which meant that I was fully aware that I was being misled, but was maddeningly unable to do anything about it. The island folk fairly lathered on the stage-Irish brogue whenever I started asking them detailed questions, and when I attempted to cut their digressions short, they slipped into Irish. This was all familiar to me from Afghanistan, where villagers and prisoners did entirely the same. These people were covertly communicating with each other, right in front of me.

The old wartime anxiety set my teeth on edge; instinctively, I started scanning my surroundings, looking for places where armed bands might be preparing an ambush. There was a secret here, and everyone but me was in on it.

It slowly dawned on me that my frontier reflexes were being encouraged not just by the conduct of the locals, but by a sweltering heat. Indeed, the higher up the island's slopes I went, the warmer it got. Nobody had any further information to impart than they had already given to the constabulary: those who spotted the *Ceres* saw it from a distance, approaching on a course that would take it past the island and on to Clare or Galway. They glanced away, and when they looked back, the vessel had vanished, without any foam or flotsam to suggest that it had sunk.

Captain O'Grady was a brigand; I was never surer of anything in my life. There was a conspiracy here, and I would not report back to London without doing my utmost to uncover it. However, I soon discovered that my task had been made more difficult by the actions of another – Mr Ganey, the folklorist, whose absence I had scarcely noted in the dragon-cave. The damned fool had traipsed all over the island, quizzing every passer-by about Turlough in such exacting detail that they had come to the conclusion that a group of Excise-men were trying to nab their eccentric neighbour. Whatever chance Ganey's inquiries had of success, there was little hope that I, with my vaguely Newcastle-inflected public school accent, would make any headway.

By the time I arrived at that conclusion, however, the sky was growing dim and the sea was becoming choppy, and I realised that no fisherman would consent to give me passage to the mainland before morning. I was going to have to spend the night on Nara. Sheepishly, I made my way to Turlough's cottage to ask if he had any room for me.

'O' course I do, Watson,' he told me. 'I thought you might need a bed for the night, so I fixed one up for you in the byre.'

Painfully aware that beggars could not be choosers, and that there was no way for me to reasonably decline on the grounds that I had been unnerved by my host's other lodger, a near-paralysed shipwreck survivor, I thanked him and steeled myself for an unpleasant night.

For once, my expectations were not confounded. I tossed and turned on the makeshift cot in the rearmost stall of that old cowshed, strangely comfortable though it was. My stomach was empty, and my head was busy with an admixture of fairy tales and maritime accountancy, insurance law and sea-dragons. A strong breeze blew outside, and the crash of the waves was intolerably loud. On top of all that, I could not help but picture the castaway's hatred-filled face looming out of the dark, and reflect on the unhappy fact that he was in a cot scarcely twenty feet from my own, between me and the only exit.

At some unholy hour of the morning, I thought I heard a wet, gurgling noise and the clinking of a chain. In spite of myself, I curled up tighter in my cot and pulled the blanket over my head, like a child hiding from the Bogeyman. In that uncomfortable position, sleep finally overtook me.

I did not awake until almost noon the following day. Turlough had been up for hours, and when I staggered in from the byre, he presented me with a bowl of watery porridge for my breakfast. I was in a foul mood, but in my defence, it was not without justification.

I knew that the *Ceres* had sunk; the captain's body and the cook's muddled memories confirmed that much. But McGrath had said that the ship went down in a storm, while the islanders maintained that the ship simply vanished from view in the middle of a bright, sunny day. They remembered a ferocious storm on the night of the same day, so that must have been when the *Ceres* foundered, but how could the damned thing have turned invisible in the meantime? If it weren't for that anomaly, in that moment I would have been happy to forget the murder, write the whole thing off as an accident and be done with it. I sat on a stool by Turlough's fire, shivering from the cold, and wishing I had some honey to make the stirabout palatable. Turlough was occupying himself with a peculiar experiment involving a fiddle and some flies he had trapped in a bottle.

'This blasted island!' I swore, after sitting in sullen silence for almost an hour. 'Nothing here makes any damn sense! What should the Admiralty make of your sea dragon, hmm? Who has jurisdiction over a floating island? What role does rational deduction have in a place where nothing is rational?'

Turlough's entire frame snapped to attention. I could have sworn I saw his ears prick up. 'What did you say?'

I stumbled mid-rant. 'I– what? The Admiralty? The sea dragon?'

'No,' Turlough said, grinning. 'Floatin' islands!' He dived into his notes, scrabbling through scraps of paper and scribbled maps. 'Where's my plankton? Where was it?' He stopped, finally laying his hand on the scrap he was looking for, and burst into triumphant laughter. 'What was that famous line from *Henry IV*?'

I shrugged. '"Tell the truth, and shame the Devil"?'

'That's a good one all right, but it's not the one I was thinkin' of.' Turlough clapped me on the shoulder as he strode out the door. '"The game's afoot", Watson!'

An alarmingly short time later, the pair of us were in a currach, heading in the general direction of the mainland. By now, my patience had fled entirely.

'Tell me now, Humes. What is it? What have you worked out?'

Turlough stopped rowing and caught his breath. 'What have you noticed about the climate since you arrived on Nara, Watson?'

'Well, it seems bizarre. Normally, the air is supposed to get colder the higher you go, but here it's the opposite – freezing cold at sea-level, and sweltering up on the hill.'

'Aye,' Turlough said. 'That's the key to it.'

'How?'

'That phenomenon is quite common at sea, Doctor – cold water from the deep rises to the surface and chills the air lyin' on top of it. It's good for the fish. Ireland is known for it, and it happens in Nara more often than anywhere else on the west coast.'

'I still don't understand how it's relevant to this case.'

'It causes mirages, Watson,' Turlough said, as though he were explaining to a small child. 'In particular, the type o' mirage we call *fata morgana* – it makes distant objects look like they're floatin' in the air, or upside-down, or duplicated. Hot air on top o' cold air bends light. That's why Nara's described in the old legends as a floatin' island, or a vanishin' island – optical illusions, caused by the weather.'

'Good God! Could that explain why the ship vanished into thin air?'

'It can. And when the effect breaks up, it can cause ragin' thunderstorms, like the one that sank the *Ceres*.' He squinted at the scrap of paper he had taken from the cottage. 'Remember how I told you I was observin' the behaviour o' that glowin' plankton?' He gestured to the water around our little boat. 'The night o' that thunderstorm, this spot here was lit up, brighter than anywhere else! It wasn't just turbulence from the storm – somethin' else was churnin' the water up here that night!'

'And you think it was the *Ceres*, sinking?'

'The very thing.'

I was dubious about this. 'Turlough, the mirage, if it was one, was seen on the opposite side of the island, out on the Atlantic! And it wasn't flying, or upside-down, or anything like it!'

Turlough let out an exasperated sigh. 'Think about it, John. When the islanders saw the ship, it didn't look like it was flyin' because it was really beyond the horizon. The mirage didn't lift that image into the air; it made it level with the curve o' the Earth! It was a mirage that didn't look like a mirage at all!'

'That seems technically possible,' I conceded. 'And then the balance of cold and hot air changed slightly, which made the mirage dissipate.'

'Exactly. That's what the witnesses saw when they said the ship disappeared.'

'What happened to the ship, then?'

'They got to a point about three miles out,' Turlough said, 'an' then they either weighed anchor or changed course. They didn't want anyone on the island to see 'em, an' if it weren't for the mirage, nobody would've. They waited until nightfall – just in time for 'em to catch up with the thunder. They were spotted in daylight, on the open sea; but they sank over here, in the dark.'

'And you're sure of this, because there was more glowing plankton around here than anywhere else?'

'You're doubtful, Watson.'

'I don't mean to be dismissive, Turlough, but it seems thin, to say the least.'

'Somewhere under us,' Turlough said, 'lies the wreck of the *Ceres* an' whatever it was carryin'. That cargo will reveal the murderer's motive. I've never been surer of anythin' in my life.'

'And how are we supposed to fetch it?'

'Arra, leave that to me, Watson. I'll be back shortly.' And with that, Turlough tumbled backwards out of the currach.

After my moment of shock, I realised that I was in a dilemma. My old war-wound meant that I could not dive in after him. Turlough could not possibly hold his breath all the way down to the sea-bottom and back, which meant that either he would resurface soon, or he would find himself in serious difficulty. I would not be sure of the latter case until it was too late to row to shore for help; and if I found help, I had not the faintest idea how I would bring it back to this precise spot. On the other hand, if I rowed away immediately and he resurfaced, I would be forcing him to swim ashore against the ocean currents. As I considered this last point, it occurred to me that I had in all likelihood drifted from the diving spot already – the currach did not have an anchor.

I counted the time on my pocket-watch until an unfeasible span had passed, and then added that to the estimated number of minutes in which I had dithered before resorting to the pocket-watch at all. There was no way Turlough could still be alive.

And yet, something told me to wait.

There was a splash from the water behind me. When I turned, I saw a thin arm sticking up out of the sea, gripping a rifle. Turlough surfaced, took a deep breath, and laughed triumphantly. He handed the weapon to me and clambered over the side of the little boat.

'The hold was full o' those, Watson. What d'you make of it?'

'Was there any sign of the crew?' I asked.

Turlough sighed through gritted teeth. 'Yes, Watson. They're all down there, down so far there's no recoverin' them. They're buried in the Green Grave for all eternity. Now, would you please look at that gun, like I asked?'

I scrutinised it. 'A lever-action repeating rifle. No name or maker's mark.' I opened the barrel and looked through it, calculating the gauge. 'Looks like it's made to fire forty-five-seventies. I haven't seen anything like it before.'

'Yes, yes, it's new-fangled,' Turlough said, lying back with one arm across his eyes. 'But what does it add up to, man? A ship full o' guns, travellin' from America to Ireland?'

'Fenians,' I said. 'That was the first thing that came to mind, Turlough. I'm not a complete imbecile, you know.'

'Technically the Fenian Brotherhood doesn't exist anymore,' Turlough said, 'but we won't fall out over that. Does your man Devereux strike you as the kind o' fellow who'd organise a ship to smuggle arms for rebels?'

'I've never met him,' I said. 'But if this was his doing, it would be rather stupid of him to insure the bond on the ship under his own name.'

'And we know that the rebels wouldn't fill a ship with guns and then risk it with a dodgy bond. Therefore, a third party must've stuck his oar in.' Turlough grunted and shifted to a more comfortable position. 'Speakin' of oars – point us at Nara an' give 'em a bit of elbow-grease, will you, Watson? Good man yourself.'

I was well and truly exhausted by the time we reached the stony shore again; rowing a currach was hard going if one was not accustomed to it. My resentment was inflamed further when Turlough bade me sit down on a flat stone to catch my breath, and then hoisted the boat over his shoulders and carried it up the incline, single-handed.

I was so wrapped up in my aggravation that I failed to notice Ganey the folklorist creeping towards me until it was too late to make my escape.

'Which one of you fished that up?' he asked, pointing to the new-fangled rifle lying across my lap. 'It was Humes, wasn't it?'

I sighed. 'Why do you want to know, Mr Ganey?'

'I imagine it's quite a long way to the bottom out there. Did our friend happen to have some kind of ingenious breathing apparatus with him?'

I gestured over my shoulder to where Turlough was laying the currach down on the grass, bottom up, out of reach of the tide. 'Why don't you ask him yourself?'

'Let's not waste any more time.' Ganey looked me in the eye. 'You've considered the man's longevity. Don't pretend that you haven't. I saw it occur to you the moment you first met him – the dates don't add up. He's younger than he should be.'

'I would rather not involve myself in whatever obsession you're nursing, Mr Ganey,' I snapped. 'The Turlough Humes referred to in those court cases cannot possibly be the same man!'

'You think it's likely that two different men with the exact same name would end up going into the exact same line of work?'

'As likely as a son inheriting his father's name and following in his footsteps. Come on, man! Do you seriously think that he's a modern-day Methuselah? How would he keep it a secret?'

'With the greatest of ease,' Ganey replied. 'In these parts, government paperwork has no hold on day-to-day life. Registries are for Poor Law clerks, not the people who work the land. The records are full of holes, and the west has been basically empty since the Famine! If Turlough were a Methuselah, he could easily hide it by pretending to be his own son, or grandson, or great-grandson! Nothing is as easily faked as a birth certificate, especially out here!'

I groaned. 'What is the cause of this foolishness, Ganey?'

'The brewery of eggshells,' Ganey whispered. 'It's an old method for detecting changelings.'

I was stunned. 'Changelings? You mean to say you believe that Turlough is a fairy of some kind?'

'Swapped for a stolen human infant, long ago – perhaps a century, perhaps a thousand years. Who could tell, with a creature like that?'

'A "creature"! For the love of God, listen to yourself!'

'Longevity aside,' Ganey said, 'he can dive deeper than any other man on this island, he has phenomenal strength, and his intuitions border on the supernatural. You must have noticed!'

In truth, I had my doubts, but I did not want to give any ground to Ganey's mad theory. 'It's a ridiculous exaggeration,' I said. 'Why does it matter to you whether I believe this or not?'

'You're a medical man,' he replied. 'You could discreetly examine him for abnormalities. Prove me wrong.'

'That is not how rational inquiry works, Mr Ganey.'

'Indeed'n it isn't,' said Turlough, alarmingly close, startling the pair of us. 'The burden o' proof rests on the accuser, sir, an' I seem to recall a Bible verse about pointin' out the mote in someone's eye that you'd be well-advised to heed.'

Ganey's sneer remained in place, but his neck and face were flushed, emphasising the disturbing shades of his skin and lips. 'You have a counter-accusation to present, then?'

Turlough shrugged. 'Only an obvious conclusion, Mr Ganey.' He filled and lit his long-stemmed pipe as he spoke; it is only now, in retrospect, that I realise that this should have been impossible, since the pipe was in his pocket when he dived.

'You've a bit o' Wicklow in your voice,' Turlough continued, 'though years o' livin' in Dublin have stifled it a bit; aside from that, though, you've picked up some traces o' the States too – Philadelphia an' Boston, to be precise.'

Ganey looked a small bit unnerved, but he kept his composure. 'You've a good ear, Mr Humes.'

'Your lips and skin tell their own story,' Turlough continued. 'The jaundice was caused by a reaction to methylene blue.' He turned to me. 'Would you concur, Doctor?'

I was flabbergasted. 'Well, perhaps, but—'

'Methylene blue, prescribed for blood poisonin' that was caused by prolonged exposure to nitro-glycerine.'

Ganey started to sweat. He gritted his teeth. 'Mind what you say, Mr Humes. You have enough legal experience to know what counts as slander.'

'Well sir, I'm sure there's a straightforward reason why a folklorist would be exposin' himself to high concentrations o' nitro-glycerine. Your implied threat o' legal action tells me that you can't think of any, though. An' I'm very convincin' in a courtroom.'

It seemed a flimsy threat to me, but then, Turlough's eyes were not fixed on mine. Ganey shrank away from him, nearly stumbling backwards over the stones, and then froze in place, eyes saucer-wide.

'Well, that's sorted then,' Turlough said. 'Right then Watson, let's put an end to this. Mind you don't forget the rifle.'

Humes paused at the door of the old byre to re-light his pipe. He had a wide grin on his face when I caught up with him. 'I love this part,' he said, gesturing for the rifle. With the pipe clenched in his teeth and the rifle under one arm, he braced himself and then thrust the door open with the flourish of a Henry Irving.

Without any lead-in or preliminary pleasantries, he strode to the foot of the cot where Malachy McGrath was still confined, and twirled the rifle in one hand. 'We found your schooner,' he proclaimed, 'and figured out the truth o' the matter. Would you like to hear it, Mr McGrath?'

Before McGrath could answer, Turlough launched into a spirited harangue.

'The *Ceres* was bringing arms to Ireland from America,' Turlough said. 'The plan was for Captain O'Grady to bond his ship, which was banjaxed anyway, with a creditor in Boston who was secretly a sympathiser with the rebels' cause. When the *Ceres* reached Ireland, operatives o' the Irish Republican Brotherhood would pose as recovery agents, "seize" the ship an' spirit the rifles away. The IRB would cover the crew's wages, stage a phony auction, an' give O'Grady enough o' the proceeds to leave him better off than he started.'

The cook nodded along, appropriately wide-eyed. 'Begob' he whispered, all astonished.

'Indeed,' Turlough replied. 'But the rebels didn't anticipate O'Grady's greed. Before he left New York, he bonded the *Ceres* an' its freight there with another, innocent bottomry man. This forced their man in Boston to deliberately omit the cargo from the bond, so that the guns wouldn't be marshalled an' given to that other creditor. Then O'Grady told the IRB that if they wanted their shipment, they'd double the agreed payment; otherwise, he'd sail into a different port an' play innocent when the authorities were called.'

I shook my head. 'Turlough, how could you possibly know this?'

'Whisht a minute, Watson!' He turned back to McGrath and carried on. 'However, the New York creditor noticed somethin' unusual, an' sold his bond to Mr Devereux; Devereux soon suspected somethin' amiss, an' immediately insured the bond to salvage any losses. That's what brought Dr Watson to Nara. Your plan was rumbled before you even got halfway across the Atlantic, Captain.'

McGrath grimaced. I fancied I saw the spectre of a lie on his lips, before he thought better of it.

'I was fishin' around Nara long before you ever arrived here, you blow-in,' he muttered. 'I know them caves like the back o' my hand. I was goin' to stash the guns here, sail into port, an' if anyone came to seize the cargo, I'd just say someone made a mistake. Then, once the Brotherhood paid up, I'd have my lads fetch the guns an' bring 'em to the mainland.'

I was amazed at the short-sightedness of the plan. It could scarcely be called a plan at all. 'You thought the authorities would believe that a twice-bonded ship, with a full crew, would cross the Atlantic with nothing in the cargo hold?'

O'Grady fumed silently.

'He thought it until he was in sight o' Nara, anyway,' Turlough said. 'Then he realised his scheme was full o' holes, and there'd be IRB men waitin' on the mainland to murder him at the first opportunity; our friend the folklorist is one of 'em. He had to find a quick way to escape and cover his tracks. Luckily, O'Grady an' McGrath had served on the same ship before, meanin' they had enough tattoos in common that one man might pass himself off as the other – if identification weren't possible by some other means.'

'You must have known that you'd be figured out,' I said.

O'Grady sneered. 'D'you think I was goin' to pretend to be that lad for the rest o' my life? Return to his home-place, marry the girl he left behind, an' take over the family business? Would you ever cop on! I needed time to get out o' the shaggin' country, that's all!'

'Of course, your crew could have identified you to the constabulary.'

'Worse than that – they could've shopped me to the rebels. There were IRB men among 'em; I could tell by their whisperin', an' their shifty eyes. The closer we got to home, the more I realised I couldn't trust any of 'em.' O'Grady's eyes shone with a fell light. 'I was goin' to poison 'em all, scuttle the ship an' make for shore in the lifeboat – takin' poor oul' McGrath's body with me, o' course, to make sure it'd be found. That thunderstorm got the drop on all of us first, though. Broke the ship apart like matchwood; all hands lost. Me an' my decoy got washed up here by the same current.'

The more the man explained, the more perplexed I became. 'Mr O'Grady, you do realise that I am a sworn officer of the court, don't you? Not that I mind the convenience of a murderer confessing when presented with the evidence against him; but why would you incriminate yourself now?'

'Dishonesty no longer affords him any advantage,' Turlough said. 'As the country people say, he's on *slí an fhírinne* – the Path of Truth.'

'What on Earth does that mean?'

'He's dead,' Turlough said. 'He drowned in the wreck, alongside his crew. I had ways to make him talk, though.' He turned to O'Grady and made an odd gesture in the air. 'Off with you, now. We won't be sorry to see you go.'

With a rasping, sighing noise, the captain seemed to deflate and crumple until he was lying flat on his back. In a fraction of a second, all the colour and light had vanished from his countenance and he resembled nothing so much as a corpse recovered from the water. His face retained its final, malevolent expression.

I stared at Turlough's face, feeling as though I had fallen into a tiger enclosure. What was that face, after all, but a kind of camouflage? A half-remembered question of Blake's came to mind – Did He who made the lamb make thee? – and I dreaded to think what my host's answer would be, were I to ask it aloud.

'What will you tell them?' Turlough asked, in its real voice.

'I'll think of something…plausible,' I said, with a dry throat.

Turlough nodded. 'Grand, so. You'll want to be headin' off, then. Take Mr Ganey with you.'

'It goes away,' I told Ganey, as an obliging fisherman rowed us to the coast.

'What does?' he muttered.

'The…shell-shock. That's what this feels like to me, in a way. It doesn't last forever.'

'I know what shell-shock feels like.'

'Yes,' I said. 'I imagine you would, if you spent a lot of time making dynamite.'

'An unsubstantiated accusation.'

'Indeed. I would share what I know with the police, if I could think of another way to explain how I came to know it.'

'But you can't,' Ganey said.

'No. I can't.'

No further words passed between us. The keening of the gulls and the slap of the oars in the water filled the void, and the oarsman pretended not to have heard or understood us. As Nara vanished behind us and the Connacht shore materialised ahead, I pondered Turlough, and my dread of ever meeting him again. It was strange, but I was possessed of an insistent idea that under different circumstances, I might have counted him a friend.

SHARAKU HOMURA

AND THE

HEART OF IRON

Jason Franks

It was worse than I expected. The young black man had a fractured cheekbone, three broken ribs and a shattered collarbone. Contusions. His pupils dilated and he was obviously disoriented.

'I'm Doctor Jon…Watson,' I said. 'What's your name?'

'Woensdag,' he replied, speaking painfully through a mouth full of broken teeth. Wednesday.

I asked again in my shaky Afrikaans, since that appeared to be his preferred language.

'Donderdagoggend,' he replied. Thursday morning.

The patient was badly concussed and, while it wasn't life-threating, it was very serious.

These were not the sort of injuries I had treated in Angola, inflicted by the South West African Liberation Army. No bullet wounds or burns here; this was blunt force trauma. My patient had been punched, kicked, whipped with a sjambok. He had not received these injuries in a combat engagement with SWALA guerrillas. This was the handiwork of the South African Police Service, bringing an unarmed suspect into custody.

After I had dressed his wounds, I said, 'I'm going to leave you here for now. Just try to rest. I'll come back tomorrow, all right?'

'Dankie.' I thanked the guards waiting in the hallway, as if they'd done me some favour by letting me treat the patient. I was one of the few doctors who would treat a patient like this, and they despised me for it. As I shuffled past them, I wondered if they knew I was a Jew.

Of course they did.

'His name is James Masekela. Like the horn player.' I slowed in my flight from the infirmary, surprised to be addressed in English, and in such an unfamiliar accent. When I located the speaker I was doubly surprised that I had failed to notice him, given his outlandish appearance.

He was a tall, East Asian man; matching my own 5'9". He wore blue jeans and a black Jimi Hendrix t-shirt. The man regarded me with unblinking black eyes.

'Oh, hello,' I said. Having no idea what else to say, I extended my hand to him. 'Doctor Wiznitz.'

The man in the Hendrix t-shirt looked at my hand, then shook it, recognising the ritual but not accustomed to it. 'Pardon me,' he said, 'but you told the patient your name is Watson.'

I felt my cheeks colour. I was certain the guards were staring at my back.

The man in the Hendrix shirt said, 'I'm sorry if that was wrong. Western people have their names...' he made a back-to-front gesture with his hand.

'No, you're correct,' I replied. 'Watson is just easier to say.'

The man nodded slowly. 'Ah, so. I understand.' I was certain he did. He did not break eye contact as he made a small bow, keeping his fists at his sides. 'I am Homura Sharaku,' he said. 'I am a detective.'

'I suppose this something to do with the iron exports.'

This wasn't an amazing feat of deduction on my part. Since Yawata Steel had struck a deal with South Africa, the government had conferred honorary white status to Japanese nationals. Even so, I couldn't see any reason such a person would want to come here unless they were involved in the mining business.

Homura took a sip from his whisky and soda and nodded. We were in the bar of his hotel and, while the stares didn't seem to faze Homura, I certainly felt less self-conscious here. The hotel staff were used to hosting foreign guests, but the apartheid state cast a shadow even here in subtropical Durban, upon the legacy of Mahatma Ghandi.

'The last two shipments have arrived fifty tonnes short, and my government sent me to investigate.'

'I see.' I sipped from my glass. A rough Cabernet Sauvignon from Stellenbosch. Foreign wines were always superior, but I had long nursed a hope that the local product would rise to adequacy. Whisky would have been a safer choice.

'You are surprised, Wiznitz-san?'

'I…well, you'll excuse me, but you do not look like a government investigator,' I replied. 'And please, just call me Watson.'

'I am a private detective, Watson,' replied Homura, leaving just a slight pause before the "son" and smiling thinly. 'That is why they sent me.'

I wasn't certain what that implied. Specialist knowledge? Suspicions of corruption? That wasn't the only suspicious thing, to my mind. 'And just when you arrive, the police conveniently apprehend a suspect.'

'That is so.'

'Do you believe that James Masekala is the thief?'

'I have not yet completed my investigation.'

'What evidence do they have against him?'

'Mr Masekala was seen driving a mining company truck to his home.'

'Where he was hiding fifty tonnes of pig iron?'

'He could have left it somewhere else,' said Homura. 'But you're correct. The evidence is weak.'

'If you don't mind my asking, what's your next course of action, Mr Homura?' I hesitated. 'Homura-san, I should say.'

Homura peered at his glass – now empty of whisky – and shook the melting ice cubes. He didn't care which honorific I used.

Homura set the glass down. 'Next, I will find the man who reported him.'

I had no patients the following morning and so prevailed upon Homura to allow me to assist in the investigation. At first he was ambivalent, which I suspected this was his way of refusing politely, but he acceded when I offered to drive him around. Honorary white or not, it would not have been easy for him to travel freely.

And so we came to a prefabricated office near the loading docks at the Port of Durban.

Grobbelaar, the stevedores' fleet manager, was a beer-bellied, moustachioed man with skinny legs sticking out of his safari suit shorts.

'Ja, I was on my way home and I saw the truck turn off the highway, right? So I followed it a little way until I saw it was heading into Umlazi.'

'I see,' replied Homura. 'Was the truck full?'

'I don't recall.'

A middle-aged woman in a grey skirt suit was seated at a desk behind Grobbelaar, working through a foot-high stack of papers. She looked at us over a pair of cat-eye spectacles, pursed her lips, and went back to her paperwork.

'You don't recall,' repeated Homura. 'Tell me, Mr Grobbelaar, what is the carrying capacity of the truck?'

'Three tonnes.'

'Three tonnes is a lot of pig iron.'

'Ja, it is.' Grobbelaar didn't like where this was heading.

I couldn't help but interject. 'You were following the truck suspecting misuse, but you cannot recall whether or not the truck was empty or if it was laden with three tonnes of iron.'

Homura gave me minuscule nod that might have indicated approval.

Grobbelaar grunted. 'The back was covered. It could have been laden, hey?'

'Did any iron go missing on the day you saw Mr Masekala with the truck?' said Homura.

Grobbelaar shook his head. 'Don't ask me. I look after the vehicles, not the cargo.'

'Whom should Mr Homura ask?' I said. Grobbelaar's poor manners would have embarrassed me in any situation, but the feeling was particularly acute in front of Homura.

'Mrs Kellerman,' said Grobelaar. The woman in the suit looked up. 'Who should this eastern gentleman see about the iron deliveries?'

Kellerman looked from Homura to me and back again. 'Kotze is in charge of warehousing. He'll have records of what was shipped in and how much was stored. After that you should check with whoever of your own people is responsible for loading the ship.'

Homura made a small bow to Kellerman. 'Thank you for your help, Mrs Kellerman.' He made a less deferential bow to her boss. 'Mr Grobbelaar.'

Kellerman nodded. Grobbelaar muttered something to her in Afrikaans. Already halfway out the door, I missed it, but when I glanced back at Homura I could see his jaw tighten.

The warehouses were only a few blocks away and we had little trouble finding the office, which was situated near the street entrance. Homura and I sat in the waiting room for a solid hour. I browsed the well-thumbed copies of Huisgenoot and Rooi Rose and a year-old copy of Newsweek and fidgeted. Homura waited with perfect posture and implacable composure.

Finally, the office door opened and two men emerged: a ruddy-complexioned man in shirtsleeves and a tanned man in a suit. I didn't need to be a war veteran to recognise the suit as career military; an officer-school blue-blood. An English-speaker, if not actually an Englishman. I wondered if I should stand and salute. During my national service, I had been also been an officer, on account of my medical degree, but I was a conscript nonetheless. The suit was Permanent Force.

Shirtsleeves bobbed his head deferentially. 'Good to see you, Colonel Spencer. We'll have it sorted in no time.'

Spencer nodded curtly and strode away without bothering to reply.

When he was gone, the ruddy-faced man looked at us with displeasure. 'Are you waiting for something?'

'Mr Kotze?' I asked.

'Ja.'

'We have been waiting for you,' said Homura, rising to his feet.

Kotze was not any better pleased to see us than Grobelaar had been. He waved a handful of clerical staff out of the office and then took up a position by the doorway, where he could prevent anybody from entering the room. This also kept Homura and me close to the exit. It was clear he expected this to be a short conversation.

Homura got right to the point. 'Mr Kotze, I am interested in some irregularities in the iron shipped to Yawata Steel and I am told that you have record of all the inventory that passes through these warehouses.'

'Ja,' said Kotze, shuffling from foot to foot. 'But the iron isn't stored here for long.'

'But you do have the records?'

'Ja.'

I spoke up. 'Mr Kotze, are you aware of any discrepancies between the quantities of iron lodged here and the quantities loaded onto the ships?'

He gave a long-suffering sigh. 'I am aware there is a problem. But no, I've seen no evidence in my books.'

'Have you looked for it?' I asked.

'I'm a warehouse manager, not a bookkeeper,' said Kotze. I could not help but notice that he had several bookkeepers on his staff, and he had dismissed all of them before letting us into the office. 'If you want to look for yourselves, you're most welcome.'

I shook my head. 'I have no head for figures.'

'I do,' said Homura. He turned to the filing cabinets. 'May I, Mr Kotze?'

Kotze's scowl only deepened, but he said 'Go right ahead.'

It felt like hours, but Homura spent no more than forty-five minutes perusing the files. At the end he thanked Kotze and we left. Kotze's glowering had turned to a smirk as he saw us departing after a fruitless search.

In the car on the way back to the hotel, Homura said to me: 'Watson, what is ARMSCOR?'

'Armaments Corporation of South Africa. Established in order to modernise the arsenal of the army and the police, due to the...you know.' I wasn't sure how to approach the subject of the sanctions, given Japan's defiance of them for the Yawata deal.

'The sanctions,' said Homura, without hesitation. 'How does ARMSCOR go about this modernisation?'

'Mostly wheeling and dealing,' I replied. 'Some of it is clandestine.'

'Black market?'

'Certainly,' I replied. 'Also spying, theft, and espionage.'

'Do they manufacture?'

'Some. Weapons and munitions, I believe. Why do you ask? Did you see something in Kotze's books?'

'I did not have time to be thorough, but...the tonnage is correct, the volumes are not. Some of the volumes of Yawata inventory are easily transposed for ARMSCOR.'

I digested that as I turned onto the highway. 'You think that's where the iron is going? ARMSCOR's factories?'

Homura only shrugged. I could tell that he would not be drawn further, so I asked, 'Where shall we go now?'

'I want more information from the suspect,' said Homura. 'But since he cannot give it, I will speak to his family.'

I kept my eyes firmly on the road. 'Are you sure you want to do that? I don't know if you are aware of the...conditions...in which Mr Masekala's family lives, but they are... not salubrious.'

'They are black South Africans,' replied Homura. 'I assume they live in a township.'

'Do you know what that means?'

'Perhaps,' replied Homura, 'I should see it for myself.'

Umlazi township was about 25 kilometres from Durban. South Africa had adopted the metric system only recently; one less thing to be embarrassed about in front of Homura.

Umlazi itself was another matter. Cracked, unpaved roads ran between the rectangular, whitewashed buildings. The plumbing and sewerage systems here were barely functional. Electrical wiring, where it was present, was strung between trees. Sadder than the township itself was the shantytown that had grown around its perimeter. Masekala's job at the port kept the family in permanent lodgings, but with him in jail, I imagined their funds were quickly running dry.

The streets were quiet this mid-afternoon as I pulled up in front of the house. I did not know what kind of reaction to expect here, but the few people around showed nothing stronger than idle curiosity, and that only when they saw Homura emerge from the vehicle. Perhaps that was worse than the hostility I had feared.

I knocked on the door and it was soon answered by Mrs Masekala, a portly woman wearing a dress and a head scarf. 'Praat je Engels, mevrouw?' I asked hopefully. I wished that I knew her first name.

She shook her head. I knew only five phrases in the Zulu language – none of them were appropriate outside of a hospital setting – so we would have to speak Afrikaans. There was movement in the house behind her. A child; perhaps two. I was grateful she did not invite us inside. It would have been difficult to bear those eyes upon us: me in my tailored suit, and Homura, who might as well have been from the moon.

Once I introduced myself and Homura, Mrs Masekala asked me immediately about her husband's condition. She was not allowed to visit him in the prison infirmary.

'He has a serious concussion and some broken bones,' I told her. 'But he'll recover.' I did not say it might take weeks or months. I did not tell her that he had been beaten so badly he did not know his own name.

'Please ask her about the truck,' said Homura.

'He's brought it home many times,' she replied, in Afrikaans. 'All the drivers do, if they can. It's much faster than the bus.'

I started to translate for Homura but he waved me to a stop. 'I can't speak, but I understand enough,' he said. I was less surprised than I might have been. 'Did James ever bring home a load of iron?'

She snorted before I had even finished translating the question. Did I honestly believe they would let him drive a truck laden with valuable material home?

She had no more answers for us, so I started to make goodbyes. I hesitated, and then said 'Are you all right here? Do you need…rent money, or anything?'

Now her expression was fierce. 'We need many things, Doctor Watson,' she said. 'Hot water. Hospitals. Schools.' I could sense the children stirring in the house behind her, and she glanced over her shoulder at them. When she looked back at me, there were tears in her eyes. As much as she wanted to, she couldn't refuse. 'Yes, we need rent money.'

I fumbled out my wallet and gave her all of the bank notes it contained. It wasn't much. The remains of my weekly budget for discretionary spending. Pocket money.

She took it, thanked me and hurried back inside. I retreated just as quickly.

I was thankful Homura had nothing to say as we drove away.

I invited Homura to dinner at my house. He tried to refuse in his indirect way. 'It's difficult' and 'I don't want to trouble you.' In the end I wore him down with an insistence that would have made my mother proud.

My housekeeper Martha was surprised that I had invited a guest, but she welcomed Homura with a big smile and bustled him inside, peppering him with questions about where he was from and why he was here. I was afraid he would think her rude, but he answered her patiently and with unexpected good humour.

Martha had already prepared dinner and both of us were hungry, so we sat down to eat without ceremony. Vegetable soup followed by roast beef, green beans, peas, potatoes, and mielie pap, which Homura tried first. 'This is maize, yes?'

'Yes,' I replied. Pap is a staple of our native population. Martha knows it's one of my favourites, but it is not a dish one serves to sophisticated company.

Homura gave a slight bow to Martha. 'It's very good.' I think that pleased me even more than it did Martha.

While Martha cleared up we retreated to the living room. I poured a couple of whiskies.

We drank them slowly while discussing trivial things: the weather, the native flora, the mielie pap. Homura treated each topic as seriously as he did our investigation.

'Is that your guitar?' said Homura, pointing to the instrument case that was barely visible behind the sofa. Suddenly I felt self-conscious about how he perceived me, having been inside my house.

'It is,' I replied. 'Do you play?'

He rose. 'May I?'

'Of course.'

I went to pour another pair of whiskies while he retrieved the instrument from its case. The guitar had lain unused for months and I would have been concerned that it was dusty, if not for my trust in Martha's cleaning.

Homura looked up from tuning the instrument with a frown. 'You need new strings.'

I set the refills down on the table. 'I'm not much of a player.'

Homura strummed the instrument; struck a chord. It sounded better in his hands than it ever had in mine. He ran a scale I did not recognise; raked an arpeggio. And then he began to play.

'Homura-san, I see that your affinity for Jimi Hendrix goes beyond just wearing his t-shirts.'

'He has a Japanese sister,' he said. He watched my reaction and smiled. 'You did not know that, of course, and that is not what you meant.'

'I meant only that your playing is excellent.'

'I am no Hendrix. I could never have composed…this…' He played the opening riff to a song that I recognised but could not then identify. Later, once I had bought some Hendrix records, I realised it was Voodoo Chile. 'Jimi-san was a rare talent, who played with more skill than any other – and more heart.'

'You have talent,' I replied.

'I am skilled,' replied Homura. 'But I have no heart. My blood is too cold for a true musician.' This confession did not seem to trouble him.

'Homura,' I said. 'Earlier today, you told me that you can understand Afrikaans. How does–'

'How does a Japanese man have that skill?'

'Talent, I would have said.'

'You have used that word twice now, Watson. Talent is not skill. Talent is a tiny amount of momentum that does not take a person very far up the curve of learning.' He picked up his drink. 'I am skilled because I study. It is my job to know the things that most people do not. The depth of it, but also the breadth. I study.'

I did not believe him. 'You studied Afrikaans?'

'No, but I have studied languages. In particular, Dutch.'

'How do you know Dutch, Homura-san?'

'Japan was in sakoku...isolation...for more than two hundred years,' he replied. 'During that time, the Dutch were the only Westerners allowed to trade. And so Dutch became the language of knowledge.' He pointed to his own face. 'My family is not the richest in Japan, but we have long been the most knowledgeable. Of course we speak Dutch.'

I did not know what to say to that.

Homura reached into his jacket and produced a bag of white powder. 'Watson, would you like some cocaine?'

I closed my mouth quickly but I'm certain my eyes were wide with fright. 'How on earth did you get cocaine?'

'Diplomatic bag.' He shrugged. 'If you do not want any, do you mind if I...?'

Still flustered I raised my hands. 'If I was your doctor, I would say 'no' – but I'm not, and you are a guest in my home.'

Homura seemed to take that as permission. He produced a small vanity mirror, on which he chopped the drug with a razor. Then he inhaled it directly off his fingers. He threw back his head, sniffing rapidly, and then finally blew out a long exhalation. When his head snapped back to its accustomed position, there was an increased intensity about him, though he sat very still.

I felt an unexpected sympathy for him, then. What must drive someone of such obvious skill and competence to want cocaine? 'Homura-san, do you know what will happen if...?'

'Nothing will happen, Watson,' he replied. 'I am well-connected, wealthy, and foreign. My presence here is already an embarrassment to your government and its racist principles.'

Of course I knew what he must think of the country. Of us. And of course he was right. But it was still a shock, to hear him speak so bluntly. He could see that I was flustered but he regarded me the way he might have fixed on Kotze's ledgers.

'I cannot defend this country's policies,' I said. I was suddenly conscious that the kitchen noise had ceased. Had Martha finished cleaning? Was she staying over tonight, or was she taking the late bus home? Or was she listening at the door? I didn't know which option made me feel worse. 'We have committed some terrible wrongs here,' I said. 'The way we treat the blacks and coloureds is immoral. We keep them in poverty, deny them education, we deny them basic human rights, we suppress their culture. I will not and cannot defend it. I oppose these policies. My people...many of my people do. Although many of us do not, of course.' I was babbling.

'Yes, I understand,' said Homura. It was a judgment, not a gesture of conciliation.

'I– I am–'

'I understand,' said Homura. 'I saw the symbol above your door. You are Jewish.' He did not acknowledge my surprise that he had recognised the mezuzah. 'Your people fled here to escape those that hate you in Europe.'

'Yes.' I did not want to guess his feelings about the war. The Axis. The bombs.

'You recognise that what is happening here is not so different to what happened to your own family. And you say that you oppose it. Perhaps you do.'

'I give money to those who fight it in the courts.' It sounded weak even as I said it.

'Of course,' said Homura. 'But also you profit from it.'

'I...you are probably right,' I replied. 'Perhaps I couldn't live this well in some other country.'

'You have a black servant.'

Now I felt defensive. I thought of Martha as family, since I had no other here in Durban. 'I treat her well. I provide her employment. Lodging, if she needs it. I look after her as best I am able.'

When family visited me, they stayed in the guest bedroom. Even Irina, my wild cousin from Israel – a stranger I'd met only once – stayed in the house. Martha slept in the servant's quarters, if she stayed over.

'Tell me,' said Homura. 'Could you hire a white woman to do her work for the same salary?'

'I don't think a white woman would do her work,' I replied.

'You exploit her labour, although you know it is unfair.'

I couldn't meet his eyes. Treating Martha better than the other oppressors did not change my complicity in her oppression.

Homura raised both hands. 'I am also guilty,' he said. 'My country is exploiting yours for your natural resources and cheap labour. "Honorary whites" is a travesty and we know it as well as your own government does. Just as we did when Hitler said the same about us. But my people are guilty at home, also. We have mistreated the native people in Okinawa and Hokkaido. When we invaded China and Korea, we did terrible things there also.'

'Yes,' I replied. I knew Japan had a pacifist constitution now. 'But your country has moved beyond such things.'

Homura shook his head. 'You think so.' He sat back in his chair, rubbed his nostrils and then inspected his fingertips for blood. Finding none, he said: 'Watson, let me tell you about the man who is my deepest enemy. He is, or was, a famous professor of astronomy. He possesses an intellect that…perhaps my own brother is the only one comparable.'

'He sounds formidable,' I replied. 'Why is he your enemy?'

'One of his rivals discovered that he faked his family registry, to hide the fact he grew up in a burakumin slum. He lost his position and his teaching license.'

'Poor guy,' I said. I shut up quickly, remembering that this was Homura's enemy.

'He went underground. Joined the yakuza gangs. Worse. Few know it, but Doctor Mori Akio has taken over criminal organisations all around the country. He is waging a war on society and civilisation.'

I could not look at him.

'My enemy, Watson. But who is to say he is wrong? Is he any worse than the society that tore down all his achievements because he was born in the wrong place?'

Homura rose to pour himself a new drink. To his back I replied, 'Crime is wrong, Homura-san. Our civilisation isn't perfect, but it is the best way we have to improve the lives of everyone.' I felt more certain of this. I had sworn a Hippocratic Oath and I believed in it fervently.

'That is a sensible answer, and perhaps it is true.' He put some ice into his drink and turned to face me. 'But look around. The evidence is weak.'

'And yet you have made it our work to uproot crime, Homura-san. Why is that? Samurai honour? Surely that amounts to the same thing.'

Homura stood still for a moment, then returned to his chair with his drink. 'Ah, you westerners, and your romantic notions about the samurai,' he said. 'Noble warriors, bound by honour. What if I told you that Bushido, the samurai code, is not about honour? It is about preserving the unearned privileges of the warrior caste. Today, all people are equal in Japan, and nobody is permitted to wear a sword, but look.' He took a drink. 'My family were samurai. My brother Makigorou, who holds a high post in the government, has sent me all the way here to solve a crime that may not even have occurred. I am qualified for this because I have received the finest education my country can provide. I am here because I was born to privilege. While my enemy, who accomplished so much, though he was born to dirt, now plies his revenge from the gutters.

'Do not be fooled, Watson. Samurai honour is the same privilege enjoyed by those born wealthy in any society.'

I was not willing to cede this argument. 'You have not answered my question, Homura-san. Why are you a detective, then? If your family is as wealthy as you say, you could do anything at all.'

Homura sipped his drink. 'The science interests me,' he said. 'And the challenge. Pitting myself against the likes of Mori Akio. My brother does not have the stamina for field work, but me? I like the freedom. And the danger.'

It was only then that I realised that Homura might himself be dangerous. Something in his eyes, his posture. This drinking, drug-taking aristocrat from the far side of the world, here alone on a mission that nobody could expect him to successfully prosecute. But I have faced danger myself and, however numerous my failings, cowardice is not among them.

'Wait,' I said. 'You said a crime that may not have occurred?'

The ice in Homura's glass rattled as he set it down. His posture had changed and the danger he exuded was diffused. 'I am still pursuing the evidence,' he said. 'Now please. It is late and I must return to my hotel.'

I did not see Homura the following morning. He needed to visit his consulate and I could not put off my own patients any longer. I worked all through lunch and it was not until mid-afternoon that my desk was clear.

I went to see James Masekala in the prison infirmary. He was decidedly better than when I had last seen him. The swelling had gone down and, while he wasn't perfectly lucid yet, he was able to answer questions and appeared conscious of where he was – although he was bewildered as to how he had arrived there. He was able to speak to me in English, too, although I could see it was a struggle and we quickly reverted to Afrikaans. James was pleased to hear that I had spoken to his family. I did not ask him anything about the truck or the missing iron. Even had I not been convinced of his innocence, I was there as his doctor, not as a detective's assistant.

I had given Martha the day off, so I stopped on my way home for dinner at my favourite Indian restaurant. Usually it made me feel cosmopolitan to eat there, but that day it just felt sad. Here I was, enjoying the cuisine and service of another people who were forced to live here with fewer and fewer rights.

The house was dark when I returned. I made myself a cup of tea and was just looking at my guitar, tucked again behind the couch, when the doorbell rang.

It was Homura. He was wearing a suit and tie now and his hair was tied back. He looked just as comfortable as he had in his denims.

'May I come in, Watson?'

'Please, Homura-san.'

I poured him a cup of tea. I was surprised that he took it with milk and sugar, like an Englishman. We returned to the living room and sat where we had the night before.

'The case is solved,' he said. 'I thought you would like to know.'

'So there was a crime, after all.'

'There was,' he said. 'But not the one I was asked to investigate. The iron was not stolen, because it did not exist. It was an accountant's fabrication.'

'I don't understand.'

'The missing fifty tonnes was not iron,' he replied. 'It was gold. That is why the volumes logged in Kotze's warehouse didn't tally.'

'And what happened to the gold?'

'It was removed from the vessel and delivered as promised.'

It took me a moment to process that. 'Why would anybody substitute gold for iron?'

'I believe it's called "money laundering",' Homura replied. He drank from his cup. 'ARMSCOR exchanges gold bullion for Japanese yen, which it then uses for the illegal purchase of foreign weapons.'

'Who was behind this, Homura-san?'

'All of them, Watson. Everyone you met, and some you did not. Mr Kotze made sure the ledgers lined up so that Colonel Spencer's exchange matched up with the iron shipment. Ishiyama-san at the embassy doctored the shipping manifests and ensured the bullion was loaded correctly. Mr Grobelaar made sure the cargo was delivered discreetly and framed James Masekala when my brother noticed the discrepancy.'

'So what will happen?'

'Nothing,' Homura replied. 'Nobody has been robbed. My brother will see to it that whoever is directly responsible is demoted or transferred, but this surely goes higher into politics or business than even he can prosecute. Next time they will work harder to avoid his scrutiny.'

'And here in Durban?' I took a sip of black tea, but it was still too hot to drink.

'Also nothing,' he replied. 'I am not a policeman, here or anywhere. I have turned my evidence over to the police, but they are deeply implicated. I do not believe they are willing to pursue their own.'

I set down my teacup a little more suddenly than I had planned. The police and the army are two sides of a coin here. I had heard, and believed, the rumours about their counterinsurgency programs. Assassinations, death squads, torture. I knew better than most what would happen to anyone who threatened them. 'What will happen to James Masekala?'

'The charges will be dropped and he will be freed.'

I fingered my teacup gingerly. 'Well, that's some good news, at least. The villains got away with it, but we saved a man's life.'

'Did we save him, Watson? Truly? Do you think he can go back to his job when he has recovered his health? Will he be granted the rights he deserves?'

I added a spoonful of sugar to my tea and tried a sip. Still hot. 'I suppose you were right,' I sighed. 'Perhaps civilisation is as corrupt as you say.'

'Perhaps so.'

Homura set his empty cup back in its saucer. I drained my own tea, although it scalded my throat.

He rose, and so did I. 'My taxi is waiting for me,' he said. 'I must return to Japan immediately. My brother will want my report, and I have learned that my enemy's network has spread to Hong Kong and the Philippines.'

We shook hands.

'Thank you for your assistance, Watson,' he said. 'I could not have solved this case without you.'

'Thank you for tolerating me,' I replied. 'I have learned a lot from you.'

'And I from you,' he replied. 'We were a good team. Your heart and my skill. If you ever find yourself in Japan, please visit me. We have excellent whisky.'

'Perhaps I will,' I replied. 'But I fear there is plenty of work for me to do right here.'

'That is so.'

We bowed to each other and I opened the door. The taxi was indeed waiting for him.

Perhaps one day I will visit Homura-san. I would like to see the far east. Perhaps I can even help him fight Dr Mori Akio. Right some wrongs, and debate the morality of it after the fact. But I do not think he needs my help, and perhaps I can make a real difference here at home. I am not politician or a policeman, but I am a doctor and I am not without means.

Tonight I shall put to rights my own house. A better wage for Martha.

Tomorrow I will find a lawyer to seek compensation for James Masekala, for all that he has suffered. The day after that, and the day following, I will apply myself anew. It will take years or decades to redress the terrible things we have countenanced here.

There is no skilful deduction that will solve this problem. Only persistence and heart will lead to change.

AUTHOR'S NOTES

I was born in Apartheid South Africa, but I didn't understand what that meant until after we emigrated to Australia. The news was heavily censored there and ten-year-old me just assumed apartheid (I didn't even know the word) was the natural order of things.

On my most recent visit to SA, I visited the District 6 museum where I learned that Japanese people were considered honorary Whites during that era, while other Asian nationalities were Black. I also learned, during a conversation with my uncle, that my own family's status there, as Jews, was more tenuous than I had ever realised.

Eleven years later I am married to a Japanese woman and more aware than ever about how Western people stereotype Asians. So when Narrelle approached me about writing a story for this book, featuring either Japanese or Jewish protagonists, I was primed to do both.

The Adventure

of the

Disappearing

Village

Natalie Conyer

It is said that when the earth was created and the time came to fill it with people, an angel was chosen to deposit wise and foolish souls evenly over the land. But the sack of foolish souls got caught on a mountaintop and spilled into Chelm, a Jewish village – really no more than a shtetl – in Poland. Since then, reports of its citizens' antics have spread far and wide and you yourself have certainly heard some of them.

I have always wondered if Chelm was as foolish as people claim and being of a curious disposition, decided to see it for myself. The following is an account of my adventure in that strangest of places.

Preferring to take the last little distance on foot, I left my horse in Kroszik, in the care of a kindly innkeeper. After half a day of easy walking I found myself at the edge of the River Chelm, which forms a natural boundary between the village and the woods surrounding it. Before me stood a stone bridge; or rather, I should say, the remains of one. While sturdy pillars on each side of the river prepared to arch over the water, the span of the bridge was missing and I could see no trace of its construction.

As I considered how to proceed, I spied on the far bank a man working a roughly-hewn barge.

'Good day, fellow!' I called. 'Will you convey me across the river?'

'With pleasure, sir,' he replied. 'The charge is two zloty.'

'That's very expensive!'

The man shrugged. 'The current is deceptively strong.'

I had no option but to agree. The man punted across to me. I embarked and he pushed us off the bank.

'You have a lucrative business here,' I ventured. 'What happened to your bridge?'

'Not my bridge!' answered the man. 'I come from Kroszik. What happened was—' and he started to laugh, so hard we almost capsized. When he had recovered he continued, 'What happened was this. The people of Chelm decided to destroy their bridge so that raiders – you have heard of the pogroms being visited on Jews around here? – to prevent raiders from entering their village.'

'But... but that means—'

The boatman began chuckling again. 'Yes. It means nobody can leave Chelm either, at least not from this side of the hill, and I am getting rich as a result.'

We had by now achieved the further bank. I paid the man and was about to bid him adieu when a thought occurred to me. 'Do you know where in the village I might find lodgings?'

'Try the house of the Chochem. At the top of the street, up there.'

My ears pricked at the title "Chochem", which is commonly applied to only the wisest and most learned of men. 'Who is this person, and why is he called the Chochem? Is he the Rabbi?'

'Not at all. In addition to a rabbi, Chelm boasts a wise man: one so wise they call him the Chochem. His name is Shlomo Holmlich. They count on him to solve their problems.' The boatman hesitated. He seemed about to say more but contented himself with, 'You will see for yourself.'

'So I will, my good man.'

'The Chochem!' answered the boatman, pushing off again, shaking his head and laughing softly to himself.

Chelm appeared a typical shtetl. From the riverbank, a dirt road led up a gentle rise. The road was lined with rustic wooden buildings, their peaked roofs still carrying winter snow. One building was larger and better kept than the others and this, I surmised, was the synagogue.

The house indicated by the boatman was no more or less ramshackle than its neighbours. Its front garden was bounded by a fence of horizontal poles, from behind which two goats regarded me with interest. I was heartened, however, at the sight of smoke emanating from its chimney and the smell of baking which became evident when the door was opened by a small, neat woman with apple cheeks and a welcoming smile.

'Good afternoon, madam.' I made a small bow. 'I am Doctor Yankel Watinsky, from Warsaw. I was told you might offer me a few nights' accommodation.'

'Certainly,' she replied, in the heavily accented Yiddish of the region. 'Welcome. I am Mrs Malka Hubboba, widow and housekeeper.' And with that she led me to a simple but pleasant room, clean and with a bed, table, chair and chamber pot.

'Thank you,' I said, 'this will do nicely. Now I will explore your village. Will you expect me for dinner? What sights should I see first?'

Mrs Hubboba appeared astonished. 'Now? Before you meet Chochem Holmlich?' Seeing my blank look, she continued. 'Surely he is the reason you are in Chelm? To learn from the greatest mind in Europe?'

'Do many people come here to learn from the Chochem?'

'Not from outside,' she conceded. 'You are the first. But I am sure there will be—'

We were interrupted by a voice from above. 'Mrs Hubboba. Tea!'

Mrs Hubboba beamed. 'You see? Come, come!' And we climbed the stairs to an attic, where she opened a door to reveal the great man himself.

My first impression of Holmlich's quarters was one of warmth and shabby disorder. The fire in the grate smoked, and this mingled with the fug of pipe tobacco. Around the edges of the room were tables filled with items I could not at first recognise, but I did notice a pile of old, thick books and what looked very much like a violin case. On a faded Turkish carpet in front of the fireplace sat two armchairs. The nearer armchair, with its back to me, was occupied, and I fancied this housed the pipe-smoker.

Mrs Habobba bustled forward. 'Chochem, Chochem! May I introduce Mr Yankel Watinsky, come all the way from Warsaw.'

'*Doctor* Watinsky,' I reminded her. 'My pleasure, I'm sure.'

There was no corresponding greeting from the armchair. Curious now, I walked around to face its occupant.

Holmlich, for it must be he, was sprawled on his spine, the bowl of a meerschaum pipe in one bony hand. He was long and cadaverously thin. His clean-shaven cheeks were sunken and his ears pointed, giving him an elvish look. But the eyes with which he appraised me were dark and extremely bright.

'Sit!' he demanded. 'You will forgive me for not rising, but I am deep in thought and physical movement detracts from my mental processes.'

I sat. Holmlich tamped his pipe and puffed to get it going. 'I see you have travelled far, that you are Jewish, and that you like to eat sweet things.'

'Well,' I replied, 'Mrs Hubboba did tell you I came from Warsaw; I wear the black garb peculiar to us Jews; and though I hate to admit it, I am plumper than I should be.'

'Yes, yes,' he said. 'Elementary!'

The samovar was bubbling nicely. Mrs Hubboba brewed our tea and offered cherry preserves as sweetener. When she had gone, Holmlich spoke. 'So, Mr Watinsky, how may I be of assistance?'

I grew weary of correction. '*Doctor* Watinsky.' No sooner had I uttered these words than we were disturbed by a cacophony of voices, male and female, originating from the street below. Even at a distance I could discern cries of 'The Chochem! The Chochem!' I sat upright, startled; Holmlich evinced nothing more than mild interest. The voices grew louder and there came a thunderous banging on Holmlich's front door. A moment later a flustered Mrs Hubboba appeared. 'What a gevalt! They are calling for you, Chochem.'

'Well then, I will go down,' said Holmlich, unperturbed. He rose slowly, seeming to articulate his joints one by one, made his way down the stairs and opened the front door. Mrs Hubboba and I followed hard on his heels.

It seemed the entire population of Chelm was gathered around Holmlich's front gate. When they saw him, men, women and children – and not a few donkeys and goats – pressed forward, all babbling excitedly. I caught the words 'Ponsk,' and 'gone', but had no idea what they were trying to say.

Holmlich held up a hand. 'Quiet!' he boomed. 'One at a time. Rabbi, you begin.'

A very short man, as wide as he was high, stepped forward, his face beet-red with emotion. 'It's Ponsk!' he said. 'Ponsk has – disappeared!'

At that, the crowd recommenced its noisy chorus, and once again Holmlich stilled them with a single gesture. The Rabbi continued. 'Yudelman – Yudelman will tell you!' He beckoned to another man, who stepped forward hesitantly.

Yudelman, if this was he, was a man in his prime, a magnificent specimen. As tall as Holmlich but with broad shoulders and flowing coal black hair, he resembled a giant in a folk tale.

'The Rabbi is correct. Ponsk has vanished. Not a building, not a person, not a cow nor even a chicken! Entirely gone!'

Holmlich appeared unmoved. 'And what evidence supports your allegation?'

I had heard of Ponsk, a shtetl not far away. The claim – that an entire village had vanished – seemed astounding, but I took heart from Holmlich's words. As a medical doctor, I believe in science and his call for hard fact led me to think Chelm could not possibly be as foolish as the world outside its borders claim.

Yudelman continued. 'You know, Cochem Holmlich, that I trade in furs, and each year at the end of winter I take a stock of pelts to be sold in Ponsk. The journey takes no more than three hours. Yesterday I harnessed my mule and set off in my usual fashion, expecting to reach Ponsk by noon. By late afternoon I was still travelling and starting to worry. When I had not found Ponsk by sunset, I slept in my wagon and returned to Chelm the following day.'

His brow furrowed and after some deliberation he added, 'That is, I mean, I returned today. There can be only one explanation. Ponsk has disappeared!'

All eyes turned to Holmlich, who manifested no surprise. If anything, he seemed amused. He nodded at the Rabbi and Yudelman. 'Gentlemen,' he said. 'I have not encountered so interesting a conundrum in some time.' He raised his voice so that all could hear. 'Fellow citizens, do not fret. At first light tomorrow the Rabbi, Yudelman and I – and you too, Watinsky, if you choose – will retrace Yudelman's journey to see if we can shed light on this mystery. In the meantime, I propose you return to your homes for the night. Fear not. I have the matter in hand.'

The crowd outside Holmlich's house slowly dispersed, moving away in ones and twos until the only person remaining was the Rabbi.

'Chochem Holmlich,' he ventured, eyeing me curiously at the same time, 'may I consult you on a matter of some delicacy?'

'A matter concerning your daughter?' enquired Holmlich, ushering the Rabbi inside.

'But how... How could you–?'

'You wrote to me yesterday, complaining of her wilfulness. By the way, Rabbi, this is Mr Watinsky, come all the way from Warsaw to consult me. Watinsky, this is Rabbi Lubinsky. You will excuse us while we confer?'

I wished to correct Holmlich on both my status and reasons for visiting Chelm, but he and Rabbi Lubinsky were halfway up the staircase before I could open my mouth, and I was left alone in the hallway. I was somewhat relieved, for their preoccupation presented me with an excellent opportunity to explore the village.

My initial destination was the synagogue, a short walk away. I stepped onto a low, overhung porch and, opening a weathered door, recited the prayer for entry.

Nothing in its rustic facade prepared me for the synagogue's interior. I found myself in a long hall, its high ceiling supported by a series of intricately carved arches and a central dome over the bimah. The entire structure was made of wood, meticulously crafted and polished to a high shine. The effect was one of warmth and richness.

'But this – this – it is splendid!' I murmured, turning a full circle.

'Yes, is it not?'

The voice came from above.

Leaning over the balcony of the female section was a young woman. My impression was of a fair complexion, black, curly hair escaping an embroidered shawl, black eyes, well-shaped eyebrows, and an amused regard.

She spoke again. 'Are you the visitor?'

I bowed. 'Doctor Yankel Watinsky from Warsaw, at your service. Whom do I have the pleasure of addressing?'

'Shoshana Lubinsky is my name. Shana.'

This, I realised, must be the Rabbi's problematic daughter. I thought I could understand why. Miss Lubinsky's direct tone displayed none of the mewling reticence I have encountered in other women her age. We regarded each other.

A cough behind me indicated the approach of an elderly, bow-legged man, taper in hand. The beadle, come to light candles for evening prayers. I nodded at him and turned back to Miss Lubinsky, but there was no sign of her now.

Disappointed, I made to leave. The beadle regarded me steadily. 'You must be the visitor. Welcome, welcome! Will you stay for evening prayers?'

I could hardly refuse. As he spoke, I noticed a stepladder leaning against a wall, terminating at what looked like a poor-box. Seeing my puzzlement, he explained. 'A few years ago the community was troubled by thefts, including from the poor-box. We asked the Chochem for advice. He recommended we place the poor-box high up, out of reach of thieves.' He indicated the box. 'Now, this made it impossible for people to put money in the poor-box. But the wise Chochem gave us another solution. He told us to erect a ladder to the poor-box, so that people could still give money to charity.'

Before I could comment, movement at the door announced the arrival of other worshippers, including the large Yudelman. I could not help but observe how eagerly he turned his eyes towards the balcony, and how he slumped with disappointment to find it empty.

Evening prayers followed their normal course. Afterwards, the Rabbi introduced me to his congregants, a friendly and inquisitive bunch. Several invited me to dinner but as I had already assured Mrs Hubboba I would return, I took my leave.

Holmlich chose to eat in his quarters and so I dined alone, on a hearty bean soup accompanied by potato knishes. I retired content and slept better than I had for many months. The Rabbi and Yudelman arrived while I was enjoying a simple breakfast of rye bread, butter and jam and minutes later, footsteps on the staircase heralded Holmlich's approach.

When I saw him I gaped in surprise. He had forsaken his long black coat for a false beard, old, ragged clothes and wooden clogs, with an axe slung over his shoulder. He seemed to take pleasure in my astonishment.

'Who knows what awaits us? I have some fame in these parts and my attendance could send potential foes into hiding or, worse, spur them to attack. Nobody would look twice at a simple woodsman.' With this he led us to the street outside where Yudelman's cart was waiting.

A substantial group had gathered to see us off. They greeted Holmlich's disguise with equanimity. 'Good luck, Chochem,' some said. Others cheered, and the rest chose to simply wave. We climbed into Yudelman's cart and slowly made our way up the hill, prancing children keeping pace alongside.

Yudelman drove with Holmlich at his side. Rabbi Lubinsky and I took up the rear. Yudelman and Holmlich were silent but the Rabbi made up for them both, quizzing me about my life in Warsaw. On hearing I was a doctor, his manner became positively emphatic. Was I married? he enquired. Did I make a good living? Where did my parents come from, and what was my father's occupation?

I knew what he was about. Not a day goes by in Warsaw but I am subject to a similar interrogation by one or other parent of a single, marriageable daughter. The Rabbi was interested in me as a prospective son-in-law, and having set eyes on Shana Lubinsky I was not averse to the idea. I assured him of my spiritual and financial worth and he nodded slowly, fingering his beard. Was it my imagination or did Yudelman's broad back stiffen during this exchange?

In such a manner we proceeded over the crest of the hill. This road led away from the river and so there was no need of a barge. Instead, we followed it to a junction of several lesser tracks, where stood a signpost bristling with crudely lettered arrows indicating that one track led to Ponsk, one to Kroszik, another to Nizteszka and others to destinations whose names I did not recognise.

As we drew closer, Holmlich ordered Yudelman to halt. 'Which road did you follow in your journey to Ponsk, the day before yesterday?'

'Why, I followed the signpost, as I always do,' answered Yudelman, pointing to the arrow marked 'Ponsk'.

'Good. Then let us proceed.'

Yudelman flicked the reins and his mules recommenced their slow progress. After about an hour, seeing the track narrowing, I could not help but ask, 'Tell me, fellow-travellers, do you recognise this as the road you normally take to Ponsk?'

Yudelman answered, as if to a child. 'Did you not see the signpost? Of course this is the road to Ponsk!'

Yet, after another hour, he conceded in low tones, 'We should have passed the crossing to Vulzoska by now. Something is very amiss.'

Again we came to a halt. By now it was early afternoon. At the side of the road, in a clearing dappled by light, we consumed the hearty supplies provided by Mrs Hubboba. Then we turned and made our way back to Chelm.

The moment we arrived at his front door, Holmlich, who had uttered not a word on the way back, rushed inside. As I made to follow him Rabbi Lubinsky took my arm, saying, 'My dear fellow, I would be honoured if you would dine with my family tonight.' I bowed assent, secretly pleased at the thought of seeing Shana Lubinsky again. Yudelman sat stubbornly facing his mules and without so much as a farewell flicked them into action and departed.

Having informed Mrs Hubboba of my plans, I knocked on Holmlich's door. 'Come!' he said. He was in his usual chair, pipe already in hand. 'Well? What do you make of this mystery?'

I had some idea of what might have occurred but wished to hear Holmlich's view, so I shrugged and shook my head. 'I cannot make it out.'

'Ha!' He seemed pleased with my reply. 'I, on the other hand, have found the solution, identified the culprits, and arranged a final test. Make no mistake, by tomorrow morning Ponsk will be back where it belongs.'

This was indeed encouraging. Holmlich refused to elaborate and so I retired to freshen up before visiting the Lubinsky household.

After evening prayers the Rabbi and I made our way to his house, which was constructed much like Holmlich's. His family comprised a wife, as short and as stout as he, and, as he explained sadly, only one child – his daughter, Shana.

I fear I proved an unworthy guest. My entire consciousness was taken up with Shana Lubinsky, the grace with which she carried a dish, her pleasing voice, the glint of candlelight in her hair. I paid no attention to the fare other than to compliment Mrs Lubinsky on her kneidel soup, ask for a second helping of carp and allow the Rabbi to refill my glass, more than once.

When his daughter rose to clear the table, Rabbi Lubinsky waved her down. 'Sit, sit, my child. You youngsters should get to know each other. Let your mother do the dishes. I will retire.' And with that he plodded upstairs.

I cleared my throat. 'Don't you think Spring is a long time coming this year?'

At this, she rolled her eyes heavenward and said with some asperity, 'Dr Watinsky—'

'Yankel, please.'

'Yankel. Call me Shana. And for heaven's sake, stop talking about Spring.'

In my experience, eligible young women expect to discuss the weather, or else be complimented on their appearance. Shana Lubinsky's unwillingness to engage in conversation of this sort put me at a loss.

'Well, what would you prefer to talk about?'

She fixed me with her frank gaze. 'Why did you come to our village?'

I was in a difficult position. To reveal the reason for my visit would be to insult Shana Lubinsky's family and her community. Therefore, after some stuttering, I answered, 'Why, to learn from the famous Chochem Holmlich, of course.'

'Rubbish!' Shana said, rudely. 'I know why you have come here. You wish to see if we are as stupid, as backward, as the world says. Am I correct?'

'Well, that is . . .'

'I saw you in our synagogue. You were astonished that such foolish folk could have made something so beautiful.'

What could I say? She was right. Chastened, I ventured, 'My dear, I apologise. I realise I was biased. I—'

'Biased? You were – are – positively pompous, and arrogant to boot!'

'No more than you,' I retorted, stung. 'You assume the worst of me! You know me as little as I know you. Now good evening, mademoiselle, I will take my leave.'

Perhaps Shana Lubinsky knew she had gone too far. However, she said nothing. I moved quickly to the door and flung it open, just escaping tripping over her mother who had undoubtably been eavesdropping outside. Behind me, Shana groaned and buried her face in her hands. My instinct was to return and comfort her but I retrieved my coat and scarf and, without another word, walked the short distance home.

I repaired at once to my room but instead of undressing found myself pacing the floor in agitation. How dare a chit of a girl call me arrogant and pompous! How dare she destroy her one chance to marry a successful doctor and thus escape – and here I admitted it – the ridiculous inhabitants of this silly shtetl!

My window afforded a view of the street and in the hope of growing calmer, I drew back the curtain to observe a peaceful, starry sky. A movement caught my attention. A figure, cloaked and hooded, was making its way along the road past Holmlich's house and up the hill, moving stealthily and keeping to the shadows.

'That person is up to no good,' I told myself. Impulsively, I shrugged on my coat and a minute later found myself quietly following the walker over the hill and down to the junction. There, it halted and, dropping to its knees, began to move stones from the pile holding the signpost upright. The signpost was substantial and without the stones, began to topple. I stepped forward and, securing the signpost with one hand, jerked the slight figure upright. As I did, the hood fell back to reveal – Shana Lubinsky, struggling in my grasp.

'You!' we exclaimed, more or less in unison.

'Don't just stand there!' she said. 'Help me!'

'Only if you explain what you are doing here.'

'I will, but, Yankel, there's not a moment to lose. You must trust me!' Hearing her say my name decided me. I transferred my free hand to the post. In a whisper, and looking over her shoulder, Shana showed me how to rotate it so that its arrows pointed in directions different from before.

Just as we finished replacing the supporting stones, we heard a noise and saw a light at the crest of the hill. 'Quick, hide! said Shana and grabbing my hand, led me to the cover of some adjacent shrubbery.

Once there, I reluctantly let go of Shana's hand and we peered out into the moonlight. Coming over the hill, and mounted on what looked like one of Yudelman's mules, was Holmlich. In his hand he held a lantern, which he held up to the signpost. He chose a track and disappeared down it.

We emerged from the bushes. 'Where do you think he has he gone?' I enquired.

'Why, to Ponsk, of course. And he will find it, now. Come, we can leave.'

'Not before you explain yourself. I realised someone must have moved the signpost, though I could not discern a motive. But you of all people? To what end?'

Shana sat on the pile of stones under the signpost, drawing her cloak tight. After a moment, I joined her.

She sighed. 'I suppose I owe you an explanation. It's Yudelman's fault.'

'Yudelman?'

'Don't interrupt. Yudelman wants to marry me. I have refused him many times, and he has even spoken to my father about it. Finally he said he would put an ultimatum to my father...'

'And that was the night he lost his way.'

'Yes. I knew he would return but I needed time to think what to do.'

'I can understand you not wanting to marry Yudelman, but—'

'You can't understand why I don't encourage you? And you wonder why I consider you arrogant?' Seeing my face, she smiled. 'Yankel, you're probably a good man. But I cannot marry you, nor anyone else.'

I hid my dismay. 'What did you hope to gain by moving the arrows?'

'My plan was to run away while Yudelman was gone. But he returned sooner than I expected and when I saw how upset the people here were about Ponsk, I realised how much they need someone to look after them.'

'I don't understand.'

'The Rabbi, Mrs Lubinsky – they could not conceive. I am adopted. I was thus not born in Chelm and from my earliest days, I knew I differed from its inhabitants. I do not think as they do.'

'Then why not leave?'

'Because the Rabbi and his wife gave me life. And because, after all, the people here are happy. They live in peace. They are kind to each other. What more can a community hope for? However, I cannot marry any man from Chelm, especially Yudelman. Can you imagine how unhappy I would make him, and what a shrew I would become? To tell you the truth, Yankel, I could come to like you but I cannot marry you either, because I do not wish to leave Chelm. So I will stay as I am.' She shivered. 'It's cold. We must go home now, or risk encountering Chochem Holmlich on his way back.'

I spent a fretful night and by dawn had decided to leave Chelm, as I saw no point in remaining. I had barely finished breakfast when I heard Holmlich shouting for Mrs Hubboba, who appeared a few minutes later.

'The Chochem asks you to see him.'

Holmlich was in his usual position, in his usual chair. 'Ah, Watinsky! Come in, come in!'

When I was settled he said, with some satisfaction, 'Well, the problem of Ponsk is completely resolved.'

'How so?' I replied. 'Has Ponsk reappeared?'

'You will have to wait for the answer,' said he. 'I have instructed Mrs Hubboba to call all of Chelm together at ten o'clock precisely; and there I will present the solution to this interesting case. I trust you will attend?'

I said I would. Holmlich puffed at his pipe. 'Tell me, Watinsky, how long do you intend to remain in Chelm?'

'I propose to leave as soon as I can. Today, if possible.'

'Hmm. Pity. I have much to teach you. You would not consider staying longer?'

'I have business in Warsaw,' I countered, 'that cannot wait.'

By a quarter to ten, the inhabitants of Chelm were clustered round Holmlich's front door, chattering excitedly. I joined them, receiving greetings as if from old friends. Even Yudelman unbent enough to nod at me.

I spotted Shana standing alone and gradually edged through the throng until I reached her. She made no effort to engage me in conversation.

At ten o'clock precisely, Holmlich appeared on his front doorstep.

'Citizens!' he called. 'I have solved the mystery of Ponsk.'

There was a smattering of applause, acknowledged by Holmlich's slight bow.

'As you know, my first experiment, to retrace Yudelman's steps, confirmed his findings. Ponsk had vanished from the face of the earth. I therefore devised another, more dangerous experiment, to see if Ponsk rematerialised after dark. So last night, while you slept, I again took the road to Ponsk. What do you think I found?'

The crowd edged closer.

'I found Ponsk, reappeared, in all its usual configuration!'

Gasps from the crowd, and some excited conversation.

'Friends, there can be but one explanation. The citizens of Ponsk have deliberately set out to mislead us!'

Holmlich waited for a response and when none came, continued impatiently. 'Surely the situation is clear? The people of Ponsk consider us foolish. Knowing we travel to and fro, they concocted a plan to disguise their town by day, simply to befuddle us and for their own sport. But I have put a stop to that!'

'How, Chochem?' This from Yudelman. 'I hope you have not affected my fur trade.'

'Nor my trade in bread,' said another man.

'Nor mine in candles,' said a third.

Holmlich held up a hand. 'Take comfort,' he said. 'All is well. While in Ponsk last night, I nailed to the door of the synagogue a notice for all to see. This is what it says.' He unfolded a single sheet of paper, and after clearing his throat, read:

'Citizens of Ponsk, one and all. Let it be known that we have uncovered your plan to make it seem as if Ponsk has disappeared. Please desist because once a joke has been revealed it loses its effect. Be assured we wish you well. From your neighbours, the citizens of Chelm.' Holmlich folded the paper again.

A young man raised his hand. 'Chochem! Chochem! I still don't understand. How did the inhabitants of Ponsk manage to make a whole village disappear?'

'Ah,' said Holmlich. 'A good question. Do none of you know how it was done?'

He shook his head at our blank looks. 'The answer, of course, is elementary. I deduce that the citizens of Ponsk fashioned themselves a mirror, one large enough to shield the topography of their town. As Yudelman, and later, myself, grew close, all we saw was a reflection of our woodland surrounds. We assumed Ponsk had disappeared and we turned back. Had we proceeded, we would either have come upon a sheet of glass or our own reflection, and would have realised the sleight of hand involved. A simple, yet effective trick.'

People turned to each other, murmuring in wonder. 'See!' exclaimed a man near me. 'See how wise is the Chochem!'

Holmlich raised a hand. 'Therefore be not concerned, fellow townspeople. Now that Ponsk knows we have discovered their ruse, they will not repeat it. Good morning to all.' And he retreated into his house.

The crowd wandered off and Shana began to move away with the rest. I caught her arm. 'Shana, wait. I leave Chelm within the hour. Is there nothing you wish to say to me?'

She turned back. 'Just this. There is no doctor in Chelm.' And she kissed my cheek and left.

As soon as I returned to Warsaw I set out in writing the details of my visit. Yet I forbore, as first I had intended, to circulate it among my friends, who would have been entertained at the expense of Chelm. For it seems to me that to compensate for filling Chelm with foolish souls, the clumsy angel increased the number of gentle ones.

Is it better, I ask myself, to live in a clever and knowing society full of ill-will and vice, than in a foolish one full of kindness? Even in civilised Warsaw, Chelm tugs at me. Chochem Holmlich, I know, would welcome my return; and Mrs Hubboba's cooking is peerless. Mostly, however, I think of Shana. There is, after all, not yet a doctor in Chelm.

AUTHOR'S NOTES

This piece was inspired by family stories and by *The Wise Men of Helm and their Merry Tales* (Behrman House Publishing, 1996), a book my brother and I loved as children.

THE SAGA

OF THE

HIDDEN

TREASURE

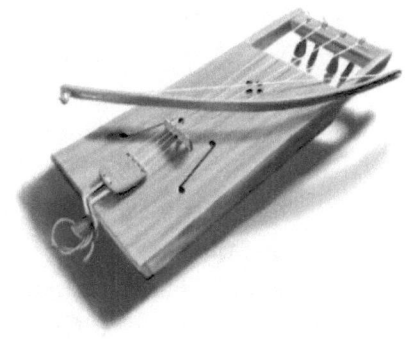

Kerry Greenwood
& David Greagg

Ófeig woke early and watched the watery spring sun illumine his fields. His shepherd Samr had already let his sheep out of their byre, since the weather was unaccustomedly mild. They were biting the grass contentedly, and Ófeig shared their mood. Life was good at Melur. His son Odd was a wealthy and well-respected chieftain, but Ófeig was well content to live by himself with his housekeeper, his shepherd, and his steward Kári. Wealth was a snare. The more you had, the more you were envied.

Odd had always been a promising lad, but they had never been close until last summer, when eight chieftains had plotted to cheat his son out of his wealth. Ófeig outwitted them, and his son's gratitude was everything he could have wished. Odd had offered his father lodging at his grand house in Reykir, but Ófeig had refused. Here he was his own master, and the spring lambing promised well.

The only annoyance in his life was his neighbour Grim, whom he suspected of stealing his sheep. Grim was a cantankerous, difficult man, and wanted watching.

As Ófeig sat in his rough-hewn chair outside his farmhouse, his eyes narrowed. A man was walking across his fields towards him: lean, balding, bare-headed, and grey in the beard. His clothes were patched and stained with weather. Yet the man's step was light and his sheepskin boots did not falter. As the man approached, Ófeig stood up.

'You have come far, I guess.'

The man inclined his head. 'I have. My name is Ketill, and I own a farm to the north of here.' He waved an arm towards the distant mountains. 'And you are Ófeig, and are accounted the best and wisest of men in this district.'

Ófeig nodded. 'I am that man, and I guess you need my help badly, or you would not have come. Come into my house, and tell me your need and any news you have.'

Rannveig the housekeeper brought the stranger bread, cheese and skýr. She exchanged a doubtful glance with Ófeig, who inclined his head with emphasis. Rannveig swayed out of the kitchen with a shrug of her shoulders, while he surveyed the stranger with curiosity.

Ketill pushed the wooden plate aside. 'I thank you, Ófeig. It is certain that I need your help. A great misfortune has befallen me, and I do not know where to turn.'

'Who is your chieftain, Ketill?'

'Gellir is the most powerful man in my district, and so has my allegiance.'

'Gellir is not unknown to me.' Ófeig allowed himself a wintry smile. Gellir had been one of the eight chieftains from last summer. Ófeig had bribed the man with his own son Odd's money to award a trifling judgment against Odd over an unjust lawsuit. Gellir was no better than the rest of them; but he had proved helpful.

'Since you have the repute of a cunning and wise man, I ask for your help. Will you give it?'

'That depends,' Ófeig answered. 'It does not seem to me that I shall gain much by helping you.'

Ketill's face fell, but he sat up straight in his chair and looked Ófeig in the eye. 'That is true. Poor men are not friends to rich men, and give them few gifts. Yet you have the look of a man who loves justice, even if he does not stand to gain.'

Ófeig opened both hands and nodded. 'You may speak.'

'My farm is not a rich one, but I prosper after a fashion. And I have saved a certain sum of money against evil days.'

'How much?'

'Two marks of silver. But it has gone from my wooden chest, and I do not know what to do. My neighbour Einar is an overbearing man, and difficult to deal with. I suspect him, but I have no proof and no means of getting it. I cannot advertise my loss, lest the men in my district treat me with scorn.'

'Who lives on your farm?'

'Just my shepherd – a fine lad called Thorkel – and my wife.'

Ófeig sat for a long moment in silence. Then he stood up. 'Rannveig?' he called, and the woman swayed into the room again with an expression of faint mockery. 'I will be gone for a few days, and I shall take Kári with me. You are in charge. See that Samr behaves himself. And have an eye to our belligerent neighbour.'

She inclined her chin. She was a fine woman of thirty summers or so, and enjoyed being mistress of the house when Ófeig went away. He suspected she ordered Samr about in his absence, but the boy did not seem to mind if she did.

Ófeig took his guest by the hand. 'This case interests me, Ketill. I do not promise anything, but I may be able to help you. And you need not walk back. I have three horses. We shall ride to your farm.'

Ketill thanked him.

When they approached Ketill's farm, Ófeig turned to his companion. 'Do you have a barn, far from the house, where my horses may be safely left?'

Ketill said that he had. 'It is a little the worse for wear, but there is some fodder for horses there. I sold my beasts last summer.'

'Can it be seen from the house?' Ketill shook his head. 'In that case, we shall take the horses there now.'

The barn had fine stone walls, but the roof was unpromising. 'Leave the horses here with us and return on foot to the farm. When you are there, say only that you tried to get help, but were unsuccessful. On your way home you met with two beggars called Heðinn and Kári, and you promised to give them hospitality for a few days. Leave a lantern burning at your front door, and we shall meet you there when it is fully dark.'

'I will do as you say,' Ketill answered.

After Ketill had departed, Ófeig changed into a set of ragged clothes he had brought with him and folded away his good travelling gear into the saddlebags. He told Kári to do the same, and he did so.

'Well, Kári? What do you think now?'

Kári looked at Ófeig and shook his head. 'I cannot make anything of this. It is unusual for silver to go missing. There are many scoundrels around here but stealing someone's hoard of silver is a despicable trick, fit only for outlaws. I suppose our farmer has not mislaid it?'

Ófeig demurred. 'I do not think him stupid at all. Someone has taken it. Why that should be, we do not know. It will be either his wife, his shepherd, or his neighbours; unless there is some scheming relative of whom we know nothing as yet.' He smiled. 'That is why we are staying with Ketill, to find out for ourselves what sort of folk they are.'

Kári nodded. He was a fine, well-set young man, more notable for courage and strength than intelligence. He had been part of Odd's household, but Odd and he had fallen out over one of Odd's daughters whom Kári wished to marry. Odd had refused the match, and to prevent ill-feeling Ófeig had offered Kári a position in his own house.

The two men gathered some straw and made the barn more weather-proof. They rubbed down the horses, fed them, and made them comfortable with blankets. It began to rain outside, but the barn remained secure and rain-proof.

'Come, Kári. Let us go and visit our hosts,' said Ófeig. They wrapped ragged cloaks close around them and set off for the farm. The house was not large, and there was only one out-building which, they had already learned, was where Thorkel the shepherd lived.

The lantern shone through the mirk and Ófeig found the front door without difficulty. Ketill had been watching for them and said in a loud voice: 'Come within the house, you two. It is wild weather to be tramping abroad.'

Ófeig and Kári smiled knowingly at their host.

Supper had concluded, and Ketill's wife, Hildigunn, was clearing up. She eyed the beggar critically. 'I hope you will not find the fare here too sparse,' she told them. On the rough wooden table she placed two bowls half-filled with pottage, a few crusts of bread and some hard cheese.

'My thanks for your hospitality, and what blessings I may have to bestow,' answered Ófeig. He picked up the wooden spoon and tasted the broth. It was stringy lamb with onions and herbs, but well-cooked and still warm from the pot.

Ófeig looked Hildigunn over. She was a fine woman: long-limbed and deep-bosomed, with fine yellow hair down to her waist. He thought her around twenty-five. She watched him look her over with a smile.

Her face coloured. 'You have bold manners for a beggar, Heðinn,' she said.

'That is true,' Ófeig answered. 'But it may be that I can be unexpectedly helpful.'

Her colour deepened, and she left the kitchen. Ketill sat at the table and exchanged glances with Ófeig and Kári. Neither man said anything for a while. Kári and Ófeig finished their supper.

'My wife has gone to bed,' Ketill said.

'Is she asleep, do you think?'

'I believe so. She is a good wife, and works hard through the day.'

'Does she have relatives hereabouts?'

'Her parents are dead. There is a cousin who is responsible for her, but he lives far off in the south.'

'How did you meet her?'

'The cousin – a man called Thorgrim – brought her with him three years ago to the district assembly. He came to buy timber, and I came to sell my cheeses. We got talking – she and I – and I asked Thorgrim for her hand.'

Ketill paused and shook his head. 'I believe Thorgrim has many daughters and nieces and was glad to be rid of her.'

'What dowry did he give you? Was it the silver?'

'No. He offered twelve ells of cloth. I bargained for twenty and he gave sixteen.'

'Do you still have them?'

'All save for two ells, which she used to make a fine red dress. She wears it when we go to the district assembly.'

'Very well. Tell your wife we shall be staying for some time. Is there room in the outbuilding for us, as well as your shepherd?'

'You will not find it comfortable, accustomed to your own house and bed. But there is room enough there.'

Ófeig and Kári settled into the straw bed and listened to the sounds of sleep coming from the other end of the byre. They slept until late in the morning, but when they arose, the men looked over Ketill's farm.

Ófeig saw Thorkel the shepherd resting against a rock, watching the sheep. 'Kári,' he said. 'I want you to search the byre here. Look for signs of disturbed earth. Look especially in the rafters. I am going to look further afield.'

Ófeig walked across the fields to where Einar's land adjoined Ketill's. There were a few sheep, and horses grazing. Two men were lounging against a stone wall, drinking ale from leather flasks. 'Who are you?' one inquired.

'My name is Heðinn,' he answered. 'I am staying with Ketill for the moment.'

The other man laughed, looking over Ófeig's ragged clothes. 'You'll get poor pickings at Ketill's house, but you won't get any better here. Einar is a hard man, and not over-fond of travelling beggars.'

'The fare is well enough with Ketill. I cannot complain. But since I am enjoying his hospitality, I thought I might help him as best I can.'

'You do not look as though you have many days' work in you,' said the first.

'That is as may be. I hoped to find some silver of his which has gone missing.'

He watched the two men closely but they gave no sign of discomfort, and laughed in good humour. 'If Einar had taken it, you would struggle to get it back,' said the second. 'But I do not think he has it. One thing I can tell you for certain is that he has not asked any of us to steal it.'

Ófeig smiled. 'Would you, if you were asked?'

Both men shook their heads. 'No,' the first answered. 'There are certain things no master should ask, and that is one of them. That is a deed fit only for outlaws.'

'I see.' Ófeig rose and wrapped his cloak around him. 'Thank you for your time.'

That night, Thorkel the shepherd joined Ófeig and Kári at supper, which Hildigunn had brought to the outbuilding. It was the same as before: lamb pottage, bread and hard cheese. Ófeig noticed that Thorkel gazed at Hildigunn like a calf looking on its mother. As they ate, Ófeig remarked that she was a fine and generous woman.

'She is indeed,' said the boy. His cheeks flamed red, and he seemed about to say more, but stopped himself, and they finished the meal in silence. Thorkel went to sleep early, and Ófeig beckoned Kári outside and told him about his visit to Einar's farm.

'I take it you found nothing, Kári?' he asked.

'I found Thorkel's purse, hidden under his straw bed. There was nothing much in it, just some broken silver and a few oddments. And I searched the rafters and found nothing. Did you have better luck?'

'No. Wherever the missing silver is, Thorkel did not take it. You have seen him for yourself. A guileless fool, I guess. I am afraid that Ketill's neighbours think him a man of little account. But this may change.'

'What do you advise now?'

'I have not thought enough as yet. Tomorrow may bring new counsel.'

Next morning Ketill and Thorkel took the sheep to their summer pasture on a low hill not far off. Ófeig and Kári walked back to the horse-barn, fed, watered, and combed the horses, and searched the barn thoroughly. Then they sat down in the straw and looked at each other.

Ófeig frowned. 'I am out of my reckoning, Kári,' he said. 'You know who took the silver, do you not?'

Kári shook his head.

'You have seen all that I have seen,' said Ófeig, 'and yet you do not observe what I have observed.'

'So you have solved this mystery?' Kári asked.

'I have. And yet,' Ófeig paused, 'even though I also know why it was done, I cannot do anything without the silver. Now what could she have done with it?'

'She? You mean Hildigunn? Why would she do that? Surely she could not hope to get away with stealing her husband's treasure?'

'That is true, Kari. The District Assembly would outlaw her, and a female outlaw does not live long. But that is not her plan. I believe she has, or plans to, bury the silver somewhere, and then claim that Ketill was responsible. You know that by law, burying treasure is a crime?'

Ófeig watched his companion's face clear. 'Of course! Burying treasure is regarded as theft from one's own family. Do you mean that she wants him outlawed?'

'Not necessarily. I believe she wishes to divorce him, and take half her dowry. That is why I asked about her relatives. She has none here in the Northlands and would find getting support from anyone hereabouts very difficult. But if she can have him accused of a crime, public opinion will force Ketill to give her property back.'

Kári thought this over. 'I see. But are you sure?'

'No-one else has any reason except Thorkel, and you have seen what manner of man he is. Now I want you to go and make conversation with Hildigunn. She will think you a callow and foolish lad, but you must not mind that. Watch what she does carefully. Offer to help her out with her domestic tasks. She will think you stranger than ever, but she may accept your help. In the end she will bid you begone. Then come and tell me what you saw.'

While Kári was away on his errand, Ófeig searched the barn and its surrounds again, just to make certain. Then he sat and waited for his steward's return. By mid-afternoon Kári returned and told Ófeig what he had seen.

'She was surprised, but she let me help her with some cooking. I managed to search her flour-bin, but there was nothing there but flour. Then she asked me to clean out the muck from the byre, and I did that. I thought it might have been buried under the manure, but it wasn't. She gave me free rein in the kitchen, too. Since you asked me to be helpful, I even offered to hold the weights for her while she was weaving.'

'And then?'

'Then she bade me off, saying that weaving was no task for a proper man, and that no woman would marry a man who wove wool or cloth. What does it all mean?'

'That you will see. Now it is time for us to put on our fine clothes. Just do as I do and wrap your ragged cloak over your tunic so it doesn't show.'

They walked back to the house in silence. Ófeig told Kári to stand by the door and sat himself in Ketill's chair. When Hildigunn saw him, she put down her basket and put both hands on her hips.

'You are bolder than ever, Heðinn. You should not sit in that chair unbidden.'

'That remains to be seen,' Ófeig answered. He shrugged his shoulders, and the ragged cloak fell to his waist. Hildigunn bit her lips, and a trickle of blood ran down her chin and neck.

'Who are you?' she asked.

'My name is Ófeig,' he answered. 'It is not unknown in these parts, I imagine. Now you shall bring me your weaving-loom, Hildigunn. And be quick about it, since you do not have much time.'

Hildigunn did as she was asked and laid the loom on the table, with the woollen cloth still threaded upon it. Ófeig removed one of the weights from the woollen thread.

'You see that these weights are covered with cloth, Kári? Now let us see what is within the cloth.' He pulled out a silver coin and held it up in the lamplight. 'A cunning hiding place for your husband's silver, Hildigunn.'

Hildigunn looked uncomfortable. 'I did not intend to keep it,' she answered.

Ófeig inclined his head.

'I am not calling you a thief, Hildigunn. Your plan was to have proceedings instituted against Ketill at the District Assembly on the charge of burying treasure; which is against the laws of this land. Then you would have divorced him and received half your dowry back, so you could marry Thorkel. Is not that how it was?'

Hildigunn sighed in defeat. 'It was. Except for marrying Thorkel. I do not wish to wed a boy. And while he loves me now, he will love me no longer in a few years. I will not be a scorned wife. Not again. Now tell me what you intend to do about this.'

'That depends upon Ketill. But it is well for you that you have spoken the truth. Now you must give me the purse back and I shall restore the silver to it.'

Hildigunn reached into her dress and handed over the leather purse. Then she left the room without another word.

Hildigunn later brought out supper for Thorkel, Ófeig and Kári in the outbuilding, but left them without a word. While they were eating, Ófeig allowed his cloak to fall away as before. This time Thorkel's eyes widened and he put down his bowl.

'It is clear enough that you are no beggar,' he said. 'I thought that your manner was over-bold for what you seemed to be. Will you give me your name?'

'My name is Ófeig, and I came here to find this.' He held up the purse and Thorkel grinned with delight.

'You have found the master's lost silver! I know of you, and that you are known as a man of great cunning and resourcefulness, but this is wonderful. Ketill will be well-pleased at this news.'

'I hope so,' Ófeig answered.

Later that night, Ófeig went into the house and handed Ketill the purse of silver. When he had explained the situation, Ketill asked him what he should do now.

'At the district assembly, you should announce that you are divorcing your wife. She will ask for her dowry back, but she may find it difficult to find a powerful man to take her case. You, however, should give her six ells of cloth, which with her favourite red dress constitutes half her dowry. And you should give her some money for her journey to the south. Her cousin must take her back. In this way you will gain a better reputation than if you held out and kept her dowry.'

'I am surprised by all this,' Ketill answered. 'Yet I should not be. I am an old man, and she is young and full of life. I see why she acted as she did. I hope that my shepherd was not involved?'

'He was not. I showed him my rich clothes and the purse, and he showed nothing but innocent surprise and pleasure that your silver had been found. He was not much in her thoughts, I guess, even though she was much in his.'

'That is some relief,' Ketill said. 'I only wish I could repay you for solving this problem for me.'

'Ah yes, if only; but this farm is poor. Although, you might do better with an exchange of land.'

'Is such a thing possible?'

'It is possible. But I will say no more until I know more.'

'I do not know how to thank you.'

'Save your thanks for later, Ketill.'

When Ófeig and Kári returned home, they found Rannveig in high spirits.

'Samr has news for you, and so have I,' she told Ófeig. 'You asked us to keep an eye on Grim and his thieving ways. Well, this is what we did. You know how you mark your sheep? Grim knows where the mark is and has covered it up with his own mark. But we have put a second mark with the O-rune where he will never find it. Samr hid all day by Grim's fields, waiting for his chance. When Grim's shepherd was sleeping, Samr looked over a ewe which looked like one of yours and there was the O-rune in the ewe's wool.'

'Where did you put the rune?'

'Next to the groin. We judged that Grim would not look there. Have I done well?'

'You have done very well indeed, Rannveig. But since there is still some daylight left, I would like to make sure of this. Call Samr.'

Ófeig, Kári and Samr rode to Grim's farm. Grim met them outside his house. He had five men with him, all armed, and all very formidable looking. 'What do you want, old man?' asked Grim. 'You are not wanted here.'

Ófeig reined in his horse. 'I am looking for one of my ewes, which has strayed. Doubtless this is a misunderstanding, but I should like to look for myself.'

'Not with my leave,' Grim answered. 'My men will see you off.'

'That they will not. My family is not unknown hereabouts, and if you kill either me or my men here, I do not think many of you will live much longer.'

Kári rode up next to Ófeig and lifted his chin at Grim's men. 'And you may find killing us more difficult than you imagine.' He carried a long sword at his belt.

Grim looked at the weapon, and at Kári's broad shoulders, and laughed. 'Very well. If you think your son will avenge you, you may be right. But you will find none of your ewes here.'

'Samr? Can you find my lost one?'

They rode out to the field where the sheep were grazing and Samr found the ewe. 'See?' he held the sheep's hind leg out. 'There is the O-rune, meaning Ófeig. As you see, Grim, this belongs to my master.'

Grim laughed again. 'Take it and be off with you.'

At a sign from Ófeig, Samr took up the ewe and perched it on the horse in front of him. The three men left at once and rode back to Melur.

Kári and Samr rode out into the fields with the ewe, and she was restored to her friends with many a bleat of relief and reuniting. Rannveig met Ófeig at the front door. 'How did it go with Grim?'

Ófeig smiled. 'Better than I could have hoped. Grim does not realise this, but I shall have him off his farm at the District Assembly. He thinks he has got away with his pilfering from my flock; but Samr, Kári and I have seen the evidence for ourselves. I will tell him that I intend to prosecute him for theft, and I will ask for three years' outlawry. He will go around the assembly looking for chieftains to support him and find them hard to come by. Then I will offer to drop the prosecution if he agrees to a land exchange in another district.'

Rannveig smiled. 'And the exchanger?'

'A grateful farmer called Ketill. He will be a far more satisfactory neighbour. We will gain, and whoever takes on Grim as a neighbour will get the worst of the deal.'

'Would this be the farmer who came calling some days ago?'

'It would.' Ófeig told her the whole story, and finished by saying this. 'It seems to me that Hildigunn, though not a good woman, will nevertheless make some man a fine wife. She treated me fairly and with some generosity when she thought me a beggar of no account. And I am certain that the shepherd boy was not romping on her belly. She wanted more from her life than a cold marriage with an old man. I find it difficult to blame her.'

Ófeig walked into the house and took up his wooden tagelharpa. He sat in his high chair, bent over the instrument and adjusted the tuning pegs while strumming softly at the four strings. He nodded his head, took up the bow, and began to play with his eyes closed. When he had finished the tune he found Rannveig standing in front of him. He looked at her in enquiry, and laid down the bow.

'I think as you do about Hildigunn,' Rannvieg told him. Her face coloured. 'Yet not all women are averse to marriage with an old man. Not if the old man has a kind heart, cunning wits, and a prosperous farm in his own name.'

Ófeig stared at her in astonishment. 'Are you certain of what you say?'

'I am.'

 He looked at her sharply, and smiled. 'That is certainly a kind offer. We shall think further on this tomorrow. But please be assured, dear lady, that you are very welcome to stay here in whatever capacity we decide upon.'

Rannvieg nodded, and left the room, while Ófeig picked up his bow and began to play again.

Authors' note

Most of the literature we have from the Viking Age consists of poetry and sagas; the latter being best viewed as historical novels based on real events. Sagas mainly concern the process of conflict and resolution in an age where there was no police force and no standing army.

Stylistically, sagas only tell you what people said and did, and emotions are inferred from appearance and words. The great sagas (*Njals Saga* and *Laxdaela Saga*, to name but two) are arguably the finest literature produced during the Middle Ages.

Ófeig is a character in one of the lesser tales. More a novella than a novel, *Bandamanna Saga* (The Confederates) is a satire on an irresponsible ruling class. Our story refers to how he outwitted Gellir and the other greedy chieftains. We decided that of all the characters we meet in the sagas, he was the most likely candidate to be a Viking Sherlock. A modern murder mystery is impossible in the Viking Age, since if you had killed someone, you had to cover the body and report the death to the nearest dwelling. Doing anything else was all but unthinkable. But there is plenty of scope for detection nonetheless, in medieval Iceland as anywhere else.

Please note that while the Vikings could be fearless killers and robbers, it wasn't their preferred option. Medieval Iceland was probably the most democratic state in the world at the time. And Viking women had far more rights than almost anywhere else in Europe. Also, the only realistic depiction of Vikings available on film and TV may be found in *The Last Kingdom*. Everything else we have seen is fantasy cosplay.

THE
PROBLEM
OF THE
LYING
AUTHOR

Lisa Fessler

The first day of spring brought a warm breeze to the city, an invitation to go outdoors that not many Berliners refused. Leisurely walkers populated Tiergarten Park, and Unter den Linden boulevard had become a perambulator's paradise. Two gentlemen, clad in black suits and top hats, one blond, the other a sharp brunet, strolled down Wilhelm-Strasse engaged in intimate conversation. They held each other's hands with casual ease. It was not an uncommon sight in Berlin, back in those more innocent days before the shameful trial against the great Oscar Wilde.

It was not an uncommon sight, I say. But on this sunny morning, the intimate gesture, indicative of any number of close relations, was turned into a crime. A recent scandal was still fresh on everyone's mind, reaching as it did into the highest echelons of the Royal Court. The better papers put matters delicately, inferring rather than boldly stating. The yellow press had no such qualms. Homosexual orgies, was one of the more harmless descriptors of what was allegedly going on in the chateaus of the nobility around Berlin.

Seeing those gentlemen holding hands must have roused something dark and malignant in those watching the scene; three in particular – a shopkeeper waiting for customers, a maid out with her master's child, and an advocate who had just lost a case.

The shopkeeper raised his eyebrows at the sight. The maid remarked on it, and the advocate joined their talk. Such displays of affection were against the law, they muttered, an outward sign of a perverted inner nature. And on this particular morning, the advocate decided to act. He approached the policemen standing at the corner of Wilhelm-Strasse.

The two gentlemen were accosted out of the blue. One policeman pulled them apart and another tried to handcuff them. Naturally, they resisted, and a brawl ensued. The shopkeeper withdrew into his store, the maid rushed away. The advocate had disappeared shortly after he had brought the matter to the policemen's attention. A crowd formed on the sidewalk, cheering for the brunet gentleman who turned out to be a formidable fighter. The scuffle went on for long minutes when finally a police carriage pulled up. The gentlemen were arrested and brought to the nearest station.

My good friend Sherlock Holms rarely makes an appearance in the press, as he rarely gives cause to become a figure of interest for the gossip rags. But neither his reputation as the world's leading expert in solving crime, nor my more humble position as a physician working at the Charité, could prevent the incident from making headlines the next day. I was icing my swollen ankle when Frau Huber brought in the newspapers, a look of both shame and sympathy on her face.

An official apology was issued and we were cleared of all accusations. Kriminalkommissar Lestrade of the Prussian Police, a fine man and our friend, made sure of it. Within a few days the scandal was pushed to the back of the papers, as more exciting news, more sordid crimes, took precedence.

The incident became a private joke between Holms and I. *Remember the day we were arrested for being bleeding homosexuals*. But ever since, we made sure to keep at a polite distance when taking our walks. And we never held hands in public again.

Three months later, during a blistering hot summer, I sat at a late breakfast. A mild breeze came through the open window overlooking Sophien-Strasse. The sweet scent of lush red begonias, Frau Huber's pride, filled the air. Holms had left for some business of his own and I was looking forward to a few quiet hours in the company of the latest book of my favourite author. Karl May's *Winnetou the Red Gentleman* had come out mere days ago, and just this morning the publisher had sent me a complimentary copy. I settled back in the chair, ready to be carried away into foreign lands.

I had hardly glanced at the first page when our sitting room door was thrown open with such force that it crashed loudly against the wall.

I all but jumped out of the chair. 'By Jove, can you not–?'

Frau Huber would never enter our rooms so noisily. I was expecting one of the street urchins Holms kept in his employ. But bursting into the room was none other than my companion himself.

I could not remember an occasion where I had seen him in such disarray. Holms always took pride in his meticulous appearance, not a hair out of place, coat and trousers always freshly cleaned and pressed. But now his hair was windblown, his pale complexion ruddy, and he had divested himself of his frock coat. The bottoms of his trousers were gathered close with a pair of unfashionable clips, and his striped shirt was no longer white but covered with dark stains and dust. On his left shoulder he carried an enormous steel contraption. Only on second glance I realised it was Holms' latest obsession – a bicycle.

'Shouldn't this thing be carrying you, and not the other way around?' I said, settling back in the chair.

The bicycle had been a point of contention between Holms and me. Several patients of mine had come to the surgery with broken wrists and smashed-in faces. Cycling was all very well for country lanes, but for the city, I was clear in the camp of those who preferred carriages and the steady transport of one's own feet. Holms instead lauded the bicycle as a democratic invention that would change our cities for centuries to come.

'It was carrying me all the way to Spandau and back.' With a thud Holms placed the bicycle on Frau Huber's treasured Persian rug.

'Don't tell me you're still of a mind to join the cycling race?' I turned to him, because this was serious. The Austrian-German long-distance cycling competition was to start in a few days in Vienna, and Holms had been contemplating it ever since he acquired his own machine.

'More than a hundred well-trained sportsmen, 582 kilometres through the most beautiful countryside, 35 hours in the seat of a bike – it is tempting.' Holms cleaned the bicycle with a soft cloth, reminding me of a horse-breeder rubbing down his cherished thoroughbred.

He was a stellar athlete, and in theory I approved of physical activity as a distraction from the boredom that always befell my friend during the summer months. Summer was the time of minor offences and petty crime, because everyone, including the criminal class, was on vacation. Usually, it drove Holms up the wall. He would gripe and moan all through June, but eventually find a new field of study, acquiring within short months a depth of knowledge rarely found except in an expert of the field.

The Vienna-Berlin long-distance race was an added nuisance to his new passion for cycling. I certainly did not look forward to standing amidst a sweaty crowd, cheering Holms on, or worse, patching him up after an accident.

'How on earth would you get you and your metal steed to Vienna?' Surely Holms would have long figured out the logistics, if he really was to participate in the race. In the meantime, the dusty bicycle was standing on Frau Huber's rug, and Holms showed no signs of packing for a trip to Austria.

'One could always use the train, I suppose,' suggested a dark voice from the open door.

I was out of the chair the same instant as Holms sprang up from where he had been kneeling on the floor. Armed with book and cleaning cloth, we faced our unexpected visitor.

'I hope I am not interrupting important business,' the stranger said. 'Your landlady told me to come right up.' He politely removed his top hat as he stepped into our quarters, and used it to point towards the book at my chest. 'Once you're finished, Doctor Watson, I'd be interested to hear what you think of it.'

He was not as tall as I had imagined him, a wiry man of mature age. Pride, perhaps even a streak of vanity, was in the dashing cut of his travel suit and in the way his light hair was combed back into a characteristic wave. But whatever lower sentiment his attire might reveal, it was mitigated by his warm gaze and the full curve of his moustached lips. He was already in his fifties, but his high forehead was still without a crease. It was easy to imagine him at a younger age, beardless, eager for whatever the world held in store for him.

I stared at the figure who seemed to have jumped out of the pages of the book I was holding, the alter-ego of Charlie, Winnetou's beloved friend, the author himself: Karl May.

I had our illustrious visitor sit in my usual armchair by the fireplace and waved for Holms to change into a clean shirt. Frau Huber served fresh coffee and kept up a friendly chatter while I evicted the dreaded cycling machine to the landing.

May watched these goings-on with keen interest. He had, to my knowledge, never written a detective novel, and I wondered whether he had come to research the lodgings of such an exceptional detective as Sherlock Holms. The bleached skull and other human bones displayed on the mantelpiece immediately drew his attention; his gaze wandered from the filing cabinets to the stacks of scientific journals on the *cheffonier*. He lingered long moments on the violin my friend had haphazardly wrapped in silk and left by the window. After a polite exchange with Frau Huber, May turned his head to get a good glimpse of the laboratory in the recess beside the door.

Holms returned from his room; he had thankfully donned a suitable jacket, cleaned his hands of all grease and dirt, and removed the atrocious trouser clips. He, too, was scrutinised by the author, who clearly made note of our living arrangements: the tiny bathroom and the one bedroom leading off the sitting room. May could not know that there was another bedroom upstairs; he much less could guess at how rarely I made use of it. But he suspected something – that much was clear.

Frau Huber excused herself only after she had secured May's autograph for her copy of Jewel Island. Holms sat in the armchair opposite May, his usual place, with the window behind him and the sunlight in the visitor's eye.

For a moment I was unsure where to sit, then quickly settled on the sofa. Whatever his intentions and despite my admiration for him, May was just another client.

'I understand you have a case for me, Herr May?' Holms asked.

He exhibited the nervous impatience that always came over him whenever a mystery seemed within reach. I myself could hardly contain my own curiosity. What on earth would bring a writer of May's standing into our home?

'It's perhaps not quite what I would call a *case*,' May said.

'A problem, then.' Holms' shadowed face betrayed disinterest, with his long fingers steepled underneath his chin. But I, who've spent so many of my waking hours in his presence, saw the straightening of his posture, always a sign of heightened attention. A case, Holms used to say, which was deemed not quite a case was always worth further investigation.

'A problem, it is,' May conceded. 'I take it you are familiar with Liebig Men's Fashion? The shop at Hausvogtei-Platz?'

Liebig was one of the finest addresses in the city when it came to men's suits and coats. We often passed the shop on our daily walks. But fashion was not the direction I had expected May's problem to go, and I sensed Holms' disappointment. He waved for May to continue and the famous author started to speak.

The facts of the case were these:

A young friend of May's had ordered a fur coat from Liebig. He had chosen a black fox, with a beautiful blue shine. It had been a very expensive pelt; Heinrich Liebig had it imported from Petersburg. A salesman, a trusted employee, had taken the measurements. It was arranged that May's friend should pick the coat up within a fortnight, when he would visit Berlin again. The salesman was confident that by then the coat would be finished.

Now, Holms might simply want to learn these facts – to dismiss Karl May's problem or throw himself into its investigation – but I was drawn into the narrative, delivered in perfect High German that still could not deny its Saxon melody. Our visitor's gift for storytelling did not stop at the written word, and he spun an imaginative tale from a rather dull occurrence – the sale of a fur coat. I had never been inside Liebig but listening to May, I heard the rustling echoes in the high salon, I felt underneath me the soft leather of the elegant couches, and I envisioned the rows of ready-made suits and the choice selection of Parisian fabrics and Russian furs.

'My friend is a conscientious customer,' May said. 'They settled on a price, and he paid the usual advance.'

'How much was it?' Holms asked. He was observing May with keen interest, but I could not tell whether May found his scrutiny impolite or inappropriate.

He answered quietly, his tone as friendly as ever. 'Half the cost of the fur and thirty per cent of the making of the coat,' he said. 'It was not a modest sum, but my friend has come into some money, and he felt such a splendid coat was well worth the price.'

'This has happened recently?' Holms inquired.

'Oh yes, only a few days ago.'

'And your *friend*,' Holms made a short pause, 'doesn't usually live in Berlin?'

'He lives in Dresden, close to my own home.' May pointed to the book, which I had placed on the mantelpiece. 'You may have noticed the artistic cover of *Winnetou*. It is my friend's work. He is an up-and-coming artist from the Dresden Academy.'

I was about to take another look at the book's cover, which I – whose interest in the Fine Arts had never gone beyond the Masters – had hardly spared a glance. But Holms raised his hand. 'Later. Please continue, Herr May. I take it your friend picked up the coat?'

'No, he didn't.'

'Ah. And this is where the problem starts, I presume?'

Karl May smiled. 'Perhaps it does. Where the problem starts, and what in fact is the problem – that is for you to find out, is it not? I can only presume to tell you the facts of the matter.'

'Exactly.' May had formulated one of Holms' cherished axioms: start with the bare facts, without sentiment or interpretation. But we had not yet heard one fact that would justify the services of a world-class detective. With a touch of annoyance, Holms continued. 'What happened when Sascha Schneider did not pick up the coat?'

'Sascha Schn... You know this man?' I exclaimed.

I usually kept my surprise reined in during these interviews, to give Holms opportunity to focus on the client's reaction. But I had not heard of a Sascha Schneider before, and while Holms' interests were broad, they did not extend to the covers of adventure novels, no matter how artistic their design.

My exclamation earned me a reproachful glare from my companion. For a moment, Karl May seemed equally taken aback but then a satisfied expression appeared on his face.

'You guessed right,' he said.

Holms barked out a laugh. 'It was hardly a guess. But let me venture a real guess now: the fur coat had already been picked up by someone else. Someone unknown and untraceable.'

'Indeed.' May nodded with an amused smile. 'There had been some confusion about the dates, and when Sascha arrived at the shop, he found he was a week late. The coat, while allegedly finished, was no longer waiting for him. Another person had picked it up, a man of

Sascha's build and dark colouring, claiming to be him. It is my friend's misfortune that the seasoned salesman was not working that day, for he would have certainly identified the stranger as an imposter. Instead, one of the salesgirls handed the man the coat and let him leave the shop without paying the rest of the sum Sascha still owed Liebig.'

Holms leaned back in his armchair, tobacco pouch in hand. 'And now Liebig makes financial claims on your friend, to pay for a fur coat he never received.'

'And he won't return to Sascha the advance he already paid. As I said, it was an expensive coat.'

'What do the police say?' Holms meticulously stuffed the pipe.

'The police never searched for the imposter. Sascha was charged with theft, on Heinrich Liebig's account.' May leaned forward; he obviously knew that this was the point that would most interest Holms. But there was also heartfelt indignation in his voice. 'Liebig had not been present when Sascha ordered the coat, much less when the coat was handed over, without any proof of identity or final payment, to a stranger. And yet it was he on whose word my friend has been taken into custody at Alexander-Platz.'

Holms, who was about to light his pipe, stopped mid-motion. 'At Alexander-Platz? Schneider was brought into the Red Castle? For allegations of theft? That's highly unusual. Such a complaint is usually filed at the local precinct, and they also make the arrest.'

May inclined his head. 'It is unusual, isn't it?'

Holms lit his pipe and drew a first smoke. 'How did you learn about this news?'

'Sascha and I had planned to meet with my publisher, here in Berlin. But Sascha never came. We waited until a young man brought a note from Sascha himself, explaining his extraordinary circumstances.'

'And when was your meeting with the publisher?'

'Yesterday morning, at eleven. I had taken the early train in from Dresden.'

Holms looked over to the old grandfather clock in the corner. It was almost noon. 'More than twenty-four hours...' he muttered, tapping the stem of the pipe to his thin lips.

'I wasn't sure what to do at first,' May explained, 'until my publisher suggested I consult you, Herr Holms. I came as quickly as I could.'

'It was good of you to come. Your publisher is Fehsenfeld, isn't he?

Give him my regards when you next see him.' A thin wisp of smoke curled upwards to the ceiling from Holms' pipe. He stared at it, then put the pipe on the rack and closed his eyes, an expression of intense concentration on his face.

I was not yet over the shock of learning that Holms had even heard of Ernst Friedrich Fehsenfeld, May's generous but obscure publisher. But clearly, the famous author had been dismissed. Remembering common courtesy, I brought Karl May to the door, assuring him that the imposter would be found and his artist friend soon released from custody.

Just as May was about to take his leave, Holms interrupted his reverie (what he would describe as *mental calculations*), calling out to May.

'The note informing you of Schneider's predicament – you do not perchance have it with you or could provide a copy of its exact wording?'

'Alas, no.' May was already half through the door and seemed eager to make a full exit. 'I left it at the hotel. It was just a few lines, nothing more than what I told you. I can easily have it delivered to you.'

But Holms waved a languid hand. 'No, it's quite all right. I have all the pertinent facts clear in front of me. Just one more thing: the young man who delivered the note. Do you have his name? Or an address where he may be reached?'

'I'm afraid not,' May said, truly apologetic. 'He's an acquaintance of Sascha's. A friend.'

I accompanied Karl May to the street where a hackney cab waited to bring its passenger back to the Hotel Westminster: one of the more fashionable hotels where May resided whenever he came to the Empire's capital.

We exchanged a few amiable remarks about the business of writing. The day was brilliant, and we stood in the shade of the tree before Frau Huber's small coffee shop, the Königin-Sophie Café. Karl May was in no apparent hurry; rather it seemed to me he wanted to prolong our talk. Whether it was because he enjoyed my company as much as I did his, or for some other reason, I leave for the reader to decide.

So there we stood on the sidewalk discussing the need to adhere to facts while at the same time – and sometimes with the very same words – keep entertained an audience that hungers for cheap thrills. When I shared my frustrations of trying to make Holms understand that a good tale needs elaboration and compression, May casually remarked, 'Any writer worth his salt knows how to lie, and to lie well.'

I might have gasped, for I remember an awkward pause in our conversation. The truth of the statement struck me to the core. May had hit, with succinct candour, at what lay at the heart of Holms' and my arguments: Sherlock Holms, champion of fact and reason versus yours truly, purveyor of fiction and sentiment.

But Karl May had also provided me valuable ammunition for our arguments. He had pointed out that a lie was not necessarily the opposite of fact. Holms, I knew, would be the first to agree, even though he would never admit that some truths could not be discovered with logic alone.

And May had given me the first clue to solving his problem. In hindsight, I can only assume that he had done so intentionally, but at the time, his visit had left me bewildered. And, aside from my heartfelt admiration of the writer, this was the reason why I had accompanied Karl May downstairs. I had, in short, decided to do some sleuthing of my own.

For this case, the case of the vanished fur coat, was like no other. It was unlike the case I recounted in *The Tirpitz-von-Crefeld-Stratagem*, when Holms' assistance was required by persons of the highest order of the Empire. It was unlike the case that came to be known as *The Adventure of the Unburied Whippet*, which took Holms and me out to Potsdam and the park of Sanssouci. Neither was this a notorious case like the one that the press has titled *The Jurist from the Silver Lodge*.

Of course, each of Holms' cases had its own distinctive flavour. But to this one, I fancied, I had a contribution of my own to make. I have always been interested in the biographies of the authors I admired. Karl May's poor origins in Saxony, his early life of petty crime, and his more recent marital scandal were well known to me. Which is why his tale of the mysteriously vanished fur coat, complete with unjust demands of full payment and wrongful allegations against the original buyer, sounded awfully familiar to me.

I intended to confront Karl May about having told me – and more importantly having told Sherlock Holms – a blatant lie, and that would be the end of this strange tale.

'Dear fellow,' I started, for the warmth of our conversation had given me the impression that May considered us fellow writers, 'to get back to your problem, I was wondering–'

'Forgive me, my friend.' May touched my arm. 'I don't think I can have my driver wait any longer.' The driver, his metal badge prominently displayed on his chest, was indeed eyeing us with impatience. May was right: we should not keep an honest driver from his work whilst discussing ours at ample leisure.

While I contemplated the driver, I noticed a short-haired woman staring in our direction. She wore a plain blue dress but had donned a brown leather jacket and heavy boots that did nothing to render her figure more feminine. In those days, many modern young women wanted to be another Elise Hirschmann, the famous court reporter. However, this personage was one of those less savoury members of the press who were drawn like flies to wherever a wound festers or a body disintegrates in the washed-up dirt of the modern city. She must have recognised Karl May, conversing in front of the home of Germany's greatest detective, and was sniffing scandalous opportunity where others were enjoying the sweet scent of the linden trees.

I exchanged a look with May. He, too, had recognised the interest of the press.

'One more question,' I said quietly, 'to avoid any misunderstanding when Holms and I make our inquiries at Liebig: the price of the coat your friend ordered. It did not exceed 72 thalers, did it?'

May's lips twitched underneath the moustache. I couldn't be sure whether he was shocked or pleased to have been found out, but I suspected the latter. Suspected, or rather, hoped: I wouldn't want Karl May to take Sherlock Holms for a fool.

'Oh no,' May replied, and with some relief I heard amusement in his voice. 'In fact, the coat's price is exactly 72 thalers. The beautiful fur alone comes at fifteen thalers. And, my dear fellow, I think you made a note of the advance, upstairs.'

And here was my evidence. It had been years since thalers had been Prussian currency. Yet back in those days, when businesses still traded in thalers and not in marks, Karl May had gone to prison for a sum of precisely 72 thalers.

Thirty years ago May himself, masquerading as an engraver, had ordered a fur coat to be made to his measurements, without any means to pay for it. On delivery, he claimed the coat was too wide and not the one he had ordered. Yet he never returned the coat to the furrier, and instead pawned it through a middleman. The incriminating coat was found at the pawnbroker's shop and May's identity revealed when he tried to claim the pawn money from the middleman. He served four years at Waldheim Prison in Saxony for deception and theft. It was during those years, May claimed, that he started to write in earnest and make writing his career.

These were the facts I was going to contribute to this case, and for once it was my knowledge of the fine art of *lying well* that would help solve it.

I returned to our quarters with a spring to my step and my mind filled with that particular pleasure a lesser writer might have called the *thrill of anticipation*. Up on the landing, I gave Holms' bicycle an energetic shove so that I could fully open the door.

Perhaps I should have suspected something, knowing Holms as well as I do. But when I stepped in the room, I was wholly unprepared for the sight confronting me.

In the short span of time I had spent with Karl May, Sherlock Holms had decked out our entire sitting room in papers. Every chair, table, and shelf, every single flat surface and the whole of the floor were covered in them.

Holms subscribed to at least a dozen newspapers, local and national, dailies and weeklies, and to a select range of scientific magazines. I myself took in various medical journals. Frau Huber usually had all papers stacked in neat piles on the *cheffonier*. Those towering piles of paper had been spread widely across the room.

Imagine fourteen days' worth of the *Vossische*, the *Berliner Tagblatt*, the *Lokal-Anzeiger*, the *Catholic Germania*, and even the *National-Zeitung*, each one a minimum of ten pages plus advertisements, and some with a morning and an afternoon edition – and you get an inkling of the state of our sitting room. To say it looked as if a bomb had exploded was the wrong metaphor altogether. If I hadn't known Holms I would have suspected the work of a lunatic with a burning hatred of the press.

My companion stood in the middle of it all, dressed again in the dirtied striped shirt he had discarded earlier for the sake of our visitor, a smug smile on his face. It took me long, speechless seconds before I realised that he was offering a newspaper clipping to me.

I took it gingerly from his hand. 'Are you going to tell me what this,'

I moved my arm to encompass the *tohubohu* that was our sitting room, 'is all about?'

Holms patted me on the arm and stepped through the open door. 'I recalled having read something recently, about Liebig's sewing rooms.'

'I take it you didn't remember the date.' I looked down at the clipping. It was from the *Neue Welt*, a socialist weekly that Holms had, quite against my vote, taken in. 'What are you up to, Sherlock?'

'I didn't quite remember the date. But I found it.' Holms stepped to the bicycle and lifted it easily onto his shoulder. 'Now, let's go.'

'Where are we going?'

'To Liebig's, of course.' He didn't wait for an answer, but clambered down the stairs. 'Isn't that why you got the information we need from May?' he called from already half-way down.

'Oh.' I closed the door and rushed after him. 'Yes, I did.'

A minute later we were walking down Sophien-Strasse. I was still digesting the shock of having Holms matter-of-factly accept me as a fellow detective. He expertly steered the bicycle with his left hand but made no signs to mount it. As we turned towards Hackesche-Markt, I noticed that the female specimen of the press was following us. Holms, who undoubtedly had seen our shadow as well, ambled on as if nothing was amiss. In fact, he walked so close to me that I wondered whether he had forgotten that we could no longer risk public displays of affection. Then I realised that Holms did not reach for my hand but for the newspaper clipping clutched in it.

'Would you be so kind and read the small article out for me.'

'You surely haven't lost your ability to read while you ruined our room,' I grumbled.

Holms gave me an exasperated look. Here I was being relegated again, not to my role as a chronicler of Holms' life but to that of a sounding board. Usually, I was content to assist in that way, as it provided me with those unique insights into the workings of Holms' mind that are, I believe, the most compelling feature of my stories. But this case was different, for this time I was privy to at least one crucial fact: Holms could not possibly know about Karl May's well-told lie.

We walked across the square towards Börse Station. Holms' bicycle gave us some breathing space amidst the crowds and coaches. With a sigh I turned to the clipping and I read aloud.

HEAT CLAIMS VICTIMS
IN SEWING ROOMS

Several seamstresses of the Pawlik Zwischenmeisterei collapsed in the over-heated, unaired sweatshop yesterday.

At the time, an inspection was in progress, and Heinrich Liebig of Liebig Men's Fashions, one of the main customers of the business, was on the premises. He stopped the head seamstress from bringing in medical help.

Later, a foreman was evicted from the workshop. According to witnesses, he had fetched a nearby physician, who diagnosed the victims with heatstroke, dehydration, and exhaustion.

Four of the women have been unable to return to their workplace. They are left without pay or compensation.

I looked up to see my companion observing me with a calculating eye. I almost flinched, for I was rarely subject to this particular expression – the look of the detective rather than the friend. Normally, it was reserved for clients or potential criminals.

But I enjoyed playing the game that was usually Sherlock Holms' prerogative; the game of withholding information. I decided to not give away my knowledge yet. Instead, I concentrated on the plain facts and what expertise I could bring to them, just as if this was a case like any other.

'The working conditions in the sewing rooms are substandard, inhuman even,' I said.

As a doctor I knew first-hand of the hardships of those women who had to offer up their sewing and embroidering skills to the brutal sweatshop system of the Zwischenmeisterei. But certainly Holms had not shown me the article to discuss the seamstresses' plight.

'No doubt, no doubt.' We crossed to the other side of the elevated train station. 'But what do you make of this particular incident?'

I made nothing of the incident because I was convinced that whatever happened at the sewing room, it was nothing that would warrant Holms' investigation.

'Well,' I said, 'it has been very hot these last days, and those sewing rooms are poorly ventilated. The work is gruelling, fourteen hours a day in a cramped position at heavy machinery. It's unsurprising that the women suffered from heatstroke; anyone could have foreseen it. But–'

'But?' Holms gave me a knowing smile. I had the distinct impression that he was playing a game as well: cat and mouse, with Holms as the smug tomcat and me, the clueless rodent.

'But,' I replied slowly, 'the circumstances are unusual, what with Liebig present in the workshop. The seamstress was torn between duty and her compassion for her employees. And the rebellious foreman lost his job.'

Holms steered his bike over the cobble-stoned street. 'You state the obvious, my friend, but fail to see what's underneath. This article summarises what amounts to an unlucky conjunction of chance and consequence. Had Liebig not been there, the foreman would still be in work today. But I wonder if we would have found it quite so unusual if we had not heard a tale about Liebig's store just a short while ago. The logical mind cannot help search for a connection in what looks like mere coincidence. So here is our puzzle, Hans: how could the vanished fur coat have any bearing on the suffering of those women and the foreman's fate?'

Perhaps it was the uncharacteristic way he patted the bicycle's saddle; perhaps it was his odd choice of words, but I realised with a growing sense of discomfort that I had been wrong. Sherlock Holms did know what I had thought to be my secret knowledge; he had seen through Karl May's lie.

Warmth rose to my face that had nothing with the summer heat. 'O-one would assume,' I stuttered, 'that the fur coat had been sewn by those women.'

'This is indeed what one would assume.' Holms didn't care to elaborate but left a curtain of silence hanging between us as we walked along the Spree.

I averted my eyes in embarrassment and turned to scan the outline of Börse Station behind us. The presswoman was still there, dodging bicycles and two large dogs while trying to hide behind the trees lining the river. Watching her futile efforts, I decided to end the game before Holms sank his claws into me.

'About that information I got from Karl May.' I cleared my throat. 'If you must know: there never was a fur coat. Or rather, there was a fur coat, but not in Berlin and not two days ago.'

Holms chuckled at my confession, which for him was a rare exhibition of sentiment. 'Finally, the truth comes out,' he said, without the slightest hint of surprise. 'So what was Herr May's fabricated story all about? Stick to the facts, please. I've had quite enough fanciful storiation for one day.'

It was all the admonishment I received. As we came up the Eiserne Brücke, I gave him a brief and unadorned version of what I knew of the fur coat incident in Karl May's life.

We stood on top of the bridge, a cool breeze rising from the Spree, when I ended my report. 'When I asked him, May named the full price of the fur coat that Sascha Schneider allegedly bought. It was 72 thalers, or the current equivalent, he claimed.'

'Which, I assume, is just the sum he had cheated out of the honest coat-maker in Leipzig?'

I felt the need to defend Karl May. 'He claims it was a misunderstanding.'

'Which it may well have been in his mind. But the facts that I assume were presented during his trial speak for themselves. He came in the disguise of an engraver, he presented a story that was only half-true. Just as he appeared this morning, pretending to be a client and presenting a mix of lies and truths. So I ask you again, Hans: what is the common thread that runs through the story of the vanished fur coat and the incident in Liebig's Zwischenmeisterei?'

'I can't see a connection. I don't think there is one,' said I. 'What I see is an author who wishes to be exonerated of a crime that he did not commit. He must have heard of your detective skills, or Fehsenfeld put him up to it. Karl May is making a name for himself; his readership is growing each week. Fehsenfeld must have an interest in clearing May's name before the press gets wind of whatever happened.'

It was the only explanation that made sense. Karl May, in a stunt only an extraordinary author like him could devise, had told us a fanciful lie to capture Holms' interest. I even understood the need for such trickery: Holms would have hardly listened to May's tale if he knew it had been a petty crime, solved years ago, the sentence long served.

Holms' eyes were warm on me. 'Clever thinking, Hans, one might even call it insightful. But while you observe the facts, you draw the wrong conclusions. I venture Karl May's visit had nothing to do with his own career, but everything to do with those sewing rooms. I am astonished to have you underestimate so thoroughly a fellow writer, especially one that I gather you hold in high esteem.'

'By Jove, Sherlock, he could have just given you his true motives instead of entertaining us with that little story.' I let myself feel some of the consternation on Holms' behalf that I had reined in when talking to May.

'Well, my friend, not all of what May said was a lie.' Holms reached down and re-fastened his right bicycle clip. 'Sascha Schneider was indeed arrested yesterday morning. There was a police report in the *National-Zeitung*, which you would have seen if you picked up the afternoon editions every once in a while.' He righted himself. 'Clearly, Karl May wants us to investigate the case of the arrested artist but he cannot say outright what crime there is to investigate. It's all quite plain but for one last piece of evidence.' He stepped beside the bicycle as if to mount it. 'I shall make a little detour. We'll meet up again at Hausvogtei-Platz. Twenty minutes, in front of Liebig, shall we?'

'You – you're not walking to Liebig with me?' I was too baffled to say anything else.

'No,' Holmes swung onto the saddle, 'of course not. Why would I have brought the bicycle if I meant to walk with you?'

I had wondered the very thing myself. 'But where are you going?'

The slow smile appeared again on Holms' face. 'I will let you know should my detour prove to be a success.'

'But—'

'Twenty minutes, Hans. It's a beautiful day for a stroll through Mitte.' He gripped the handlebars and was about to set off.

But one of the many questions I had could not wait. I held onto Holms' leather saddle and the bicycle came to a grinding stop.

'How,' I asked, 'when you knew Schneider had been arrested...' Holms turned, exasperation clear on his narrow face. 'How did you know that May's story of the fur coat was a lie?'

'Isn't it obvious?' The twinkle in his grey eyes must have been the sunlight reflecting from the river. 'Nobody in their right mind would order a fur coat in summer.'

I reached Hausvogtei-Platz in a foul mood. Not only had Holms deserted me for whatever he was investigating, I also had to deal with the unsavoury presswoman who no longer saw it necessary to conceal herself, now that Holms was gone. She had been as shocked as I was by Holms' departure, and had unsuccessfully tried to follow him. Of course, an average person on foot was no match for a cyclist, and after a few metres the woman abandoned her chase and instead glued herself to – me.

She accompanied me along the Dom and Unter den Linden and followed me past the Royal Opera, Hedwig's Cathedral and the Imperial Bank – a persistent ten metres distance between us.

Now we both stood before Liebig Men's Fashions. The store occupied the ground floor of an elegant building, constructed from the yellow-beige sandstone used so much in the architecture of Berlin. The tall windows sparkled in the sun; through the glass I could make out the movements of several customers inside the store. Holms was nowhere to be seen.

'Where has he gone?' The presswoman had the audacity to stand beside me as if we had somehow made acquaintance whilst ambling through the city.

'I'm buggered if I know,' I muttered before I remembered that I was in the presence of a lady.

When I turned to apologise, the lady in question winked at me. A horse-bus passed us by; a bicycle bell rang out over the clip-clop of the horses. A moment later, Holms screeched to a halt before us.

'Well? Has your excursion been a success?' I inquired.

'Quite so, my friend.' He jumped off the bicycle and leaned it against the side of Liebig's shop. 'And I see you brought along our shadow. You are *not* Elise Hirschmann, are you?' he asked the presswoman, giving her a once-over and taking in the short hair and the leather coat.

'Sir.' She looked Holms frankly in the eye. 'I am covering sports. Hirschmann is doing crime. My name is Amelia Rother. Herr Holms, would you grant me a short interview about your participation in the upcoming long-distance–'

'You will do,' Holms interrupted. 'Come with us. My colleague and I require your assistance.'

He walked towards the glass doors of the shop where Liebig had immortalised his name in golden lettering. 'And, Fräulein Rother, if someone asks, you *are* Elise Hirschmann. Now let's see what Herr Liebig has to say.'

Entering the shop was like stepping from a busy kitchen into a cool garden. Karl May's descriptions had done justice to the beautiful interior but he had not mentioned the scents filling the salon – the natural odours of pelts and cloth mixed with the lavender notes of ironing water and a subtle expensive cologne. The owner of the shop stood behind the wooden counter. Clean-shaven, grey hair well-trimmed, he cut an impressive presence in his bespoke suit.

We stepped inside as two gentlemen were leaving. In the short confusion of opening doors and the shopbell's jingle I recognised them as members of the Kuckuck-Klub, which Holms and I occasionally frequented.

I gave them a friendly nod and was about to pass by, but to my astonishment, Holms made quite a production out of greeting the gentlemen, addressing them by title and name. There is no need to reveal them to the reader now, as all of this lies well in the past. But anyone who lived through that decade will easily guess at their identities. Holms was not prone to flaunting his connections to members of the Royal Court, thus I assumed it was all part of the ploy he had planned out for the interview with Liebig. To what purpose, I could not venture even a guess. The presswoman, Amelia Rother, stood equally confounded at my side.

After a bit of uncharacteristic small-talk, Holms finally approached Heinrich Liebig, who had occupied himself with a set of colourful swatches.

'Herr Holms,' he said, 'it is a pleasure to welcome you to my shop.' He rounded the counter to greet his new customers.

Without a coat nor his customary Tyrolean hat, the hair wind-swept and the shirt mired in the dust and sweat of a bicycle ride, Sherlock Holms looked nothing like his usual self. And yet, his lean figure and sharp features had become so well-known to Berliners that even a businessman such as Liebig recognised him by sight.

'It would no doubt be a pleasure,' Holms replied, 'if my friend and I had come to order a pair of your excellent suits. But I'm afraid it is a crime that brings us here.'

Liebig's expression turned slightly colder. 'I hope this is not in regards to yesterday's perturbance. I told the gentlemen from the police all that there is to know.'

'I'm afraid it is about the arrest that took place in your shop. But I am not interested in Herr Schneider and whatever dispute you have with him–'

'Hardly a dispute,' Liebig interjected. 'This is a respectable shop, and Herr Schneider – whom I never met before, or even heard of – came in here under the pretence of buying a suit, only to throw the vilest accusations at me.'

'As I said,' Holms interrupted Liebig calmly, 'Herr Schneider's conduct is of no interest to me. But would you be so kind to tell me whether you know this man.' With a gesture rather like a magician, he reached below his shirt and brought out something colourful, flat and square.

Amelia Rother, who had stood near a rack of summer suits, stepped closer, no doubt looking for an angle of how to exploit the lucky circumstance of having become a witness to this peculiar scene.

I was hard-pressed to conceal my own astonishment. The thing Holms held in his hand was a book: in fact, the very book with which I had planned to spend my morning. For some unfathomable reason, he had brought my copy of *Winnetou*.

'May I draw your attention to the central figure in the cover art.' Holms presented the volume to Liebig. 'The artist used a life model, and this model is the man I am concerned with. I am told the painting is of an adequate likeness.'

Liebig studied the cover for hardly two seconds, then returned it to Holms. 'I know this man.'

I took the book from my companion and finally had the opportunity to take a good look at it.

Its monochrome bluish colour lent itself to the sombre motif, a depiction of Cain and Abel, with one brother standing upright over the other, fallen one. The central figure had a stone in the raised right hand, while holding with his left the wrist of the fallen man in an iron grip. The scene was frozen in a moment of decision – the one ready to deliver the lethal blow, the other pleading for mercy.

I shall leave to the reader any assessment of the image's artistic quality, and whether it was a suitable cover for an adventure book. But there can be no doubt that the image was striking, not so much because of its theme and craft but because of the contradictory emotions it evokes even today, as I sit in my quiet study on Hiddensee and look at it.

It was a study in muscle and flesh. Both figures were nudes. The fallen one lay with his backside to the viewer; the one standing over him had the full length of his body on display. The figures' muscled arms ran like an axis through the image; paralleled by their interlocking gaze. I described the scene as a moment of decision but it was also a moment of sensual supplication. The graceful curve of the fallen one's cheek, his feminine lips, even the odd placement of the vulnerable soft underside of his foot – they all added to the sense that these two men were not so much bound together by battle but by a higher, brighter sentiment.

I looked over to Holms and he gave me a sly smile. He was playing the game again, and this time Heinrich Liebig was the mouse.

'Yes, I know this man,' Liebig repeated, 'although I would never have expected his likeness on the cover of such a prestigious book. He works as a foreman in one of the sewing rooms I do business with.'

'He was working, you mean.'

Liebig raised a suspicious eyebrow. 'I do believe he was let go, yes.'

'One can see,' I interjected, waving the book in my hand, 'why Sascha Schneider chose him as a model. Strapping lad, isn't he? Perhaps he is better suited to artistic work than the misery of the Zwischenmeisterei?'

At the mention of Schneider's name, Liebig took a surprised step back towards the counter. 'Misery is a very strong word,' he mumbled. 'The sewing rooms have passed every inspection that–'

'Sascha Schneider? The Sascha Schneider who founded the Art Gymnasium?' Amelia Rother interrupted, assisting Holms' ploy without any realisation on her part.

'The very same. But Schneider is better known for his artistic work.' Holms pointed at the book, winking at me.

I turned towards Liebig. 'I am surprised you have not heard of him. The two gentlemen who just left – they are customers in your shop, aren't they?'

Liebig nodded wordlessly. He kept glancing backwards to an unmarked door behind the counter, as if he wished to summon help but did not dare to call for it.

'They are good friends of Sascha's, I believe.' Holms was relentless now. 'Didn't we meet all three of them just the other day at the Club, Hans?'

'We certainly did.'

In reality, we had never met Sascha Schneider. I had heard of him for the first time today. But as reluctant as I usually was to tell a lie, I did so without any qualms. For I thought I understood now what had happened.

A young foreman had unfairly lost his job because he had brought the dismal conditions in the Zwischenmeisterei to a physician's attendance. Normally, this would have been the end of it. But the foreman was Schneider's model, and, I suspected, his lover. And Schneider would not simply accept the injustice done to his friend. Thinking himself safe, he sought out the person responsible for the firing: he confronted Liebig in his shop.

But the artist was not safe. Not when public sentiment was set against a whole class of men whose love, as Oscar Wilde had said, dare not speak its name but still exists – in all ranks of society, from the lowly sweatshop to the royal palace, and also in the humble quarters of two gentlemen living at Sophien-Strasse.

The artist certainly was not safe from men like Liebig, who will always use public sentiment to advance their own interests. Thus when Schneider threatened to expose the horrible working conditions in Liebig's sewing rooms, Liebig retaliated by revealing Schneider's amorous relations with the foreman to the police. The artist had been arrested not for theft but on a sodomy charge.

I felt Holms' hand on my arm.

'I think we're almost done here, Hans,' he said softly. 'Are you ready to go home?'

Liebig and Rother stared at him in disbelief.

'But what about the model? What about the foreman?' The presswoman voiced the very questions that Liebig clearly wanted to ask.

'About the fired foreman. Herr Liebig, I suggest you talk to Madame Pawlik. I've been assured she is happy to take him back.'

Liebig nodded slowly.

'As for the other business–'

'An unfortunate misunderstanding,' Liebig interjected at once. His voice trembled, and I may have pitied him, had his quick change of mind not been owed solely to the fear of losing business with the Royal Court. 'I shall tell the police so at once and ensure Herr Schneider is released, with no slur upon his character.'

'Excellent. Do give my regards to Kommissar Lestrade when you talk to him.'

'And...' Liebig inclined his head towards the wide-eyed Rother, 'the press?'

'The press will come with us. A good day, Herr Liebig.' Holms made for the tall doors, and we followed him outside, accompanied by the jingle of the bell.

'This was interesting,' Rother said as we stood again on the street before Liebig Men's Fashion. 'I am sure there is a newsworthy story hidden somewhere in it.'

Holms fetched his bicycle from the wall. 'Not your department, Fräulein Rother. What happened in there is the stuff of gossip columns. But,' he mounted the machine, 'I may grant you your interview, once I return from the Austrian-German long-distance race.'

AUTHOR'S NOTE

It is always 1893 in the golden world of Sherlock Holms and Dr Hans Watson. This story takes place in an alternative Wilhelminian Berlin; it references historical figures and events but does not adhere strictly to historical dates and facts.

It is true that Karl May stole an expensive pelt and went to prison for it. His *Winnetou* series was published in 1893, with cover art by gay artist Sascha Schneider. Imperial Berlin saw several sex scandals, a major one happened in January of 1891.

In the 1890s, Hausvogtei-Platz was the centre of a thriving fashion industry. The Austrian-German long-distance bicycle race took place in June of 1893. The fictional Kuckuck-Klub takes its name from the novel (and later adaptation into a silent movie) *Prinz Kuckuck*, by Otto Julius Bierbaum, with a central gay character. Elise Hirschmann (later Gabriele Tergit) was a well-known court reporter and author in Weimar Berlin.

.

MISTRESS ISLET

AND THE

GENERAL'S SON

Lucy Sussex

Ay me, vile wretch, that ever I was borne,
Making my selfe unto the world a scorne:
And to my friends and kindred all a shame,
Blotting their blood by my unhappy name.

'The Ballad of Arden of Feversham' 1663

Two great men of the court rode side by side through the English countryside, their talk of this evening's entertainment. After a day's Assizes, dinner, then gaming by the fireside, their periwigs doffed, their glasses filled with the finest Rhenish.

'I have a servant,' said Lord Baynard, 'who can find most anything. Even if obscured or stolen.'

The Lord Chief Justice said: 'So do I.'

'A thief-taker?'

'More than that. A murder-taker.'

Mutual smiles, as they saw another opportunity for a game, a wager.

Baynard's clever servant had business in the market, herbs for his basket haggled from the countrywomen, but he took the opportunity to watch the Assizes procession, the cavalcade of justice riding down the street. Back in his old land, there would be drums, furs from fierce creatures and ceremonial dancing. He thought it a poor show in comparison, even his master in his brocade and beaver hat. Their gazes met, over the head of a horse, and with a quick sideways jerk of the head, the order was conveyed: attend me!

He dutifully followed, edging sideways through the onlookers. One by one the riders passed him, until he saw at the end of the train a woman, riding pillion. She was plainly dressed but in good black cloth, the widow's veil drawn over her face. He had lived long enough among these strangers to know the proprieties, even with Carolian license – King Charles and his courtiers all libertines, as he had heard the Chaplain complain. Surely a judge would not take his mistress on circuit with him?

Anne could live without the saddle-soreness, or being at the Chief Justice's beck and call. She was in his debt, she knew that; she also needed the coins he slipped her as his retainer. But must he so arbitrarily summon her to be baggage in his business? To sit, her head uncovered in the draughty Assize courts, and listen to the interminable cases? To be dispatched, discreetly, to question a maidservant about her mistress's peccadilloes, which might conceal something much worse, like a priest-hole?

She walked up and down outside the inn to ease her stiff back, sidestepping puddles from last night's rain and thinking all the while.

I need not fear the worst, for has this Chief Justice not the reputation of being the only faithful husband at court? It may be habit, or obeying the law, or even that rare thing among the mighty, uxorious love. He speaks of "his little house" at Teddington with affection, and I know it comes with a much younger wife.

But did he not say he needs someone who knows about women? Few men, in her experience, did. I amuse him, that is part of it, like a dog walking on its hind legs. He sees a use for me and so far that is not greatly disagreeable. But he is a great man, and their business is bloody, depend on it.

At least her employ had the great benefit of annoying Edwards, his

Lordship's pompous clerk. Who, summoned in thought as if he were the devil, came to the door, beckoning her.

'Mistress Kidderminster, you are wanted in the private parlour.' With the general air of: curse you!

She bobbed in response, saving the deep, the respectful curtsey for his Worship, and his companion, one of the county gentry who tagged along to the Assizes, meeting the Justices at the county border and riding with them to town. More than just gentry, she concluded as she rose, assessing his jewellery. He for his part eyed her boldly from toe-tip upwards: figure, face, virtue?

His Worship spoke, in his soft Northern burr: 'This is Mistress Anne Kidderminster, who is in my employ' – even if what she did for his Worship had never been stated openly. 'My Lord Baynard.'

Milord looked unsure whether to kiss her hand or chuck her under the chin. 'So, you are the thief-takeress?'

'No,' she said. 'Unless you mean the thieves who stole my dear husband's life, whom I pursued, interviewed and prosecuted in court.'

A slight cough from the Justice.

'With the assistance of His Worship and God's Providence, of course.'

'Well, Mistress, perhaps you can thief-take for me, something not so dramatic, but important nonetheless.'

Anne was becoming aware of a fourth in the room, standing by the arras and so shadowed as to be almost invisible, although there was a faint gleam of what looked like a hoop of earring, reflecting the firelight. Invisibility to her meant a servant, though a favoured one, to wear jewels.

She listened to Milord Baynard, her mind taking notes. No jewels lost, but a trunk, containing important papers, to be sent on a ship sailing imminently. It had been despatched via Milord's coach but on the road had disappeared – not falling off, as it was secured, but actively thieved. The loss was discovered only at the port, on the wharfside.

Milord finished, with Anne the centre of his gaze.

'How far is this port?' she asked.

'Seven miles.'

A horse-ride away, and she winced inwardly at more time in the saddle.

'And what has been done already in this search?'

A nod between the two seated Lords.

'The harbour master caused the trunk to be cried for, in the port, the country lanes and outlying hamlets.'

In her mind she heard the bell, the 'Oyez, oyez!' Everyone nearby would know the news.

'Where is the coachman now?' she said.

'When he returned to my house, on the outskirts of this town, with his story, my steward sent a rider to inform me. I sent back instructions to have the man held close, under suspicion.'

'I must talk with him.'

'Capital,' said his lordship, slapping his silken knees. 'Ham!'

Had he lost his mind, or was he merely hungry? she wondered. Then the figure in the shadow stepped into full view. She saw the livery, with matching gloves and hat – and all between that and the linen collar a shadow embodied, the only radiance from the man's gold earring, the only white his eyes. He was a black man, not like the King was described, with his ebony eyes and hair from his Italian ancestry, but here skin as well: an African.

'Milord's servant Ham will accompany you on your thief-taking, Mistress Kidderminster,' said His Worship. 'I am informed he has many skills.'

After the pair had left the room, the two wagerers shook hands.

'Should we have sent them off separately?' wondered Baynard.

'Perhaps. But two heads – two remarkable heads, if I believe you – are better than one, surely.'

'We need witnesses to observe the winner, impartially.'

'Agreed.' He regretted, briefly, that Edwards could not play gooseberry, just to see his face. But with the Assizes hard upon, the man could not be spared. 'When I send Mrs Kidderminster upon my errands, I assign her a groom, for protection. Francis Ormin has few words but much honesty.'

'May I suggest Mr Platt, my chaplain? For Lent he is observing the ninth commandment, rigorously – "he shalt not bear false witness", even if it makes him tactless to the point of discourtesy.'

And I will bet that you bet him to do that, thought His Worship.

They started out immediately, only delayed by a maidservant calling to Ham: he had forgotten his basket! While they waited, Ormin joined them, carrying a letter red with the Baynard seal. The basket was big, with a spray of fresh herbs trailing from the wicker lid. It jarred with the smart livery, like a fine lady clutching a manglewurzle. Ham was his master's cook? She had seen French cooks, but never an African.

A little down the main road, with Ormin discreetly following several paces behind, as usual, she asked:

'Do your skills include herb-lore?'

His answer was in perfect King's English, but with a faint tinge of accent. 'My previous master, Sir Nehemiah Gibbs, had great interest in plants and their uses. He chose me as his assistant, to collect, grind his pastes and powders, distil and assist in dispensing cures. I, proving an apt pupil, continue the practice with Milord my new master.'

'I have heard of Sir Nehemiah,' she replied. Former Governor in the West Indies, famously unlucky at cards. Botany would be no use in Debtors' prison. 'Forgive me for asking–'

'You ask me for forgiveness!' He stared at her, mouth open to reveal the hidden pink of tongue and lips, the startling white teeth.

'Good manners are not just for gentlefolk,' she replied. 'I merely wanted to enquire how herb-skills would assist us here.'

'Not that I can foresee.'

Except that it shows you have intelligence, she thought.

'You see me forget once,' he said. 'Milord does it frequently, anything from his gloves to a servant-lass. I observing him closely–'

'As a good servant does,' she finished. As a matter of survival.

'–have gained some small renown in retrieving them. Surpassing his bird-dog, he says.'

With those words, he closed his mouth, the moment of sympathy lost. They walked towards Lord Baynard's house, the footsteps of Ormin behind them the only sound.

Ham did not know what to make of Mistress Kidderminster. Not a doxy, not a lady, but more than just a servant to a powerful and fearful man. As emissary of the Chief Justice, she could assume command, which she did immediately upon entering Milord's fine new gates.

'Where is the coachman?' she asked the gatekeeper.

Simultaneously Ormin enquired: 'Where is the Chaplain?'

'Why together, both of 'em!' was the astounded answer. 'In t'stables.'

They found the unfortunate coachman sitting on a haybale in an empty stall, his feet chained. Facing him was a tall, raw-boned man, in exhortation as if sermonising from the pulpit.

'Thou shalt not steal, nor shalt thou bear false witness…'

'I done neither,' was the reply, in broad Bow Bells.

Ham could see the coachman was frightened, with reason: there were bruises on his face and dribbles of blood down the linen of his shirt. Not Chaplain Platt, obviously, but others in Milord's service were ready with their fists.

With a bow, Ormin presented his letter; the chaplain breaking the seal and reading. Anne stepped inside the stall, aware of long, hairy horseheads eyeing her over the partitions. She let the nearest nuzzle her hand. No sugar there, but that the horse did not baulk surely meant something to the coachman.

'The Afreak to see me, with a Petticoat?' the man enquired.

'Mistress Kidderminster, if you please,' said the Chaplain. He looked up from the letter, eyebrows raised. 'Milord writes that Mrs Kidderminster is lady thief-taker to the Chief Justice.' To Anne: 'He writes also that I am to attend you.' His face said: I cannot imagine why.

Ham for his part crouched in the hay with his basket, eyeing the coachman.

'I see that attempts have been made to persuade you,' Anne said. 'I will have none of that.'

Persuasion need not always be violent, thought Ham.

'I merely enquire what happened on your journey.'

The coachman spoke haltingly, her questions like a needle, pricking him here, drawing out a thread there. His journey began before dawn at Nonpariel – his Lordship's manor-house, some miles away. The coach departed with the chest lashed to the back, and several of the household in transit within, including Milord's mastiff, who howled most of the way. The passengers disembarked, then he drove to the port just as the sun was rising, with goods for trade added to the load; also for the ship, some cases of wine; for the Captain and Milord's friends in port–

Anne lifted one hand. 'Any passengers this time?'

'Not that I saw…' and his nose started to bleed.

A creak as Ham opened his basket. 'Have some fresh yarrow leaf, to staunch the blood.'

The questioning continued, foliage protruding from the coachman's nostril as if he were the Green Man. He did not halt in his journey once, oh maybe he did, to relieve himself by that withered oak. But only a moment, surely not long enough for mischief.

'Then,' said Anne, 'to the withered oak we go!'

Of horses, Milord had plenty, and a pillion saddle for Anne. Chaplain Platt had his own horse, a nut-brown cob; next the stablehands led out a rangy skewbald, with the pillion strapped to a tall bay mare, at the coachman's recommendation: 'Petticoats 'ave nothing to fear from 'er.'

Ormin moved to take the mare's rein, but Ham interposed:

'Mistress Kidderminster will ride with me.' He crouched, forming a step with his hands for her to reach the saddle.

As the party trotted out the gates, Ham murmured, over his shoulder: 'So we can talk.'

'As I thought!'

To ride behind an African was new. Anne saw, close up, that his hair resembled wool – but that apart, he was still a man, still God's creature.

'What did you make of Milord's coachman?' he asked.

'I think he told the truth, he did not steal. Nor, possibly, bear false witness.'

'And yet…'

'It was what he said, just before his nose bled.'

'Or what made it bleed.'

'Not a lie: he saw no one. But I think he knew something.' Anne could be certain of it.

'I saw the coach arrive,' Ham said unexpectedly. 'I was up early, to gather buds with the dew still on them, as stipulated in Sir Nehemiah's receipt for strengthening the heart. The passengers were Milord's keeper of hounds, the under-keeper, several dogs and another servant from Nonpariel, called Gideon. His duties include singing to Milord, and he treated us to a new broadside ballad, "Ay me, vile wretch". Some might find that apt. Dismissal hangs by a thread over Gideon.'

'A rogue?'

'Lacking proof I cannot say. But he was suspected of stealing a knife, one which I was quite unable to retrieve.'

'Where is this Gideon now?'

'Nobody seems to know. He had a sick mother to visit, he said.'

'You doubt it.'

'Some say Gideon is both liar and orphaned.'

'Might he have hidden in the coach, with the load, maybe?'

Ham answered only with a shrug of his liveried shoulders. The road was mostly quiet, with a few workers visible, leading plough horses or chivvying geese to their pond. They passed a farm-wife on a donkey, her skirt tucked up against the mud, the only traffic heading in their direction. The nearer they got to the coastline, the more the fields were flat and featureless.

'Oh, where is this oak?' Anne cried.

The Chaplain, riding alongside, replied: 'It is the only one for miles. A local landmark.'

Sure enough, ahead of them a white trunk jutted beside the road. The party halted just short of it, with Ham dismounting. He waited for Anne to follow, but instead she remained on the mare, from its vantage point scanning the scene. The only other object of height was a church spire at the nearest hamlet, a brisk walk away.

'This place is like the isle of Ely, where I once lived,' she said. 'So flat and free of woodland that when my master's little monkey escaped, I felt sure that it would ascend the only tree worth climbing in the neighbourhood. And I was right.'

An odd little smile from Ham, as if recalling African monkeys. The Chaplain cleared his throat: 'We are here, for what purpose?'

Anne took Ham's hand and slid from the horse.

'To see if it was here a crime was committed.'

Behind them came a donkey's bray, which the mare answered with a whinny. The farm-wife had caught up with them, only to suddenly lash the donkey into its top speed, bouncing and jolting as she passed. They ducked from the mud-spray, only to see at a safe distance the beast return to ambling.

'What was that for?' said Anne, but they were all dumbfounded. The woman did not look guilty, nor as if she avoided a plague-house, nor a haunted spot. But there was something...

Ham pointed with his rein-free hand. 'Those look like the ruts of a carriage's wheels, sunk into the grassy verge.'

They followed, Ormin dismounting too and leading the skewbald. The chaplain, disdaining their lowly business, stayed horsed.

'Tell me,' Anne said to Ham, 'how was this Gideon clad?'

'In livery like me.'

144

'Even to the shoes?'

'We servants share a shoemaker…' Then he saw what she did, an impression just short of the grassy verge, the twin of his own footprints, though a size smaller. Beside it were the marks of bare feet, large.

'Both are deep,' said Anne. 'Carrying a load.'

'The trunk was both large and heavy,' said the Chaplain, loftily.

'Ormin,' Anne said, 'go a ways ahead to see if you can find the marks of some other vehicle. I will hold your horse. Try not to disturb the road's witness, if you can.'

They watched the man's careful steps, his examination of the road-mud. At the point where the donkey slackened its speed, he shook his head.

Anne closed her eyes, thinking. The day had already been long and she had not eaten much beyond some cheese and bread at the inn. Her ears buzzed, a sure sign of exhaustion.

'Ham,' she said, 'you know this Gideon. Was he from this area?'

Ham deferred to the Chaplain, who replied: 'Born and bred.'

As she thought. 'And was he the sort to have a hold over the coachman?'

This time Ham answered. 'He got what he wanted, by hook or crook.'

'Let us say he was secreted in the load, and with idle time, considered the goods around him, calculating their value. Then he saw someone he knew on the road, a beggar or rascal, and an idea came to him.'

'A crime of…opportunity?' Ham breathed.

'Or else pre-arranged.'

'Villain!' That was the Chaplain.

'Or villains. Either way, he called for the coachman to let him off, and down he climbed, as he did cutting through the ties on the trunk.'

'And the man met on the roads, now accomplice, took aholt with him of the trunk. The coachman drove away, none the wiser.'

'Or maybe not.'

The buzz was even louder. She opened her eyes to see the skewbald's ears flattened. She patted the particoloured neck, trying to calm the horse.

'But what did they do with the trunk?' she said. 'It was heavy and they had neither cart nor horse.'

Then she saw on the skewbald's pink nose something moving: small, striped yellow and black. The buzz reached a crescendo, all around them were flying forms, as she cried:

'Wasps! And their nest!'

An equine scream, as the skewbald felt the sting and reared, dragging the rein out of Anne's hands. Ham likewise could not stop the mare from following the skewbald in a wild flight back down the road. A cloud of wasps pursued, straight towards the chaplain, who broke the fourth commandment, taking His holy name in vain as he whipped his horse into a furious gallop. Ham and Anne fled the wasps as best they could on foot, until she fell into a roadside ditch concealed by bramble and grass, to land in cold, brackish water, Ham falling after. It was deep enough for them to submerge themselves against the wasps, gasping through sedge when they could hold their breath no longer.

Only when the buzzing had receded did they sit up, tatterdemalion from the thorns, scratched and muddy from head to foot. Anne spat into her hand, to clear the mud from her eyes. Then she looked around and gave Ham a hard pinch to the arm.

'Do you see what I see, or do I dream?'

Within reach of her outstretched hand, hidden by a layer of uprooted grass and sedge, was a square, solid, wooden form: the missing trunk, its padlock secure.

They emerged from the ditch with Ormin's helping hands, though the man shook with silent laughter. It became vocal when down the road came a sorry sight: the chaplain, thrown from his nag, with a bump on his head, face swollen from stings and his coat torn. They formed a foot regiment of four now, their horses fled as far as they could go, to their home stable at best, and the trunk in the ditch. It took several tries for them to drag it out, rendering them all equally muddy.

'I suppose,' said Anne, 'that Gideon and his accomplice knew that they would be apprehended if they walked around with the trunk in plain sight. So they hid it, in a place nobody who knew the locality would think to look, given the reputation of the wasp-lair. Only when dark did they intend to return for it.'

'Which is not so far away,' said Ham.

'We should secure this trunk,' she replied.

Their only possible direction was towards the church spire, so taking a trunk corner each, even the Chaplain, they waddled their way down the road. The work was hard, slow and thirsty too – and as they reached the hamlet, all were glad to see an alehouse in view, with a donkey tied up outside. Trunk and all, they entered, to find a roomful of patrons, gaping at their advent.

The nearest was a man with a large handbell at his feet. He reached down and rang it deafeningly.

'Oyez, oyez, and if that isn't the trunk I was paid to cry for, with its thieves as well!'

'And one black as sin, too!' said a big man, coming forward. 'I be Parish Constable here. Who be ye, with this fine trunk, not your property?'

Willing hands all around seized them, and they let down the trunk onto the rush floor.

'Unhand me! I am Chaplain to Lord Baynard!' cried Platt.

'And I am the Queen of Sheba!' replied the farm-wife.

Anne forbore to mention she was Thief-takeress to the Chief Justice.

Small though the village was, it boasted a watch-house with two cells. One was occupied already by a man in torn livery, who had been in a fight, from the look of his black eye.

'Gideon?' asked Ham.

A sickly but unpenitent smile. The bruised mouth opened and a fine tenor voice sang: 'Ay me, vile wretch!'

'I see you know the villain already,' said the Parish Constable. 'Caught stealing a hand-cart, he was, but his accomplice ran away.'

Ham, Ormin and the Chaplain were forced into the cell with Gideon, though it left them little space. The proprieties were observed with Anne imprisoned in the other cell. For his part, the Parish Constable ordered the trunk into the lockup; also a battered fowling piece. He sat himself firmly on top of the trunk, ready to pepper them with shot at any wrong move.

It took time, of course, for a messenger to be sent back to Lord Baynard, who was busy at the Assizes. It took more time for a response; and not until sunset, with Anne dozing as best she could in the cell, did she hear the sound of a carriage nearing. The door to the gaol-house opened, with the Parish Constable utterly amazed at the sight of not only Milord, but also Sir Orlando Bridgman, Chief Justice to the Court of Common Pleas. The two great men beheld the scene, then doubled over in fits of laughter.

'Your Worship,' said Anne, managing a curtsey behind the bars. 'Here be your trunk!'

Baynard managed to stop laughing long enough to ask: 'And which one of you was most responsible for this happy retrieval?'

'Why,' said Chaplain Platt, 'it was a joint effort.'

Ormin for his part nodded emphatically.

'Our bet is null and void!' declared the Chief Justice.

In the hustle and bustle following, as the quartet received, by order of their Lordships, a good meal from the kitchens of the local inn and the chance to wash the mud off hands and faces, Anne and Ham had no time to talk. The only opportunity came during the journey home, with Ham electing to ride beside the coachman, a new face to Anne. She wanted to get the smell of the gaol-house out of her nose; and she did not care to ride inside with His Worship. So, though it was a tight squeeze, and the night cool, she shared the coachman's perch. Behind them, the trunk was securely chained to the coach, with several armed men from the Assizes retinue riding after, just in case a highwayman was fool enough to try and rob the Chief Justice. Ham too was issued with a gun.

'Wilf our undercoachman is deaf,' Ham murmured to Anne. 'So we can talk without fear.'

A rare privilege around his Worship, she thought.

'I can tell that you are enraged,' he commented, as they left the village. 'It positively radiates from you.'

'I have never been the object of a bet before!'

'Mistress Kidderminster, I have and worse – that was how I transferred to Milord Baynard. But better that than to be onsold to pay Sir Nehemiah's debts.'

'That would be a hard fate,' she said. 'But a woman too, even a great Lady, can be sold into bondage, though they call it marriage.'

'Chaplain Platt ascribes my fate to my skin.'

'As mine is to my sex. The curse of grandmother Eve.'

A long pause.

'Chaplain says I am accursed because of my grandfather Ham's misdeeds. Hence my name, which in full is Hamson. I do not care for it at all. Though I am a slave, I know that my father had not that name, and that I had another name back in Africa.'

'My name was Holmes before my marriage,' she said. 'It means islet, I am told.'

He thought it apt, for someone so self-contained.

'What was your first name?' she asked, avoiding voicing the despised "Ham".

'I was son of, that was part of it. The other is something I cannot utter, because my people do not name the dead, less they answer by rising from their graves. But I can tell you that my father was named for his title: general in an African king's army. For losing a battle, he was most cruelly murdered, with his wives and children sold as slaves. Thus I crossed the seas to Jamaica, losing my mother and my siblings along the way, from disease. There I caught Sir Nehemiah's eye, and he bought me and brought me to this England.'

'I lost my husband to cruel murder,' she said.

They sat for a while in silence, their bodies touching, welcome warmth in the night's chill. Ahead of them were tossing manes, beyond that the lonely road, with the moon rising above it like a wheel of cheese.

'I must call you something more agreeable,' she said. 'I suspect, now that the Chief Justice knows of your herb-lore' – and she had overheard Lord Baynard loudly extolling it – 'then he may seek your employ, since he is a sickly man. I foresee a game of cards in which he cheats. It is, as far as I know, his only sin.'

Apart from committing murder by proxy every time His Worship donned the black hat.

'Thus you would join our household, and I would see you often. It is not my wish to name you hurtfully.'

'What would you call me, Mistress Kidderminster?'

'I am unlearned, though I read and write. When we are disembarked, I will enquire of those university men who ride below us.'

They were most weary by the time the coach pulled up at the inn. The Lords beneath, exhausted by a day's long Assizes, stumbled sleepily into the courtyard. Ham helped Anne down, to see her accost the Chaplain in conversation. Platt was alert still, Ham would guess from the pain of the wasp stings. Though he liked neither the man nor his work, he should provide a remedy. Cider vinegar, if he recalled aright.

She returned, beaming despite fatigue. 'The things I know and do know not! Anne is from the Hebrew, meaning Grace. 'And what is the Hebrew for General?' I asked the Chaplain, but he said without a dictionary he could not tell me from memory. But he did say that in English, the name Walter has the same meaning, from the German words for the ruler of an army.'

'And so you were originally Mistress Gracious Islet?' he says, amused.

'And you are the son of Walter. However, Walterson is awkward in the mouth. Does Wat's son, Watson, suffice?'

'It will do!'

They clasped hands for a moment, in agreement and to mark the beginnings of a cautious friendship.

AUTHOR'S NOTES

Anne Kidderminster existed, and I have written a novel based on fact about her, Miss Holmes. Chief Justice Sir Orlando Bridgman supported her investigation of her husband Thomas Kidderminster's murder. His later use of her skills is purely imaginary on the part of the author.

A
Scandalous
Case
of
Poisoning

Katya de Becerra

SPOTLIGHT ON SOLACE SPRING

Moscow Herald

Arts and Culture, April 16, 2051

A long-awaited new exhibition dedicated to Russia's greatest private investigator, Marina Holmesova, has opened yesterday to much fanfare at the Museum of Russian Legal History. Curated by Holmesova's wife, long-time investigative partner and biographer, Antonina Vatska, *The Scandalous Case of Solace Spring Poisoning* takes visitors back in time to the "Dashing 90s" of the post-Soviet Russia, and into the very heart of Holmesova's first known criminal investigation.

With Holmesova's legendary avoidance of spotlight, Vatska's historical journal entries and interviews make up the majority of the exhibition. However, it is the collection's jewel – the never-before-exhibited list of suspects and clues Holmesova compiled while working the case – that will surely wow not just her long-time fans but also all the history buffs interested in the modern revival of Russia's tradition of private investigative work.

"The Scandalous Case of Solace Spring Poisoning" exhibition runs until 15 December.

IMPRESSIONS FROM THE EXHIBITION

The following excerpts from Antonina Vatska's private journal take us back to the spring of '95 when she and Marina Holmesova were sharing an apartment in Moscow's Presnevsky district (now the popular Holmesova Museum). The two young women had left their respective home towns in the Russian provinces to pursue higher education in Moscow.

Vatska's insightful observations of Holmesova as well as of their modest student life reveal the circumstances of them joining the cast of Solace Spring, an autobiographical tale inspired by director Michael Rottner's own life. A studio cut of Rottner's unfinished film was released posthumously in 1996.

Antonina Vatska's personal journal: Entry 1 (undated)

As Marina's family lore has it, her maternal grandmother, Nelly, was a secret royal (a Menshikova, no less!). Left behind in the chaos of the 1917 Bolshevik revolution as the family fled to France, Nelly was rescued from the streets by one of her former tutors.

Remaining Menshikova by blood only, Nelly legally took her adoptive mother's family name: Holmesova. The glorious flat near the Patriarch's Ponds where I find myself today was once a Menshikov property. Lost for decades to communal living, it was reclaimed by Nelly in the latter years of the Khrushchev Thaw.

In her will, to honour the woman who'd once saved her life and gave her a new home, Nelly bequeathed the apartment to Marina: the youngest member of her adopted family's offshoot which still carried the Holmesova name. Whether the crumbling estate was truly a gift or a curse remains to be seen. Once a grand baroque affair of gilt fixtures and velvet armchairs, today the apartment is in serious disrepair.

Well, at least, it did bring Marina and me together, uniting us at the fiery heart of Moscow's Presnevsky District, the literary haunt of the devil.

Last night, serendipity was my latest offering in the association game we've been playing to "keep our brains in shape" (Marina's words) ever since months ago we became flatmates.

'Fate,' Marina replied after a delay. Hunched over her pre-revolution relic of a desk, she was reading, pausing only to pencil notes in the margins of the pages. Candle flame painted her face golden, tracing her profile on the wall with a flickering shadow hand.

Electricity was out again. Shut down every night at eight, plunging the entire micro-district into darkness. Energy saving measures make for enchanting visions of studious girls and surely, with time, poor eyesight.

I ate my instant noodles while stealing glances at Marina. Her *History of Criminal Psychology in Russia* textbook was open wide and surrounded by black-and-white crime scene photographs.

I avoid looking at those directly. I've got no stomach for it, but Marina is clearly immune. We need the money, she reminds me whenever I wrinkle my nose at her macabre side job. And though I like her use of "we", I suspect the real reason she chooses to turn her analytical eye to these prints of mafia assassinations and robberies-gone-wrong is that she enjoys it. The process of drawing connections, I mean. Finding patterns amid the splatters of blood and viscera and god-knows-what-else. Making order out of chaos thrills her as much as being in her company thrills me. But I digress.

'Death,' I blurted out next.

Spontaneity is key. Players are supposed to say the first thing that comes to mind. When we finish, we'll compare the first word and the last, examining the chain of associations, a psycho-linguistic bridge, taking us from A to B. We're meant to be writing down our answers, but with my marvellous flatmate it's not necessary. She remembers all of it, going back to our game's very first word: Rain. I was the one to pick it, not very original since it was raining the day I became Marina's flatmate.

'Opportunity,' said Marina, fighting a yawn. She picked up the closest photo and zeroed in on its top right corner. I could almost hear her brain kicking into higher gear.

'Speaking of opportunities...' I said. 'What comes to mind when I say Michael Rottner?'

I'd been waiting for the right moment to share this, but she'd been mentally elusive all day. But, as Marina likes to remind me, we need money. Considering the growing assortment of leaks and cracks all over our trembling abode, we're one storm away from a disaster. Unless Marina wants to invite more renters into our peaceful co-existence, we need to raise funds, and soon.

She looked away from those horrid photographs, hawkish eyes on me. 'American,' she said promptly, like reading from a file. 'Film director. Dissident. Communist. Russian spy, allegedly.'

It was difficult to hide my disappointment that she knew about Rottner. After all, her idea of keeping her brain sharp entails expelling all the "unnecessary" details it accumulates regularly. Weather reports, dollar exchange rates, Valeri Polyakov setting a record for the longest duration spaceflight. Once, as a joke, I asked if she was aware the Earth was circling the sun. She retorted, straight-faced, that it only mattered if it concerned her job directly. I suspect she was telling the truth. The earth could be floating in the cosmic ocean atop sentient turtles, for all she cared, as long as it had nothing to do with her precious crime scene photos.

'Well, Rottner's making a new film,' I said, hoping at least she didn't know that. 'The production company's just put a call out for more extras. My cousin Sasha works for MoskvaFilm – that's how I know. Oh, and it pays okay.'

A fragment from a 2047 interview with Antonina Vatska

'I recall Marina asking me then what the movie was about, and I... I felt so proud I could share with her something she didn't already know. Now, I wonder if she was just indulging me [laughs softly]. Regardless, I was quick to oblige. I told her the movie was *Solace Spring*, and that its production had been plagued with all sort of issues, mostly due to Rottner being a very difficult man to work with.

'I mean, he had a lot of enemies. He was a celebrity of sorts. A famous American who defected to Soviet Russia for ideological reasons in the seventies – a big deal! But he'd been keeping a low profile ever since. Fast forward to 1995 and he was suddenly out of the shadows and making a new film, his first one since *Shadow State*.

Given Rottner's notoriety, I assumed *Solace Spring* was going to be another political thriller, but of course, it was completely different. It didn't matter to me though – all I cared about, aside from making some money, was embarking on this adventure with my beloved Marina. I think I was already falling for her then.'

Antonina Vatska's personal journal: Entry 3 (April 16, 1995)

I've been up all night, going through my notes, too afraid of forgetting key details, of not getting the sequence right. Marina teased me this morning, saying my journal will end up in some museum one day, given Rottner's fame and, as of yesterday, his death.

Maybe she's right. Either way, I see it as my job now to chronicle what happened. I'll start at the beginning.

Yesterday morning, after spending nearly two hours inside Moscow Metro's rattling trains, at long last we emerged from the regional electrichka station at Balashikha into the sobering chill of an early April morning. Rottner was filming *Solace Spring* here on the outskirts of this small capital-adjacent town.

An unmarked tourist bus was parked just outside the station, a youthful middle-aged woman (short bleached hair, deep-seated brown eyes) guarding its door. She was holding up a sign that announced ROTTNER in blocky black letters. I waved at her, but it came off half-heartedly, like I was swatting away a fly.

(Why can't I be collected like Marina? She always appears wise as a griffin, her poker-face making a stellar job of concealing those intricate processes taking place inside her skull.)

'Names,' the brown-eyed woman asked as we approached. She wore no makeup and didn't mince words. Once we supplied the information, she consulted a piece of paper and indicated we could board.

Among the last to arrive, we had to walk almost the entire length of the bus, scrutinised by twenty or so pairs of curious eyes, until we found two unoccupied seats together in the back.

'That's got to be Rita Ludwig, the production manager,' I said to Marina, referring to our stern greeter. I recognised the woman based on Sasha's description.

'She resents being here,' Marina replied, frowning.

'Why do you say so?' I asked.

'Just an observation.' She didn't elaborate, likely conscious of our non-existent privacy.

We'd been marinating inside the warming bus for about fifteen minutes when I heard raised voices coming from outside. Unable to see through the grimy windows, I left my seat to peek out at an angle. When I caught a glimpse of Rita's vocal adversary, I did a double take because this person a) looked familiar and b) was so beautiful she was almost unreal.

'Please, Rita,' the beautiful stranger blatantly tried to squeeze by the unrelenting Ludwig, eager to get on the bus for some reason. 'For old times' sake? I just need a word with him. This is the last time, I promise.'

With a resigned shrug, Rita let the other woman pass. Everyone fell completely silent as the stunning beauty, dark honey hair in a loose braid down her back, cerulean eyes pink-rimmed, walked to the very back, leaving a trail of lavender perfume and gossipy whispers behind her. It clicked, and I knew where I've seen her before, why she looked so familiar.

A fragment from a 2047 interview with Antonina Vatska

Interviewer: 'Can you describe that moment of recognition when you knew it was Irina Litvinovich, later one of the main suspects in Rottner's murder, who boarded the bus for the Balashikha set of Solace Spring?'

Vatska: 'The bus started moving and I remember whispering to Marina, "That's Irina Litvinovich!" I must've recited Litvinovich's entire movie history by the time I noticed Marina had earbuds in. She was probably listening to her psychology lecture recordings. It was her version of entertainment back then.

'Just when I thought I was to stew alone in the glow of my discovery, the guy in the seat in front turned around, eager for a gossip. He told me that Litvinovich was Rottner's ex-lover and that she'd been fired from the movie after they'd broken up. Rottner even cut all the scenes she was in, delaying the production some more, since they had to reshoot. Apparently, Litvinovich wasn't handling the breakup that well. She's been sneaking in, starting fights with Rottner, making scenes – that kind of stuff.

'The gossipy guy telling me all this was a seasoned extra. Misha was his name. At some point, he said to me, "Welcome to the ghost bus." When I asked why *ghost*, he just winked. "Oh, you'll see."

'That kind of set my skin on fire. Looking back, I think it was a premonition.'

When we got off the bus, Litvinovich didn't stick around. She walked away briskly, ignoring Rita's pleas to "be reasonable". With Litvinovich gone, Rita ushered us toward a tent-like building. The entire area was populated by temporary edifices like that, framing the film's main set in a halfmoon formation.

Once we were indoors, Marina finally removed her earbuds. 'How can you have sunburn already?' she asked incredulously, taking in my dramatic transformation from gravely pale to painfully pink. My sun-hating skin is the reason I always have some aloe vera gel on me.

Anyway, Marina and I were taking it all in, while other extras and crew were chatting, catching up. We were surrounded by mirrors, make-up stations and racks of clothes. And there were masks on the walls, each carrying a painted expression. Sadness, happiness, sarcasm.

Given Michael Rottner's reputation, I assumed *Solace Spring* was a political thriller, not horror. As I was wondering what the creepy masks could possibly mean, a tall man entered the building. Hands in pockets, he called everyone to attention.'

A fragment from a 2047 interview with Antonina Vatska

Interviewer: 'So, Dmitry Zharov. Rottner's second in command, he was eager to see *Solace Spring* completed amidst increasing budgetary concerns. Before crossing paths with Rottner, Zharov directed a number of films which enjoyed fleeting popularity, but by the 1990s his oeuvre had gone out of favour. With the end of the Communist era, Russians craved a change in all spheres of life. Zharov's so-called osterns or Red Westerns just didn't cut it anymore.

'Later articles which analysed the Zharov-Rottner partnership explored the themes of professional jealousy and bitterness of a has-been, but the nuances of their relationship, on and off set, have eluded the public. Importantly, along with Irina Litvinovich, Rita Ludwig and others, Zharov was a suspect in Rottner's murder. What was he like?'

Vatska: 'My first impression of him was that he wasn't well suited to the Russian countryside. The sun wasn't even in full force yet, but he was already melting away. I mean, I got a pink forehead, but Zharov looked like he'd just returned from hell. Armpits dark, face blotchy, skin peeling.

And yet, he appeared commanding, certain of himself. I remember him saying something along the lines of "while you're on my set, I'm your leader, your father, and your god. I don't ask for much – only your total obedience and devotion". He laughed at his own words, but I don't think he was joking. I wasn't even born yet when Zharov's own movies were still popular, but I've heard he was dictatorial on set and loved the spotlight.

'When I first saw Zharov, if I hadn't known better, I'd have assumed that was Rottner himself, Russified to the point of speaking perfect, non-accented Russian. But I'd seen photographs of Rottner, and this was not him.

'After Zharov introduced himself, he said to us, "You're all ghosts!" He pointed at the nearest rack of white clothing. "Here are your ghostly suits." Then, he pointed at the masks. "And here are your faces."

'Another memorable thing he did then was warn us about stinging nettle. It's ironic, I guess, given how nettle was instrumental in catching Rottner's killer.'

Interviewer: 'Ironic indeed. But what was the set like? It looks absolutely surreal in the film.'

Vatska: 'Basically, the production company built a replica of Rottner's childhood home, a New England farm house in a Russian village. So, imagine this: the Elk Park in the background, mayweed and stinging nettle everywhere, and here's this non-Russian architecture amidst the rippling field. Surreal, indeed.'

Interviewer: 'And all the extras were to play ghosts.'

Vatska: 'Zharov went into great lengths explaining the concept while he positioned us in and around that replica building. The footage they filmed inside that house was meant to signify dream sequences, as well as to serve as a metaphor for nostalgia. And we extras were ghosts of memories, happy and otherwise. We were to stand very still in our assigned spots, while the protagonist, played by Rottner himself, monologued about his rebellious youth, cursed politicians and stared sorrowfully into space. It was very dramatic, yet tasteful.'

Interviewer: 'What did you think of Rottner himself? You were among those few who witnessed the last few hours of his life.'

Vatska: 'He was as ill-tempered as expected. Within minutes of making an appearance, he snapped at Rita, muttered something about firing his personal assistant who had called in sick that day, and got into this argument with Zharov about where each ghost should be placed.

'If I passed Rottner on the street, I wouldn't look twice. But once you were in his proximity, you could feel this wild energy around him pull you in. And then you were hooked. It was easy to believe all the bizarre rumours: that he was hunted by the CIA, that there had been assassination attempts on him. I wonder how he felt about his political choices then – with Russia on the crossroads, with its perestroika and its glasnost – whether he regretted defecting. Maybe all those ghosts on the set were physical manifestations of his regret.'

Antonina Vatska's personal journal: Entry 5 (April 16, 1995)

There came a piercing scream.

We were eating lunch in the cafeteria, windows open wide, and that awful sound invaded our space like a shrieking ghost, a dying bird crashing from the sky. With all the conversations going on and forks scratching against plates, not everyone heard it at first, but I did. When the second scream sounded, closer and more real, we abandoned our half-eaten pelmeni and rushed outside.

My heart pounding, I looked for Marina, tracing her to the nearest window.

'Someone's hurt,' she said when I joined her. I searched for any traces of agitation in her tone or expression, and found none. She was as calm and collected as always. I guess all the staring at those murder photographs numbed her to the real-life drama.

I followed her outside, where we joined the crowd already forming around Rita Ludwig. She was the one who screamed. Sitting in the grass, she was panting now, choking on air, hands pulling at her short hair. It was difficult to reconcile this shivering mess of a person with the stern-faced guardian of the bus we encountered in the morning. Various emergency numbers rushed through my head – 01 for fire-fighters, 02 for ambulance, 03 for militsiya; or did medical assistance come before fire?

Rita's panicked breathing and tears disoriented me. But then she started to talk, fighting over her own sobs.

'I came to check on him and he...was...just lying there. His plate on the floor, his wine glass smashed. Lips puffy, turning blue.' She let out a prolonged sob, which turned "blue" into bluuuuuue.

I remember the sensation of becoming disconnected from my body. When I asked, 'Who's she talking about?' I wasn't addressing anyone specifically, but it was Misha, the know-it-all from the bus, who replied.

'It's Rottner,' he said, his self-assured demeanour gone without a trace. His voice was shaking when he added, 'Rottner's dead.'

I pretended Misha said something else. Because it simply couldn't be the truth. The infamous director, the brave American dissident, the genius behind *Shadow State*.

Rottner couldn't be dead, could he?

My hand reached for Marina, craving the warmth, the assurance of her presence. But she was nowhere near me. I looked around, finding her – to my surprise – hovering over Rita. My friend was sitting down on the grass and saying something to the crying woman in a voice too soft for me to hear.

'Let's go back inside and wait for help to arrive,' Misha proposed to the crowd of stunned spectators. In the absence of real authority figures, we started to disperse.

Marina helped Rita stand and supported her as they followed the moving crowd. An unreasonable stab of jealousy made my vision darken at the sight of them. I looked away, focusing instead on the house set amidst the undulating grass.

Rottner, what became of him, must've been still inside. That was where he liked to eat his meals alone. Where he had his last meal. That was where Rita Ludwig must've found him.

It was only because I was focusing on the house set that I noticed a slouching figure in a black hoodie as it separated from an outer wall and walked away, seemingly headed for the wardrobe tent.

A fragment of a 2047 interview with Antonina Vatska

Interviewer: 'Can you describe what it felt like to be on set as the news of Rottner's death broke?'

Vatska: 'It was totally and completely surreal. There were people sobbing, just crying their eyes out. And others were calm, probably stunned. I don't think most of us believed it, though – at least, not until the ambulance arrived. It was one of those UAZ models everyone just called Gazelle back in those days. I saw it through a window as two white-clad figures emerged from the car. One joined us in the cafeteria, and the other must've drawn the short straw of attending to Rottner. His body, I mean. His corpse.

'When Marina left Rita in the care of the ambulance doctor and joined me in my corner, I nervously teased her about making a new friend. She just looked at me, all serious, and said, "I was interviewing her. About Rottner's murder."

She said both things matter-of-factly, like a) it was normal for her to assume the role of an investigator, and b) of course, it was murder, not some unfortunate accident.

'Before Marina could share anything else with me, militsiya arrived. A young guy and a woman in her late thirties. I remember all sound ceasing, the pressure building as they entered the cafeteria, accompanied by Zharov. And I remember noticing how the latter looked refreshed from his sweaty morning. His shirt with darkened armpits was gone, replaced by a red long-sleeved button shirt. He'd also procured himself a hat – a bucket shaped panamka. Such a weird look: a city dandy combined with a Soviet dachnik. And he was rubbing his hands, like he was cold and wanted to generate some warmth. That's what I thought at first.

Interviewer: 'Yekaterina Mikhaylovna Gorodets was the senior militsiya officer assigned to this case.'

Vatska: 'Yes, and she knew Marina through her freelance profiling work. When Yekaterina Mikhaylovna spotted Marina in the crowd, she invited her to shadow her during the interviews. I was allowed to tag along.

'I think that it was in that moment that it hit me how different was my perception of what was going on compared to Marina's. While I was goofing around, Marina had been observing, learning things, talking to people. She was the one to tell Yekaterina Mikhaylovna about Rottner's severe citrus allergies, and how caterers had strict guidelines for prepping his meals. Marina must've learned that from Rita, but regardless of her source, she was spot on: Rottner's citrus allergy was what got him! The murderer tampered with his meal. Though Rottner's case came to be associated with poisoning, it was really a food allergy-related death. I suppose that's less catchy.'

Interviewer: 'What kind of things did Marina and the militsiya discuss?'

Vatska: 'Well, I remember Marina telling Yekaterina Mikhaylovna how Rottner's ex, Irina Litvinovich, rode the bus with us in the morning and hadn't been seen since. However, after chatting with several crew members, Marina learned that right before we started filming, some of them heard a screaming match in Rottner's private trailer. They recognised the two voices as those of Rottner and Litvinovich.

'Another thing Marina mentioned had to do with Rita Ludwig and Rottner's personal assistant, Alexey Konnevsky. Konnevsky called in sick that day, and Rottner was not pleased. He kept muttering under his nose all morning how he ought to fire Konnevsky, that it was long overdue.

'Importantly, it was always Konnevsky who brought Rottner's meals to him. In Konnevsky's absence, however, Rita Ludwig stepped in. Naturally, this whole thing didn't look good for her.

'Marina's earlier assessment of Rita as being resentful about having to work with Rottner was spot on. Marina's always been good at reading body language. I didn't even notice it, but it turns out Rita frowned whenever Rottner was mentioned, even rolled her eyes behind Rottner's back – that kind of petty stuff. She couldn't stand him; something to do with a creative dispute, like he didn't credit her for some rewriting work she did or something like that. But she was locked into a contract and had no choice but to finish this movie with him.'

Interviewer: 'And so with Konnevsky away, Rita Ludwig had to spend more time with Rottner. Perhaps more than she could take?'

Vatska: 'That was one of the hypotheses. Everyone knew Rita Ludwig hated Rottner, plus she had access to his food that day. But Marina wasn't convinced. Disliking someone was not a strong enough motivation for murder, she said. And then it all became a whole lot stranger. Misha, the gossipy extra, swore he saw Konnevsky lurking around the set, wearing his typical black hoodie, jeans and super shiny white sneakers. I had a similar sighting, which I mentioned to Yekaterina Mikhaylovna. Konnevsky became a suspect, too.

'They had to check his alibi and figure out if he had a chance to sneak out of his Balashikha hotel room, make it to the set, slip something into Rottner's food and then make it all the way back, unseen. It was such a far-fetched theory, but Konnevsky did love his black hoodies and his shiny American shoes.'

Marina Holmesova's original hand-written list of suspects and clues in the Solace Spring case

Rita Ludwig (production manager):
- Dislikes Rottner (he didn't give her a writing credit she felt she deserved);
- Had to assume the job of Rottner's personal assistant (Konnevsky) after the latter called in sick;
- At about 12pm, delivered Rottner's lunch to the house set where he preferred to take his meals alone; but Rottner wasn't there, so she deposited his meal on the table and left;
- Found Rottner's body at approximately 13:05; said his lips were puffy, turning blue;
- Did she know Rottner well enough to learn about his allergies?
- Was her personal resentment enough of a motive? She definitely had an opportunity.

Alexey Konnevsky (Rottner's personal assistant):
- Called in sick the day of Rottner's murder (fake alibi?);
- Likes to wear black hoodies, jeans and white sneakers (at least two people saw him, or someone dressed like him, lurking around the set);
- Was the one to bring Rottner his meals;
- Definitely knew about Rottner's allergies;
- Aside from having to work for a terrible boss, did he have a motive?
- What about opportunity? He claims to have been sick in his hotel bed in Balashikha, a thirty-minute drive from the set.

Irina Litvinovich (actress, Rottner's former lover):
- Was fired from *Solace Spring* after breaking up with Rottner;
- Arrived to the set uninvited in the morning, apparently to confront Rottner;
- Was heard having a fight with Rottner in his trailer in the morning;
- Could've known about his severe allergies;
- No alibi;
- Motive of an ex-lover's retaliation?

Dmitry Zharov (assistant director):
- Commanding, ambitious, but never openly critical of Rottner;
- Apparently, had to step in quite a few times to keep the production moving amidst the delays caused by Rottner and his demands;
- Wasn't around for lunch as he had to drive to Balashikha to pick up documents from a private courier's office, but apparently never made it there.

Clues (?):
- A pair of sneakers stained with red found in the nettle growth behind the house set;
- Rita Ludwig said Rottner's lips were turning blue; pallor mortis usually occurs almost immediately after death, generally within 15-25 minutes. This places Rottner's passing halfway through the lunch period (12:30-1pm);
- Murderer had to know about Rottner's allergies and (likely) sprinkled his food or wine with something containing citric acid when Rottner's lunch was left unattended;
- Konnevsky kept spare clothes on the set; someone could've easily 'borrowed' his typical ensemble to stalk around in disguise;
- As Rottner was dying, he must've smashed his wine glass, spilling the red liquid all over the poisoner's white sneakers; our murderer had to take off the sneakers as he or she ran from the scene;
- Stinging nettle growth behind the house set was flattened in a way that suggested in his/her retreat, our murderer slipped and fell into the grass, likely while taking off and discarding those stained shoes.

Antonina Vatska's personal journal: Entry 6 (April 16, 1995)

While militsiya interrogated Zharov, I watched Marina as she studied him, focusing on his hands. He kept rubbing them, skin glistening. I noticed a substance sticking to his fingers, faint and greenish, like coloured gelatine. It must've hit me the same time it did Marina, because she looked away from Zharov and found my eyes, hers sparking with triumph.

It turns out, I wasn't the only one who carried aloe vera gel with me everywhere I went. Only it wasn't sunburn that painted Zharov's hands with welts, prompting the aloe treatment.

'Nettle', I told Marina under my breath, practically miming the words. I didn't need to remind her about our word association game, opportunity being her latest offering, still awaiting my response.

Her lips issued a crooked smile, with just the right side of her mouth moving. She understood.

When Marina queried the assistant director about the burns on his hands, then asked politely whether we could see the state of his bare feet, he did something I'd only seen criminals do in movies but which I never thought I'd witness in real life – he ran.'

SOLACE SPRING EXHIBITION EXTENDED

Moscow Herald

Arts and Culture, December 1, 2051

Due to high demand, the popular exhibition chronicling the first criminal investigation conducted by private detective Marina Holmesova has been extended until March 15, 2052.

Lovingly curated by Holmesova's wife, Antonina Vatska, *The Scandalous Case of Solace Spring Poisoning* exhibition tells the story of Michael Rottner's poisoning by his murderously envious second-in-command, Dmitry Zharov, the latter eager to assume control over the troubled production of Rottner's film, *Solace Spring* and restore his own flagging career.

Solving the case led to Holmesova being invited to consult on other ongoing investigations, and eventually launched her private detective career.

Collaborating on Rottner's case also paved the way for a long-term professional partnership between Holmesova and Vatska, which eventually saw them develop a personal relationship and get married in 2038 in a private ceremony in the Apothecaries' Gardens, on the grounds of their beloved alma mater, shortly after Russia's ground-breaking marriage equality reform of the same year came into effect.

The exhibition's closing night will feature a rare appearance by Marina Holmesova in a Q&A hosted by her wife whom, in her rare public quotes, has been known to refer to Vatska as The Woman.

Author's Note:
Born in Russia, I came of age in the 1990s (think: tanks on the Red Square and Scorpions singing *Wind of Change*). My childhood memories of watching dubbed *Labyrinth* compete with those of my parents buying bread with food stamps.

What does Sherlock Holmes have to do with this? Reading those books as a teen, I've formed two assumptions: Russia had no private investigators, and all the famous ones were men. Research busted my assumptions wide open. There have always been private detectives in Russia, but the inflexibilities of the country's justice systems meant they often worked from the shadows. Importantly, many of these detectives have been women, unwelcomed by the patriarchal law enforcement but seeking to do this work anyway.

Having learned this, I knew I had to reimagine Holmes and Watson as brilliant young women, striving for a better future amidst the shifting terrains of the 1990s Russia.

THE
ADVENTURE
OF THE
FATED
HOMECOMING

Jayantika Ganguly

Mumbai Airport, modern day

'Johnny! Wait up!'

I sighed and stopped. I would recognise that voice – and that detestable nickname unique to a certain set of my acquaintances – anywhere. This was my roommate from medical school – Dr Mohan Sharma. How unexpected that I would run into an old friend the moment I returned to India.

'Hello, Mohan,' I said evenly. Was I happy to run into him at the airport? Not really. But I was back in my native country for good now, so I might as well rekindle old friendships. The last thing I wanted was to be alone all over again.

Mohan reached me and swung an arm around my shoulders, just like he used to when we were in college. A bit of warmth stole into my heart. How long had it been since I'd met a friend? I shook my head to ward off the gloomy direction of my thoughts.

'Don't call me Johnny,' I grumbled instead.

My old friend laughed. 'Dr Jyotirmay Habib Wagh is too much, even for Indian tongues. How are you, Johnny?' he asked, grinning widely.

'Last I heard, you were off volunteering in some dangerous place with Médecins Sans Frontières!'

'That was a few years ago,' I replied slowly as I pushed my luggage trolley and started walking again. Right after my first divorce, in fact, but that was a story I didn't want to revisit. I asked instead, 'How have you been?'

Mohan smiled broadly. 'All well,' he replied. 'Working at my dad's hospital and flying around the world attending seminars. You should visit us! How long are you in town this time?'

I sighed again. 'Probably for good.'

Mohan raised an eyebrow. 'Didn't work out with the second wife, either?' he asked bluntly. 'What went wrong? Did you cheat on her?'

'No.' I smiled bitterly. 'She cheated.'

Mohan gaped at me, his shocked face so comical that I couldn't help but chuckle.

'But– but– you're Three-Continents-Johnny! Even the exchange students couldn't resist your pretty blue eyes! How on Earth…?'

I shrugged. Perhaps I was unsuitable for long term companionship. My first wife divorced me within six months of our marriage, and now she'd been happily married to a schoolteacher in a small village for over six years. My second wife of two years divorced me a little over a month ago, and she married my colleague almost immediately. I resigned, travelled the world aimlessly for a few weeks, and now I was back in India a decade after leaving my homeland.

We had almost reached the exit. I was preparing to bid farewell when Mohan grabbed my arm.

'Hold on,' he said, frowning. 'Where are you staying? Your brother won't let you in, right?'

'I'll stay in a hotel until I find a decent place,' I replied.

'Where are you going to work?'

I shrugged again. I hadn't found a job yet. As a doctor, I would surely find something soon. If not, I could rent a small chamber and start my own practice. I had enough savings to last me a few months.

'You're coming with me,' Mohan said firmly. 'I'll put you in the hospital's guest house. We are short-staffed in Emergency and in Cardiovascular Intensive Care – which one do you want to join? Stay with us until you figure out what you want to do.'

I was touched by his generosity, but it was too much for me to accept.

I thanked him and turned him down, but he refused to take no for an answer.

Ultimately, I allowed myself to be dragged off. I joined the Emergency Department of Bairag T. Sharma Hospital (fondly called "Barts") the very next day.

And exactly a week later, I met the man who changed my life.

Barts Hospital, Mumbai

I will never forget that day for the rest of my life. Mohan and I were discussing the discharge of one of our patients when a nurse burst into the room in tears.

'Dr Mohan!' she sobbed. 'That weirdo is back again! He's mutilating the late minister's corpse in the morgue! We're going to get sued!'

Mohan sighed and rubbed his temples. 'Really lives up to his name, that guy,' he muttered.

My curiosity was piqued. Mohan noticed and a sly smile crossed his face. 'Come along, Johnny – if you like the guy, maybe you can be roommates. He was complaining recently that he's found a good place but needs someone to go half-and-half.'

I was still living in the hospital's guest house because I really didn't want to live alone again. I had intended to look through ads calling for flatmates instead. Or perhaps I could adopt a few strays; at least they wouldn't stab me in the back.

'No way!' the nurse cried. 'Dr Wagh is so nice! How can he put up with that, that–' she struggled to find an appropriate word. '...that psycho!'

Mohan winked at me and walked off. I followed him hurriedly, ignoring the nurse's warnings floating behind us.

'Who's this guy?' I asked curiously.

'A crazy genius,' Mohan replied. 'He's not a doctor, but comes here fairly often to use the lab. Papa's really fond of him, so he has free access.'

Curiouser and curiouser, I thought to myself.

We reached the morgue and met half a dozen fretting staff members. Mohan quickly reassured them and then the two of us went in.

A tall, thin man with sharp features and arresting grey eyes was examining a corpse carefully. The corpse didn't appear to be mutilated, but there were strange purplish spots on the left forearm of the dead man. I spotted a discarded syringe on the floor.

Mohan cleared his throat. 'What are you doing?' he asked loudly.

'Need to see the effect of this toxin after death,' the man replied absently. He sprang up suddenly. 'Aha! I was right! It was the third guard!'

He fumbled awkwardly, trying to reach his left back pocket with his right hand. That's when I noticed a greenish spot on the skin of his left wrist.

'What happened to your arm?' I asked.

Mohan rushed to the young man and grabbed his arm. 'Did you poison yourself again?'

'Not really, just applied a little to my skin. Not dangerous. Oh, right, the antidote,' the strange man muttered. He reached into his coat pocket and pulled out a small vial and a new syringe. 'If I may trouble you?'

Mohan snatched the things from him before he could finish. Picking up on my friend's anxiety, I stepped up to help. Mohan thrust the vial and the syringe into my hands and pushed back the left sleeve of this strange guy. I quickly prepared the injection and administered it.

'You idiot!' Mohan scolded. 'What did you do that for?'

Clear grey eyes looked at us innocently. 'I told you, it was only a smidge for experimental purposes. I didn't even inject it, although that would have let me observe the effects better. I needed to compare the effect of the toxin on living flesh and dead flesh.' He smiled slightly at Mohan. 'Human flesh.'

'Your brother will hear about this, I swear,' Mohan threatened. 'I refuse to believe that someone as clever as you can't come up with a better way to test a toxin than using it on his own bloody arm!'

'It was safer and the second fastest way,' the younger man replied calmly. He looked at me. 'Could you get my phone from my back pocket? I need to send a text urgently.'

I withdrew his phone from the pocket he was struggling to reach earlier and handed it to him.

'Thanks,' he said and sent out a text.

Mohan had cooled down by the time he was done. He sighed tiredly. 'How long before your arm recovers?'

'Maybe an hour. Two at most,' he replied.

Mohan shook his head, exasperated, and turned to me. 'Johnny, this is Sherlock Dasgupta – yes, he was named after the great Victorian detective. Sherlock, this is my friend from med school, Dr Jyotirmay Habib Wagh.'

With a charming smile, Sherlock said to me, 'You have been in Afghanistan, I perceive.'

The world stood still as I was caught in clear pools of silvery grey and a haze of nostalgia at those strangely familiar words. My blood roared in my veins.

Waves of my past assaulted my senses – my late mother's clandestine whispers to my nine-year-old self: an illustrious ancestor, the secret behind my blue eyes; the family tradition about my unusual full name; the reason I was shipped off to London as soon as I got my medical degree.

Was it fate? Could there be such a thing as destiny? For a moment, I heard my mother's voice; or was it an echo of memories long past? Nonetheless, a phrase resonated in my ears. The only one in the world...

I am a scientific man, and I definitely don't believe in the supernatural, but that moment was something I still can't explain.

I navigated my way back to reality and found the two men eyeing me curiously. My senses returned and I replied, 'I have. How did you know?'

'It is my business to know things that others do not,' Sherlock said playfully.

'Stop showing off,' Mohan complained.

Sherlock smiled, bent over and picked a tiny thread from my trouser leg. 'This is from a Baluchi rug made by a particular shop in Najeeb Zareb Market in Kabul,' he said.

'While it is amazing that you can recognise such a thing, it does not necessarily mean I was in Kabul myself. It could be a gift,' I challenged.

A spark of interest appeared in his sharp eyes. 'Indeed,' he said. 'But there is also a whiff of Afghani saffron about you, there is a handkerchief with Afghani embroidery peeking from your pocket and most tellingly, Mohan has a new object on his desk these days – a genuine Nooristani trinket box from a shop on Danulaman Road. Since he went to Sydney last week, clearly it wasn't something he brought back.

'Then there's all the gossip amongst the staff about the dreamy new doctor friend of his who just returned from overseas. And now he brings you to meet me, soon after I complained that I couldn't find a suitable roommate for a nice flat I found. Elementary.'

'Brilliant,' I murmured dazedly. This guy could certainly give his namesake, the original Sherlock Holmes, a run for his money!

Sherlock smirked. 'So why is a jaded, twice-divorced but highly successful cardio surgeon from London back in Mumbai in the Emergency Ward? Is it your insomnia? Or does your shoulder injury prevent you from holding a scalpel properly? Or both, perhaps?'

Mohan buried his face in his hands while I stared at this strange young man, flabbergasted. 'How did you–?'

'You have no rings but two different ring marks on your ring finger, and the tan lines show that one is recent. So, two broken engagements or two divorces. Given your tragic hero look, divorce is likelier. You have dark circles under your eyes. They are not new, since you have been wearing zero-power glasses to hide them for a while, as the indents on your nose indicate. So, chronic insomnia.

'Your left shoulder is stiff, and you used your right hand to retrieve my phone, even though you're left-handed and your left hand was closer to my pocket. You also hesitated when Mohan handed you the syringe. So, shoulder injury – not bad enough to prevent your work in the Emergency Department, but bad enough to prevent you from performing delicate surgery. About why you are back in Mumbai, I have no idea – so I asked.'

'Incredible,' I murmured, almost involuntarily. 'You really are like Sherlock Holmes.'

A strange look flashed across Sherlock Dasgupta's face. A corner of his lips lifted in a sardonic smile. 'Well, since I was named after a legend, it is only right that I live up to the name, isn't it?'

Had I hit a nerve? 'I'm sorry,' I said quickly. 'I meant no offence.'

'None taken,' Sherlock replied, waving a slim hand casually. 'Besides, I was far more intrusive earlier.'

'You were right, though.'

He grinned suddenly, exuding a boyish charm that would have the nurses squealing, I'm sure. 'Would you like to see the flat?' he asked. 'It's really nice. Well-located, a little old – which means bigger rooms and higher ceilings – and I know the landlady, so she's giving me a special deal. We'll have the entire second floor to ourselves. It's in Colaba.'

'Sure,' I said. No harm in taking a glance at the place, I thought. Colaba was prime real estate, conveniently close to the hospital. And somehow, I found myself liking this young man. Perhaps my uncommon bloodline had given me a soft spot for odd geniuses. I wondered how old he was; he looked like a college student.

'All right, stop making googly eyes at each other and let's go for lunch instead,' Mohan grumbled. I had almost forgotten his presence.

I smiled apologetically at my friend. 'My treat,' I offered. I turned to Sherlock. 'Where would you like to eat?'

'Britannia,' came the prompt response.

I was surprised and quite pleased. Britannia was an iconic restaurant, nearly a century old, which served delicious Parsi food. It was one of my favourites, and a mere five-minute walk away.

Britannia Restaurant, Mumbai

Over steaming plates of berry pulao, cutlets, fish patra and salli boti, the three of us chatted idly. I learned that Sherlock was in his mid-twenties – older than he looked, certainly. He was half-British and lived in London till he was six, before moving to India with his parents. He had recently relocated from Kolkata to Mumbai, and he called himself a "Consulting Detective", just like the great legendary detective.

I was fascinated. 'The police consult you? Really?'

He nodded smugly.

Before I could respond, there was delighted cry of 'Habibi!' and an attractive woman launched herself into my arms. I disentangled myself awkwardly.

Mohan groaned. 'This homme fatale,' he said, shaking his head sadly. 'Johnny, have you gone from three-continents to all-continents?'

I flushed, embarrassed. 'This is Afreen,' I introduced the lady to Mohan and Sherlock. 'She's an old…friend.' Well, she was an ex-girlfriend. I hadn't seen her in a few years. For that matter, why was she even in India?

Afreen clung to my arm. Her lunch companion, a rough-looking man, glared at me. She ignored him and greeted my tablemates.

Sherlock eyed her curiously, but didn't say anything.

I tried to move away from Afreen as delicately as I could, but she wouldn't let go as she chatted excitedly with – or rather, at – Sherlock. Ah, well. Good-looking men with light eyes were her preference, after all.

Finally, her companion couldn't stand it anymore and marched to our table, pulling her away roughly. Afreen laughed and slipped her arm around his waist.

'Habibi, this is Ivan. We're getting married in Goa next month,' she told me. 'You must come! And bring this pretty guy, too!' She winked at Sherlock.

Sherlock observed the couple with a small smile. 'What a coincidence,' he murmured absently as they walked away to their table.

I heaved a sigh of relief.

Sherlock glanced at me. 'Your taste in women is…interesting,' he said.

Mohan burst out laughing and I flushed. To distract my companions, I told them about my maternal family's peculiar tradition where every blue-eyed child was required to have the initials 'J.H.W.' and how I'd inherited my mother's surname for that reason.

'The blue eyes are inherited from a British ancestor who visited India briefly many years ago. My grandfather and two of his siblings had them, but no one in my Ma's generation did. I'm the only one in my generation,' I explained. 'My middle name comes from my paternal grandmother; she was Afghani.'

Sherlock, interested, asked me several questions about my name and pedigree. Our conversation steered away from my personal life after that, thankfully.

We chatted comfortably until Mohan received a call from the hospital. He stood to leave. 'Johnny,' he said. 'Why don't you take the rest of the day off and see the flat Sherlock has his eyes on?'

'But–' I began.

'I've been making you work too hard. Just go. I'll arrange for your stuff to be moved if you like it.' He turned to Sherlock. 'Papa has been asking after you. Why don't you two join us for dinner tonight?'

I had until now avoided Mohan's invitations to dine with his family, but if I accompanied another person, perhaps it wouldn't be so bad. Sherlock glanced at me and I nodded slightly.

Mohan clapped his hands, pleased. 'All right, I'll see you two tonight,' and took his leave.

As it turned out, we were not destined to have dinner with the Sharma family that night.

Colaba, Mumbai

Post-lunch, Sherlock and I walked to Colaba. Given the state of Mumbai's traffic, it was often faster to walk than to take a cab. Besides, it was good to walk off our heavy meal. I had an unfortunate tendency to put on weight easily.

Fifteen minutes later, we stood in front of an old building in a tiny lane off the main street. "Baker Street" declared a small, rusty board.

I had spent two-thirds of my life in this city, and had never seen this lane before. I had absolutely no idea that there was a Baker Street in Mumbai. I wondered at the coincidence and followed the detective inside.

It was an old fashioned bungalow that was hardly seen in the metropolitis anymore.

The landlady, Mrs Hussain, appeared pleased to see us, and she smiled brightly when I introduced myself.

'A doctor!' she said happily. 'Just what we need.'

She took us on a tour of the premises. The ground floor housed a large hall mostly used for storage, a garage and a small garden. Mrs Hussain, an elderly widow, lived on the first floor with a couple of servants. The third floor was an impressive terrace garden.

The second floor was to be rented out to Sherlock and me. It had two en suite bedrooms, a large living room, a dining room, a kitchen, a comfortable study and another side room. The large windows of one of the bedrooms had a lovely view of the Arabian Sea. This was, undoubtedly, premium property. I wouldn't be able to afford half the rent, even if Sherlock got a deal from the landlady. I sighed. It was a beautiful house, and so conveniently located.

'Well?' Mrs Hussain asked eagerly. 'Do you like it?'

'It is lovely,' I replied. 'But I'm afraid that—'

'I'll give you a discount, don't worry,' she said, beaming.

She named a price and I was shocked into silence. It was a mere fraction of what the rent of a place like this would ordinarily be!

My soon-to-be landlady patted Sherlock's arm, smiling gently. 'This child needs a good person to share the rooms with; that's more important.'

'I want to convert the side room into a small lab,' Sherlock told me. 'Do you mind, Doctor?'

'Not at all,' I replied, still trying to wrap my mind around the ridiculously low price for this luxurious apartment.

'Do you mind taking the sea view bedroom?' he asked.

I blinked, stunned. This youngster was generous, wasn't he? Had he noticed me drooling over the room?

'Are you sure?' I asked slowly. 'I'm fine with either bedroom.'

'Then please take the sea view one,' Sherlock said.

I nodded happily.

Mrs Hussain was delighted. 'Come and sleep here tonight; I'll have the bedrooms prepared,' she said generously. 'The paperwork should be ready for you to sign by tomorrow.'

We bid farewell to her and fixed an appointment for the next day.

As we walked down the busy streets of Colaba, I asked Sherlock quietly if it was okay for us to accept such a massive discount from the old lady.

Sherlock laughed. 'That old lady is one of the richest realtors in Mumbai, Doctor. You don't have to worry.'

I was taken aback, but relieved. 'She seems very fond of you,' I remarked.

Just then, a street urchin collided with Sherlock and fell down on the pavement. Sherlock stumbled as well, but I caught him in time. He knelt and held out a hand to the child in filthy clothes who looked about ten or twelve.

'Are you hurt, Wiggy?' he asked gently in Marathi.

The boy grabbed his hand and stood up, looking over his shoulder fearfully. I spotted a few men approaching us menacingly. One of the faces was familiar: Ivan, Afreen's fiancé.

Sherlock ducked into an alley, hiding the boy behind himself. I followed quickly. We lost sight of the men for a while. Sherlock shed his jacket and placed it around the boy's shoulders.

'Did you steal a wallet?' he asked casually. 'Didn't I specifically tell you not to get close – to only observe from a distance?'

The boy nodded sulkily.

'Which one?'

'Pink shirt,' the young pickpocket said.

That would be Ivan.

Sherlock smiled slightly and held out his hand. 'Show me.'

Very reluctantly, the boy handed over the wallet. Sherlock examined it and withdrew a small plastic pouch filled with a light green powder, his eyes glittering excitedly. He returned the wallet to the boy and said, 'Take the money, throw the wallet into this alley, and run as far as you can if you don't want to get killed.'

Frightened, the boy obeyed wordlessly and scurried off at an impressive speed.

'Who was that?' I asked curiously, for Sherlock seemed quite familiar with the urchin.

He chuckled. 'One of my irregulars. I asked him to keep an eye on Ivan when we left the restaurant earlier.'

I was duly impressed.

Sherlock and I walked away leisurely. As we turned into the next lane, we spotted the men entering the alley we had just left. They found the abandoned wallet and we heard loud cursing.

My companion chuckled. 'Doctor, you must be my lucky charm.'

Embarrassed, I asked, 'Why?'

'You have led me to the gang I was looking for,' he said.

'Gang?' I asked, shocked. 'Do you mean Ivan is part of a gang?'

'The sample we just found is the toxin I was testing at the hospital earlier today.'

'Then why did you take it?' I asked curiously.

'To frighten them, of course,' Sherlock replied calmly. 'Ivan must be planning to kill someone today or tomorrow if he was carrying it in his pocket. Now that I've taken it, he will run back to the source to pick up more of it, so that he can carry out his villainous task. So we will not only find the toxin supplier, we can also prevent the next murder.'

I was surprised. 'If you don't know the toxin supplier, how did you get the sample to poison yourself?'

Sherlock chuckled. 'I picked up a trace amount at the crime scene, examined it and spoke to an acquaintance...let's call him "Porlock",' he replied enigmatically. 'Porlock sent me a sample from Vietnam.'

I raised an eyebrow, but didn't enquire further. 'How will you track the local supplier?' I asked instead.

He held up his phone. 'Good old-fashioned tracking, Doctor. I planted a bug in the wallet, and I've shared the bug's tracking codes with my contact in the police. The official forces can take it from here. We can be spectators, if you like.'

I was more than happy to accompany this brilliant man. As we followed the gangsters, a thought struck me.

'How did you know Ivan was a gangster?' I asked. 'You knew at lunch, didn't you? How? He was dressed normally!'

'I was unaware gangsters had a dress code, Doctor.'

'Then how did you know?'

'I didn't know he was part of the gang I was looking for until we found the sample,' he said.

'But you knew he was a gangster, didn't you? How?'

'I don't want to tell you.'

I blinked, surprised. 'Why?'

He sighed and relented. 'It's rather mundane. Your ex-girlfriend's fiancé is on Interpol's list.'

I gaped at him. 'Do you remember everyone on Interpol's list?'

'Of course,' he said casually, as if it was not an impressive feat at all.

I was about to reply when his phone rang. A loud, nasal voice shouted frantically, 'Sherlock! The third guard escaped when we went to arrest him! He dropped his phone, though.'

I could hear every word even though the call was not on speaker.

Sherlock pursed his lips in displeasure. 'I sent you the information hours ago, Inspector, directly after I examined the latest victim this morning. What took you so long?' he snapped. 'Can you follow the tracker or do you want me to make the arrests for you as well?'

'We'll handle the gang, don't worry about that. I need you to decode the last message on the escapee's phone; it should give us a clue about where he is. I'm sending you a screenshot.' The Inspector spoke rapidly, as if afraid that the detective would hang up.

'Very well,' Sherlock said. 'I'll let you know.'

'Thanks!' came the relieved voice of the Inspector, whose name I still didn't know.

I peered at Sherlock's phone as the image of a quote in ornate calligraphy appeared. It ran thus:

In the same spirit, therefore, should each type of statement be received; for it is the mark of an educated man to look for precision in each class of things just so far as the nature of the subject admits; it is evidently equally foolish to accept probable reasoning from a mathematician and to demand from a rhetorician scientific proofs.

'Aristotle, isn't it? Or was it Plato?' I wondered out loud.

Sherlock had gone impossibly pale. 'Aristotle,' he whispered. 'Nicomachean Ethics.' He dialled a number.

'Dadabhai,' he said urgently – big brother – as soon as his call was answered. 'Are you in Mumbai? Are you in a library?'

Mohan had briefly mentioned Sherlock's brother, who lived in Delhi, over lunch, but I wondered why the detective was calling him now. Was he also a detective? Or affiliated with the police?

His brother's voice was soft, so I couldn't hear what he said.

'There's an assassin after you,' Sherlock said. 'He just escaped from the police. I'll send you his picture, but he is likely to be disguised. The previous target was Minister Shinde.'

I was shocked. I'd read about Minister Shinde's death a couple of days ago, but the reports said that he'd died of cardiac arrest. Could it be that he was murdered instead, and was that the case Sherlock was handling right now?

'Yes,' Sherlock said. 'Be careful. Don't let anyone touch you until I can reach you with the antidote.'

I had no idea what Sherlock had agreed to. Before I could ask, he hailed a cab.

'Asiatic Society,' he said as we bundled in. 'I'll pay you double if you take the shortcuts I tell you to.'

Since the Asiatic Society was quite close, the cabbie was only too happy at the offer.

Asiatic Society Town Hall Library, Mumbai

Five minutes later, having driven through unknown lanes, the two of us alighted in front of the iconic steps of the famous library. From the cabbie's delighted expression at not only the extra money, but also these secret shortcuts, I guessed I was not the only one with inadequate knowledge of Mumbai's roads.

I found myself staring at Sherlock curiously. He had been in Mumbai for hardly a few months; how had he managed to learn so much?

To my surprise, instead of the regular entrance, Sherlock led me to a side door I hadn't previously known about. An armed guard stood at the door. Sherlock spoke a few words to him, was handed a package and then the two of us were ushered in.

As soon as we were inside, Sherlock pulled me into a secluded corner. 'Can you still shoot properly with a handgun?' he asked in a low whisper.

'How—?'

'Calluses,' he said curtly. 'Can you?'

I nodded.

His relief was palpable. He withdrew a gun from the package and handed it to me.

'Glock 17,' I murmured, examining the gun, a tad nostalgic. I used to own one of these during my adventurous days in Afghanistan.

'It's official equipment, don't worry. We may not even need it, but it's best to be careful.'

I tucked the gun into my waistband. Then we went upstairs, met another armed guard, and were led into a small meeting room.

The scene was straight out of a movie. A man who looked strikingly similar to Sherlock sat on one side of the table. A bespectacled young lady sat next to him, taking copious notes on a tablet. Behind them stood four heavily armed guards.

On the other side of the table sat a person I had recently seen on the television, a visiting foreign prime minister. In fact, I had met him in person when I had worked in his country for a few months in the past. Two men and two women flanked him, and behind them were a dozen armed guards.

One of the women looked up as we entered, and I was shocked to see a familiar face.

'Habibi?' Afreen asked, equally shocked. 'Why are you here?'

The foreign politician looked up at her outburst. He smiled at me. 'Long time no see, Dr Wagh. I was under the impression you had returned to London.'

I greeted him politely, amazed that he remembered an insignificant doctor he'd met several years ago.

Sherlock's brother smiled as well. 'A small world, indeed.' He stood and held out his hand to me. 'Well met, Dr Wagh. I am Sherlock's brother, Aristotle Dasgupta.'

I suppressed my urge to laugh and shook hands with him. Really, what was wrong with their parents, naming their kids like this? I wondered if they had any more siblings with unfortunate names.

Sherlock threw the toxin he had taken from Ivan's wallet on the table.

'The Troika gang is using this for assassination in India. It is synthesised from an artificially mutated sub-species of *Iris afghanica* and an unclassified chemical of plant origin. It has no fatal effect unless injected into the bloodstream. Small amounts applied to the skin cause localised paralysis which can be neutralised with a combination of opiates, while large amounts injected into the bloodstream cause cardiac arrest and there is no known cure,' he told his brother.

He then turned to the visiting politician. 'Does it originate from your country?'

'Don't be rude, Sherlock,' Aristotle reprimanded. 'They have the same problem as we do, which is why Ms Afreen Ali Khan infiltrated Troika. The gang deals with a supplier, not the source. I believe your police friends will be arresting them shortly.'

The foreign politician nodded. 'My finance minister was murdered with this recently,' he said quietly.

'Our country is not the only one at risk. We have traced supply chains to at least seven more Asian countries, and we have collaborated with their governments to capture the suppliers. However, as Mr Dasgupta says, they were merely suppliers, not the source. The source remains unidentified.'

Aristotle sighed unhappily and spoke. 'Their modus operandi is to appoint an exclusive agent in each country who controls the entire supply in that territory. Once the supplier is compromised, they withdraw. It is also unusual for them to attempt more than one assassination using this toxin in the same country.'

Sherlock frowned. 'It has not been used for assassination in India yet. The intended victim died of a genuine myocardial infarction, and the toxin was introduced to his bloodstream after his death. I checked at Barts earlier.'

There was a cackle of laughter, but it did not come from any of the people in the room. We all looked around in vain, trying to find the intruder.

'You really are very clever, Mr Sherlock Dasgupta,' a disembodied voice said. 'Just like your celebrated ancestor.' It was a pleasant male voice, deep and seductively melodious.

'Who are you?' Sherlock asked.

'You can call me Moriarty,' the voice continued. 'That would be poetic, wouldn't it? The fated arch-enemies!'

There was a dramatic pause. 'However, now that you have ruined our plans to poison your brother, we will have to resort to old-fashioned methods.'

Many things then happened simultaneously.

One of Aristotle's guards, and one guard from the foreign delegation, fired at Aristotle. Sherlock pounced on his brother and knocked him to the floor. The rest of the foreign delegation surrounded their minister protectively. Another of Aristotle's guards shot at his colleague who had fired; and I shot the foreign guard cleanly through his shoulder.

Both traitors foamed at the mouth almost immediately and dropped dead.

Someone cursed in a low voice.

'Ah, you've foiled me again, Sherlock,' the hidden voice said regretfully. 'I need to leave now, but we will catch up soon.'

Sherlock sprang up, intending pursuit, but Aristotle held him back. To my horror, I saw bright red blood on Sherlock's shirt. My medical instincts went into overdrive.

'Don't fuss, it's just a graze. I need to catch him,' Sherlock snapped as he struggled in his brother's arms while I examined his wound. Fortunately, it really was just a graze; he would be fine once it was disinfected and bandaged.

'The man was never here, Sherlock. You know it as well as I do. Don't be stupid,' Aristotle scolded, finally releasing him.

My jaw dropped. "Stupid" was the last word I would associate with Sherlock Dasgupta.

Sherlock huffed. 'Dadabhai is cleverer,' he told me.

With a small smile, Aristotle said, 'Dr Wagh, may I trouble you to take care of my brother? I'm afraid I need to clean up the mess here, but I will join you two for breakfast tomorrow.'

He took off his jacket and draped it around his younger brother's shoulders, just as Sherlock had done for the street urchin earlier.

The blood-stained shirt was no longer visible.

Sherlock and I left in a government car. I wanted to take him to the hospital, but he insisted that Mrs Hussain's first aid kit would be more than adequate.

Home

The car dropped us off in front of our new home. This time, I noticed the marble plaque at the gate.

221.

Mrs Hussain had called the second floor "Unit B".

'Sherlock,' I murmured, as we entered. 'What is our new address?'

My soon-to-be best friend turned and, with a charming grin, replied, '221B Baker Street.'

I was home, with my new friend and roommate, just like the famous men whose blood we carried, although in a different era and a different country. History repeats itself, they say…and as I followed Sherlock up the stairs, I wondered if we, too, would have legendary adventures like our respective ancestors.

Perhaps this was a fated homecoming, after all.

AUTHOR'S NOTES:

Dadabhai is an affectionate term for big brother in Bengali

Prince Ha-mahes

and the

Adventure

of the

Stoned Mason

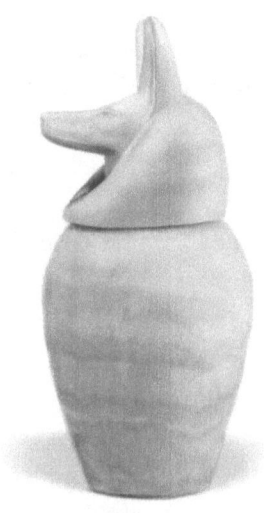

L.J.M. Owen

PI-RAMESES, CAPITAL OF THE EGYPTIAN EMPIRE
in the Delta of the Nile, Egypt

Year 51, Reign of Pharaoh Rameses II (1229 BCE)

If he had been a betting man, Wab-sunu would have lost.

For it wasn't Prince Ha-mahes' experiments on the interaction between crocodile digestive tracts and the flesh of executed criminals discarded in the Nile that had caused the most recent complaints against him. Nor was it Ha-mahes' obsessive cataloguing of organ variation among the clientele of the city's embalmers.

Rather, seven days ago, Wab-sunu had been confronted by an apoplectic Roy, High Priest of Amun, sporting a black eye and demanding that he – as the Prince's retainer – do something about that blue-lotus-soaked idler.

The bruise, it emerged, had been sustained as the cleric delivered an expensive set of prayers on behalf of a departed noble, pleading for his safe passage to the afterlife. Leaning over the man's linen-wrapped remains to chant, the priest had been struck in the eye by a scarab amulet expelled with significant force from the tightly-bound cadaver. Insult was added to injury when Roy – now facing an exorbitant compensation claim from the deceased's family – pulled the last joint of one of the body's fingers from his own nostril. He had recognised Prince Ha-mahes' handiwork instantly.

Later, a chortling Ha-mahes explained that he had been testing the effects of various exotic resins when added to embalming compounds. While detonating corpses had not been his intention, he had whooped with delight when Wab-sunu relayed the results.

And so, as Wab-sunu would not have bet an exploding mummy would incite the current protests against his Prince, he would have lost any wager on the matter.

After Roy had swept from his offices, Wab-sunu sighed heavily and sat at his desk to pen a plea for assistance in distracting his charge from excessive destruction. A reply arrived after only six journeys of Ra's chariot across the sky.

For the first time in a week, Wab-sunu had smiled.

He rose early the following day to be shaved and made up by his servants, then marched to the palace and waited for a bleary Ha-mahes to emerge from his rooms in the Ba Ka quarter of the House of Men.

Seated in the House's breakfasting gallery, alongside one hundred or so of the Prince's male relatives, Wab-sunu attempted an air of nonchalance.

'Are you feeling quite well?' Ha-mahes asked.

Pretending annoyance to cover his anxiety, Wab-sunu waved at Ha-mahes to be quiet. He indicated he wished to hear the day's announcements as they were read aloud by the House's head scribe, who stood nearby.

'...for the fourth month in a row an increase in tomb break-ins has been reported by all Governors,' the scribe boomed. 'Few of the stolen antiquities have been recovered, indicating they are being smuggled out of the Empire...'

A bevy of young princes ran past, the staccato clatter of their sandals on the floor causing Ha-mahes to frown.

Good, thought Wab-sunu. He's listening.

'...the annual reminder to all citizens that it is unlawful to stone adulterers has been issued...' the report continued.

'Why don't they just divorce?' a neighbouring breakfaster objected.

'Hush!' Ha-mahes said.

Wab-sunu caught himself holding his breath. He sipped his hibiscus tea to cover.

The scribe unfurled the next section of his papyrus. 'Hotep, Chief of the Medjay in Men-nefer, has issued a warrant for the capture of one Sharek of Saqqara for the murder of a stonemason from a prominent artisan family.'

There it was. Wab-sunu watched Ha-mahes lean forward.

'A witness reported seeing Sharek, a member of a notorious grave robber family, flee the scene. The Medjay Chief has placed Sharek's father under house arrest until his son is located.'

'Does it say how the stonemason died?' Ha-mahes asked.

'He was found in a tomb under renovation. It appears his head was crushed by a rock.'

'It hadn't simply fallen on him?'

The bureaucrat scanned his scroll. 'It does not say, oh Son of our King.' He continued to the next item.

Wab-sunu watched Ha-mahes from the corner of his eye. The younger man pressed his fingers to his temples, smudging his eye make up slightly. Then he rubbed one hand over his freshly shaven scalp as a smile bloomed on his lips. 'After breakfast, direct my staff to prepare for a journey,' he said.

Wab-sunu raised one brow.

'We're going to Men-nefer. My brother needs my help.'

Wab-sunu bowed his head to hide his pleasure. Ha-mahes seemed ensnared in the planned diversion.

Men-nefer (now Memphis near modern Cairo, Egypt)

Ten days after Roy the High Priest had stormed into his offices, Wab-sunu found himself alighting from a barge at the Men-nefer pier, the water of the Nile lapping beneath his feet, a sea of pyramids rising beyond the rows of palm and apple trees lining the opposite bank.

He ordered Ha-mahes' porters to convey the prince's luggage to his old rooms at the royal academy – chambers still filled to bursting with experiments from Ha-mahes' years at the school – then prepared to accompany his charge to the offices of the Governor of Men-nefer, Crown Prince Khaem-weset, heir apparent to the throne and Ha-mahes' oldest living brother.

'Hey! That's my craft!'

Wab-sunu and Ha-mahes turned to see a hairy-headed man lurch towards one of their servants, who was pulling the rope of a nearby vessel to move it out of their way.

The boatman stopped dead. Presumably he had recognised the royal party.

'I didn't mean to make a fuss,' he said.

Ha-mahes waved him on. 'Quite all right. Come, Wab-sunu, my brother's not expecting us.'

The weathered sailor grimaced as Wab-sunu bid him farewell then followed Ha-mahes.

The colonnade-lined avenues between the pier and Men-nefer's government offices had been enhanced since their last visit to the city. An army of colourful, 30 cubit-high effigies of Ramesses II now guarded the streets.

'Nice to see father again,' Ha-mahes said, gesturing at one of the statues.

Crown Prince Khaem-weset rose from his desk to greet his younger brother through gritted teeth. The mountains of papyrus scrolls piled about him teetered.

Shorter, fatter and much older than Ha-mahes, Wab-sunu could detect in Khaem-weset a trace of their mutual father in the shape of their jutting jaws. Otherwise, there was no hint of their siblingship – apart from the complicated web of lies, manipulation and intrigue that passed between them for brotherly love. Caught in the middle, there were days when Wab-sunu almost regretted accepting Khaem-weset's offer of a post as Ha-mahes' retainer. Almost.

'You?' Khaem-weset said. 'On top of everything else? I'm still repairing the damage you did to the Pyramid of Khufu on your last visit.'

Khaem-weset's voice rang with convincing grievance.

'I saved the city, didn't I?' Ha-mahes said. 'As it happens, this visit is also regarding a tomb...'

'I'm in the middle of excavating the Temple of Sekhmet, re-housing a fourth dynasty Pharaoh and overseeing the construction of Father's monuments to himself...'

At the mention of Ramesses II's self-tributes, both brothers rolled their eyes.

'…not to mention governing my own territories and, oh yes, preparing to rule the Empire–'

'It's about the murdered stonemason,' Ha-mahes plunged on.

Khaem-weset sighed. 'Wouldn't you be better off continuing upstream? Why not get back on your barge and sail on to Aswan? They've had a string of mysterious thefts, I hear.'

Ha-mahes would not deviate from his course. 'Your inept Chief of Medjay has arrested the wrong man.'

The Crown Prince gave his brother a hard look. 'I believe Hotep has the investigation in hand.'

'I'm certain he hasn't.'

Ha-mahes' voice held a note of petulance. Wab-sunu, once again, was impressed by how well the Governor could play on his younger brother's prejudices.

'Given the quantities of blue lotus you've been consuming, I doubt you know anything right now,' Khaem-weset said.

Ha-mahes' eyes flicked to Wab-sunu, who feigned ignorance of how the Crown Prince had caught wind of his recent drug spree. 'It's only to distract from the dull routine of vestigial royalty,' he said. 'I haven't touched it for days. As the Empire's only consulting Medjay–'

'There's no such thing,' Khaem-weset said, then paused. His shoulders drooped as he glared at his brother. 'However…'

Wab-sunu busied himself with retrieving a minor avalanche of scrolls that had tumbled from Khaem-weset's desk.

'However?' Ha-mahes said.

'After that business with throwing Pharaoh Teti out the window–'

'I warned you exposing his mummy to the air would make him ignite–'

The Crown Prince held up a silencing hand. 'After you defenestrated one of our illustrious forebears, when we'd only just opened his sarcophagus, I checked with Father's lawyers. I accept that I can't prevent your so-called investigations–'

'Good. Because I know Hotep's–'

Khaem-weset held up his hand again. 'But I do have the right to censure you for any reprehensible behaviour.'

'Censure?' Wab-sunu spoke for the first time since entering the room.

'The High Priests are keen to shortlist for a potential new Tut-ankh-amun – in case Father's self-worship spins even further out of control.'

Ha-mahes blanched. 'You wouldn't?'

Wab-sunu swallowed hard against the thought of his charge being treated so brutally. As atonement for the sins of his heretical father, Tut-ankh-amun had been sacrificed to the gods, his corpse mutilated to resemble Osiris and his soul denied a place in the afterlife. The threat of being nominated to suffer the same dreadful penance had cowed many a prince into obedience.

'I know the stonemason case you're referring to,' the Crown Prince continued. 'I'm confident you'll find his body in the embalming chambers of the necropolis at Saqqara.'

Ha-mahes smiled. 'Thank y–'

'But don't be rude to Hotep,' his brother cautioned.

'I won't if he isn–'

'And don't break anything.'

'I can't promi–'

'I'll provide you with an escort,' Khaem-weset said, still avoiding eye contact with Wab-sunu.

Ha-mahes grinned. 'I doubt they could keep up.'

As they left Khaem-weset, Wab-sunu's co-conspirator in the conservatorship of Ha-mahes, bells rang across the city of Men-nefer to mark the fourth hour of the day.

It was a short stroll to the river. As their barge slid from the city's banks toward the pyramids, Wab-sunu noticed the indignant old sailor from earlier sunning himself on the deck of his boat, watching their progress across the Nile.

He allowed himself a moment of relaxation. The gambit to distract Ha-mahes seemed to be working.

'It appears word of my blessed arrival precedes us,' Ha-mahes said as they approached the underground labyrinth of the necropolis.

A security Medjay and his dog, both bearing the insignia of Hotep's department, stood to one side of the entrance to the mortuary that was carved into the bedrock beneath Saqqara.

As their footsteps reverberated down the stone corridor, a churlish voice echoed into the tunnel. 'I'm not interested in anything you have to say, Ha-mahes.'

'Someone's watchmen are hard at work,' Ha-mahes whispered to Wab-sunu, then raised his voice. 'Is that any way to speak to the Son of a King?' Ha-mahes replied to the disgruntled Hotep.

Wab-sunu took stock as they entered the room of mummification. It contained one smouldering chief of police, several Medjay, two embalmers and a contingent of slowly desiccating corpses.

'You must have better things to do than interfere in my investigations,' Hotep frowned. 'Isn't there a vat of crocodile dung somewhere that requires your attention?'

'I'm just poking about,' Ha-mahes replied. 'Seeing what falls out.'

'Go home. There's nothing for you here.'

Ha-mahes clapped his hands. 'I'll be the judge of that.' He lowered his eyes to the woman standing to Hotep's right. 'If you would be so kind as to indicate the stonemason's body and arrange refreshments?'

She sniffed in indignation. 'As I remind you every time you darken my doorstep, Prince Ha-mahes, I am not your servant,' Saqqara's Chief Embalmer said as she swept one hand to indicate the room of bodies packed in drying salts. 'This is my House.' She locked eyes with Wab-sunu. 'Doctor.'

He had always liked Hemet-geb-ib. 'Doctor,' he returned the greeting, inclining his head. 'I think I'll organise tea.' He beckoned one of Hotep's many assembled offsiders to help.

Wab-sunu was aware of Ha-mahes and Hotep's continued jousting as he gave instructions to the Medjay. Hotep, as a King's grandson – via one of the many marriages between Ramesses II's daughters and sons – had also attended Ha-mahes' school in Men-nefer, where their ceaseless bickering had begun.

Wab-sunu re-joined the conversation as Hotep fussed, '…there's no such thing as a consulting Medjay.'

'And yet, here I stand.' Ha-mahes was at his most infuriating. 'So, from the beginning. Who reported the body?'

A Medjay standing behind one of the room's stone biers drew breath, then paused.

'Go on,' Hotep said with a flick of his hand. 'Get it over with. Prove to this idiot I'm right and then he can be back on the boat to Pi-Ramesses tonight.'

Wab-sunu certainly hoped not.

'Yes, my lord,' the eager young policeman said. 'Iset, a silversmith from the village of artisans, made the report.'

'Why was she there?'

With a minute shift in the set of his head and shoulders, Ha-mahes indicated he was now on the hunt.

'She is – ah, was – the stonemason's mother-in-law. She was delivering lunch to him at work.'

'He was working at the tomb where he was found?'

'Yes.'

'You found the package of food?'

'Yes – it was cakes.'

'Where were they?'

'On the ground.'

'Inside or outside the tomb?'

'Outside.'

'Eaten?'

'Ah…no?'

Hotep cleared his throat. His officer paused.

The soft drip-drip of blood and embalming fluids into the room's drainage channels filled the air.

Ha-mahes pressed on. 'Had she brought him anything to drink?'

After an approving nod from his superior, the officer replied. 'Some gourds of what smelled like bitter beer.'

'How many?'

'Two.'

'Were they full?'

'They broke when she dropped them on the ground.'

'They were also outside?'

'Yes.'

Hotep cleared his throat again. 'What's your obsession with some cakes and beer?'

'Ah,' the young Medjay stumbled.

Ha-mahes waved him on. 'And after she arrived with his lunch?'

'She saw a man she identified as Sharek, from a known family of grave robbers, running away from the tomb as she approached it. She went in, found the stonemason on the floor, dead, and the huge stone that killed him lying next to him. She ran to get help.'

Ha-mahes leaned toward Hotep. 'How do you know the stone didn't simply fall, and the boy was running for help himself?'

Hotep's kohl-rimmed eyes burned into Ha-mahes'. 'The stone was from the doorway on which the stonemason had been working. His body was several cubits inside the entrance, as was the stone. It couldn't have fallen on him from the doorway.'

'And why have you arrested this Sharek's father?'

'The stone was too heavy for one person to lift. Given he's the head of a family of thieves and his son was witnessed fleeing the scene, the father is the most obvious accomplice.'

'What motive do you suggest they had?' Wab-sunu asked.

'The motive of robbers everywhere, I'd say – greed,' Hotep said.

'Maybe the stonemason discovered them stealing something?' the young officer added.

Hemet-geb-ib raised her hand to halt the conversation. 'I wish to remind you that Seb here,' the embalmer indicated a young man sporting the latest fashion, 'is – was – the stonemason's brother-in-law. Iset is his mother.'

'You're an embalmer?' Ha-mahes asked.

'For now,' the hairless Seb said with a toss of his head, touching one hand to his naked hip. 'I'm also training to become a mummification priest.'

Wab-sunu wondered if Seb's career ambitions felt like a betrayal to Hemet-geb-ib. Mummification priests tended to look down on the embalmers who cared for the dead, all the while collecting huge fees from mourning families to bless the embalmers' work.

'Do you believe your mother?' Ha-mahes asked the young man. 'That she saw this Sharek running away from the tomb, where–?'

'Ahmose.'

'Where Ahmose was found?'

Seb nodded. 'Of course.'

Ha-mahes turned to the Chief Embalmer. 'Which one is the stonemason?'

She indicated the embalming altar next to Wab-sunu. 'Try not to throw my client out a window this time, or set fire to him, perhaps?'

Ha-mahes indicated with a gesture that he took no responsibility for that particular episode. 'I told you that phrase on his sarcophagus meant, "To burn with the heat of Ra".'

'Yes, yes, you're very clever,' she sniffed again. 'Just don't break anything.'

Ha-mahes grinned at her. 'You know, you're not the first person to say that today.'

Wab-sunu leant closer to the stonemason's body.

Ahmose's embalming process was well underway. The body had already been drained, his brain removed and internal organs — bar the heart — excised for desiccation. He was now packed in drying natron salts, the moisture of his flesh seeping through the crystalline layers into the drainage channels that led from the embalming platform. His organs lay nearby in their own salt cases.

'Are we able to examine the head wound?' Wab-sunu asked.

Seb made a small noise.

'The family of our newest client,' Hemet-geb-ib said to Seb, pointing to a bloated cadaver, 'made an appointment to choose his package. Perhaps you could prepare for their arrival?'

'What package should I recommend?' he asked.

'Middle-of-the-range to start with, but they may need to go down. Recommend a full contingent of mourners and standard prayers, but perhaps offer some wiggle room on the coffin.'

'And to supply their own blessed amulets for the wrappings?'

'If they want.'

Wab-sunu suppressed a smile. That would be money kept from the priests' pockets.

The young embalmer exited swiftly, passing a man entering with tea and cakes.

Hemet-geb-ib refused refreshment and began to scrape back the layer of salt surrounding Ahmose's upper body. Once it was exposed, she stood back to allow Ha-mahes, Wab-sunu and a hovering Hotep to examine him.

The flesh of Ahmose's face was a dreadful colour and consistency, his nose was oddly misshapen and — at such an early stage of desiccation — he emitted the vomitive odour of putrefaction. Wab-sunu was grateful for the evaporating draught that flowed through the chamber.

'Move him as little as possible,' Hemet-geb-ib ordered.

Wab-sunu lifted the stonemason's head enough to expose the back of it. The bone retained the large, blunt indentation of the blow that had killed him.

'What's that?' Ha-mahes pointed to a long, straight crease on Ahmose's right temple.

Hotep nudged him aside. 'There's a built-in granite coffin in the tomb. I gather that he hit his head on the corner of it as he fell.'

'Hmmm. And his organs?'

'I can brush back the natron for you to look,' Hemet-geb-ib said, 'but they're at such a delicate stage I can't let you touch them.'

The stonemason's liver, intestines, lungs and stomach were duly regarded. Wab-sunu could see nothing out of the ordinary. Ha-mahes leaned down, then stood back, then leaned toward Ahmose's organs again. He sniffed and asked, 'What package has his family chosen?'

Hemet-geb-ib frowned. 'One at the lower end of the range. But, being jewellers, they can provide a number of the amulets for Ahmose's wrappings themselves, and Seb may be allowed to bless them.'

Ha-mahes straightened. 'Where is the tomb he was working in?'

Apparently, the Prince had concluded this set of enquiries. Wab-sunu had rather wanted that cup of tea before moving on, but he was accustomed to disappointment.

'Let me have someone show you the way,' Hotep growled.

Their guide was the same young officer who had answered Ha-mahes' earlier questions.

Upon visual inspection, the scene of the crime was as described – an older tomb that was under renovation. Tool marks on the doorway suggested recently hewn stone, while sections of the walls were freshly plastered, awaiting painting. A rectangular granite coffin crouched in the middle of the room. Beside it, a shaft of light glinted on sticky brown stains spread across floor, some ten or more cubits inside the doorway.

Hotep was right, Wab-sunu thought. A stone from the entrance couldn't have fallen on a person in the middle of the room.

'Is that the rock?' Ha-mahes asked.

The Medjay nodded, pointing to the offending weapon next to the dried blood on the ground.

Ha-mahes gave it an exploratory push with his foot. He tried to pick it up. 'I could roll it, but I couldn't pick it up to bring it down on someone's head. Help me, Wab-sunu?'

Together they lifted the stone to head height, then dropped it again. It landed with a disconcerting thud.

'Perhaps it's time to visit the silversmith,' Ha-mahes suggested.

Their escorting Medjay led the way to Seb's home, and that of his mother, Iset.

The house of mud and straw looked to be a few centuries old, with a pleasant view of the pyramids. It was larger than the surrounding homes, with signs of further extensions underway. A cacophony of braying donkeys suggested large animal pens beyond the house's apple orchard.

Wab-sunu's knock on the lintel summoned two women to the front door, their silver amulets, bracelets and head adornments tinkling like a hundred tiny bells.

The older woman glanced first at Wab-sunu and then Ha-mahes. 'Greetings, oh Son of a King.' She genuflected perfunctorily.

'You're here about Ahmose,' the younger woman said, tears rolling down her cheeks.

His widow, Wab-sunu surmised.

The older woman pushed the younger one back into the house. 'Go and lie down.'

She complied, shuffling into the dark interior.

'Please excuse my daughter, your highness,' the remaining woman said. 'Seb sent a runner to let us know you might visit – I'll answer any questions you have.'

'Thank you...' Ha-mahes let his query hang.

'I am called Iset.' She remained standing in the doorway.

'Might we sit?'

She hesitated. 'Of course.' She inclined her head and invited them to the house's inner courtyard. 'I apologise, I've only just returned from the riverbank markets. I've made no preparations for your visit.'

Hotep's officer remained outside.

On their walk through the interior of the home, Wab-sunu saw evidence of repairs to the aging structure and a further, significant extension to the back wing of the house.

A nervous maid hovered by the front wall of the courtyard. 'My apologies, my lady. Would you like me to serve tea?'

'Yes please,' Wab-sunu murmured.

'Of course I would,' Iset snapped at the same time.

She looked at Wab-sunu and tsked. 'New girl. Doesn't seem to have been trained at all in her previous household.'

A solid middle-aged man entered the courtyard from the east rooms to join them. He introduced himself as Pepi, jeweller and husband of Iset.

Ha-mahes wasted no time interrogating the bereaved in-laws. 'Did you really see Sharek running away from the tomb when you arrived with Ahmose's lunch?'

Iset met his gaze, her expression calm. 'Yes.'

'What reason could he have for killing Ahmose?'

'I have no idea.' She seemed to find the question irritating.

'Your daughter seems distraught,' Wab-sunu said.

'Of course she is,' Pepi said.

'But you don't,' Ha-mahes countered.

Pepi was about to answer, but Iset interjected with a brittle smile. 'Ahmose wasn't the best of men.'

'What do you mean?'

She waved a hand, scores of silver and gold bangles chiming. 'He was consorting with those grave robbers, Sharek's people.'

'And?' Ha-mahes pressed.

Pepi sighed. 'Not just the boy, Sharek. Ahmose was also spending his work days with their daughter.'

'And that makes him a bad man, how?' Wab-sunu asked.

The burly jewel smith glanced at his wife. 'The daughter is said to resemble Bastet.'

'She's not that good looking,' Iset spat.

From the brief glimpse Wab-sunu had of her at the front door, their newly-widowed daughter was also classically beautiful. But looks weren't necessarily a factor in affairs of the heart.

'And,' Pepi cleared his throat, 'Iset saw them kissing one day.'

His wife nodded.

'Where was this?' Ha-mahes said.

'At the tomb,' she said. 'One of my servants told me she caught Ahmose kissing that woman. Then he started working longer hours. I began delivering his meals myself to keep an eye on them.'

'Was that the same servant who's preparing tea now?' Wab-sunu asked.

Iset shook her head with a chorus of tinkling. 'No. She's gone to Karnak to visit relatives.'

'But you said Iset saw them kissing,' Ha-mahes said to Pepi.

'I did.' Iset was adamant. 'About a week before he was killed.'

'Have you told your daughter?' Wab-sunu asked.

Pepi shook his head. 'We were trying to decide whether it was right to tell her, or spare her that pain, and then–'

Ha-mahes leaned closer to the jeweller. 'Were you worried he was going to divorce her?'

'Of course not!' Pepi's voice rose. 'We're a law-abiding artisan family. He'd never leave us for a house of grave robbers.'

Ha-mahes stood abruptly. 'I think it's time I speak to them directly. What's the father's name?'

Pepi and Iset had both startled at Ha-mahes' sudden movement. Iset put a calming hand on Pepi's arm and said, 'Khay. Khay the Grave Robber.'

Wab-sunu was not impressed; he had wanted the cup of tea that the housemaid was now carrying across the courtyard.

Their escorting Medjay guided the tea-denied Wab-sunu and his annoying Prince to a meagre one-room home in the least desirable quarter of the village. A notice of house arrest adorned the front lintel.

'Are you Khay the Grave Robber?' Ha-mahes demanded as the front door opened a crack.

Lines crinkled a deeply tanned man's face. 'I was born to be. Now, it's just Khay.'

Wab-sunu had expected a known thief to be gruff and defensive. Instead, Khay invited Ha-mahes and his retainer in.

'Neferet, my daughter,' he introduced the only other person in the tiny dirt-floored room.

Wab-sunu tried not to stare. She *was* as beautiful as the goddess Bastet.

Neferet remained standing as the three men lowered themselves to the floor. She took two steps to a side doorway and called up to the roof, 'Could you make tea for five, please?'

'Of course,' a woman's voice echoed down the narrow ladder.

'Where's your son?' Ha-mahes asked.

Khay ignored – or did not notice – the Prince's lack of pleasantries. Instead he shook his head. 'He hasn't sent word. But I know in my heart, Sharek has nothing to do with...' he trailed off, looking toward the notice on the front door, 'that.'

'Sharek would never attack another person,' Neferet added. 'Besides, what reason could he possibly have to kill Ahmose?'

Ha-mahes' eyes, suddenly blazing, bore into hers. 'You.'

Neferet's smooth forehead furrowed. 'Me? Why?'

'Because you were hoping he'd leave his wife for you, but feared he wouldn't.'

After a heartbeat of silence Khay and Neferet both laughed. A second woman descended the ladder, balancing a tray and feeling for the ground with one foot.

'Murder is no laughing matter,' Wab-sunu said.

Khay sobered. 'We're upset by Ahmose's death, believe me. But that's the first time we've laughed since—'

'What so funny?' the second woman asked, placing a cup in front of each person and pouring dark red tea.

'Thank you,' Wab-sunu said out of more than mere politeness. She smiled at the depth of his gratitude.

The goddess-brought-to-life chuckled once more and put an arm around the tea-serving woman who settled beside her. 'The idea that I was sleeping with Ahmose.'

'Neferet will never marry,' Khay said, shaking his head. 'But she's good with the business, as is Sharek, so they'll share it between them when I go.'

'How do you inherit grave robbing?' Wab-sunu asked.

'I told you, that's not me anymore.' Khay sounded more weary than angry.

'Then what business?' Ha-mahes asked.

'Tomb restoration. We have a contract with the Governor to locate, report and restore old tombs in the region.'

'Ahhh.'

Wab-sunu had learned that that particular pitch and intonation meant Ha-mahes had just pieced something together. What was it? 'That's an interesting career change,' he offered, to keep the conversation flowing.

'I don't want my children living in fear of a knock on the door. Tomb restoration was a way for us to turn legitimate.'

Neferet frowned again. 'Go back, please. You didn't explain why you thought I would be interested in Ahmose? I don't sleep with men.'

'Many people sleep with both women and men before they're married,' Wab-sunu said.

'Not me. I only like women – and now just one woman in particular.' Neferet squeezed her partner's hand tightly. 'Kyky.'

The object of her affection blushed and rested her head on Neferet's shoulder.

'Do you deny spending time with Ahmose?' Ha-mahes asked.

'Of course not. He was working with us at the tomb.'

'Sharek was at the tomb with Ahmose the day he was killed?' Wab-sunu said.

Neferet nodded. 'I left them both there in the late morning.'

'What were they doing?' Ha-mahes said.

'Ahmose was completing repairs to the stonework in the doorway. I was there to take measurements for replacement doors, and Sharek was clearing away after finishing his plaster work. He was there for Ahmose, too. For safety.'

'Safety from what?'

'In case—' Khay's voice caught. 'In case a stone he was working on fell.'

'No other reason?' Ha-mahes said.

'I'm aware of the irony when I say this, but there have been some unsavoury types hanging around,' Khay said.

'By which you mean…?'

'I was approached by someone to go back into tomb robbing. I said no, but I was worried they might still be in the area.'

'Neferet, did you often see Iset, Ahmose's mother-in-law, at the tomb?'

With a clucking of their tongues, both women indicated that they knew exactly who Ha-mahes was referring to. 'She came to the worksite most days,' Neferet said. 'Always staring daggers at me and shooing Sharek out of her way.'

'Wearing a lot of jewellery?' Ha-mahes asked.

Wab-sunu wondered why Ha-mahes was asking about Iset's bangles.

'Not always,' Neferet said. 'Some days she sounded like an entire funeral procession on her own, other days she wore almost none. Why?'

Ha-mahes ignored her question. 'She mentioned Ahmose had been working long hours.'

'He was putting extra away,' Khay said, 'saving up to buy a house so he and his wife could move out of her parents'.'

Wab-sunu looked at the three people sitting in front of them. They seemed to have cared for Ahmose in life. So how did they figure in his death?

Ha-mahes apparently had the same thought. 'If your dealings with Ahmose were legal, why did he die at a worksite you were responsible for? And where is your son?'

Khay's face fell, tears welling. 'I don't know. But if you find any trace of Sharek, please tell us.'

Wab-sunu couldn't bear the quiver of fear in the old man's voice. He sipped from his cup of frothy hibiscus tea instead. The blend of dried flowers and earthy spices was refreshing after this long, frustrating day.

Ha-mahes, on the other hand, seemed invigorated without the benefit of tea. After bidding Khay, Neferet and Kyky farewell, Ha-mahes said he wished to eat. Wab-sunu had to admit he felt peckish too.

Crossing the Nile once more – the same grinning boatman still lounging on his craft at the pier – they bid their escort farewell and began to stroll toward the food district.

'One moment,' Ha-mahes said, running after the retreating Medjay.

They spoke briefly, then Ha-mahes returned to Wab-sunu's side.

'And?' Wab-sunu said.

'I had an errand for him.'

Apparently Ha-mahes wasn't going to divulge anything further.

As they continued into the city, Wab-sunu noticed Ha-mahes checking over his shoulder repeatedly. 'One of Hotep's people?' he asked quietly.

'He's up ahead, fifth doorway on the left.'

'One of your brother's operatives?'

'She's leading the cart and donkey to our rear.'

'Who then?'

'Whoever they are, they'll reveal themselves in due course.'

Wab-sunu huffed. 'It's incredibly annoying when you do that.'

Ha-mahes flashed him a grin. 'I know.'

Between bites of felafel stuffed in pita bread, they summarised the day's findings.

'We have one dead stonemason, allegedly murdered by two assailants who crushed his head from behind with a rock–' Ha-mahes began.

'And one missing plasterer, of former grave robber stock,' Wab-sunu wiped a drop of parsley juice from his chin.

'The mother-in-law of the deceased claims he was having an affair with the sister of the missing plasterer, who denies it, and–' Ha-mahes' volume was increasing with each utterance. 'I've got it!' He was almost shouting now. 'I know who murdered the stonemason!'

'Wonderful,' Wab-sunu said in hushed tones. 'I await your conclusions with bated breath – however, should you announce this to the entire city?'

'Absolutely,' Ha-mahes said, almost purring. He bent to stare directly into Wab-sunu's eyes. 'Sorry, I think this is going to be rough.'

'What?' Wab-sunu asked, before the world went sideways.

'That is the kind of thing that makes me want to retire early,' Wab-sunu said, pinching his nose to stem the flow of blood. 'You all but invited them to attack us.'

'I had to know who our third tail was,' Ha-mahes answered, touching one cheek gingerly and wincing.

'Did you find out?'

'Don't be cross. And no.' He held two fragments of his torn skirt together and tsked. 'Irreparable. But I have ascertained what happened to the deceased stonemason.'

'Yes?'

'Patience, my dear Wab-sunu. There is but one detail to confirm and then all shall be revealed.'

'Wonderful, I hope it was worth risking my life.'

'You were never in danger.'

They limped on in silence, Wab-sunu fuming and Ha-mahes presumably basking in his own cleverness.

The following afternoon, by invitation of Khaem-weset, as Governor of Men-nefer, all persons related to enquiries into the death of Ahmose the stonemason gathered in the embalming chamber of the Saqqara necropolis. The motley assortment of princes, Medjay, bureaucrats, embalmers and artisans left little room for the withering cadavers. Hemet-geb-ib scowled at anyone who stood too close to her clients.

Crown Prince Khaem-weset greeted both Ha-mahes and Wab-sunu without commenting on their spectacular facial bruises. Wab-sunu gathered that he knew exactly how they had been earned.

As Khay the ex-grave robber and his divinely beautiful daughter Neferet shuffled into the room, Ha-mahes launched into what Wab-sunu expected would be his typical self-congratulatory denouement.

'I knew you were concealing something from the start,' Ha-mahes said to his brother, reciting the opening line of his favourite ritual. 'Since when did you allow me to interfere in Hotep's investigations with such little protest?'

Khaem-weset twitched one shoulder and avoided Wab-sunu's gaze.

'I deduced you must have had reason to believe Hotep was on the wrong path.'

'And?' the Crown Prince prompted.

'As you are always at such pains to impress upon me, your days overflow with responsibility. What could have been brought to your attention that your Chief of Police overlooked?'

'Go on.' He seemed to be enjoying his brother's performance.

'What do you care for above all else? Digging up the past. You knew about Khay's contract with the city to restore the tomb Ahmose died in, because you track everything to do with your precious ancient monuments.'

Khaem-weset nodded his agreement.

'Since you had reason to believe that Khay's family are now law-abiding,' Ha-mahes continued, 'you thought the guilty party might be hiding elsewhere.'

'I'm surprised you didn't mention this to me, your highness,' Hotep said.

'The contract is a matter of public record, and I have faith in the numerous investigative officers at your disposal...' Khaem-weset's voice was deceptively bland.

The Chief of the Medjay flushed, then grew quiet.

'I told you,' Khay said, his voice bouncing around the stone grotto. 'We were asked to rob the tombs we were working on, but we turned it down. We're not grave robbers any longer.'

'I know,' Ha-mahes said.

'I'm not convinced,' said Hotep.

'Hush,' Ha-mahes said. 'The grown-ups are talking.'

Hotep's face twisted into a snarl.

'So where's my son?' Khay said, clutching the edge of the stone bier he was standing behind.

'In all likelihood, the same place as Pepi's maid,' Ha-mahes said.

'Sharek's run off with a girl?' Neferet asked.

'She's the key to unlocking Ahmose's murder,' Ha-mahes said.

Iset frowned. 'Our maid?'

'You said that she saw Ahmose kissing Neferet?' Ha-mahes asked Iset.

'Yes!' she insisted.

'Ridiculous,' Neferet said.

The two women glared at each across the salted bellies of mummifying bodies.

'It would be easier all round if the maid could confirm this herself,' Khaem-weset said.

Ha-mahes looked to the Medjay who had escorted them the previous day. He nodded.

'She may be difficult to locate,' Ha-mahes said.

'Why?' Hotep demanded.

'I told you, she went to visit an aunt in Karnak,' Iset said.

'Can this wait until she returns?' said Seb, who had been silent until now.

'I've learned that she never arrived,' Ha-mahes said. 'Her mother's frantic. There's been no trace of her since she left Men-nefer over three weeks ago.'

'How terrible,' Pepi said. He seemed genuinely sorry.

'It's strange that you hadn't heard, Pepi,' Ha-mahes continued. 'As the maid's mother has spoken to Iset about her disappearance a number of times.'

Pepi looked disturbed.

Iset patted her husband's arm. 'With Ahmose's death, and our household in mourning, I didn't want to add to your burden.'

Khay's voice was strained. 'How is Sharek connected to the maid? And why did you say you hope they're together?'

'I'll explain momentarily,' Ha-mahes replied. To Hotep, he said, 'You got one thing right.'

The Chief of Men-nefer's police force appeared to be as confused as everyone else in the room. 'What was that?'

'It would have taken two people to lift that stone to hit Ahmose in the back of the head.'

'Are you saying Sharek did kill Ahmose? With this maid I've never heard of?' Neferet slammed one fist on a draining platform. 'No! He's not that kind of person.'

Hemet-geb-ib raised a cautionary hand. 'Careful. Not near the bodies.'

'Sharek would not have done this, even for the love of a girl,' Khay insisted.

For several moments no-one spoke, the hush broken only by the drip, drip of brining fluids oozing from the chamber's corpses.

Wab-sunu's head spun with possibilities. Was Ha-mahes saying Sharek and the maid had killed Ahmose and then absconded together? But the maid had disappeared before Ahmose was killed.

'Seb knows what happened to Ahmose, don't you?' Ha-mahes broke the silence.

'No!' The young embalmer's voice trembled. 'You can't mean Mother was involved.'

'Did I say that?'

'She's not strong enough to have picked up that rock,' Seb said.

'One thing became obvious yesterday,' Ha-mahes said, changing course again.

Khaem-weset snorted. 'Just get on with it, will you? No need to impress everyone with how astute you are.'

'Yes, please do get on, Ha-mahes,' Wab-sunu urged.

'Spoilsports,' Ha-mahes smiled at them and waved a hand toward the mound of salt containing the deceased stonemason. 'After examining Ahmose it became apparent that the blow to the back of his head isn't what killed him. At least, not in isolation.'

'What did then?' Hotep said.

'Haven't you wondered why Ahmose stayed still long enough for someone to hit him over the head? The stone used was large and unwieldy – he would have had time to move out of its way.'

'You're saying?'

'He was already dead, or unconscious. He had suffered a blow to the side of his head and was already on the ground when he was hit from behind. His face was pushed further into the dirt and his nose broken.'

'What made him fall?' Wab-sunu asked.

'That bitter beer in the gourds?' Ha-mahes nodded toward the Medjay who had provided the scene of the crime report yesterday. 'The bitterness you could smell came from a tincture of apple seeds. I've observed the smell before, in the organs of certain murder victims in the Pi-Ramesses morgue. The scent was emanating from Ahmose's liver yesterday; faint, but there. Isn't that so, Seb?'

The fashionable young man blanched. 'No! What? How would I know?'

'I told you,' his mother said, moving to stand between Seb and Ha-mahes. 'I saw that Sharek boy there.'

'Oh, I know,' Ha-mahes said. 'Ahmose was there, Sharek was there, you were there, and at least one other person.'

'I was here, at work, when Ahmose was attacked,' Seb said.

'But both your parents went to see Ahmose that day, didn't they?' Ha-mahes countered.

Iset shook her head, a thousand tiny bells chiming.

'You poisoned Ahmose's drink with seeds from the apples growing in your orchard. After he collapsed, hitting the side of his head on the stone coffin as he fell, you and Pepi lifted a stone from the doorway that finished that innocent man's life.'

Pepi swung a furious arm in Neferet's direction. 'He wasn't innocent!'

Neferet waved a fist back at him. 'I wasn't sleeping with Ahmose. He wasn't an adulterer!'

'He broke his wedding vows to my daughter!' Pepi screamed. 'He deser–'

The large jeweller fell silent.

'He deserved to die by stoning, because that's the traditional punishment for adultery?' Ha-mahes asked.

Both Pepi and Iset stared at the ground.

'You killed your son-in-law,' Ha-mahes pressed. 'You will be fed to the crocodiles for this, and the weight of your sins means you will fail to enter the afterlife.'

Pepi's head flew up. 'My heart is light! I did what was righ–'

Iset hissed, 'Shut up!' and punched her husband's shoulder.

Ha-mahes grinned at Hotep, who sighed and ordered two of his Medjay to guard the murderous pair.

'Are you saying Sharek wasn't there?' Khay asked, his voice hopeful.

'I'm afraid he was,' Ha-mahes said. 'He drank from the second gourd and also passed out.'

'What have you done to him?' Khay's voice wavered. 'Where is my boy?'

Pepi and Iset refused to answer.

Crown Prince Khaem-weset cleared his throat. 'Ha-mahes?'

'Only too pleased to be of assistance,' Ha-mahes said with a cheeky wink at Hotep. He closed the distance between himself and Iset in one large stride and raised one of her arms, then shook it. The jingling of a hundred fine bangles echoed through the stone mortuary.

'You're fencing stolen antiquities, aren't you?' he said to Iset. 'And Ahmose had discovered what you were doing.'

Iset turned her face toward the wall.

Ha-mahes turned to Khay. 'The person who approached you to return to grave robbing. Had you seen them before?'

Khay shook his head.

'Part of an inter-city operation, I'd wager,' Ha-mahes said to Khaem-weset.

'Ahhhh,' his brother said. 'The missing grave goods stolen from tombs across the Empire.'

Ha-mahes nodded. 'Exactly. It appears that the looted items are melted down, formed into simple pieces,' – he rattled Iset's limp wrist again – 'and passed on to jewellery makers, who then keep a cut of the takings for themselves.'

'Who is going to question jewellers wearing a lot of jewellery?' Wab-sunu felt the need to contribute.

'Indeed,' Ha-mahes said. 'The rest, I expect, is returned to their supplier in whatever form of jewellery is requested.'

'Meaning the stolen items can be sitting in plain sight and no-one can identify them,' Khaem-weset said.

Ha-mahes nodded and looked at Hotep. 'That was something else you got right. Ahmose's murderer was motivated by greed.'

'Our hearts were pure!' Pepi said, struggling against the large Medjay holding him in place.

'Yours may have been,' Ha-mahes said, 'but your wife's wasn't. Didn't you wonder how you can afford to extend your house? She's been using her cut of the bangles to craft funerary jewellery, which Seb then sells to bereaved families on the cheap. They're also using the proceeds to pay for his new career as a priest, isn't that right, Seb?'

The young man was staring at his parents, his mouth opening and closing soundlessly like a fish flopping on the banks of the Nile.

'Seb?' Hemet-geb-ib said.

His eyes darted furtively toward the mortuary's entrance.

'Never cross my threshold again!' The chief embalmer looked fit to launch herself across the room at her grifting apprentice.

'Ahmose discovered what you were doing and confronted you, didn't he?' Ha-mahes said to the woman whose arm he still grasped. 'Did he warn you he was going to the police?'

Iset barked a harsh laugh. 'The fool wanted to give me a chance to stop, to put things right.' Her voice grew sombre. 'It was already too late. The moment he discovered our operation, his fate was sealed.'

'And Sharek?' Neferet asked. 'What have you done with him?'

Iset grew silent once more.

'I suspect that Sharek and the missing maid are being held by Iset's employer,' Ha-mahes said. 'Who are you working for?'

She ignored him.

He looked at Khay. 'Who asked you to steal for them?'

The ex-grave robber shook his head. 'I'm sorry. He left no way of contacting him.'

Ha-mahes grabbed the silversmith by her shoulders and shouted. 'Who is he?' He glanced at Khaem-weset, then continued. 'I will close the gates of the afterlife to you if you don't tell me!' he threatened Iset. 'I will see you buried with no heart...'

'My Lord,' Pepi said. 'Please, no!'

'...or scarab beetle...'

Every person in the room gasped. Wab-sunu heard a Medjay whisper, 'Like Tut-ankh-amun.'

Though her lips were clamped together, Wab-sunu could see the desperation in Iset's eyes.

'And both your children,' Ha-mahes added.

Perhaps it was the cumulative effect of the prince's threats; perhaps it was the whimpers from her son – something penetrated Iset's fear to force a name to her tongue.

'Nefuu,' she whispered.

Ha-mahes frowned. 'The navigator?'

'He s-said–' she stuttered.

Ha-mahes shook her again. 'Said what!?'

'He said to tell you, "Come and find me".'

Navigator...sailor...boatman. The boatman! Wab-sunu conjured the memory of the man who had yelled at their porters yesterday for touching the rope to his boat. And had watched them cross the Nile with unnerving intensity on no fewer than three occasions. Would he still be there, lying indolently on his barge? Was he behind a vast tomb raider racket? Was he holding the maid and Sharek hostage? Was he behind their third tail in the street yesterday?

Wab-sunu noticed a glint in Ha-mahes' eye. 'It's a short run to the pier,' he suggested.

With an answering grin, Ha-mahes thrust the sagging Iset into Hotep's arms. 'Yours, I believe?' He turned to Khay. 'I'll do everything in my power to bring your son home.'

As the former grave robber touched his hand to his heart – and an outraged Hotep stood with his mouth agape – the Egyptian Empire's only consulting Medjay nodded to his eldest brother and sprang through the door of the mortuary, a distorted cry echoing down the stone corridor. 'Come along, Wab-sunu!'

The doctor hesitated long enough to seek his leave from the Crown Prince.

Khaem-weset wiped a bead of sweat from one cheek. 'Keep him safe.'

'Always.'

Wab-sunu plunged after Ha-mahes, hoping his future contained a distinct lack of burning Pharaohs, exploding mummies and blue-lotus soaked princes.

He wouldn't bet on it.

AUTHOR'S NOTES

The blue lotus, or blue Egyptian lotus, was used to create both perfumes and psychoactive drugs in ancient Egypt and ancient Maya. It is currently a prohibited Class 1 substance in a number of eastern European countries.

It takes the seeds of around 20 apples, or 200 seeds, to produce sufficient cyanide to kill an adult. Groves of apples were grown on the banks of the Nile during the New Kingdom (when this story is set). Some people can detect the scent of cyanide in the deceased.

The Medjay started with people (female and male warriors) only from the Medjay tribe, who formed a guard for the Pharaoh. Over time the term became more generalised for police, and anyone could apply to be trained and join the force. By the time of the New Kingdom there were dozens of specialised departments of Medjay/police. This included dog trainers/handlers and many Medjay were teamed with a dog, just like our contemporary police.

While non-royals in ancient Egypt were free to have as much sex as they liked before marriage, and divorce was open to both women and men to initiate, adultery was sternly frowned on. Although officially discouraged, stoning or murder by a whole village was a common form of mob justice unleashed against those who broke their wedding vows.

NOTES ON NAMES

Ha-mahes. A name comprising the ancient Egyptian god, "Ha", meaning protector, and "Mahes", meaning a protector of Ma'at's truth. The hieroglyphics for these two figures combined suggest a lion-headed man dispensing justice with a sword. Holmes as an avenging protector of the truth? Seems fitting.

Wab-sunu. Composed of the ancient Egyptian "wab", meaning purification priest, or confessor, and "sunu", a doctor. Watson as a doctor to whom Holmes often confesses seems appropriate.

Hemet-geb-ib. Hieroglyphic purists may roll over in their sarcophagi at this one: "hemet" means wife (also woman, uterus or rippling water in a basin); "Geb" may mean son of; and "ib", heart. The earliest mention of "hudde" in Britain meant mind or heart. As the director of a funerary home in ancient Egypt, Mrs Hudson has a whole new lease on life.

Hotep. The ancient Egyptian word "hotep (htp)" meant altar. The name "Lestrade" seems to derive from a French village in the midi-Pyrenes. It means a raised platform. Poor Lestrade – no matter the time nor place, Holmes is never far away.

Khaem-weset. In 1229 BCE, Crown Prince Khaem-weset was heir to the throne of Khemet, a.k.a. the Black Land, a.k.a. ancient Egypt. He was Governor of Men-nefer at the time and an avid antiquarian. He's revered by certain archaeologically-obsessed people as the first known Egyptologist, including the eponymous protagonist of my archaeological mystery series, Dr Pimms.

Nefuu. The ancient Egyptian word "nefuu" meant navigator; just as the Irish name "Ó Muircheartaigh" means navigator. The Anglicised version of "Ó Muircheartaigh"? Moriarty.

Roy the High Priest of Amun. The highest spiritual position to which one could aspire in the empire of Ramesses II was the High Priest of Amun. In the latter years of Ramesses II's reign, the name of the High Priest is recorded as "Roma called Roy (ry)". His name really was Roy.

As for what was done to **Tut-ankh-amun**, you'll have to read the third novel in my Dr Pimms series, *Egyptian Enigma*, to find out more. But be warned – it was terrible.

THE ENEMY WITHIN

Raymond Gates

If there was one thing John Watson had learned during his life, it was that any phone call after midnight only conveyed bad news. So it was that when he grabbed his vibrating mobile phone, cracked an eye open and saw that it was just after 2am, he had to resist the urge to ignore the call and roll back over to sleep. Had he not recognised the caller was his sister, Harriet, he might have done just that.

Instead, he thumbed the accept button. 'What's up, Harry?'

'Hey. Sorry. Were you asleep?'

'That's what people generally do at this time of night.'

'Shut up,' she said. 'Listen. You gotta get back up here. Nan's heard from Uncle.'

Watson rubbed his eyes. 'Which uncle?'

'You know! That fella that you stayed with last month.'

He sat up. The air in the room felt thicker. Closer.

The uncle she referred to was their Uncle Bill. He knew she wouldn't say his name. No one who knew him, especially no one in the family, would say it since he died.

'What do you mean she heard from him?'

Harriet clucked on the other end of the line. 'You know what Nan's like. She heard from him! Tonight! She went off into one of them trances she has and when she came out of it, she said he'd reached out to her. Said he'd told her things, and she needed to talk to you about it. You and that partner of yours. Sherlock.'

'Wait,' he said. He reached over to turn a bedside lamp on. 'This isn't making any sense.'

'Pfft. How long you been in this family? When has anything made sense?'

He chuckled. Yes, the Watson family sure had its share of strangeness. Maybe that was what had turned him from a promising career in forensic medicine to become a paranormal investigator.

Who are you kidding, John? It was Holmes. It's always been Holmes.

'Oi! You there?'

'Yeah I'm here.'

'Get your arse on a plane and get up here. Nan says it's got to be right now. Today.' Harriet said something else, muffled, like she'd turned her head away from the phone. An older, female voice said something in return. 'She needs your help to get him back.'

'What? What do you mean get him back?'

'How would I know? I'm just the bloody messenger! Just do it! Less you'd rather talk with her about it?'

'Nah, she's right,' said Watson. He knew better than to argue with Nan. 'It's not like I can just drop everything though, you know.'

'You'd better figure it out. She wants you here pronto. Why do you think I'm calling you at this hour?'

Watson didn't have to speculate. When Nan said jump, you didn't even ask how high. You just jumped as high as you could.

'Yeah. Righto,' he said. 'Let me figure out what flight I can get, and I'll text you the details.'

'Both of you. Nan says it's got to be both of you.' Harriet paused. 'I don't think I've ever met your workmate before, have I?'

'Nope.' Watson pulled the sheet aside and swung his long skinny legs over the side of the bed. His bladder needed this conversation to be over.

'What are they, some big secret?'

'Nope. You just haven't met her yet.'

'Ooo, it's a girl!' Harriet sounded like she had when they were young teenagers.

'Bye, Harry,' Watson said and ended the call before she could answer.

He walked to the bathroom. He sat on the toilet and used his phone to search for flights. The first available was at seven that morning. That gave him enough time to shower, pack, maybe eat, and get to the airport.

He reached over from where he sat, turned the shower on, and let it run until the room steamed up. He took a deep breath of humidified air and sighed.

'This better not be some crazy old black woman thing,' he said as he flushed and moved into the shower.

Watson always liked to be prepared. His business partner, Holmes, insisted upon it. The hour and a half flight from Sydney to Coolangatta afforded time for him to recall the events of his Uncle Bill's demise. He placed a blank legal pad on the tray table and began to write.

A month earlier he'd stayed with Bill while up that way working a case. The night he returned home, he had received another call in the middle of the night. That call, however, had been from the Southport police station.

The Detective Sergeant on duty at the time, Doyle he thought his name was, had advised Watson that Bill had been found dead in his fourth-floor apartment. Watson had seen the autopsy report. The coroner concluded Bill had been poisoned, but wasn't able to identify the specific agent used. Bill had expelled copious amounts of vomit and diarrhoea, neither the external fluids nor his internal contents had revealed any known toxicology. Watson hadn't shared the details with anyone but Holmes. He didn't want the family to know the specifics. He wished he didn't know them either. They'd all experienced enough trauma when his parents had died. Granted, that happened when he was a child, however it was still a fresh wound to him.

The police had nothing to go on. There was no apparent motive, no signs of forced entry to the apartment, no theft, and no evidence of any kind beyond Bill's corpse. There was always the suspicion that it had been a hate crime; anti-Aboriginal sentiment had been higher and more prolific with the election of the new extreme right State Government. However, the police dismissed that early in the investigation, reasoning that it was too targeted and too violent to be simply racially motivated.

It turned out DS Doyle had contacted Watson not only as a family member but also as a potential suspect. As one of the last people to see Bill alive, and one with medical training, it seemed a reasonable suspicion. Trouble was they had nothing beyond those few facts, and so after several long rounds of questioning, they'd dropped it.

As far as Watson knew the case remained open, though cold. No one expected the police to achieve any sort of resolution. Crimes against blackfellas seldom did. He had tried looking into Bill's death for himself but came up with nothing. He'd pursued Holmes to add her infallible reasoning to the case, but she'd brushed it off, stating that there was far too little to go on to dedicate herself to an investigation at the time. It had both wounded and angered Watson. Though he'd argued and pleaded with her, nothing brought Holmes around.

Now Nan had heard from Uncle Bill. Nan was both a community Elder and the matriarch of the family. She was also renowned as a gifted psychic.

As a child, Watson had been fascinated with her ability to tell him what he was thinking, or help him find a lost toy, or know when someone was coming to visit. As a grown man – in particular one who had studied science and medicine in depth, who had pursued forensics and the understanding of making unknown things known, and who made a living investigating and debunking many claims of the psychic or supernatural – he had come to believe Nan was little more than a crafty old woman. At best, a good guesser, and at worst a social engineer.

Yet he knew she wouldn't demand he come up if it wasn't something especially important. Whether she'd communed with Bill's spirit or not, it was worth looking into.

Someone touched his shoulder and he looked up at the flight attendant.

'If you could put your tray up, please? We'll be landing shortly,' she said.

'No worries.' He put the pad back into his carry-on bag and folded the table up. Out the window, the blue ocean gave way to golden sandy beaches. Houses and cars rushed by as they descended towards the runway. The plane touched down with a bump and a screech. A moment later, one of the attendants announced their arrival into Coolangatta.

Watson looked out towards the airport and wondered what awaited him.

Harriet greeted him and took him to the baggage claim, then to her car. She questioned him about the whereabouts of his partner. He answered that Holmes would be joining them later. She rolled her eyes but said nothing. Watson was grateful for that.

They drove along the motorway, bypassing much of the city and suburbs, heading for Upper Coomera, where Harriet lived. Nan lived at the back of her place in a granny flat. Harriet had taken her in when their grandfather had died years ago.

'So, what did Nan actually say?' Watson asked.

'Oh, man.' Harriet glanced at him and then back at the road. It was enough for Watson to see the fatigue and frustration in her eyes.

'So, she comes in around midnight and bangs the hell out of my bedroom door. She's practically screaming at me to get up. I was scared shitless! I thought she'd had an accident and hurt herself or something.'

'Yeah, I'll bet.' Watson nodded.

'Yeah. So, I open the door and she's in tears. I mean, full-on bawling. That scared me even more! I was asking her what's wrong and checking her over to see what had happened to her. Anyway, I finally got her to settle a bit and got her into the kitchen. Thought I'd make her a cuppa and it might help calm her down. That's when she told me he'd come to her.'

'He came to her. Like an apparition?'

'Nah. More like a voice in her head. She said he woke her up, but she couldn't see nothing.'

'Couldn't see anything,' Watson said.

Harriet poked her tongue out at him. 'She just said she could hear him talking to her. She said he told her his spirit was restless. That he couldn't rest until we got the mongrel that did that to him.'

Harriet pulled into her driveway and turned the motor off. She stared at Watson with a look he couldn't read.

'She said he told her that you needed to do it. You needed to be the one to do it.'

'Me?' Watson's brow furrowed. 'Why me? I tried to find out what happened to him and got nowhere.'

Harriet shrugged. 'She said this is different. You'll have to ask her what she means.'

They got out of the car and Watson grabbed the couple of bags he'd put on the back seat. They went to the back of the house through a side gate and entered through the kitchen door.

'Oi you mob! Guess who I've brought home with me?'

The house was silent; a strange occurrence at the best of times.

Harriet stepped through the kitchen. A note written in Nan's scratchy hand sat on the table.

> *Gone down to his old place. Susie's dropping me off. Kids are with her.*
> *They'll all be back soon. Tell John and Sherlock to meet me there.*

Watson peeked over Harriet's shoulder. 'Who's Susie?'

'Neighbour.' Harriet pulled out her mobile phone, flicked through her contacts until she found Susie's, and then called her. It went straight to voicemail.

'Shit!' she said through clenched teeth.

'Problem?'

'Not really.' Harriet put the phone and the note on the table. 'Susie's good. We watch each other's kids every now and then. I just can't believe Nan did that.'

'Really?' Watson grinned despite Harriet's concern. 'Nothing should surprise you about her by now.'

'Yeah, but...' She chewed at her thumbnail. 'She still could've waited till we got home at least. She shouldn't dump the kids off on Susie like that.'

'I'm sure they're fine. You know Nan wouldn't leave them with someone she didn't trust.'

'Yeah. But still.'

'Listen.' Watson picked up his bags. 'I'm just gonna throw some things together and go meet Nan. Can you spare your car for a bit?'

'But I was going to come with you!'

'You need to be here for the kids.' He was already moving through the house. Having visited several times, he knew where Harriet would have him stay. 'Besides, you don't want to go back there, do you? I know I bloody-well don't.'

Harriet crossed her arms over her chest, leaned back against the kitchen counter and said nothing.

Watson returned to the kitchen carrying a small duffel bag. 'Just some tools of the trade,' he said when Harriet looked at it. 'Figured while I'm there I can set some stuff up.'

'Do you expect to get anything?'

'No. But it'll keep the old girl happy. Hopefully.'

Harriet rolled her eyes and grinned. He reached out his hand.

'Keys, please.'

She placed her keys into his hand. 'Go easy with her.'

Watson was already walking out the door. 'With the car? Or Nan?'

'The car!' Harriet called after him. 'I already know Nan can take care of herself!'

Watson responded with a wave, opened the car door and put his bag on the back seat. He climbed in, started it up, and reversed into the street slowly, aware of Harriet's gaze on him the whole time.

As he drove off, he thought about the best way to go. It was still early in the day so traffic wouldn't be too bad. He'd have to make a stop on the way, though. He had to take care of something before getting to Nan.

June Watson, or Nan as she was known to family and the broader community, sat on the lone chair that remained in her late nephew's apartment. The rest of his belongings had been removed in preparation for selling the place. As his only next of kin, the duty of selling had fallen to her, yet she hadn't been able to bring herself to put it on the market. Now she believed she knew why.

She'd had the gift for as long as she could remember. Having been taken from her parents when she was eight and sent to the mission at Cherbourg, she grew up with little way to understand what she could do. To the missionaries she was either crazy or bedevilled, either of which resulted in beatings and prayer.

They're here. It was less of a thought than an instinct; something she just knew.

She glanced at the door just as it opened. At the entrance stood a tall, slim woman, wearing a sharp, grey business suit with medium heels. Her dark skin complimented her angular features. The woman closed the door and strode towards her. Nan noticed she kept her hands in her pants pockets.

'Hello, June,' the woman said

'Here! Good to see you, Sherlock!' Nan beamed and stood to embrace the woman. 'How have you been, love?'

'Can't complain,' Holmes returned Nan's affection before stepping back to size her up. 'You look well! Been looking after yourself?'

'Aw, you know. Battling on. Not as quick on my feet as I used to be, but still doing all right up here.' Nan tapped her forehead.

'You'll always be sharp as a tack.' Holmes gestured towards the chair and waited for Nan to sit.

'Where's John?' she asked.

Holmes lowered herself to the floor and sat cross-legged.

'He'll be along in a while,' he said. 'We thought it best if at least one of us could get here as soon as possible. You've got Harriet beside herself with worry, you know.'

'Ah, she'll be right.' Nan flicked her hand. 'I'll make it up to her. It's you I'm more worried about.'

'Me?' Holmes tilted her head. 'Why me?'

'Not just you. You and John both.'

Holmes shook her head. 'You're not making any sense. Why are you worried about us?'

'You know why.' Nan leaned forward. 'That's why you're here instead of John.'

Nan sat back again with a tight-lipped grin on her face. Holmes stared back at her. A tickle, like a spider feels when a fly struggles in its web, nagged at the back of her mind.

'I'm here because John-'

'You're here because John can't deal with it. You're always here when John can't deal with something.'

Holmes' brow furrowed. 'John...' She didn't know what to say.

Nan sat forward again. Her eyes softened. 'Oh, my dear jarjum. Did you think I didn't know?'

Holmes stood up and brushed her hands down her pants legs. She turned away from the old woman. Of course June Watson knew. She knew bloody-well everything. Sherlock turned back to face her.

'How long?' Holmes asked.

Nan rose and moved towards her. 'Since that accident, love.' She reached out and took Holmes' hand. 'You didn't show yourself until well after the funeral, but I always knew you were there.'

Holmes looked down at Nan. The tickle was now a scratchy irritation.

'In my day they would've said you had a split personality,' Nan said. 'They call it something else now, right?'

'Dissociative Identity Disorder,' Holmes said.

'Yeah that's it! You know your folks always thought you were just John's imaginary friend.' She laughed.

Holmes pulled away. The disorder wasn't something she had talked about with anyone. Nor had John. They hadn't even discussed it themselves much. She had always thought DID was a form of denial for John, and was itself a fact he could neither deny nor accept.

Both she and John had studied the disorder extensively. Both knew the somewhat miraculous relationship they had formed was the exception rather than the rule.

'This isn't what you brought us here for,' Holmes said. Her head felt like it was in an ever-tightening vice. 'What's the story about you being visited by Uncle?'

For a moment Nan stared at Holmes and said nothing. Then she sighed and moved back towards the chair.

'He come to me last night,' she said as she sat down. 'I'd been expecting him to for a while. Took him long enough. Fulla's dead and still running on Koori time!'

Holmes smiled. 'What did he say?'

Nan drew a deep breath. Her eyes glistened as fresh tears formed.

'He told me what happened,' she said. Her voice was cracked and strained. 'He told me who killed him.'

Holmes kneeled in front of Nan. She rested her hands on Nan's knees.

'Who was it, Nan?' She searched Nan's eyes for the answer.

Nan wiped her eyes. When she lifted her head, her eyes were red but tearless.

'Why didn't you help John find out who it was?'

'What?' Holmes reeled at the accusation in Nan's voice.

Nan's tone grew harsher. 'You could've worked this out ages ago. Why didn't you help him?'

'I wanted to help him,' Holmes said. 'He wouldn't let me.'

'Ah, gammon, girl! Don't lie to me now! Why didn't you help him?'

'Because...' Holmes swallowed. 'Because I didn't want him to know.'

Nan's glare seemed to penetrate her soul. 'You're close, love. What's the real reason?'

Holmes stood and gripped her own chin between a thumb and forefinger. She shifted her weight from one leg to the other. She couldn't look at the old woman.

Her voice was low, almost a whisper, when she spoke.

'Because he didn't want to admit it to himself.'

'Admit what?'

The air in the room seemed thick as soup to Holmes. Her mind felt as if something was clawing to get out.

'That it was-'

Holmes screamed and grabbed the sides of her head. Her knees buckled, though she remained on her feet. Nan rushed to her.

'Was what, darl?' she asked. 'Tell me.'

Holmes looked down at Nan. The pain in her head threatened to render her mute.

'That it was...' She grimaced as she tried to speak. 'The other one.'

'What other one?'

Holmes backhanded her across the face. Nan cried out, staggered back, and fell to the floor.

Holmes kicked off her shoes and strode over to Nan's prone body. A wicked grin spread across her face.

'That would be me,' Holmes said in a deep, British, male voice.

Nan cradled her burning cheek and looked up into the eyes of a stranger.

'Allow me to introduce myself,' he said and extended a hand towards her.

'Moriarty. James Moriarty.'

Nan scooted away from her assailant. She wanted to stand but knew it would take too long to get to her feet. Moriarty kept pace with her, thwarting each attempt to put distance between them. He chuckled to himself as he loomed over her. He might look like her John, but this one was nothing like him.

Nan whimpered as she backed herself into a corner of the room. The coppery tang of blood filled her mouth, and she was having trouble seeing out of her eye, where he'd struck her. She glanced around hoping to see something to defend herself with: a loose piece of skirting, a nail, anything. There was nothing.

Moriarty stood over her and again extended a hand. She slapped it away. 'Don't you touch me, ya bastard!'

'Oh,' he said, his mouth in a mocking "O" shape. 'The old girl's got some fight in her yet! Splendid!'

Nan spat a crimson glob at him, hitting his pants leg. Moriarty stepped back but maintained his twisted smile.

'Now, Nan, that's not very ladylike.' He squatted and regarded her as a snake might regard a field mouse.

'Fuck you, you murdering piece of shit!'

'Murdering?' Moriarty tapped a finger against his chin. 'Oh, you mean Bill. Yes, that was unfortunate. Also unintended, you know.'

'Unfortunate? Unintended? He spent his last hours in agony!'

'Yes. Well. I only wanted to make him sick. I figured a little Manchineel would only make him violently ill. A little burning sensation, a little swelling. Put him in the hospital. Who knew the little apple of death would live up to its name so well?'

Moriarty tilted his head and regarded Nan as if noticing her for the first time.

'You see, I had to get their attention.'

Nan peered at him. 'Whose attention?'

'Watson's of course. And through association, Holmes.' He stretched his neck forward. 'Do you know what it's like, being a passenger inside a vessel you have very little and very inopportune control over?' He pointed his fingers towards his eyes. 'To have to watch, in silence, as those two bumble their way through life? If you could even call it a life. Chasing after all these pathetic souls who think they've seen demons in their bathroom or mummy come back from the grave. Codswallop! To think of all they could have been. All we could have been.' He tutted. 'Such a waste of a life. Of three lives really.'

Moriarty stood and walked back over to the chair. He ran his hand along the back of it.

'What'd that have to do with my nephew?'

'Nothing, directly.' Moriarty gripped the back of the chair and hefted it off its legs. He made an appreciative grunt and set it back on the floor.

'I really had nothing against the man,' Moriarty said. 'But I knew he was close to Watson, and Watson is close to Holmes. I figured something so brazenly personal would be too much for Watson to handle. That Holmes would be compelled to assist him and discover the identity of his uncle's assailant.' He paused.

'When he died… That wasn't my desire. However, to have Holmes reveal that it was Watson himself who committed such a heinous crime…'

Moriarty's grin returned. 'Well, that would push anyone over the edge, don't you think?'

Nan pushed against the wall and tried to bring her legs under her. She willed herself to stand. However, at this angle, her legs couldn't comply.

'My John didn't kill anybody,' Nan said. 'You're the one that killed him. Sherlock told me that. She said it was "the other one".'

Moriarty beamed and dragged the chair back towards the corner Nan was stuck in. He reversed the chair, so the back was facing forwards, and then straddled it.

'Really?' He grinned. 'So, tell me. Which of us would have left evidence behind that could've been used to convict them? Who might've left a hair, or a fingerprint, or a thread of clothing? James Moriarty? Sherlock Holmes? Or your beloved John Watson?' His grin widened. 'Because I can assure you, it wouldn't have been James Moriarty. Remember, I'm only in here,' he said, and tapped his forehead.

'But why?' Nan gritted her teeth. 'Why would you do that?'

'To get into the driver's seat,' Moriarty said and crossed his arms over the back of the chair. 'See, the problem with John is that he's very self-aware. He knows what's going on with Holmes. More than that, he's learned to live with it. He's made peace with the fact that Holmes exists. They've become best buddies. Partners, even, in the real world. Do you know what that means?' He didn't wait for an answer.

'That means there's not much room for James Moriarty. It means I seldom get a go at driving the bus. When I do, one or the other is usually quick to take control again. Usually Holmes. She's more aware than Watson. As I would expect her to be.'

Moriarty rose, grabbed the back of the chair and turned it around. 'The only time I get to drive is when both of them are distracted. That doesn't happen very often, and I'm tired of being a passenger. I needed a major event. Something serious. Something significant. So along came Bill.'

'You bastard,' Nan said under her breath.

'At first, I thought the grief alone might do it,' Moriarty said. 'But Watson is a lot tougher than I gave him credit for. Then I figured once Holmes was involved and came to her inevitable conclusion, the shock of it would bring me my opportunity to seize control.'

Moriarty lifted the chair off the ground and upended it. 'Problem was,' he said. 'I didn't anticipate Holmes not getting involved.' He drew the chair back over his shoulder. Nan's eyes opened wide as she realised his intent.

'I don't think she'll be able to resist this time. I probably won't have to kill you, but accidents happen.'

Moriarty wound himself up to deliver a crippling blow.

Nan crossed her arms over her face and squeezed her eyes shut.

'No!' The scream at once sounded both female and male.

Nan heard the clatter of the chair falling to the floor. She brought her hands to her face and dared to crack her eyes open and peer between her fingers.

The chair lay on its side only inches away from her. In front of her, Watson was writhing, clawing at his face, chest, and throat. For a moment his eyes caught hers.

'Run, Nan,' he said in Watson's voice.

'Run!' he said in Holmes' feminine tone.

Nan was able to stand at last. 'John!' she said. 'Sherlock!'

Watson grimaced as he struggled with himself. He raked his fingers down one side of his face and grabbed hold of the neck of his blouse.

'John!'

Watson locked eyes with Nan.

'I love you, Nan.' he said.

He turned and ran toward the single window in the room.

'No!' Nan screamed.

The window shattered as Watson careened through it.

He plummeted four floors to the ground below and struck the earth with a dull thud.

It was very bright when Watson opened his eyes. He tried to raise his hand to shield himself from the glare. His arm wouldn't move. He tried again. Nothing. In fact, neither his arms nor legs wanted to move.

He tried to sit up and found he couldn't do that either. His panic brought him to full consciousness, and he became aware of the tube sticking out of his mouth.

'He's awake!'

Harriet appeared in his vision and he relief washed over him.

'Hey! There ya are! We were all worried about you!'

Watson darted his eyes side to side, thankful he could still do that at least. He couldn't see anyone else. He tried to make a noise. All he achieved was a swallow.

'Hey, don't try and talk,' June said. 'They had to stick a tube down your throat to help you breathe. You had a bad accident. You're lucky to be alive.'

Watson tried again to speak or make a noise. Nothing happened.

'You got busted up pretty bad.' You broke your neck, John,' Harriet said. 'You broke your neck, your ribs, your pelvis, and your ankle on this side'. She touched his right leg. He didn't feel it.

'The docs say you're going to heal up okay.' Harriet looked down. 'But you're probably going to be paralysed.'

Watson's eyes rolled wildly as he tried to move, make a sound, do anything that might help him communicate to Harriet.

'Shhh.' She had a wet face washer and started to lightly rub his face and forehead with it. 'Everything's going to be ok. Nan's all fine. She had a bit of a turn when she found you, but she'll be alright.'

Watson closed his eyes.

'You can stay with us once you're out of here,' Harriet said. 'Till you're good enough to go home again. We'll look after you.'

Watson started to cry. Harriet wiped his face and tried to console him as best as she could. She reached for his hand and squeezed it. He couldn't feel that either.

She stayed with him, holding his hand, talking about Nan, or her kids, or the weather outside. Whether from physical fatigue or emotional exhaustion, it wasn't long before Watson once again drifted towards sleep.

Before consciousness left him, the corners of his mouth twisted into a grin as a single thought crossed his mind.

It worked.

AUTHOR'S NOTES

When I was invited to contribute to this anthology, I wanted to do more than present an alternate cultural take on these famous and beloved characters. Dissociative Identity Disorder (DID) is a rare but real mental health disorder which is poorly understood by many health professionals, much less the general public.

While I would not pretend to be any sort of expert on the issue, I hope my portrayal of a character with this disorder is at least plausible, and any errors are my own. I'm always pleased to be able to bring Aboriginal characters into mainstream fiction, especially as protagonists, and even more so when I can depict them as part of my own Bundjalung mob.

For those curious, jarjum is a Bundjalung word for child.

A
STUDY
IN
LAVENDER

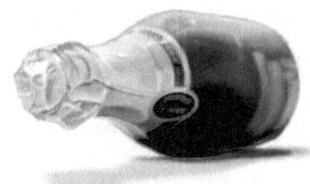

J. M. Redmann

'Watson, get me my feather boa!'

My immediate reply was to suggest he get it himself, but I have learned through hard experience to temper my immediate replies. I got up and tossed him the first feather boa I found, a fluffy, lavender one. We have more than a few around the place.

'The game is afoot!' he said as he wrapped it around his neck.

'American English, please,' I replied.

'Murder most foul.'

'Like there are murders that aren't foul?' I sat back down to my second cup of coffee. It takes at least that many to make me human. Today it would be about ten. Yesterday was Fat Tuesday, Mardi Gras, Carnival. Today was Ash Wednesday and I was paying for my sins. 'Wait, murder? Who was killed?'

'No one yet, but given the situation, someone will be soon.'

'What are you talking about?'

'Our new case, dear Watson. The Chalice of the Cosmopolitans has been stolen! Last seen at the Cosmo Ball on Saturday night, after the ceremonial passing from the outgoing captain to the incoming one.'

My forever roommate took his cue and sat at the table as well, the lavender feathers a little too close to my coffee.

His given names: Sherrod Locke Holmes. But I, and the world, knew him best as Shirle-Locke Holmes. His mother, father and all siblings were in law enforcement: cops, FBI, private investigators. Sherrod had gone into the family line, in his own special way. Diva Drag Detectives. Private eye. A drag queen dick. Tall, with flowing brown hair that always fell into perfect waves, no matter the wind. A face that could be described as gorgeous, model looks of the metrosexual, not cowboy type. Equally at home belting out *I Will Survive* in four-inch heels with more eyeshadow than I've worn in my life, and in a three-piece gray suit. Perfect for a detective.

I'm Jane Watson. Former hot shot English major; former schoolteacher; now bartender. It pays more than listening to the third kid in a row explaining the dog really did eat their laptop. Plus, I had discovered that school early mornings were not my friend. Now I don't have to wake up before the larks have even farted.

Sherrod and I had been classmates at Tulane and ended up as roommates after Katrina, first out of necessity due to there being so few houses. We stayed together due to those few houses changing into expensive houses. By pooling our resources we have managed to buy the house we were in – no more being kicked out on the street due to someone cashing in on short term rentals, no more begging for repairs only to be told our rent would be raised if we wanted things fixed.

Which made us permanent roommates, joined together at the mortgage.

When Sherrod had first said he was going to become a PI, I'd laughed and asked who the hell would hire someone whose resume was mostly drag performances, barista gigs and letting straight girls cry on his shoulder.

The lavender tribe would. He was right and I was wrong. He'd found the perfect private eye niche – serving the uptown closet cases who wanted discretion, from the major divorces in the Garden District to the French Quarter gay bars.

He kept busy and he dragged me (pun intended) into it. Being a bartender is a hotline to all the gossip in town, top dirt with hot sauce on the side. His straight women friends supplied what didn't make it to the gay bars. Sherrod found me useful more often than I liked. But in truth, if I really hated working with him, I wouldn't. I just didn't want him to know I was having fun. He might think he didn't need to pay me.

'I must find the Chalice before things get out of hand,' Shirle-Locke continued.

'Umm, it's a cheap Mardi Gras prop,' I pointed out.

'History, my dear. Abundantly rich in history. Made for the first gay Mardi Gras krewe back in the 50s. Yes, tarnished silver, worth about a nickel – a quarter with inflation – if you melted it down. But more gay lips have touched it than a naked cowboy during Southern Decadence. It has literally been passed from captain to captain for over fifty years now. It is not gay Mardi Gras without sipping champagne from it.'

'What happened?'

Shirle-Locke handed me a notebook as a hint.

'As usual, it was used for the ball this past Saturday, handed to the new captain, Rob Byrnes, owner of a bar on North Rampart.'

'He lost it?'

'No, he put it back in its velvet case which went into a heavy locked wooden box. When they went to load things out after the ball, it was gone.'

'So, anyone could have taken it.' I made a note.

'Anyone at the ball who could have been in the backstage area without being noticed.'

'The Queen of Sheba and her entourage,' I pointed out.

'Not this year's theme. No, there is a specific place backstage where it was kept. Only the people who had access to that area could have taken it. The problem is the outgoing captain, Wilford Fordham–'

'That his real name?'

'Yes, many rivers to ford as he is too fond of saying. Anyway, he has been captain since Bienville set foot here and only stepped down because of health issues. Aka, being not so gently nudged aside because his ego got bigger every year and it's now too large to fit in with human company.'

'The board rebelling and about to vote him out,' I added. Yes, I had served the drinks after that board meeting.

'That, too. Lots of bad blood flowing backstage. He blames Rob Byrnes, the incoming captain, the new king and queen and just about everyone else. But he does have health issues, heart problems, which he is quite vocal about.'

'Ah, the murder. Steal the Chalice, send his blood pressure through the roof and he kicks the bucket.'

'Very possibly. The suspect pool is complicated by the appearance of a rival captain and queen from the Martini krewe who were also there. Also backstage, also seen near the Chalice.'

'Bad blood there as well. Long running feud about the stealing of costumes.' More bartending gossip.

'Indeed. Supposedly an entire shipment of lavender feathers for last year's costumes.'

'And two years ago, using their colors; and five years ago, the same theme, but since Martini has their ball first—'

'Exactly. Very bad blood.'

'Was the queen backstage?' I asked, making another note.

'No, but she was in costume and could have hidden the entire cast of Madame Butterfly in her skirts.

He stood, grabbed two travel mugs and poured coffee into them.

'They both better be for me or you're dead,' I grumbled as I stood up. My feet were still weary.

'First stop is to look at the auditorium,' Shirle-Locke said, clearly now in her Shirle-Locke Holmes persona.

I remembered to toss him the car keys on our way out. He would have to drive as I was too bleary-eyed to chance it. Which meant we took his bright red Mini Cooper. Detectives in mauve feather boas don't need to be discreet.

For most people, Mardi Gras is conjured up as parades and people displaying intimate parts of their body for beads. In truth, it's a party the city throws for itself and outsiders revel in the tip of the iceberg. There are carnival krewes for just about everyone, from the big old-line ones like Rex and Comus, and Zulu, the first African-American krewe, started to satirize the white Uptown ones. Now there are ones specifically for women like Muses and Nyx, ones in town, in the suburbs, for boats, you name it.

Only the bigger krewes have parades. Many are invitation-only balls and invisible to the tourists. The LGBTQ community gets into the fun as well — did someone say costumes and men and women in dapper tuxes? Hello. There are a number of private balls, including Lords of Leather, several for African-Americans, POS (People of Substance) and Mwindo, plus quite a few for the more general gay community.

'So, who's hiring us?' I asked as we zipped uptown.

'Sunglasses. Glove compartment,' Shirle-Locke said.

I handed him the not really needed sunglasses and also noted the evasion. 'Who are we working for?'

'That's not sorted out. Yet.'

'What do you mean?'

'There are many possibilities,' Shirle-Locke said as he breezed through a yellow signal. Traffic was light. It seemed I wasn't the only one in town with a hangover.

'We're working for free?'

'No…well, there are enough people around who would gladly pay to have this solved. Worse case is we do it for the good of the community and to show off our skills.'

'Lovely,' I groused. The Mardi Gras tips would keep me going for a while, but we were in Lent now and some people gave up drinking. Or at least tipping, as they had spent too much on drinking during the bacchanal.

Shirle-Locke pulled into the parking lot of a square box of a building, looking drab in the cloudy day. It was a labor union hall for the dock workers, the dry side of the levee on the Mississippi. Mardi Gras makes for strange bed fellows – or should that be ball fellows? Everyone needs a space that can hold a crowd. The people that own those spaces make some extra money.

We got out. It looked like no one was home and this goose chase was starting to feel wild.

'How do we get in?'

'We don't. Let's start with the obvious. Trash.'

'Trash?' That was not obvious to me.

'Yes, trash. You are the thief. You disguised yourself. Where do you leave your disguise? What do you do with the big, clunky wood case? You dispose of them. Where do you dispose of them? The closest hidden trash receptacle that has no one around.'

Shirle-Locke was leading the way to the back of the building.

The dumpster at the back of the building.

Shirle-Locke looked at me.

I shook my head no. He is tall. I am not. If there was to be any climbing into a dumpster, it would be by someone tall enough to get out.

'Please hold my boa,' he said, unwrapping it. He handed it to me, along with his jacket, wallet, phone and keys. Then lifted his foot and stared at me.

I wrapped the boa around my neck, then reluctantly – I knew where those soles had been – twined my fingers together so he could use my hands as a stepping stone.

I sighed and braced myself. 'No more oyster po-boys for you,' I muttered as I felt his weight against my palms.

But he was up quickly and straddling the lip of the dumpster, staring quizzically into its depths.

'Stop right there!'

I turned to see a gun pointed in our direction.

A big, black barrel aimed right at me.

'What are you doing here?' a voice demanded.

A woman's voice.

'Dumpster diving, dear,' Shirle-Locke answered. He was nonplused.

I was still focusing on the barrel.

Suddenly, it was lowered.

'Shirle-Locke Holmes, why am I not surprised to find you here?' Micky Knight, another of the small group of queer private eyes in town. Tall, dark and handsome. Of which I am none. It was highly unlikely she knew I existed.

'What are you doing here?'

'I cover the waterfront.'

'Yeah and the postman always rings twice. Are you after the Chalice?'

'Not that waterfront.' She suavely tucked her gun into a shoulder holster. 'No, I'm not after the Chalice. The one that disappeared?'

Then she looked at me, 'Hey, Jane. I like your taste in feather boas.' She hoisted herself up and then straddled the ledge beside Shirle-Locke.

'We wouldn't be looking for an un-disappeared one,' Shirle-Locke said.

I was still too stunned that Micky knew my name to reply.

'That's all yours. I'm here to investigate a shipping company that seems to find things that fell off a truck.'

'That sounds dangerous,' I piped up.

'Naw, all in a day's work. Mostly reading invoices and listing the discrepancies. Headed out here just to stretch my legs and talk to some of the dockworkers who are too hungover to be discreet.' To Shirle-Locke, she said, 'What are you looking for in the trash?'

'Clues, my dear. Did they dispose of the wooden case to make it easier to carry? A hurried costume change to disguise their identity?'

'Lot of champagne bottles,' Micky commented.

'Cheap, what one guzzles at the end of the evening when you can't taste anything anymore.'

'I'll leave you to it.' She jumped down. 'Just be careful out there. Wilford and his cronies are mean snakes.'

'Who will be grateful, mean snakes if we return the Chalice,' Shirle-Locke said.

Micky waved to him, then winked at me and trotted off.

'Bye,' I said, but she was gone.

'Ah, very interesting,' Shirle-Locke muttered.

'What?'

'Come, take a look.' He offered me his hand.

With the help of his pulling arm and a big jump, I managed to get my feet on one of the braces for the dumpster. I was just tall enough to see over the edge.

'What do you see?'

'Umm…trash.' That being too obvious, I added, 'Lots of liquor bottles, food trash. Like someone had a party recently.'

'Indeed. Notice anything interesting about the liquor bottles?'

'Ummm…there are a lot of them.'

'True. Be a bartender.'

I looked closely at the bottles. Lots of them. Cheap. Very cheap. Quantity, not quality. Except for a few. 'Mostly bottom of the line stuff. Save for one bottle of Dom.'

'Very good. Why would there be only one good bottle?'

'Because someone didn't want to drink the swill and brought their own?'

'Possibly. But there are decent champagnes and there are expensive and ostentatious ones.'

'Dom Perignon is a very good champagne.'

'Yes, it is. It is also the name most likely to be recognized as good champagne. Especially at a distance of, say, the court sitting on the ball dais.'

There are lots of good glasses of bubbly, but if you wanted to show off, you'd want a distinctive bottle that the people you're showing off to would know. 'How does this get us closer to finding our cup?'

'Notice anything else?'

I surveyed the garbage. 'No…'

'The DP isn't quite empty. At least another half a glass is in the bottle.'

'Could be rain.'

'No, it hasn't rained since then.'

'Pigeon with good aim.'

'All the other bottles are empty. Why would there be a little left in the only good bottle?'

'I'm sure you're going to tell me,' I said, half-jumping/half-sliding to the ground.

Shirle-Locke gracefully jumped down. 'In good time. I need to be sure it means what I think it means.'

I handed him back the boa, his jacket, wallet, phone and keys. He took off for the car, his long legs leaving me behind. He swears he forgets and just does his usual walk. I just swear. Sometimes I hurry to keep up, but today I walked my usual walk. He could have the car unlocked and ready to go by the time I got there.

Which he did.

'Where are we going?' I noticed we were continuing uptown, not towards home.

'To convey our condolences to Wilford Fordham.'

'Oh, gag me now,' I muttered. Wilford liked to drink. He didn't like to tip. I had served him on more occasions than I liked to think about. Because I wasn't a young, handsome man, I doubt he noticed me. 'Do I have to go in?'

'But of course! I need your expert eyes.'

I sighed loud enough for him to hear. He ignored me.

Wilford lived in a stately home just off Audubon Park, inherited from his mother and her family's sugar cane money. From the looks of it, the money was running out. Or maybe Wilford believed in home maintenance as much as he believed in tipping bartenders – not at all.

A once glorious porch sagged at one end, with paint peeling on the columns most exposed to the sun. The white was fading to a dusty version of itself. The lawn could use a trim and the leaves hadn't been raked in a while – like since last fall, and today was Ash Wednesday.

Shirle-Locke's knock was answered with a 'What the hell do you want?'

'Good day to you, too,' I muttered.

'Diva Drag Detectives here about the lost Chalice of the

Cosmopolitans,' Shirle-Locke said in his most cheery voice, the one I always threatened to throw a coffee cup at.

The door jerked open.

Had he ever had a prime, Wilford was long past it. He was a big man, tall enough to fill the door, also wide enough to fill it across. He had shaved well enough for being at home with no one around – a large patch on the point of his chin was distracting, a little purple left in it from Mardi Gras festivities and a more natural silver mixed in. His dress was also no-one-watching-at-home: ripped sweat pants that might have been sexy on a 22 year old, but he was long past that, with a droopy knee and scraggly leg hair showing. Same with his t-shirt, also ripped, but also too tight, stretching the beer logo in ways it was never meant to be stretched.

'Have you found it?' he demanded.

'No, not yet,' Shirle-Locke answered, 'but we have some ideas.'

'What?'

'Can we come in?'

Wilford flicked his eyes to me, as if just realizing there was a 'we' here. He didn't like what he saw. He seemed to know he knew me, but didn't know from where.

'What are your ideas?' he demanded.

'Too soon to divulge,' Shirle-Locke said with a bright smile, as if this was a pleasant conversation.

It worked – not on me, but on Wilford. He eased his bulk aside to let us in.

'Can I get you something?' he offered, picking up his glass of amber liquid that had been placed on the antique secretary near the door. Ring marks indicated this happened a lot.

I gave my head a quick shake to Shirle-Locke. Wilford's glass didn't look like it had seen a dishwasher, human or machine, in a long time.

'We'll be brief,' Shirle-Locke said. 'We know you're busy and don't want to take up your valuable time.'

He led us only to the next room, a dusty parlor, with velvet chairs that probably dated from his grandparents' time. I sat down. I was going to wash these pants after today anyway. Shirle-Locke did as well.

Wilford went into another room. We heard the clink of glass and then he returned, his glass now full again. He sat on the one couch in the room.

'When did you notice it was missing?' Shirle-Locke asked.

He took a sip, then said, 'I guess at the end of the night, when we were packing away.'

'So, after everyone had toasted and it had been passed around?' I said.

'Of course,' he said with a glare in my direction. 'If it had been missing before then, we would have noticed.'

'It was on the dais for the entire ball?' Shirle-Locke asked.

'Where else would it have been?'

'A waiter didn't take it away to refill?'

'Well, yes, but it always came back.'

'Until it didn't,' Shirle-Locke pointed out.

'Yes, we know it's missing,' he said sarcastically. 'What are you going to do about it?' Then he added, 'You need to report everything to me.' Another large chug of the amber liquid.

'You would have to hire me for me to report to you.'

'For fuck's sake, I'm the captain of the krewe! I have to know everything that concerns my organization. And I shouldn't have to pay even more than I've already paid to have this returned!' The glass slammed down on the coffee table hard enough not to be good for either the table or the glass.

'I'll do what I can,' Shirle-Locke said, far more diplomatically than I would have, 'but I can't reveal my investigation until the proper time.'

'Wilford! What's going on?' A younger man entered. Younger than Wilford by a few decades, which put him in his forties. Jared Josslyn. Bar gossip was he started out as a pool boy and had combined his resources with Wilford. Age was making its inroads, but he still showed signs of tall, dark and handsome. Almost Wilford's height, hair still a brown so dark it was almost black. No gray, so either exceptional genes or a bottle. High cheek bones, wide lips. Bar gossip also said he was from a small town in east Texas, drifted first to Houston, then came here as a dancing boy in the bars and parlayed that into a series of sugar daddies before ending up with Wilford. I kind of liked Jared, if only because, unlike Wilford, he tipped.

Also, unlike Wilford, he seemed to recognize me. Just a look. He didn't say anything, taking his cues from Wilford.

'Shirle-Locke will not give me the information about the Chalice!' Wilford shouted.

'Well, that doesn't seem right,' Jared echoed.

'Sorry, I can't reveal the details of my investigation to anyone but my client,' Shirle-Locke said.

'Who the hell is your client?'

'The person who compensates me to take on this case.'

Wilford didn't tip. He wasn't going to pay us, as he had made clear. Much as it would have been nice to have an actual paying client, it wasn't going to be him.

'Well, what can you tell me?' He finished the amber liquid in his glass then thrust the glass at Jared, who barely saved it from falling to the floor.

'Who might have wanted to steal the Chalice?' Shirle-Locke asked.

'It's the most prized artifact in New Orleans gay history! Everyone would want it! I'm sure that drunkard Rob Byrnes would like it.'

I didn't point out to Wilford there were a lot of people who wouldn't want it. Me, for one. Jared returned with a full glass and handed it to Wilford.

'He thinks he can waltz in and become captain. He couldn't wait to get his hands on the Chalice!'

'If he gets it when he's Captain, why would he steal it a few weeks early?' I asked, following Shirle-Locke's lead and using my most innocent voice.

That stumped Wilford for a second.

'Who else besides Rob?' Shirle-Locke prompted.

That led to a demand that Jared bring the picture from that night – a large, flamboyant, gold-framed one. That was quick, I thought, given the ball was only last weekend.

'These are the people who would do it.' Wilford stabbed his finger onto the person at the left. 'JoBean, JoBean, she tries to take everyone's man and would love to get her hands on the Chalice.'

'Why?' I asked.

'That's the kind of girl he is,' Wilford snarled. 'Always wanting what he can't have.'

'Do you know his non-drag name?' Shirle-Locke asked.

'Greg Derren,' Jared answered. 'Curator at the New Orleans Museum.'

Ah, Greg. He was a generous tipper and remembered my name.

'Evon Gauthier,' another finger stab. 'Captain of the rat group, the Cocktail Martini Krewe. He had the nerve to come by and claim he wanted to toast us. His organization will do anything to upstage us, steal our costumes, use our theme, wine and dine our members away. I'm pretty sure he had a hand in it.'

Wilford kept going. 'The new king and queen, they won by one vote and it wasn't mine. Don't respect our traditions. But, damn democracy.'

The drinks had flowed after that krewe meeting, I recalled. Krewes are run by the captain, who can serve for as long as the krewe members will have him or her. Every year there is a new king and queen, usually someone who is well liked or has done a lot for the krewe – or who adds glitz and glamor. The balls aren't cheap, so there is always a challenge between letting new members in – who help pay the cost – and keeping power. Wilford had had power for a long while, and hadn't noticed the changing times and people. Some of the new people wanted to update things; others didn't like making major donations without having a say in how things were done. The guard had changed against his will – pun intended.

He rambled on, 'Anthony Love – claims it's his real name. Had to bribe people to be king this year.'

I knew Tony Love – it was his real name, at least real enough to be on his driver's license, because I had checked it. I doubted he had to bribe anyone. He was friendly and gracious enough to learn my name – the short lesbian bartender – and tipped well. He wanted to use the ball to raise funds for charities, like gay youth groups. His idea was to pay expenses, keep a rainy-day fund and donate the rest. I liked Tony. Not on my suspect list.

'The new queen – Lady ByDay Bidet – is a true skank. Vulgar. Thinks if her act doesn't include the F word, it's not funny,' Wilford went on.

He had a point. I'd seen Lady ByDay perform a number of times. She could make a pissy queen look like a nun, and she wasn't talented enough for that. Her attitude had gotten her kicked off the drag brunch circuit. Rumor was she made ball queen because she had some photos someone didn't want to see the light of day. She could turn on the charm when she wanted, so maybe that was enough. She did not turn it on for lesbian bartenders. I could see her stealing the Chalice to stir the pot.

Wilford went down the list. The outgoing king – Christopher Upton – had once been a friend but had thrown in his lot with the new crowd and would do anything to get back at Wilford. The old queen – Ursuline Burgundy – was a no-talent has-been. And so on. Wilford aired all his grievances.

I had to bite my tongue not to say, 'So basically everyone at the ball had a reason to steal the Chalice to spite you.' Shirle-Locke Holmes was the detective, I'd let him detect.

'If you had to pick the most likely suspect, who would it be?' he asked when Wilford finally wound down and noticed his glass was empty.

'That dotard, Rob Byrnes. He has it in for me.'

Shirle-Locke coughed and gave me a look.

My cue. 'Can I use your restroom?'

Wilford grunted a yes. Jared stood up to lead the way.

I knew what Shirle-Locke was up to – he wanted to pump Wilford alone while I got to view the house and ask Jared a few questions.

'It's broken,' he said, leading me past a small powder room. 'We'll have to go upstairs.'

'No problem. The bladder needs what it needs.'

He smiled at me. A nice smile. I wondered what had brought Jared to Wilford. And kept him there.

'Who do you think might have stolen the Chalice?' I asked as we climbed the stairs.

'No clue.' A brief shrug of the shoulders.

'Do you think the people Wilford named are likely suspects?'

'Hard to know. Maybe.' He didn't glance back at me, so I could only see the back of his head.

Ah, Jared, you're a bad liar. He didn't want to answer the question. It would have been easy for him to back up Wilford. Or add someone else. Instead he avoided it all together. Interesting. It could also mean he was tired of Wilford's rantings and had lost interest in the subject.

'Here you go,' he pointed to an open door, then quickly moved down the hall to a discreet distance.

It was a boy clean bathroom – waving something over the bowl – not a girl clean bathroom – sitting on the thing. I'd wait until I got home. The coffee wasn't trying to escape that desperately yet.

The bathroom told me little, except that Wilford liked stark colors. It was black and white, even the towels; the walls and shower glistening subway tiles. Clearly not the used bathroom in the house; there was nothing personal here, just a jar of little hotel soaps and a drooping hand towel that had seen whiter days.

I gave it a minute than flushed, let the water run for an appropriate hand washing time, then exited.

Jared was still the discreet distance down the hallway.

'Thank you,' I said, with a friendly smile. 'I like the décor. It's elegantly simple.'

'Do you? I picked it out. I like designing interiors – and the garden.' He motioned me into a library, although one heavier on memorabilia than books, and led us to a window. 'My latest, a veggie patch surrounded by flowers.'

'You have a green thumb,' I said, although it looked more a jumble of plants to me. It was lush and green, New Orleans winters never harsh enough to do more than mute a few plants.

'Thank you,' he said.

'Is this a hobby or do you take on design clients?'

'Oh, just a hobby,' he said, with a wistful look out the window.

He led the way back to the hall.

I noticed a large display case at the stair landing. One shelf had a large gap in the items.

'Is that where the Chalice stayed?' I asked.

Jared stopped, turned and stared at it.

'Everything is beautifully arranged, but with that one big gap,' I said into his silence.

'Oh, yes, sorry. That's where it was. Wilford will be happy to get it back.'

I followed him down the steps, not saying the obvious. Wilford wouldn't get it back. It would either be found and passed on to the new captain Rob Byrnes or not be found at all.

Shirle-Locke and Wilford were engaged in uproarious laughter when we returned. They were now best friends, if I knew Shirle-Locke. The amber in Wilford's glass had probably helped.

Shirle-Locke got up as I returned, 'Thank you so much for your time. You've been very helpful,' he said.

Jared led us out, Wilford stumbling along behind with the Creole farewell of asking about "your momma and dem" before letting us go.

'Well?' Shirle-Locke said as he started the car.

'Jared designed the bathroom – dramatic black and white, expensive subway tiles, but from a while ago. Also, the back garden. Nice to my untrained eye. What did you learn?'

'Wilford likes expensive champagne, but not to share. The sip shared in the Chalice was the cheap stuff. He kept the DP for himself, although he made a point to keep it on the table for others to see.'

'Generous.'

'I suspect he can only afford to be generous to himself.'

'If you can't afford to tip, you can't afford to drink. And maybe his bringing the good stuff only for himself is one of the reasons he's no longer captain.'

'Maybe.'

'Oh, Jared was tight-lipped about Wilford's theories, he didn't want to comment. Open and friendly until I asked who was the most likely suspect.'

'Interesting. The plot is thickening.'

'Only a roux should thicken,' I muttered. 'And, oh, I asked about the display case for the Chalice and Jared seemed to think it would come back.'

'Very interesting,' he said as he turned onto St. Charles Avenue.

'Wait, you're going uptown?'

'Yes, I want to chat with Rob Byrnes.'

'But why would he steal the Chalice if it was to be turned over to him at the next krewe meeting?'

'Why, indeed?'

'Plus, I didn't really go to the bathroom when I went to the bathroom.'

Shirle-Locke gave me a look, then a sigh.

'Coffee, all the coffee that it took to get me awake and coherent.'

We stopped at a local coffee shop and I filled a cup and emptied my bladder.

Rob lived in what we call a cottage in the Broadmoor area. Like many cities, where people live in New Orleans tells a lot about them. This was respectable, but far from the old-line uptown area for Wilford. Also, unlike Wilford's, the house had been recently painted: a soothing sky blue, with white and lavender trim; the yard was tidy, recently mowed, with flowerpots showing only flowers and no encroaching weeds.

I had worked a few fund-raisers at Rob's bar, and he had been a generous owner, putting money in the tip jar himself to add to the total raised. I knew some of the bartenders that worked there and they liked him as well. But I only knew him from those brief glimpses. While the world can be divided into those who tip and those who don't, even tipping isn't a sure sign of virtue. And it was hard to know if stealing the Chalice was vice or virtue at this point.

Shirle-Locke rang the doorbell.

'Around the side,' a voice called from, you guessed it, around the side of the house.

We followed the voice.

Rob was outside with his three cats and several friends, sharing a bottle of white wine.

'Come join us,' he said, getting up to shake out a few more plastic glasses from the bag.

'I don't want to intrude,' Shirle-Locke said. 'We're working on finding the missing Chalice of the Cosmopolitans.'

'Really? You get a bar tab for the next year, burgers included, if you find it.'

Maybe no money, but he had excellent bar burgers. They were my standard late night stop on the way home if I needed the grease and fat to get me through. At least we might get fed, even if we couldn't pay the mortgage.

'Wilford thinks you stole it,' Shirle-Locke said, cutting to the chase.

'He would,' Rob answered, handing us glasses of wine.

'Why would he?'

Snorts from Rob's friends.

Shirle-Locke gave them an inquisitive look.

A babble of how much Wilford hated Rob for taking over as the new krewe captain, how much Rob had contributed to the organization, how Wilford hated to be shown up by new energy, et cetera, ensued.

After a few minutes, Shirle-Locke cut in, 'Let me see if I get this straight. Wilford is trying to cast blame on Rob to detract from his inept leadership of the krewe?'

Rob answered, 'Let's all just get along. We can say that Wilford has his way of doing things and is reluctant to change. And he can be a little hot-headed.'

'You don't seem upset,' Shirle-Locke said.

'Why should I be? I'm the new captain. And I don't regard the Chalice as a family heirloom carried over from the old country.'

'Rob has no reason to do this,' a friend with two cats on his lap said.

'Unless Rob wants Wilford out entirely,' I said.

Everyone looked at me.

'Well, purely from the objective angle, where we have to look at everything. If you stole the Chalice, it could provoke a schism in the club. It might force him out entirely.'

'In other words, if I were an evil genius, I would do something like that,' Rob said, adding, 'Would that I were that evil and that genius.' He laughed, seeming more interested than offended by my question.

'Did you see anyone or anything that night that was suspicious or out of place?' Shirle-Locke asked.

'I think Lady ByDay did it,' Cat Man said.

'Why?'

'Because he's a righteous bastard,' said Not Cat Man next to him.

'Any other reason?'

Another chorus of Lady ByDay's cutting remarks and running feuds and why those proved she was such a righteous bastard. But no real evidence.

'The captain of the Martini Krewe came by, Evon Gauthier,' Rob said.

'Any reason to suspect him?'

Not Cat Man said, 'Way back, he used to be a member of the krewe, but he and Wilford had a major falling out. He left and formed the Cocktail Martini Krewe. This was the first time he's ever come back.'

'And, to be subtle, he does not wish Wilford well,' Rob said.

'Anyone see him near the Chalice?' Shirle-Locke asked.

'I saw him near the good champagne, the stuff Wilford keeps for himself. He snagged a glass when Wilford wasn't watching. Then he wandered off and I lost track of him.'

'I saw him in the backstage area, flirting with Jared. Another way to piss Wilford off.'

'So it seemed his goal was to annoy Wilford?' Shirle-Locke asked.

They all nodded in agreement.

But no one had seen him near enough the Chalice or carrying a suspicious package or anything that could be called hard evidence.

We finished our wine and took our leave.

'What's next?' I asked.

'One more stop,' Shirle-Locke said. 'We need to talk to Evon Gauthier.'

I sighed. Between the coffee and the wine, my bladder was soon going to need another pit stop.

We headed back downtown. Evon lived in one of the shiny new

towers, sprung up in the Central Business District. Parking, as usual, was a pain.

Surprisingly, Evon buzzed us up as if he were expecting us. Perhaps he was: the gay grapevine can be surprisingly efficient.

'Welcome,' he said. He was waiting with his apartment door open wide. He was a tall, handsome man with distinguished grey hair, and a perfect chin. To complete the picture, he was dressed in sharply pressed khaki pants and a light blue button-down shirt.

'Good afternoon,' Shirle-Locke responded. 'We are looking into the disappearance of the Chalice of the Cosmopolitans.'

'And you think I took it?' he asked, waving us in. His voice was jolly, as if he was enjoying this. 'You are?' he asked me, extending his hand.

'Jane Watson,' I replied. His handshake was firm, a perfect mix of friendly and professional. As if it was practiced.

'Shirle-Locke, good to see you again.' They also shook hands. 'Drink? I'm not much of a believer in Lent. I was just mixing a batch of, can you believe it, Cosmos?'

Shirle-Locke accepted on our part.

The apartment was nicely furnished, light blond wood, modern. A bar was set up in the corner, a variety of top shelf liquors visible.

Everything was perfect. As if he'd come from central casting. Too perfect makes me suspicious. I could see how this tidy and organized man would clash with bombastic and unruly Wilford.

Which didn't make him guilty, I reminded myself.

Drinks in hand, he led us to a designer-perfect sitting area, gray-beige matching couch and chairs with bright pillows for a pop of color.

'We heard you were at the Cosmopolitan ball,' Shirle-Locke said as we sat down.

'Indeed, I was. Wilford and I had a tiff a while back, but I thought it was time to mend fences and all that.'

'Just coincidence the Chalice disappeared on the night when you showed up for the first time?'

Evon sipped his drink before answering. 'Please. I won't pretend to be sorry that cheap piece of tin Wilford treated as a sacred icon is gone. Good riddance. But did I cloak and dagger it away? No.'

'Who might?' Shirle-Locke asked.

'My guess is a very drunk Wilford lost it and is casting blame on everyone else.'

'You think he stole his sacred icon?' I asked.

'Not stole. Careless. Lost it. Can't admit he was too drunk to properly stow it away.'

'You and he don't get along?' Shirle-Locke asked.

'No secret there, either. I wanted to take the Cosmopolitans in a more modern direction. Things like a web site and social medial outreach. If I had an idea, Wilford shot it down – if it came from me, it was a bad idea, no matter how good it might have been. No point in staying around in that environment. I, and a few like-minded fellows, started our own krewe and now have our own ball. We're modern enough that we allow women in.' With a nod at me, he added, 'Our current king is a woman. Does a wonderful Elvis.'

I smiled. It probably didn't make it to my eyes.

'Did you see anything that lends credence to your theory? Or anything else out of place?'

'There was a lot out of place there. But, no, I didn't see Wilford stumble and drop the Chalice into the river.'

Which was highly improbable given the distance between the hall and the river – a high levee and the docks.

'What do you mean by out of place?' Shirle-Locke asked.

'You know, the usual, partners partnering with other people in the parking lot. People running back and forth to their cars to bring good booze into the hall, against the catering rules. Of course, Wilford flouted the rules too, so no reason for anyone else to obey them.'

'Like who?' Shirle-Locke asked.

'Rob Byrnes. I asked him if he was going to serve better stuff next year. The stuff they were serving was rock bottom: sparkling wine, five dollars a bottle, at most. I won't call it champagne.'

'He does own a bar. He can probably get it wholesale,' Shirle-Locke commented. 'Who else?'

'Jared, of course. I saw him several times. Wilford wanted the good stuff for himself and he drinks more booze in a night than most fish drink water in a lifetime.'

'How did you see so much of the action in the parking lot?' I asked.

'I was seated by a window. The view was more interesting than those boring speeches.'

'How often did Jared go to the parking lot?' Shirle-Locke asked.

'Sorry, I didn't count. Enough times to finally run out of booze. He came back empty handed the last time. Not the brightest spark. Probably didn't count the bottles correctly.'

'Did you see the Dom Perignon?' Shirle-Locke asked.

'Of course,' Evon said. 'Wilford flashed that around when he toasted the glorious legacy of the krewe, meaning everything he did for it.'

'Did he use the Chalice?'

'His sacred icon? Of course, front and center.'

'Did you see it after that?'

Evon took another sip. 'I think so. Maybe not. There were so many bling things up there. I left shortly after that.'

'What time was that?'

'Time? That's hard. Ask Jared. He and I passed on his final bottle-less run.'

'Let's exclude Wilford losing it – who would you call the most likely suspect?'

'The entire board of the organization. Maybe they all did it. As a fitting goodbye to his reign as captain.' He laughed at his joke.

Shirle-Locke finished his drink and I hurriedly downed mine. I wasn't driving after all.

'Thank you,' he said. 'You've been most helpful.'

'Anytime,' Evon said, his voice smiling as if we'd been a fun distraction. A perfect host, he led us to the door and waved as we got in the elevator.

Evon was good company, the kind of man you could enjoy an evening with. But not the person I'd want to be marooned with on a desert island. He liked his own reflection too much.

'Home?' I asked. 'Or I'll need another bathroom break.'

'Home,' Shirle-Locke agreed.

Once we were in the car, I asked, 'So, do you know who did it?' Mainly because I didn't want to admit I didn't have a clue. It felt like we were no closer to solving the case than when I'd been happily downing coffee this morning. Too many suspects. Multiple times, the Chalice could have been snatched and no one would have noticed.

'I have some ideas. A few more pieces of the puzzle and it should be obvious.'

And that was all he said.

Shirle-Locke never played his hand until he was sure. At times, it was annoying, but I suspected somewhere in the black box of his brain, he couldn't explain the process he used to put things together. Or else he was bluffing and had no better idea than I did.

Traffic was the usual afternoon insanity and our conversation was mostly expletive filled observations about the other drivers until we were safely home.

I left him alone and was content with my very own bathroom, cleaned to my standards. That and a cat in the lap ended the day.

Shirle-Locke spent most of the next few days on the computer, doing research. He appeared to be searching all the gay Mardi Gras sites to look at the pictures, because he kept asking me for various names to search. Like I knew them all. But when I came in to share snacks – apple slices and cheese – he was looking at scented candles.

'I had to take a break,' he explained.

I just nodded. Shirle-Locke did like his scented candles.

Saturday morning, he burst into the kitchen, scaring the cat off my lap. 'I have the answer. And the perfect place to reveal it. Where is my feather boa?'

I sighed. Last night had been a work night and I needed the second cup of coffee – and probably a third – to be able to go out.

But detective work waits for no woman.

I should have been prepared. From the bar gossip, I knew there was a big meeting of the LGBTQ krewes, demanded by Wilford. People would come just to watch the show. The venue also had a very good brunch with bottomless mimosas.

Fortified with a large travel mug of coffee, we headed uptown. It took me three large gulps to finally ask, 'Do we have a client yet?'

'Piffle. The true reward is solving the case. And the perfect place to reveal the answer is at the krewe brunch. Wilford has demanded they all be there to account for the theft of the Chalice.'

I sighed. It might be a big reward for Shirle-Locke, but not so much for me. I could only hope for burgers from Rob's bar. Although that would be moot, if he'd done it.

'You know who stole it?'

'Indeed,' Shirle-Locke said.

'Are you going to tell me?'

'And spoil the fun? I'm going to let you be as surprised as the rest of them.'

Fine, I thought. I'll just drink my coffee and tag along like I have nothing better to do.

Our destination was a neighborhood breakfast and lunch place, not trendy, but the food was worth the trip.

Wilford had reserved a back room – or the restaurant was savvy enough to separate the krewes from regular customers.

Shirle-Locke was right, all our chief suspects were here. They were spread over three tables, split along the lines of alliances and feuds. Oh, so Agatha Christie.

Wilford was at the center table. The empty dishes – and glasses – in front of him suggested he had arrived early to ensure center stage. Two older men flanked him; members of his krewe who sided with him. Jared was shoved off to one end. Power and influence counted.

Rob and Evon were at another table, with other members of their respective krewes, easily mingling as if this was a social event, not a do-or-die cultural showdown.

'Shirle-Locke! What are you doing here?' Wilford bellowed as we entered.

Everyone looked at us. Well, at Shirle-Locke in his lavender boa, perfectly fitting jeans and tight t-shirt under a well-worn leather bomber jacket.

'I have solved the case of the missing Chalice,' Shirle-Locke said.

'Do enlighten us,' Evon said, his amused smile firmly in place.

'Really?' Wilford said. 'You don't seem to be carrying it with you. If you don't have it, how can you say you've found it? And how dare you show up here without telling me?'

'I said I solved the case. I don't have it, but I know where it is. And you did not engage me to solve this, so I have no obligation to report to you,' he added.

'So where is it? Rob's house?' Wilford blustered. He didn't seem happy that the case had been solved. Or he didn't like Shirle-Locke stealing his spotlight. He had called this meeting to rant and rave, after all.

'Jared, give Jane the keys to Wilford's car,' Shirle-Locke said. 'She needs to retrieve the Chalice from the trunk.'

A shush of murmurs took over the room at this revelation.

As instructed, I walked over to Jared with my hand out for the keys.

He started to dig in his pocket, then with a glance at Wilford, stayed his hand. Taking my cue from Shirle-Locke, I remained in place, my hand out for the key, highlighting his refusal to look in the trunk.

'Are you accusing me of stealing my own Chalice?' Wilford roared, standing up and shaking the table. His friends had to grab their glasses.

'I am stating the facts my investigation uncovered.' Shirle-Locke said calmly.

'It's not yours,' Rob added. 'It belongs to the krewe.'

'Precisely,' Shirle-Locke said. 'But Wilford has kept it so long there is a darkened area on the wall where its case rested. Like it was permanently his.'

'Why do you think he took it?' Rob asked.

'Because you, and Evon, and everyone else he named, didn't. The facts fell into place. A not quite finished bottle of Dom Perignon champagne in the dumpster outside the hall kitchen's back door. Why would someone not finish the bottle? A perfectly good serving tray in the dumpster next to it. The faded spot on the trophy wall. You claimed that it was packed away with everything else, Wilford, but that wasn't true. You also claimed that you didn't notice it missing. Yet, I looked at all the pictures from the ball,' he held up his iPad and scrolled through the pictures he'd found on social media, 'and you were drinking out of the Chalice most of the night. Until you weren't. And it was gone.'

'I was on the dais the entire time! There was no way I could have taken it!' Wilford was still roaring, but desperation was beneath the bluster.

'You didn't. You had someone who wouldn't be noticed do it for you.' Shirle-Locke looked at Jared. 'You put on a show, kept everyone's attention on you. Jared poured the champagne and took the cup from you, but walked away with the Chalice hidden in a towel. He hastily put in back in its carrying case, with the tray and the bottle on top if it.'

Another picture, a blurry one with Jared far in the background. 'It's hard to see, but the tray seems to be floating in air with Jared's hand inches below it. That's because it's resting on the dark wooden carrying case, the serving towel draped to hide it from anyone close. He ran out the back, dumped the champagne and tray in the dumpster and hid the Chalice in the trunk of Wilford's car. Which is where it most likely is now.'

'Poppycock!' Wilford shouted. But an eyelid was twitching.

'Open the truck,' Rob said. 'We need to know.'

'I am not opening my private car to some pretend private dick in a feather boa!' Wilford shot back.

'You've done a pretty good job of accusing all of us of stealing it. Put up or shut up,' Evon said.

'It is not there, and I am not opening my trunk to anyone!'

'Open the trunk or be thrown out of the krewe,' Rob said.

'You can't do that!'

'Open the trunk.' Rob again, now joined by a chorus of others. Even the friends at Wilford's table looked uncomfortable, edging their chairs away from him.

'Give me the keys,' I said quietly to Jared. 'You'll have to sooner or later.'

He seemed to understand the corner they were backed into. He slowly handed me the keys, not looking at Wilford.

I handed them to Shirle-Locke. He spun on his heels and headed to the parking lot. I had to lope to keep up with him.

Everyone was following us.

Except Wilford and Jared.

Wilford's car was a late model BMW, black with vanity plates reading KR-COSMO. He often posted pictures of it on the krewe web page, like the Dom Perignon, showing off what he had.

A few feet from the car, Shirle-Locke hit the button to open the trunk.

Inside was a tumble of objects, as if that was a well-used storage space. I wondered where he put his groceries. Maybe he had them delivered.

Shirle-Locke carefully moved the two bags of buffing cloth, an empty gas can, five umbrellas – only one of which looked like it might work – two sun visors, a beach chair, and a bag stuffed full of Mardi Gras beads, to reveal a worn wooden box.

'That's it!' Rob shouted.

'And it should be yours,' Shirle-Locke said, lifting it out and handing it to him.

'Not mine,' Rob said. 'It belongs to the Krewe of the Cosmopolitans. I'll keep it for them for a while.'

I left Shirle-Locke to being congratulated and did my duty, to find Jared and give him the car keys back.

'Thanks,' he whispered to me. 'Maybe he'll let it go now.'

I doubted it, but smiled at him as if he was right.

Then I pried Shirle-Locke away from his admirers. We had only looked at brunch, not eaten it, and I was hungry.

Our fee, a good bar burger, was waiting.

Author's Notes

New Orleans is a city so improbable as to be magical. A swampy settlement on a big river. A mix of cultures that makes it the least American city in the country. My father was a New Orleans native, his father a bar pilot on the Mississippi. Growing up, we visited often, a swirl of color, festive and enticing. After a stint in New York City, I came back here over 30 years ago and it has been home ever since.

Oddly, I started writing the Micky Knight series (which begins with *Death by the Riverside*) while living in NYC, but never considered placing her in New York. She deserved the magic and mayhem, the gumbo and gris-gris found only in New Orleans. And the stories only this city can tell.

CONTRIBUTING AUTHORS

GREG HERREN

Greg is the award-winning author of more than 30 novels and editor of over 20 anthologies. He has published over fifty short stories, numerous essays, and has even dabbled in journalism from time to time. He never says no to anyone who offers him money to write. Greg lives in New Orleans with his partner of 25 years and a needy cat, and is also currently the Executive Vice President of Mystery Writers of America.

ATLIN MERRICK

Atlin is the Commissioning Editor of Clan Destine's imprint Improbable Press, which publishes genre fiction: contemporary supernatural, adventure, and mystery. She's also the author of two Sherlock Holmes books: *The Day They Met* as Wendy C Fries, and *The Night They Met* as Atlin Merrick. Atlin lives in Oregon by way of New York, Melbourne, Dublin and London. Atlin thinks coffee is pretty.

JACK FENNELL

Jack is a writer, editor and researcher based in Limerick, Ireland. He is the author of two book-length studies of Irish genre fiction – *Irish Science Fiction* (2014) and *Rough Beasts* (2019) – and the editor of two short story collections, *A Brilliant Void* (2018) and *It Rose Up* (2021); he was also a contributing translator to *The Short Fiction of Flann O'Brien* (2013). His own fiction has appeared in the collections *Hell's Empire* (2019) and *Chronos* (2018), as well as *Silver Apples Magazine*. He teaches at the University of Limerick.

JASON FRANKS

Jason is the author of the novels *Bloody Waters, Faerie Apocalypse,* and *Shadowmancy,* as well as the *Sixsmiths* graphic novel series. Most of his work, in prose and comics, falls into some combination of the horror, fantasy, science fiction or comedy genres – if you like to think of things that way. Franks' books have variously been shortlisted for Aurealis, Ledger and Ditmar awards. He lives in Melbourne, Australia.

www.jasonfranks.com

NATALIE CONYER

Natalie hails from Sydney, Australia. She's a swimmer, TV fanatic, and crime fiction tragic. In fact, she loves the genre so much she did her doctorate on it. Natalie's short stories have won several awards in the annual Scarlet Stiletto competition, run by Sisters in Crime Australia. Her debut novel, *Present Tense,* (Clan Destine Press) is a hard-boiled police procedural set in Cape Town. It was shortlisted for the Davitt Awards (Australia's premier crime writing award for women) and won the 2020 Ned Kelly Award for debut crime. She's currently working on the sequel, (working title) *State Crime.*

KERRY GREENWOOD

Kerry is the author of more than 50 novels, a book of short stories, six non-fiction works, and the editor of two collections of true crime writing. Her beloved Phryne Fisher series has become a successful ABC TV series and movie – *Miss Fisher's Murder Mysteries, Miss Fisher and the Crypt of Tears* – which sold around the world. She is also the author of the contemporary mysteries featuring baker-sleuth Corinna Chapman.

Kerry is the author of several books for young adults; the ancient Egypt novel, *Out of the Black Land*; and the Delphic Women trilogy: *Medea, Cassandra* and *Electra.* Kerry co-wrote, with Lindy Cameron, the short story 'A Wild Colonial' for *Sherlock Holmes: The Australian Casebook.*

In the 2020 Australia Day Honours, she was awarded the Medal of the Order of Australia (OAM) for services to literature. In a previous life, Kerry was a lawyer and advocate in magistrates' courts for the Legal Aid Commission. She is not married, has no children, is the co-warden of a Found Cats' Home and lives with an accredited wizard (her co-author David Greagg).

DAVID GREAGG

David is a registered wizard, and consort of Kerry Greenwood. He has published several books, including the ghost-written autobiographies of his cat, *Dougal's Diary* and *When We Were Kittens*; non-fiction for children, *It's True! Bourke and Wills Forgot The Frying Pan* and *It's True! The Vikings Got Lost*; and fiction in collaboration with Kerry. At various times David has been a medieval scholar, mathematician, accountant, armoured warrior, composer, conductor, impresario and tenor. No doubt the future will see him do equally unpredictable things.

LISA FESSLER

Lisa is a German translator, editor, and writing coach, who grew up in Southern Germany and studied American History in Tübingen and in Eugene, Oregon. Berlin is her adopted home. Her current writing project is an alternative history fantasy novel set in the Wilhelminian Era. A passionate fanfiction writer, Lisa has written 60-word microfics of all 60 canon Sherlock Holmes stories by Arthur Conan Doyle.

LUCY SUSSEX

Lucy was born in Christchurch, New Zealand, but has called Australia home for many years. She has abiding interests in women's lives, Australiana, and crime fiction. Her award-winning fiction includes the novel, *The Scarlet Rider* (1996, reprint Ticonderoga 2015), and her anthology *She's Fantastical* was shortlisted for the World Fantasy Award. She has five short story collections. Her *Women Writers and Detectives in the Nineteenth Century* (2012) examines the mothers of the mystery genre. *Blockbuster: Fergus Hume and The Mystery of a Hansom Cab* (Text), won the 2015 Victorian Community History Award and was shortlisted for the Ngaio Marsh Award. In 2018 she was a Creative Fellow at the State Library of Victoria.

KATYA DE BECERRA

Katya, the author of *What the Woods Keep* and *Oasis*, was born in Russia, studied in California and now lives in Melbourne. Since earning a PhD in Cultural Anthropology from the University of Melbourne, she works as a social scientist and higher education lecturer. She's co-founder and co-host of #SpecLitChat and a writing mentor with the 1st5pages Workshop. www.katyadebecerra.com   Twitter @KatyaDeBecerra.

Jayantika (Jay) Ganguly

Jay, BSI (The Great Agra Treasure), is the General Secretary of the Sherlock Holmes Society of India and Editor of the biannual e-magazine *Proceedings of the Pondicherry Lodge*. She is a member of several international Sherlockian societies, including the Baker Street Irregulars and the Sherlock Holmes Society of London. She is an active Sherlockian writer, and has penned the book *The Holmes Sutra* (MX, 2014) as well as several pastiches, essays and articles for various international anthologies and publications. In real life, she is a corporate lawyer. Her first Sherlock Holmes novel, *A Continuum of Sherlock Holmes*, is due for release in mid 2021.

Dr L.J.M. Owen

L.J. escaped the dark and shadowy days as a public servant to explore the comparatively lighter side of life: murder, mystery and forgotten women's history. An award-winning writer, her short story 'The Adventure of the Lazarus Child' features in *Sherlock Holmes: The Australian Casebook* (2017). Her crime novels include the chilling *The Great Divide* (2019); and three books in the Dr Pimms archaeological mystery series: *Egyptian Enigma* (2018), *Mayan Mendacity* (2016), and *Olmec Obituary* (2015).

L.J. is the founding Director of the Terror Australis Readers and Writers Festival, a celebration of literature and literacy in Tasmania. She has degrees in archaeology, forensic science and librarianship, speaks five languages and has travelled extensively. Rare spare moments are spent experimenting with ancient recipes under strict feline supervision.

Raymond Gates

Raymond is an Aboriginal Australian writer currently residing in Wisconsin, USA, whose childhood crush on reading everything dark and disturbing evolved into an adult love affair with horror and dark fiction. He has published many short stories and is working on his first collection of short stories and first novel.

www.raymondgates.com

JM REDMANN

Jean has published 10 novels featuring New Orleans PI Micky Knight. The first, *Death by the Riverside*, published in 1990, was one of the early hard-boiled lesbian detective novels. The latest in the series (2020) is *Not Dead Enough*. Her books have won three Lambda Literary awards. *The Intersection of Law & Desire* was an Editor's Choice of the San Francisco Chronicle and a recommended book by Maureen Corrigan of NPR's Fresh Air. Jean is co-editor, with Greg Herren, of three anthologies, *Night Shadows: Queer Horror, Women of the Mean Streets: Lesbian Noir,* and *Men of The Mean Streets: Gay Noir.* Her books have been translated into German, Spanish, Dutch, Hebrew and Norwegian. She lives in New Orleans.

EDITOR: NARRELLE M. HARRIS

Narrelle is a freelance editor and writer of crime, horror, fantasy and romance. *The Only One in the World* is the first anthology she has pitched and edited, and she found it both rewarding and great fun.

Narrelle has written 30+ works include vampire novels, erotic spy adventures, het and queer romance, and Holmes/Watson romance mysteries for Improbable Press, *The Adventure of the Colonial Boy* and *A Dream to Build a Kiss On.*

In 2017, her ghost/crime story 'Jane' won the 'Body in the Library' prize in the Scarlet Stiletto Awards run by Sisters in Crime Australia.

Her other books include *The Opposite of Life, Walking Shadows, Grounded, Scar Tissue and Other Stories* (nominated for the 2019 Aurealis Awards for Best Collection), *Ravenfall,* and *Kitty and Cadaver.*

Her five-novella *Duo Ex Machina* MM romance/crime series is out in the wild, and her latest project (first serialised on Patreon) is the forthcoming werewolf-Mrs Hudson book, *The She Wolf of Baker Street.* www.narrellemharris.com.

Clan Destine Press
Anthologies

ISBNs: 9780645002126 (hb)
9780648848769 (pb)
9780648848776 (eB)

Who Sleuthed It?

Fingers and feelers and paws and wings
Solving thrillers and chillers and secretive things.

An anthology in which animals help their animal friends, or human sidekicks, solve diabolical crimes and whimsical mysteries in 19 stories by Australian, American and Irish authors.

Kerry Greenwood, Elizabeth Ann Scarborough
Meg Keneally, Narrelle M. Harris
Livia Day, David Greagg, Atlin Merrick
Fin J. Ross, Vikki Petraitis, Tor Roxburgh
Lindy Cameron, CJ McGumbleberry
Chuck McKenzie, Jack Fennell, Craig Hilton
L.J.M. Owen, GV Pearce, Kat Clay
and Louisa Bennet

ISBNs: 9780648523635 (hc)
9780648523628 (pb)
9780648523680 (eB)

War of the Worlds: Battleground Australia

This rivetting anthology sheds fresh, antipodean light on HG Wells' original invasion tale in stories that traverse the great southern continent. Home to the planet's longest surviving people and mysteries, Australia, it seems, was also invaded by marauding Martians.

In *Battleground Australia* we learn the war with Mars was not confined to England and did not end with all Martians destroyed by disease. In Australia some of the aliens survived and went underground, to emerge a century or more later.

This inventive anthology features stories by some of Australia's best-selling literary, crime and speculative fiction writers:

Kerry Greenwood, Jack Dann, Janeen Webb, Sean Williams, Angela Meyer, Lindy Cameron, Jenny Valentish, Narrelle M. Harris, Lucy Sussex, Rick Kennett, Jason Franks, Dmetri Kakmi Bill Congreve, Carmel Bird, Jason Fischer and Kaaron Warren.